Tender
Loving
DESIRE

Tender
Loving
DESIRE

DONNA
HILL

HARLEQUIN®
entertain, enrich, inspire™

TENDER LOVING DESIRE

ISBN-13: 978-0-373-53491-3

Copyright © 2012 by Harlequin Books S.A.

The publisher acknowledges the copyright holder of the individual works as follows:

SEX AND LIES
Copyright © 2008 by Donna Hill

SEDUCTION AND LIES
Copyright © 2008 by Donna Hill

Recycling programs for this product may not exist in your area.

Printed in U.S.A.

CONTENTS

Dear Reader,

Welcome to the TLC (The Ladies Cartel) series. In the *Tender Loving Desire* collection, you will be introduced to the two books that kicked off this popular series.

I had a great time crafting the first book of the series—*Sex and Lies.* This title reveals the torrid love and secrets between Savannah and her sexy husband, Blake. As the series continues, you'll get to know all the ladies who have secret lives and use their instincts as quickly as they use a gun or a listening device.

The second book in the collection, *Seduction and Lies,* brings fashion photographer Danielle to the front lines. With her best friend and Cartel member Savannah not around, Danielle has to take over an assignment and get a crash course in Cartel operations. She must also work on the secrets of her own identity that have always haunted her, and on her inability to commit to the unabashed love of Nick.

I have plenty of surprises in store for you, including sexy men, dynamic women and steamy sensuality— what more could a romance reader want?

Until next time, happy reading.

Donna

To all my readers who have been so supportive over the years. I thank each and every one of you from the bottom of my heart.

SEX AND LIES

Chapter 1

Tonight would change her life. She knew it. Anticipation tingled in Savannah's veins. Had anyone asked her years earlier if she would ever be able to lead a double life, lie to family, friends and her husband about what she did in her spare time, she would have laughed in their faces. She spun her office chair away from her computer screen toward the ringing multiline phone.

"Billings and Tate, Attorneys-at-Law, Savannah Fields speaking."

"Hi, sweetheart," came the always chirpy voice.

"Hey, Mom." Savannah noticed the flashing blip on her computer screen from the corner of her eye, indicating a new e-mail. "What's up?" she asked as she opened the e-mail and read the note from her boss, Richard Billings. He needed a case file pulled to prepare for court. Savannah switched the call to her headset and walked to the file cabinet.

"I just wanted to remind you about the meeting tonight."

"I'll be there. I told Blake we were having our monthly pep meeting."

Mother and daughter chuckled.

"If Blake only knew what *TLC* really was," Claudia said.

"He'd have a fit." Savannah imagined the expression of appalled disbelief on her husband's face.

To the casual observer Savannah Fields was a highly paid paralegal for a small but busy corporate law firm in midtown Manhattan and married to Blake Fields, the very sexy architect and builder of upscale apartment complexes and office buildings. They lived a solid, upper-class lifestyle and enjoyed all of its perks. But Savannah, her mother and two dozen more New York women had a life that not even their closest friends would ever suspect.

"Well, tonight is important so try to get there early. I don't want you to miss out on anything and I want a good seat."

Savannah flipped through the files until she located the one she was looking for, then pushed the metal drawer shut. "You want me to pick you up?"

"No, I'll take my car."

"See you later, Mom, and no speeding," she warned. Claudia Martin was notorious for her lead foot.

Claudia scoffed at the reprimand. "I'll try."

"If you get there before I do, save me a seat. Gotta go. Love you." She smacked kisses into the phone before disconnecting the call.

"Savannah…"

She looked up into the deep-set green eyes of her boss, who was a dead ringer for an older version of the actor Keanu Reeves.

"Hey, Richard. I have that file for you." She reached for it on her desk and handed it over.

"Thanks. Look, I know this is short notice but I'm going to need you to stay a little longer tonight."

Her stomach knotted. "Tonight!" Her normally even timbre rose two octaves as she jerked her neck to the side.

Richard held up his hands and inadvertently took a step back. His friend and business partner Jack Tate had just been talking about a book by playwright and actor Tyler Perry—*Don't Make a Black Woman Take Off Her Earrings*. He might not be up on all the black vernacular, but he got the sense that if Savannah took off her earrings at this precise moment he was in trouble.

"You know you will be paid well for the time. But I really need your help preparing for Monday."

Savannah pursed her lips and folded her arms beneath her C-cup breasts.

"Richard," she said, assuming her mother tone, "how many times have we been through this?" She pinched her lips and titled her head to the side.

Richard's hopeful expression turned sheepish. "I—"

She threw up her hand, palm facing Richard. "Don't answer. It was a rhetorical question. You can't keep waiting until the last minute. I know you're a brilliant attorney, which I hope to aspire to one day. But in the meantime I have a life, which begins promptly at 5:01 p.m." Her right brow rose to emphasize her point.

Richard took the well-deserved tongue lashing. They'd had this conversation at least once every couple of months for the past five years that they'd worked together. Savannah would chew him out, he took it and eventually she would help him out.

Any other time her "Richard traumas," which she'd dubbed these episodes, wouldn't be more than a minor annoyance, but today was different. However, she also knew that no matter what, Richard never asked her to do anything if he didn't really need her help—which was a lot.

Savannah blew out a breath. It was going to be a long night, but she could swing it.

"Fine," she conceded as they both knew she would. "But I'm warning you, I'm leaving at 7:00 p.m. sharp. And if you're not done then you explain to your client why he's going to jail."

Richard grinned, the dimple in his left cheek flashing. "Fair enough." He leaned down and kissed her forehead. "You're the best."

"I know," she grumbled, and reached for the ringing phone while waving Richard away.

"Billings and Tate…"

"Hey, baby."

Savannah's insides did a slow sensuous dance. Her eyes darkened and a warm smile moved languidly across her mouth.

"Hey, baby, yourself." She cuddled the phone close to her. "How's everything?"

"Busy as usual," Blake said with a light chuckle.

Savannah and Blake had been married for six years. Most people thought they were still newlyweds. Savannah adored her husband. He was the man she'd dreamed about since she was a little girl and when they met at an out of the way lounge in the West Village she knew that dreams did come true.

The attraction between them from the very first night was comparable to what authors who write romance novels call "hot and instantaneous." Blake wasn't just good-looking—Blake Fields was *f-i-n-e,* with a capital *F.* It always amazed her that she was the one who landed him. She knew she was no showstopper. Actually she was quite ordinary looking and had to watch her weight with the diligence of a priest trying to save souls—it was an unending job. But she cleaned up well, as she would tell herself when she looked in the mirror. She knew all the makeup tricks and what clothes complemented her solid frame. More often than not, many people mistook her for Nia Long. Not to mention that Savannah could make Blake Fields see heaven when they made love.

"Busy is good," she said in response to his statement.

"I think I'm going to have some exciting news to share but I don't want to be premature."

Savannah grew jumpy with excitement. "You know I hate secrets," she pleaded, although she kept plenty herself. "Can't you at least give me a hint?"

"Okay, you beat it out of me." He cleared his throat. "Remember I told you about the housing-complex deal that was on the table?"

"Yes." Her pulse kicked up a notch and she held her breath. The housing complex would revitalize downtown Brooklyn and was touted to be the biggest single development in decades in the area.

"W-ell…" He drew out the word.

"Come on Blake," Savannah begged.

"We won the bid and they love my design."

"Blake!" she squealed, and jumped up from her seat. "Oh, my goodness, that's incredible. I knew you could do it, baby."

Blake laughed deep in his throat. "I am sailing! This is major. This project is so high profile. I'm going to be on the map for good."

"I'm so proud of you," she said, breaking down each word.

"This calls for a celebration. I thought we could go out tonight."

The wheels of elation came to a grinding halt.

"Tonight?" she croaked.

"Yeah." He paused. "Oh, you have that thing tonight."

She heard the disappointment in his voice. She squeezed her eyes shut and tried to think. There was no getting around missing the meeting at TLC, not to mention the extra time she would have to spend at work.

"Look, I'll be finished by nine, nine-thirty. It's Friday. Let's go for a late dinner and spend the day in bed tomorrow."

"Hmm, I like the sound of that already," he said, perking right up. "I'll make reservations at The Cabaret and I'll leave tomorrow in your very capable hands."

"Perfect," she purred into the phone. "I'll meet you at the restaurant no later than ten."

"Can't wait. I've been aching for you all day," Blake said, his voice growing thick.

Savannah squirmed in her seat and licked her lips. "I'll make it worth your while," she cooed.

"I intend to hold you to that. See you tonight."

"Love you," she whispered.

"Love you right back."

Slowly Savannah hung up the phone. Well, she certainly had her day cut out for her.

Chapter 2

Blake hung up the phone just as his assistant Jasmine poked her head in the partially open door.

"Blake, they're waiting for you in the conference room."

"Thanks, J. I'll be right there." He took his jacket from the back of his chair and put it on as he walked out. Jasmine handed him a manila folder as he passed her desk.

This meeting would be brief, Blake mused as he continued down the short hallway. Tristan Montgomery said she wanted to confirm some dates. That was something that could have easily been taken care of on the phone, but Ms. Montgomery never missed an opportunity to visit his office under one pretext or another.

"Sorry for the wait," he said, opening the door and stepping right inside. He shook hands with Tristan and then her latest assistant. As usual Tristan was dressed to exploit all of her attributes. Today it was a burnt orange number that dipped a little too low for nine to five.

"Not a problem," Tristan said. "Jasmine made us very comfortable." She let her eyes wander up and down his body.

Blake cleared his throat and smoothed down his tie as he sat. "So what do you need clarified, Ms. Montgomery?"

She pouted. "Please, Blake, we're in bed together, so to speak. You can at least call me Tristan." She rocked him with her expensive smile.

Blake sidestepped the comment and straightened his tie again. He opened the folder that Jasmine had given him before glancing up and across the hard-wood table. Tristan was staring at him as if he were a rare delicacy that had been set on the table for lunch. He wanted to tug his tie off. It was suddenly cutting off his circulation. Being in the same room with Tristan Montgomery always did that to him.

She was one of the few black elite that was born into money. Her late father, Graham Montgomery, built his fortune in the real-estate game. He'd started off by renting apartments for a small agency. Learning everything he could about investment property, he bought his first building at the age of twenty-five. Upon his untimely death at sixty-two, Graham

Montgomery was a billionaire with property dotting across the country, from high-rise office buildings to luxury condos and strip malls. Before his death he started to stake a claim on one of the Hawaiian Islands. With his passing, his only child inherited it all.

"Uh, based on the rollout schedule I don't anticipate any problems," Blake said, keeping the conversation on track and his eyes on the documents in front of him.

Tristan slowly rose from her seat and rounded the table like a panther on the prowl until she stood slightly behind him. She placed her hand on his shoulder and leaned down to read the notes in front of him. Her left breast brushed his shoulder.

Blake tugged at his tie. "I was pretty sure that Jasmine gave you a copy," he said, trying to keep his voice light.

"You know how it is with copies…"

He was forced to look up at her. "No, actually I don't."

Tristan grinned and eased back. "They're nothing like the real thing," she said as she returned to her seat with the folder in her hand. She made show of reviewing the timeline.

"Were there any questions that you had in particular?"

"Actually, yes." She flipped the folder shut. "With you being so busy with the design and overseeing construction, when will you ever have any free time?"

"Excuse me?" He couldn't believe that she went there—and in front of someone else. Maybe this was all some kind of game, a test of some sort.

"You know the old saying—all work and no play…"

"I'm sure I'll find time to relax. My main priority at the moment is getting this job up and running. That's it," he added, looking her deep in the eyes.

She lifted her chin ever so slightly. "I'm sure you have everything under control. But since it's my money that is financing it, I want to make sure that every *i* is dotted and every *t* is crossed."

"Of course. I can assure you that there is nothing to worry about." He glanced from one woman to the other then stood, hoping she would get the hint. "Is there anything else that we need to discuss?"

"Yes, your availability next week."

He frowned. "Excuse me?"

"I'm hosting a dinner party at my penthouse next week." She picked up her clutch purse from the table. "There are several people I want you to meet, potential clients."

"Sounds wonderful. Both me and my wife, Savannah, love dinner parties." He reached across the table, snatched up the folder and tucked it beneath his arm.

Her eyes tightened just a hint. "I'll be sure to get all the details to Jasmine."

"Great. I'll walk you both to the elevator." He held

the door open for her. When she passed she ran her hand along the sleeve of his suit jacket.

"Armani?"

Blake swallowed. "Yes."

She grinned, her hazel eyes darkened. "I can always tell. You're a man with good taste. I like that in a man." She brushed by him and walked out.

Once they were gone, Blake released his long breath of tension. He stopped at Jasmine's desk. "Listen, the next time that woman comes here you make sure you buzz me after five minutes."

Jasmine tried not to laugh. "Don't tell me she hit on you."

"I won't." He walked off to his office.

Once inside the safety of his own space, he took his tie off completely. Tristan was a gorgeous woman, there was no doubt about that. And he knew a come-on when he saw one. In all the years of his marriage he had never strayed or contemplated straying. He was more than happy with Savannah and he didn't need the distraction of a hot socialite to ruin his track record. He certainly hoped that Ms. Montgomery stayed on her side of the dividing line. Mixing business with pleasure could bring nothing but trouble.

He reached for the phone to make reservations for dinner. A pleasant dinner with his wife and a long night of good loving was just the thing he needed to dislodge the memory of Tristan's lush body brushing up against his.

Just as he finished with his phone call and had his

reservation confirmed for ten, his close friend and business partner, Steven Long, knocked on the door.

"Come in." He hung up the phone. "Hey, man."

"Hey, yourself." He stepped inside. "I got a whiff of Ms. Hotstuff." He chuckled. "What brings her to our neck of the woods again?"

"Nothing that couldn't have been handled on the phone. She claimed she wanted to go over the roll-out schedule."

"But what she really wanted was to roll you out." He plopped down in a chair opposite Blake.

"Very funny."

"But true. That woman has a thing for you, man. Every time you step into the room her eyes light up."

Blake grimaced. "I'm a married man."

"I really don't think she cares."

"Is it that obvious that she's…"

"I'll put it this way, even Stevie Wonder could see it."

Blake shook his head. "I'm trying to keep this all on the up and up. The last thing I need is to get our wires crossed."

"Like I said, she doesn't care. But, hey, if you don't want it feel free to send her in my direction. I sure as hell wouldn't throw her out of bed."

Steve was a notorious hound from back in their college days at Moorehouse University. He'd slowed down just a little when they headed off to MIT for grad school where they received their engineering and architectural degrees, but Steven still needed a secretary to keep up with the women he dated. Not much had changed in the years since. It totally escaped Blake why Tristan had latched on to him and not Steven who was single and always available.

"She's having some kind of gathering at her penthouse next week."

"You know how I love hotsy-totsy parties," he joked.

"Yeah, anyway, she's supposed to send over the information to Jasmine. Said she has some people she wants me to meet—potential business."

Steven nodded. "Cool. I'll pencil her in. Wonder if she is going to have any of her rich, single girlfriends around."

Blake held up his hand. "Don't even think about it. I don't want to screw up this deal when some fling of yours goes bad—as they tend to do."

Steven held his hand to his chest. "You wound me, dawg. Can I help it if I have a short attention span and the ladies can't take goodbye for an answer?"

"Whatever. Just don't mess this up."

"I don't think it's me you have to worry about. Ms. Thing isn't one to take no for an answer and sooner or later she's gonna want yours."

Blake shot him a look of disregard but the truth of the matter was that Steven was right.

Chapter 3

Savannah's three-inch heels clicked like shotgun fire against the concrete of the underground employee parking lot. Her navy blue skirt suit with the pristine white tank top and a strand of real pearls around her slender neck gave her the appearance of the legal eagle she could easily become.

For a woman of only five foot five she had a long stride. She swore it came from her devout adherence to Pilates. She believed she could use all the help she could get in keeping her weight under control and giving her compact body more of a sleek and lean appearance. And as she had come to discover since becoming a member of TLC, looks were definitely deceiving.

She used her remote to disengage the alarm on

her black SUV and hopped up inside. The garage had a few cars left of those still burning the after-hour oil. She checked the dashboard clock against her watch—seven-forty. She cussed under her breath and put the SUV in gear, her skirt rising up her thighs to a provocative level. She'd wound up staying longer than she'd planned and now she would really have to make double-time.

Quickly maneuvering around pillars and yellow directional arrows, she used her monthly pass card and zipped up the exit ramp and out into the approaching twilight. As she made her way to the FDR she silently prayed that traffic would be light. She entered the FDR from 34th street and went north. Thankfully there was an open lane and she grinned as she watched the speedometer climb to 70 mph. At that pace she'd reach Harlem in about fifteen minutes.

In record time, she pulled onto the street that housed TLC headquarters, which was tucked away in an upscale brownstone directly across the street from the Pause for Men day spa. If she wasn't a married woman she could certainly spend her free time man watching with all the hotties that came in and out of there. Of course, parking was at a premium and it took her another five minutes to find a spot a block away.

Savannah checked in at reception, showing her ID, and then went upstairs to where the meeting was being held.

The main room was buzzing with chatter from the members of TLC who were using the time to catch up and share stories before the formal meeting began. Savannah waved to Leslie and Dina, two of the women she recognized. They were both high up in the ranking, having been part of TLC for about five years. As a result they got the best assignments. Savannah's goal was to one day be on par with both of them.

She walked over to the refreshment table and poured herself a cup of fruit punch just as Claudia came up behind her.

"I was wondering when you were going to get here."

Savannah turned to see her mother. As always Claudia Martin was ready for her close-up. Claudia, unlike Savannah, was tall and still slender. Her skin was butter soft, the color of warm honey and so flawless the only makeup she ever used was lipstick and mascara. Both mother and daughter loved clothes by St. John and Claudia wore hers well. Tonight she chose a red jersey sheath with a matching jacket. Gold was her accessory.

Savannah leaned up and kissed her mother's cheek. "Richard had a last-minute project."

Claudia made a face. "What else is new? One of these days you need to tell him just where he can go."

"Mom!" Savannah scoffed and bit back a laugh. "He's my boss and it's my job."

Claudia waved off the comment. "Humph."

"Ladies, if everyone could take their seats we're ready to get started," Leslie announced from the small podium.

Claudia grabbed Savannah by the arm and hustled her to the front. "I got us a spot on the antique loveseat."

The main room or ballroom of the brownstone was set up like an English parlor, with heavily decorated seating in a variety of brocades and velvets, crystal chandeliers, mahogany tables, gilded mirrors and a marble fireplace. It was like stepping back in time.

Savannah and Claudia took their seats. After several moments of shuffling and jockeying, the rest of the women found seats and settled down. As Savannah surveyed the assemblage she was still intrigued by the array of women who made up TLC—everything from business executives to fashion models, housewives to single mothers and in all shapes, sizes and nationalities. To everyone outside of the elite organization TLC meant Tender Loving Care body products and its members were the equivalent of Avon or Amway sales reps. They were far from it.

"The June meeting of The Ladies Cartel will now come to order," Leslie announced. "We have a great deal to cover tonight—old business and new assignments."

Claudia squeezed Savannah's hand with anticipation. Savannah felt the rush of adrenaline. If she was lucky she would get her first assignment. She'd only been with the organization for a little under a year but in that time she'd made great strides in learning the intricacies of the Cartel's operation; self-defense techniques, surveillance equipment and how to shoot a gun if necessary. She'd been recruited by her mother and she couldn't have been more stunned than if her mother announced that she was indeed Santa Claus.

It was a Saturday afternoon; mother and daughter were in the local supermarket shopping for their annual Fourth of July barbecue. As they were loading their packages into Savannah's SUV, Claudia out of the blue said that she was a member of a secret organization.

"What?" Savannah laughed. "What secret organization, shoppers anonymous?" Claudia was a relentless shopper, her passion for clothes and home furnishings boggled Savannah's mind.

"I'm serious," she said. "And I have been allowed to recruit someone and I want that someone to be you."

"Ma, what in the world are you talking about?" Savannah put the last bag in the car and got in behind the wheel. She put on her designer sunglasses and pulled off.

"Just listen. Four years ago I met a woman in my exercise class, Dina Fleming. She told me about this group of women who are hired to perform a variety of jobs—mostly surveillance but sometimes it's more involved. It could be anything from posing as a girlfriend to getting hired at a business to find out about illegal practices."

Savannah turned to her mother in disbelief, peering at her over the top of her shades.

"I've done several jobs myself," she said with pride.

"Are you kidding me?"

"No. Remember the big scandal about the child-care agency about a year ago?"

Savannah frowned as she tried to remember. "Sort of, why?"

"I worked that case."

Savannah tossed her head back and laughed. "Stop playing."

"I'm very serious. There are about thirty women who are part of the Cartel—in the New York chapter. For those outside of the circle they believe we are no more than a group of women who sell skin-care and body products. No one ever suspects us, that's why we're so successful at what we do."

Maybe her mother was getting senile, Savannah thought as she drove and listened to the absurd story. She'd seen her mother's case of bath and beauty products hundreds of times. Now she expected her to think it was all part of some elite organization?

"Do you really expect me to believe this? Is this some gimmick to recruit me to sell something?"

"I promise you it's not. I presented your credentials to the board and they want to meet you."

"Credentials?"

"The fact that you work for a law firm and are familiar with the law, attorneys and the court system, we believe you could be a major asset to the organization."

Her head was spinning. This was nonsense, but she figured the least she could do was humor her mother. "Mom, I'm sure you really believe all this and if it will make you feel better I'll meet your friends." She patted her mother's thigh.

Claudia pushed her daughter's hand away. "Don't patronize me! I'm not some blithering idiot. And you should know better." She folded her arms in a huff. "If I'd thought for a minute that you would react this way I would have never opened my mouth."

Savannah stole a glance at her mother and could tell by the hard set of her mouth and the deep furrow between her brows that she was dead serious.

"I'm sorry if I offended you, Mom, but you have to admit this all sounds crazy."

"I know, I thought the same thing. But it's real, very real. So are you interested?"

"Intrigued, for sure."

"Good." Her expression brightened. "I'll set everything up."

And she did. Savannah met with Dina and Leslie and was grilled as if she were applying for a job with the CIA. Then they did a background check and when everything came back clear she began her training which lasted for six months.

TLC was a secret society of highly skilled women

who were hired to perform covert operations at the behest of scorned wives, jealous husbands, business executives, government agencies and families in dispute over inheritances. It came into being more than a decade earlier, having started in Langley, Virginia—home to secrets and lies. What began as a small investigative firm headed by Jean Wallington, slowly mushroomed into TLC with branches all across the country.

Savannah was ready for her very first assignment and she hoped that tonight would be the night.

"I want to begin by congratulating Tina and Marilyn for the excellent job they did with the redlining that was happening on Long Island," Leslie said. "As a result of their hard work, the real-estate agency that was discriminating against single women home owners and black families has been closed and the owners are facing jail time."

A cheer followed by applause filled the room.

"Brenda Levin has been promoted to level two for her hard work in recruiting the most new members in the past year."

More applause.

"Tonight I want you all to give a warm welcome to three new recruits. When I call your names will you please stand? Margaret Jacobs, Mi Lin Chan and Denise Walker."

The ladies stood, smiled and waved at their fellow Cartel members to shouts of "Welcome aboard."

Leslie waited until the room quieted. She scanned

the room. "As you know from the monthly newsletter that comes with your supplies, we have several cases that need our attention. The board has reviewed the experience, skills and personal backgrounds of each of you and we've made our selections." Leslie cleared her throat and tucked several strands of her blond hair behind her ear. She opened a leather folder and pulled out a piece of paper. The room hushed.

"Serena Hamilton, Justine Parker and Savannah Fields."

The collected held breath was released. Savannah clutched her mother's hand, animation sparkling in her eyes.

"Each of you ladies will receive your instructions before you leave tonight. Of course, after reading what is required of you, you have the option to decline the assignment. Should you decide to take the assignment you will be provided with whatever support the Cartel can provide. Congratulations, ladies, and with that this portion of the meeting is adjourned. Feel free to enjoy the food and drinks and would Serena, Justine and Savannah stop in the office before you leave." Leslie stepped away from the podium and chatter filled the room.

"Congratulations, Savannah," Melonie, one of the early members of the Cartel said. "This is your first assignment, right?"

"Yes, it is." Savannah was giddy with excitement. Her mind was running in a million directions at once trying to imagine what her assignment would be.

Melonie touched Savannah's shoulder. "Well, if you need anything let me know, but you have a pro in the family," she added, looking with admiration at Claudia. "So I'm sure you'll be fine."

Savannah drew in a long breath. "That I do."

They chatted for a few minutes more and Savannah continued to get words of encouragement and support from her sister members.

Claudia yawned. "Sorry," she said. "Long day."

Savannah looked at her watch and gasped in alarm. It was nine forty-five. She'd promised Blake she would meet him at the restaurant at ten and she still had to meet with Leslie to get her assignment.

"I really have to go. I have a dinner date with my husband."

"Go, girl, go," Melonie said.

"Let me check in with Leslie. Mom, I'll call you tomorrow." She kissed her mother's cheek, said her goodbyes and hurried to the main office which was down the hallway from the ballroom.

When she got to the office, Justine was just coming out. "Good luck," she murmured as she passed Savannah.

"Thanks, you, too."

Savannah stepped up to the closed door and knocked lightly.

"Come in," came the voice on the other side of the door.

Savannah turned the knob and stepped inside. For

an instant her step faltered. It wasn't Leslie as she'd expected but the head honcho in charge.

"Savannah." Jean Wallington beamed as if she'd run into a long-lost friend. "Come in. Have a seat."

Jean Wallington rarely made an appearance. She was so high up the chain of command that you needed oxygen to hang out with her. Word had it that she was a former CIA operative who'd specialized in covert opts. Having had her fill with the old boys' club she, over time, began recruiting for her own organization. Jean firmly believed that women had just as much, if not more, skill in the field of undercover operations, primarily because no one ever suspected a woman. But mostly because women understood people. Women had instincts and they were rarely wrong. Jean banked on those instincts of her team to get the jobs done. She was never wrong.

Savannah flashed a nervous smile and sat in the high back Queen Ann chair opposite Jean. Jean folded her hands on top of the cherrywood desk.

"I've been watching you for a while, Savannah," Jean began, "and I'm very impressed by what I've seen."

"Thank you."

Jean flipped open a thin manila file folder and quickly glanced over it before sweeping her thin pink-framed glasses from her sharp nose, displaying the most intense green eyes Savannah had ever seen. They were the color of jade.

"When we make our selections, we do it very

carefully. We take many factors into account—length of membership, who you were recruited by, your education, profession and how you did during training. Most important we look at what we call the unobvious skills or attributes in our members." Jean waved her glasses toward Savannah. "In your case we discovered that you have an innate quality with people. People are drawn to you, Savannah, and for this assignment that's exactly what we need—that, combined with your legal background. We feel you are the perfect member to handle this job."

Savannah had had no idea that she was viewed that way. She was thrilled to know it yet a bit unsettled to realize that she'd been watched that closely without her knowledge. Damn, they were good.

"Your assignment will be to gather evidence on The Montgomery Enterprises. It has been brought to our attention that the corporation has been laundering money in addition to working with substandard products in the development of their housing projects and some corporate structures. We're confident that the confirmation we're seeking is buried in their legal documents. They have some of the best lawyers in the country on their payroll." She took a larger manila envelope from the file and handed it over to Savannah. "All of the information you need is inside. The information on those pages will begin to dissolve within fifteen minutes of opening the envelope and exposing it to the air. Memorize it. The tools that you need will be delivered to you in your next TLC shipment by courier."

Savannah nodded. The name Montgomery gave her an itch that she couldn't quite scratch. It was so familiar but she wasn't sure why. She held the envelope to her chest. Her racing heart thumped making the envelope vibrate like a tuning fork.

"Any questions?"

"How much time do I have?"

"Three weeks."

Savannah's deep brown eyes widened a fraction.

"Of course, you will have the full support of TLC."

"Any reason for the short window?"

"Yes, The Montgomery Enterprises is set to break ground on a new development by the end of the month. We need the information irrefutably verified before then."

Montgomery...breaking ground. It couldn't be.

"If there's nothing else." Jean stood and Savannah realized for the first time just how tall Jean actually was. She had to be at least five-eleven, Savannah guesstimated. She got up, took the envelope still clutched to her chest and stuck out her hand. "Thank you for the opportunity, Jean."

"I expect great things from all of our Cartel members," she said, shaking Savannah's hand with a death grip, her green eyes boring into Savannah's.

"I won't disappoint you."

"I know."

Savannah drew in a short breath and lifted her chin an inch in acceptance.

With her first assignment plastered to the front of her suit jacket by a damp hand, Savannah bobbed and weaved her way out of the brownstone, accepting heartfelt congratulations along the way. Once outside she gulped in the night air then sprinted down the street to her car. It was already ten-twenty. She got in the car and immediately called Blake on her cell phone.

"Baby, I'm so sorry," she said the instant his voice came on the phone.

"No worries, sugar. I ran into Mac and we were having a drink at the bar. How much longer will you be?"

"At least fifteen minutes."

"See you when you get here."

"Love you," Savannah said, truly meaning it.

"Back at ya. Drive safe."

She flipped the phone closed and put the car in gear. Her husband was the best. Damn she was lucky.

At least up to that point.

Chapter 4

The Cabaret restaurant and lounge was located on the upper Eastside of Manhattan on Park Avenue and 52nd Street. Blake and Savannah had stumbled upon this jewel during the first year of their marriage when they were still exploring each other and the city that they loved. The Cabaret became "their place" and they celebrated every event worth celebrating there.

The food was exquisite, though pricey, but it was the atmosphere that drew them back time and again. It had just the right amount of dim lighting with mirrors in strategic places, candle votives on the intimate tables tucked throughout the space. And every night there was a great jazz performance.

"So how's married life, my man?" Mac asked as

he swallowed what remained of his vodka on the rocks.

Blake grinned. "Couldn't be better. I love it."

"Get out. You, Mr. Permanent Bachelor." Mac chuckled.

Blake lowered his head, his grin broadening. "Yeah, I didn't figure marriage was for me, but when I met Savannah…" He shook his head in wonder. "All the others paled in comparison to her."

"I can't believe it. I have women still asking me about 'your friend, um, Blake,'" he said in a really bad falsetto.

They laughed at Mac's bad imitation of a female voice.

"I'm off the market, man." Blake took a swig of his drink. "What about you, ever going to settle down?"

"Why?" He signaled the waiter for another drink. "I firmly believe that men were not created to be with one woman. Why do you think they outnumber us?"

Blake cut his eyes in Mac's direction and snorted a laugh. "Maybe because we drop dead sooner from trying to keep up with so many women."

"But what a way to go!"

They clinked glasses.

"Other than women how're things going on The Street?"

Mac, whose real name was Fred McDonald, worked on Wall Street. They were both Moorehouse grads, but Blake had gone on to study architecture at MIT. After graduation, Mac went to work buying and selling.

"Crazy man. The work is grueling but the rewards are worth it. Just bought my second house out in Montclair, New Jersey."

"Congratulations! But what are you going to do with two homes?"

"The brownstone in Harlem is strictly an investment property. The one in Jersey is where I'll live."

"You plan to commute into New York every day? The traffic is horrific."

"Naw, I have enough stress to deal with at work. I'll be using mass transit."

Blake nodded. "Good move."

"What's going on with you?"

"Just landed a major development deal."

"Yeah, which one?" He angled his body on the stool toward Blake.

"Can't really talk about it right now. The ink is still drying. But I will say that it will put me on the map for good."

Mac slapped him on the back. "I always knew you would hit the big-time."

"That's what Savannah and I are celebrating tonight." He brought his glass to his mouth and took a slow swallow.

"It'll be good to see Savannah again. We all have to get together sometime. You and Savannah and me and whomever I'm so inclined to be with at the moment." He chuckled.

Blake shook his head. "One of these days the right woman is gonna come along and you will be toast."

"Like you were toast…" Savannah whispered in Blake's ear. She pecked him on the cheek. "Sorry I'm late."

Blake swiveled around on the stool and wrapped his arms around her waist. "Hey, baby." His gaze danced over her face still amazed that this woman was all his. He tenderly kissed her mouth.

"Hey, get a room," Mac jokingly cut in.

"Don't hate," Savannah teased, stepping out of her husband's arms. She came around her husband and hugged Mac. "Good to see you." She patted his arm. "Still on the prowl?" she asked, referring to his notorious womanizing.

"Like the old saying goes, can't teach an old dog new tricks."

Blake slid off the stool and turned to Mac. "Let's get together soon. It's been a long time."

Mac stuck out his hand which Blake shook. "Definitely. Give me a call anytime. All of my numbers are the same."

"I will," Blake said.

"Good seeing you, Savannah," Mac said.

"You, too," Savannah replied.

Blake slid his arm around her waist. "Our table is waiting. Let me tell the hostess you're here."

They walked to the front of the restaurant. The hostess approached.

"My party has arrived," Blake said.

"Great. Right this way." She took two menus from the holder and led them to their table. "Your server will be with you shortly. Can I get you something to drink in the meantime?"

Blake held up his glass. "I'm good." He turned to Savannah.

"Hmm, I'll have a diet cola with a twist of lemon."

"Your server will be right here with your drink and to take your orders. Have a good evening."

Blake turned his full attention to his wife. "You have that gleam in your eyes. Something exciting happen at work or at your meeting?"

Savannah inwardly flinched. "Nothing out of the ordinary. I'm buzzed about you!" She reached across the table and squeezed his hand. "Tell me every-thing—or at least as much as you can," she said.

"Well, all systems are go on the development. The entire project has been kept under wraps for months, as you know. There's been so much speculation about who was going to get the contract, if all the money would come through in time and if the City Council would approve it." He blew out a breath. "It's been an uphill battle the entire time. The surrounding com-munity has been against it from the beginning." The light in his eyes slowly dimmed. He looked at his wife. "Some folks are going to lose their homes."

Savannah heard the sadness in his voice. "But when the project is done, it will be better than be-fore," she said, hoping to lift some of the weight off his shoulders. "And this project is going to provide jobs for thousands, especially minorities."

The corner of his lush mouth curved up in a grin. "You sound like the Mayor's press secretary."

She waved off his comment with a light chuckle. "I don't mean to sound like the poster child for re-development, but it will ultimately improve the area, bring in jobs and housing. Isn't the city planning to provide relocation support to anyone who becomes displaced?"

"That's what we've been told."

"Then stop worrying. Enjoy your fifteen minutes of fame and put up the best damned development that this town has seen in decades."

"That's why I love you."

She lowered her lids and looked at him coyly. "And why is that?"

"'Cause you always know how to make me feel good in and out of bed," he said.

Her voice dropped to a husky whisper. "We all have our skills." She puckered her lips and blew him a kiss.

"Are you ready to order?"

Two pairs of eyes rose to meet those of the wait-ress.

"We're not hungry," they said in unison.

Blake sliced a look at his wife. "You can bring the check for the drinks."

Blake and Savannah tumbled through the door of their Harlem town house, giggling and groping like teenagers. The entire drive home Blake had kept one hand on the wheel and the other buried between his wife's thighs. If there weren't so many bright street lights on their block they would have made love right there in the front seat of the car. But being the respectable couple that they thought themselves to be, it wouldn't look good to get caught by one of the members of the block patrol.

Savannah kicked the door shut and tugged at Blake's shirt. Two white buttons went dancing across the sparkling hardwood floor. His tie dangled at an angle from around his neck. Blake grabbed the hem of her skirt and hitched it up around her hips. Mouths and tongues sought out any inch of exposed flesh as they tore off clothes en route to the bedroom.

Savannah and Blake tumbled onto the king-size bed, she pinned snuggly beneath his hard body.

"This is all I could think about all day," he murmured in her ear before nibbling her lobe.

"Show me exactly what you were thinking about," she whispered back.

The sublime pleasure that Blake evoked in her body hadn't waned a bit in the years of their marriage. If anything her lust and passion for him seemed to have escalated with time. He knew every one of her buttons and he expertly pressed them all until she was feverish with need.

His fingertips were featherlight as they glided and caressed her hot flesh. His mouth teased and taunted the slope of her neck, inching downward to the rise of her breasts before taking a tight nipple into his mouth and laving it with his tongue.

Savannah moaned, a sound that was filled with urgency, but Blake took his time—the scenic route as he called it—and continued to chart new territory. He slipped his hand between her parted thighs and flicked his finger back and forth across her swollen bud until her entire body trembled.

Blake reluctantly left the tenderness of her breasts and eased down toward her fluttering stomach, letting his tongue dance around her navel.

Savannah's hips instinctively moved in a slow undulating fashion. *Please* escaped from her lips on a rush of hot breath.

"This what you want?" he uttered just as his tongue slid across the pulse of her bud.

Savannah cried out and gripped the sheets in tight fists. Her pelvis jutted upward and Blake grabbed her behind and pulled her fully toward his eager mouth. He suckled and teased until he knew from her tortured mewls and the shuddering of her body that she was ready to explode into a million tiny pieces. He pushed her thighs farther apart then up and over his shoulders.

Hot tears squeezed out of her eyes as she was suddenly filled with the rock hardness of her husband. He moved into her by degrees giving them both a chance to savor those first moments of unity.

"Oh," he groaned deep in his throat. "You're so

hot…so wet." He pushed in farther and she squeezed around him while rotating her hips.

Savannah reached down between them and found his heavy, seed-filled sac and gently massaged it. Blake plunged deep inside her until there was nowhere else to go but in and out on a maddening quest to reach heaven.

Their paced picked up in unison. Savannah swore she heard ringing in her ears, every nerve ending in her body was charged. Her head swam. And then Blake did that thing he always did. He moved inside her in a circle and hit that spot.

Lights erupted. Her entire body stiffened for several seconds as if electrified. Then her *insides,* with a mind of their own, violently contracted and released around his stiff member. It felt as if he were growing inside her as he approached his own climax which set off another wave of contractions that spread up her belly and out to her limbs to explode in her brain.

She opened her mouth to scream out her pleasure, but all sound was trapped in her throat as her climax spun out of control. Blake rode her faster and faster, the words coming from his lips incomprehensible. He pulled her so close to his wet body that not even air separated them as he pushed and pushed and pushed. He buried his head into the valley of her neck barely muffling the growl of release that jettisoned from him into her.

Maybe this time, Savannah silently prayed as she clung to her husband, concentration on draining him of every ounce of his fertile seed, keeping her hips high in the air. *Maybe this time.* She felt him pulse and jerk inside her. She wrapped her legs tightly around him and used her hand to press him against her opening, not allowing even a drop to escape.

"I love you so much," Blake whispered, his voice cracking with emotion. His body convulsed one last time before all his weight eased down on her, pinning her to the damp sheets.

"And I love you, my darling man. I love you."

They closed their eyes, holding on to each other, locked as one.

Chapter 5

"We didn't get a chance to talk much last night," Blake said with a wicked grin on his face as he emerged from the shower with a towel wrapped around his waist.

Savannah had her knees drawn up to her chest, watching her handsome husband approach and wondered how she'd gotten so lucky. She angled her head to the side. "I think we did a lot of talking, just not the verbal kind."

He pointed a finger in her direction. "Touché."

Savannah patted an empty spot next to her. "So tell me about the deal."

Blake came to sit beside her. He fluffed up a pillow and leaned back against it, folding his hands across his sculpted belly.

"Well, as I was hinting at…"

He explained the details of the deal which entailed his company being the sole architect for the project, as well as handling the contract for finding the right construction crew.

"How long will the entire project last from start to finish?"

"If we get all the clearances on time and I can seal a deal with the contractors… Hmm, from start to finish, at least a year. And that's barring all of the unforeseen obstacles that come up with any job this size."

Savannah nodded. "Did I tell you how proud I am of you?"

Blake snuggled close. "Probably so, but tell me again."

She cupped his chin in her palm. "I'm so proud of you." She pecked him on the lips then winked.

"And how did your meeting go with the ladies last night?" He yawned loudly and threw his arm across his eyes. "What I wouldn't give to be a fly on the wall."

Savannah's heart thumped then settled. She still had not read the details of her assignment. But she had a very strong feeling that it wasn't going to be easy. "It went fine as usual. Girl stuff. Uh, honey…"

"Hmm?"

"What is the name of the finance people for the development again? Did you say Montgomery?"

"Yeah, The Montgomery Enterprises. Run by Miss Conglomerate herself, Tristan Montgomery."

Lord, please don't let it be her.

"By the way, she invited us to a get together at her home next week."

"Really? Then she can't be all that bad."

"I don't know what it is about the woman that rubs me the wrong way."

"But you don't work with her directly. So it shouldn't be too much of a problem."

"That's just it—I don't. But she's what you call a 'hands on' person. She's up on every detail, no matter how small."

"Don't let it bother you. She probably thinks she has to try harder because she's a woman."

"Hmm, maybe. Anyway, I don't want to talk business today. It's our day off. So what do you want to do today?"

"I was reading in the *Village Voice* that there's a boat ride up the Hudson from nine to one. Wanna go?"

"Sounds great." He turned on his side to face her. "That leaves us with quite a few hours to kill. Got any ideas on what we could do?" he asked as he trailed a finger down the center of her chest.

"We could try again to make a miracle happen." Her eyes looked at him from the depths of her soul.

Blake stroked her cheek. He knew how desperately Savannah wanted a child. They'd been trying unsuccessfully for nearly a year. He saw the sadness in her eyes when every month she'd stay as regular as a Swiss clock. They could buy stock in those little testing sticks with the amount of money she'd spent on in-home pregnancy tests.

"Listen, I don't want you to make yourself crazy about getting pregnant. The doctor said it could take time."

She pushed out a sigh. "I know." Her tone was full of dejection. "It's just that every time we make love I keep hoping...ya know?"

He kissed her tenderly. "I know. And when the time is right, it will happen." He rolled gently on top of her. "But in the meantime you know the old saying of practice makes perfect." He stroked her hip.

Savannah giggled. "Yeah, I had heard something like that..."

And as she took her husband deep into her body once more, she sent up her continued chant, *maybe this time*.

Savannah was in the kitchen fixing them something to eat before they both passed out from hunger and sexual fatigue when the phone rang.

"I got it," Blake yelled out from the bedroom where he hadn't moved from since they woke up.

Several moments later she could hear him coming up behind her chuckling and saying, "yes, ma'am." He handed her the phone. "Mom." He turned and sauntered back to the bedroom.

"Hey, Mom." She tucked the phone between her

ear and shoulder and continued to fix the western omelet.

"Hey, sweetie, can you talk?"

Savannah took a quick glance over her shoulder. "Yep. What's up?"

"You tell me," her mother said in a conspiratorial whisper.

Savannah lowered her voice. "I didn't get a chance to look at it yet."

"What? Savannah," she said in that tone she used with her as a little girl. "This is important. You wouldn't have been chosen if they didn't completely believe in you."

"Mother, I know. It's just that…well, I've been a little tied up."

Her mother said, "Chile, you're going to kill that man one of these days."

Savannah bit back a laugh. It never ceased to amaze her how out there and open her mother was about sex. "We are trying to have a baby, so I never want to miss out on an opportunity."

She turned off the flame beneath the frying pan and placed the omelet onto a platter. Savory steam wafted up to her nose.

"I told you before, stop trying and it will happen."

Savannah sighed. "Yeah, that's what Blake keeps saying."

"And he's right. Relax, sweetheart. I know you and Blake will make beautiful babies together when the time is right. In the meantime, I suggest you take a look at your assignment. I want you to do well on this. People are depending on you."

Savannah swallowed hard. "I'll take care of it. Promise."

"Good, and if you need me for anything, let me know."

"I will."

"Love you."

"Love you, too."

Slowly Savannah hung up the phone then took the platter and put it on the kitchen table. A part of her desperately wanted to read what was inside that envelope and another part of her dreaded it. But if she only had three weeks to pull off whatever it was that needed to be done, she couldn't ignore the contents for long.

Chapter 6

"I'm just going to relax and watch the game," Blake said, assuming his Sunday-afternoon position on the couch.

What else is new, Savannah's arched brow queried. She walked by and handed him the remote. It was a ritual she'd grown used to since the beginning of their marriage. Blake was willing to give all of his time and energy to her Monday through Saturday, but Sunday was sports day come hell or high water.

"Can I get you anything?" she asked.

"No, I'm good." He'd already spread out his goodies for the afternoon—chips, pretzels and an ice bucket with beer—and was surfing through the stations. The blare of a baseball game filled the room.

Savannah leaned down and kissed his forehead

then headed off to the bedroom. She closed the door behind her. Going to her dresser, she opened the bottom drawer and pulled out the envelope that was tucked beneath her lingerie.

Taking it to the bed, she felt her heart pound with trepidation. She used a nail file to slit open the top then pulled out the stapled pages. It had the TLC logo blazoned across the top. She knew she only had a short period of time to digest all of the information that was contained in the hermetically sealed envelope before the letters on the pages began to dissolve.

She read quickly, absorbing the information the way she did legal briefs, cataloging everything that was important and discarding the rest.

The more she read, the more disturbed she became. What she'd feared was no longer a bad feeling. It was a full-blown reality. The knot that had settled in her stomach since she'd gotten her assignment from Jean now threatened to loop around her lungs and cut off her air.

Her assignment was to infiltrate Montgomery headquarters on East 72nd Street, secure the original accounting documents and the legal papers that negotiated the land-acquisition deal for the development in downtown Brooklyn—the project that her husband was working on. It was believed that not only was The Montgomery Enterprises involved in illegal land deals and coercion, but several members of the City Council and the architect and developer, i.e. Blake Fields, PPC. She was to secure the necessary documents, any video tapes or audio conversations that would lead to indictments of all the parties involved—or irrefutable information to exclude them.

Her stomach roiled. Bile rose to the back of her throat and sat there burning. She stared at the pages as the words began to cloud over. She wiped the tears from her eyes as she watched the words slowly become ghostlike on the page until they were totally gone. The only thing remaining was the TLC logo.

The sudden ringing of the phone snapped through her, jerking her out of the place to which she'd descended. Dully she turned toward the intruding instrument and picked it up. She cleared her throat and sniffed hard.

"Hello…"

"Damn, girl, it's nearly one in the afternoon, you still asleep?"

Savannah laughed. Danielle Holloway was one of her two best friends, notorious for her early morning wake-up calls. One o'clock was definitely late for Dani. "What's up? And no, I'm not still asleep. Are you ill? It's after ten." She stole a glance at the now lily white pages.

"Very funny. I figured I'd give you a play since it was Sunday and all. Got any plans for today?"

"Not really. You know today is Blake's sports day, so I'm pretty much off of his radar until bedtime."

"I just got off the phone with Mia, we were thinking about going down to the South Street Seaport. They're having a jazz concert on one of the boats."

Maybe getting out of the house for the day and spending it with her girls was just the thing she needed to clear her head for a few hours.

"Sounds like a plan. What time?"

"You know me, I've been ready for hours." She chuckled. "Mia was finishing getting dressed and I'm going to pick her up. Then we can swing by and get you."

"I should be ready in about a half hour. That good?"

"We'll be there. Casual dress. I have on jeans and flip flops."

Yeah, Savannah knew what Dani meant by jeans and flip flops. Like Claudia, everything on Dani's body was high-end designer. As a fashion photographer for several leading women's magazines, Dani stayed on the cutting edge of style. "Right up my alley. See you guys in a few."

Savannah hung up, feeling momentarily better. She got off the bed and went to her closet to find something equally casual to wear.

Blake barely turned his eyes in her direction when she emerged from the bedroom in concert with the ringing of the doorbell.

"Somebody's at the door honey," he called out absently.

Savannah just shook her head and went to open the door. "Hey, Dani, wanna come in for a minute?"

They kissed cheeks.

"Just a sec to say hello to my favorite married man. Mia is in the car, we're double-parked."

As promised, Danielle was casual, at least in her mind. Her hip-hugging black Versace jeans were encrusted with what looked like cubic zirconia studs along the outside seams. A lavish silver chain belt hung from her waist and shimmied erotically each time she moved. Her petite size-seven feet were tucked into an exquisite pair of red Jimmy Choo sandals with a two-inch heel. Topping it all off was a single button, pristine white midriff blouse with elbow length sleeves. Her inky black hair that flowed almost to her hips when let loose and free was tossed on top of her head in a jazzy attempt at looking slightly disheveled and devilishly sexy.

Dani swept her sunglasses off the bridge of her nose with a flourish and sashayed inside. She struck a pose in front of Blake blocking his view of the game.

"Didn't your good southern mama teach you any manners?" she chastised.

"Yes, never to hit a woman even if she is blocking the game." Blake tried to push her aside and failed. "Come on, Dani, this is the top of the fourth. Mets at bat."

"You mean, you actually recognized me and I don't have on a sport's uniform? I'm impressed." She swatted his arm. "Say hello."

"Hello, Dani," he barked. "You're going to force

me to sit up and loose my position on the couch if you don't get out of the way," he practically whined trying to see around her.

Savannah marched over and grabbed Dani by the hand. "It's useless, sis. I could walk in front of him butt naked and he wouldn't notice." She pulled her toward the door. "See you later, baby. Going out with the girls."

He mumbled something unintelligible.

Savannah picked up her mango-colored Kate Spade purse—which matched her open-toed sandals—from the table in the foyer. "By the time he realizes I'm gone, I'll be back already," she said with a laugh of acceptance. "Come on, let's go."

"I'm determined to break that hypnotic stare one of these days," Danielle said, emphasizing the last four words.

"Good luck." Savannah shut the door behind them.

"Love that bag, by the way," Dani said with a hint of envy in her voice.

"Thanks. And no, you can't borrow it."

Dani huffed in mock offense.

They stepped out into the very warm June afternoon and down the concrete steps of Savannah and Blake's three-story town house, located in Harlem's historic Sugar Hill.

The house was originally owned by Savannah's great-grandparents, who turned it over to Claudia's mother, Sylvia, when she married and then Sylvia passed it on to Claudia on her wedding day and Claudia turned it over to Savannah as a wedding gift to her and Blake just as it had been done in the family for generations. Hopefully, one day Savannah would be able to turn the grand home over to her son or daughter. The family rumor was that Great-Granddad Jessie won the house in a high-stakes poker game from an old white land baron who figured he'd finally gotten rid of an albatross. It was no more than a rotting shell when Great-Granddad won it, but he and his four brothers worked on it for three solid years until they restored it to its former glory. It had been in the family ever since. A house that was once not worth the time it took to walk past it was now valued at more than one million dollars.

Mia waved as the duo came down the steps toward Dani's brand-new Ford Edge.

Savannah stood for a moment in front of the spanking new SUV with a hand on her hip. She snapped her head toward Dani who had a big smug smirk on her perfectly made-up face.

"So whatcha think?"

"Girl—" Savannah walked around it slowly "—when did you get this?"

"Picked it up yesterday from the dealer. Hop in."

"That little camera thing you do is really paying off," Savannah teased, and got inside the plush vehicle. Dani's job as a fashion photographer for all of the elite magazines afforded her a few luxuries; invitations to all the major events and premieres inside and out of the country along with meeting folks that the average person only reads about in the tabloids. She couldn't count the "A list" of stars and social-ites who'd become friends over the years that she had in her Rolodex.

Dani laughed, buckled her seat belt and began pulling out. "Gotta do a little something to pay the bills."

Moments later they sped off and headed for down-town Manhattan. By the time they arrived at the Seaport it was bustling with Sunday afternoon activ-ity. The day was glorious, comfortably warm with a light breeze blowing in off the Hudson River, which thankfully didn't smell like garbage, its usual aroma.

"Let's get our tickets first," Mia suggested, "then get something to eat. The first set is at five."

Mia Turner was the organizer of the trio. As a very well-respected and highly paid event planner for major corporations, she was beyond diligent when it came to scheduling and getting people where they needed to be. It got on Savannah's and Dani's last nerve at times but they still relied on her to pull ev-erything together. As typical of Mia, she had their entire day planned right down to the menu at the restaurant she'd selected for brunch.

"Mia, when in the hell do you have time to do all of this with a full-time job?" Savannah asked as Mia led the way to the ticket booth to pick up the concert tickets.

Mia looked over her narrow shoulder with a puzzled expression on her face. "Time to do what?"

Savannah and Dani stole a glance at each other, shook their heads and kept marching along.

After securing the tickets they headed over to Trio, a new Caribbean restaurant with an outdoor café that Mia had discovered and was aching to try out.

"If this place lives up to its reputation I may put it on my list of recommended locations for my clients," Mia said as they were led to their seats beneath a wide white umbrella.

That was another thing about Mia—even when she wasn't working, she was working. She found some kind of way to tie her job in to darn near everything she did. As a result, the three of them often ate for free, got free spa days, discounts on designer clothes, product samples and they were even able to finagle a trip to the island of St. Kitts as part of Mia's "focus group" for a new resort on the island. All the little perks made Mia's drill-sergeant demeanor all the more bearable. Besides, she really was a sweetheart.

"Oh, and lunch is on me," Mia announced once they were settled in their seats. "But everyone needs to order something different. I want to get a good cross-sampling of the menu, as well as the service." She snapped her menu open then put on her glasses. Truth be told, Mia was blind as a bat but hated to admit it. She spent a great majority of her time squinting, which gave her a rather sour expression to those who didn't know her. Yet her vanity wouldn't allow her to mar her near-perfect face with glasses 24/7. And she was terrified of "sticking anything in my eyes," so contacts were out of the question.

"So what have you ladies been up to?" Dani asked as she perused the menu.

"Up to my eyeballs with work," Savannah said. "But that's not unusual."

"Richard still working you to death?"

"He damn sure tries." She laughed lightly. "But it's cool. I like my job."

Mia lowered her menu and quickly tucked away her glasses before blearily focusing on Savannah. "You are entirely too talented to be someone's assistant for the rest of your life, and too damned smart. You need to take your butt back to school and finish your law degree. Then you could run the show, open your own office and work other people to death."

"She's right, Savannah," Dani chimed in. "I decided a long time ago that I was not cut out to be someone's underling. That's why I have to do my own thing. When I don't feel like working, I don't work."

This was a conversation they had at least once every three months. When she looked at her friends' busy, exciting and carefree lives she often questioned whether or not she'd made all the right choices; from settling down and getting married to settling for a job she could do with her eyes closed. Each time she

asked the question the answer was still the same—
yes. Besides, she had what neither of them had—a
loving husband and a *secret life*. Inwardly she smiled.

"Enough about me," Savannah said before they
got on a roll that would last through brunch. "What
have you two been up to?"

Dani and Mia alternated with stories about their
latest clients while Savannah tried to concentrate
on the nonstop chatter, saying all the appropriate
"Mmm, hmms" at all the right places and laughing
on cue. But her mind was elsewhere. She had what
the girls would call a DDD—*a damned difficult di-
lemma.* Under normal circumstances she would hap-
pily spill her tale all over the white linen tablecloth
and listen with amazement as Dani and Mia put their
personal spin on what she needed to do. More often
than not they were on point. This time as much as
she needed their savvy wisdom, she couldn't risk it.

As Mia predicted, the food was incredible. The
service was top-notch and Mia had penciled Trio in
as a restaurant to recommend. Of course, before they
could leave, Mia gained introductions to the owner
and manager.

"You did good," Savannah said to Mia as they
made their way to the boat.

Mia grinned, flashing a dimple beneath her right
eye. "Gotta keep my contacts fresh. My clients only
expect the best." Mia linked her arm through Savannah's. "How's the 'family planning' going?" she
asked in a soft voice.

Savannah's expression mirrored her internal disappointment. "So far, no good," she said. "But we'll keep trying."

"It will happen when the time is right."

Savannah tilted her head and rested it momentarily on Mia's shoulder. "I hope so. That's the only thing missing in our marriage."

"What's the only thing missing in your marriage?" Dani cut in with her supersonic hearing.

"A baby," Savannah said.

"It ain't all it's cracked up to be. Just think, if you had a baby, you'd be home changing Pampers instead of hanging with your girls."

"That much is true," Mia conceded. "And what about furthering your career? A baby would definitely put a damper on that."

Savannah drew in a long breath. "I could always go back to school. It would just take longer."

"Hmm," the duo hummed in unison.

"Listen, sis, if it's for you and Blake it will happen and as much as I detest stinky diapers I'd be in your corner, girl. You know that," Dani said.

"Me, too," Mia said, giving Savannah a squeeze.

Savannah smiled. "Thanks." She knew as tough as they pretended to be about permanent relationships and kids, they were true softies at heart. Beneath all the glitz and glamour of Mia and Dani they were both searching for Mr. Right.

They found the boat and got in line behind the others and spent the next two hours relaxing on lounge chairs, sipping frozen margaritas and listening to music.

Savannah tried to stay focused on the music and the lulling pull of the ocean beneath them, but her mind kept going back to her assignment and what it would mean. The results could be devastating. Although she was certain that her husband would never involve himself in anything illegal or underhanded, that wouldn't eliminate him from falling under the murky shadow of suspicion. There was a part of her that seriously considered turning down the assignment. But that, too, had repercussions. If she declined, she was sure that she'd never get another chance and she'd worked damned hard. Worse, the assignment would be given to someone else who wouldn't have the same concerns that she did regarding Blake.

Savannah jumped when she felt her shoulder being shaken. She snapped her head toward Dani. "What?"

"I was talking to you and you weren't paying me a bit of attention. The music is cool but it ain't that good."

Savannah looked around and realized that the concert was over and people were starting to leave. She blinked to clear her head and reached for her purse.

"To be truthful, you haven't been yourself all day," Mia said as they began heading out. "You've been totally distracted. What's up? It's not the baby thing, is it?"

Savannah took a deep breath. She knew that she couldn't reveal all of the details but maybe she could offer some "scenarios" to her friends and get their take on it.

"Just struggling with a case that I've been working on," she began.

"What about it?" Dani asked.

They strolled along the boardwalk to the parking area.

Savannah cleared her throat. "Well, uh, we've been working on a case…a husband and wife thing. Uh, divorce. And, well, the wife is our client and the husband claims he has no assets. But the wife believes that he does and wants us to uncover his assets that she feels she's entitled to."

Dani shrugged. "So what's the big deal? Happens every day. Bastard probably is hiding his net worth so he can keep the mother lode for himself."

"The conflict is that I know the husband." Her heart knocked in her chest.

Mia stopped in her tracks and squinted at Savannah. "You do?"

"Did you tell your boss, Richard whatshisname?" Dani asked.

Savannah shook her head. "This is a big assignment for me. Most of the time I simply do research, prepare briefs, schedule appointments, things like that. Richard is trusting me to take care of this on my own."

"So how well do you *know* the husband?" Mia asked. "Better yet, do we know him?" She shot a look at Dani who cocked a brow in anticipation.

Savannah did a rapid analysis of how long she'd known both women, where they'd gone to school, the neighborhoods they'd grown up in and the friends they had in common. It was a safe bet to say that she knew "the husband" from the one neighborhood they did not share in common. "I actually met him during high school when I would spend part of my summer with my aunt in New Jersey."

"You two didn't have 'a thing' did you?" Dani wanted to know.

Savannah shook her head. "No. It was nothing like that. He lived on the block, that's all."

Mia squinted. "I really don't see the problem. Unless you kept in touch over all those years, you don't really know him anymore, know what I mean?"

"I guess…" Savannah mumbled. "I suppose what I'm asking is what would either of you do, if you got an assignment to investigate an acquaintance—and that investigation could lead to something ugly for the person that you know?"

Dani disengaged the alarm and door lock on her SUV and the ladies got in. Dani slipped on her sunglasses. "Me, if it was a distant acquaintance like this guy and my job hinged on it, I'd do my job. If he's innocent it will all come out anyway."

"I agree. It's not like he's your best buddy or something."

But he is my best buddy, Savannah thought. *Her husband.* However as Mia said, if everything is on the up and up it won't be a problem. *If.* What if it wasn't?

Chapter 7

When Savannah arrived back home she was no closer to having an answer for her DDD than before she left. Unfortunately, she would have to make a decision and quickly. Time was of the essence.

"Hey, babe," Blake called out.

Savannah dropped her purse and keys on the hall table and followed the sound of his voice. For a moment she stood in the doorway of the kitchen observing the man she loved. A sense of warmth and peace filled her as she watched him check the chicken he'd put in the oven. What tickled her most was his attire. He had on his black-and-white barbecue apron that hung from his neck and reached his knees and nothing else.

She couldn't help but smile. Some men wouldn't

think twice about fixing a meal, especially Sunday dinner. But not Blake. He loved—among many things—cooking for his wife. He was adamant about fairness and balance and saw no reason why two people who worked equally as hard shouldn't share the responsibility of managing a home. He was like that about his work, as well. He treated others as he wanted to be treated. She'd known him to turn down lucrative deals because he didn't like the way an employer treated his employees. And that's when she made her decision. She knew her husband as well she knew herself. Blake would be the last one to become involved in something that may ultimately prove to be unjust to someone else.

"Don't get those buns of yours too close to the oven," she said, her entry line full of innuendo. She crossed the threshold of the kitchen with a wanton smile on her face.

Blake closed the oven door and slowly turned to his wife. His eyes darkened with intent. He tossed the oven mitt on the counter. "But I always thought you liked my buns warm and toasty."

They walked toward each other as if on cue. She stood before him and looked up into his eyes. "I love you," she said from the depths of her heart, and wrapped her arms lightly around his waist.

For a moment he looked at her with a question hovering in his eyes, but then it was gone. "Right back at ya." He leaned down and kissed her slow and deep then pulled back. "So how was the day with the girls?"

"Great. We did one of those afternoon jazz boat rides, had brunch at this really cool place, Trio—we'll have to try it." She leaned her hip against the counter. "Sure smells good in here. What are we having?"

"Chef's surprise. I'm trying out a new chicken recipe."

Savannah chuckled. "You and your recipes." She looked him up and down. "Uh, do I dress up or down for dinner?"

"My preference would be nothing at all, but I'll give you a break on this one." He winked.

"Can I help with anything?"

"Nope, got it all covered. About another twenty minutes for the bird and we can eat."

"Great. I'm going to change."

She walked off into the bedroom kicked off her shoes and got undressed. Since Blake had opted for an apron as his attire, she figured she'd up the ante a bit and give him a bit of Victoria's Secret to go with dessert. She giggled as she hunted through her lingerie drawer to find the perfect scanty outfit.

Just as she was slipping into her peach-colored thong, the phone rang. *Blake must have answered,* she realized when it only rang twice. Probably one of his buddies who'd bet on the baseball game earlier, she thought as she adjusted her demibra.

The bedroom door eased open.

"Phone," Blake said sticking his head in.

Savannah turned to give him an eyeful. She posed provocatively. "Who is it?"

Blake lost his train of thought when he feasted his eyes on her. He cleared his throat. "Umm, someone named Jean from your TLC group." He stuck the phone out in front of him.

Her heart jammed somewhere in her throat and she had to suck in air through widened nostrils. "Oh, thanks. Must be about my order."

She took the phone from him, gave him a "see you later" smile while holding the phone in the valley of her breasts waiting for him to leave. He took a step toward her and she wagged her finger *no.*

Pouting like a little boy Blake reluctantly backed out the door. "What's so top secret about some old body scrub anyway?" he grumbled.

Savannah waited until he was out of earshot. "Hello?"

"Hi, Savannah, is this a bad time?"

"No, not at all. We were getting ready for dinner. Is everything okay?"

"I'm doing my basic follow up that I conduct with all of the Cartel members when they get their first assignment."

"Oh." She didn't know what else to say.

"Did you read the contents?"

"Yes, I did."

"Any questions?"

"No, everything is very clear."

"Excellent. So you will be taking on the assignment?" It was more of a statement than a question.

She glanced toward the partially opened door. This was her chance to back out, stick this in someone else's hands. But she'd never backed away from a challenge. Never.

"Absolutely."

"Wonderful. If you need anything we're here to assist you. Expect your package in the next day or so. Good luck, Savannah."

Before Savannah had a chance to respond the call was disconnected. In the recesses of her mind she heard the theme music to *Mission Impossible* playing and almost laughed. Almost.

As Savannah rested in the arms of her husband later that night she wondered what she would do if she discovered that Blake was doing something wrong. She pressed closer to the warmth of his body as a slight chill ran through her.

"I'm heading to court, Savannah," Richard said, stopping for a hot minute at her desk.

Savannah glanced up at him over the rim of her reading glasses. "You look harried and your tie is crooked." She stood and adjusted his tie.

"This is a big case. If we win it will be a major coup for the company."

"You'll do fine. You're totally prepared."

"I can't thank you enough for staying on Friday.

But I couldn't have gotten it all together without you. I hope I didn't completely ruin your plans."

"Not at all. Everything worked out fine. Fortunately for you I have a very understanding husband." She tucked the hem of his tie inside his navy blue suit jacket. "Now you look like a winner." She grinned.

"Thanks. Wish me luck," he said, hurrying off.

"Luck!" she called out. Just as she sat back down, Jeremy from the mail room approached with the mail cart.

"Hey, Jeremy. How was your weekend?"

Jeremy was a college student that worked part-time at the office to help pay his tuition, and he was always full of stories about his college partying antics, which always brought back memories of her own wild college days at Spelman University.

"Pretty quiet this weekend, Mrs. Fields. Had to study." He grimaced. "Exams next week." He began piling the day's mail in her inbox.

"Still planning on going to law school?"

"Yep. That's the plan." He took a plain brown box out of the cart and set it down on her desk. "This one is for you. Kinda heavy."

She pulled it toward her and immediately knew what it was before even looking at it.

"Came by messenger." He paused, waited for a response and when he didn't get one he added, "I signed for it," in a way that hedged for information.

Savannah looked up at him and gave him a short

smile. "Thanks." Unfortunately for Jeremy she wasn't giving up the goods.

Realizing that a "thanks" was all he was going to get, he said his goodbyes and pushed off to the next office.

Savannah stared at the box for several moments. She'd seen the same kind of box delivered to her mother's door on several occasions. In the beginning Savannah always thought that her mother must be doing a booming bath and body product business. Humph, she'd sure been fooled.

She also knew that her own box would contain the tools she would need to pull off her investigation; everything from listening devices, fingerprinting equipment, burglary tools to handguns if necessary. Every member of the Cartel, upon completion of training, was issued a permit to carry a weapon. She hoped she'd never have cause to use it, but it was good to know it was at her disposal. Her fingers itched to open the box and see what goodies were inside, but it would have to wait. She'd have to compare each item with the TLC catalog to determine which bath and body products were masquerading as something else. She kept the catalog tucked away at home.

In the meantime she'd keep herself occupied by researching as much information as she could on her target. But to ensure that her snooping was never traced back to her office computer, she'd use the computers at the library during her lunch break.

Savannah glanced at her watch. It was only

ten thirty. She felt an early lunch coming on. She
couldn't wait to see what she could uncover on Ms.
Tristan Montgomery.

Chapter 8

"Ms. Montgomery, Mr. Fletcher is on the phone," her secretary said into the intercom.

Tristan grimaced. She really didn't have the time or the inclination to deal with Morris Fletcher. He rubbed her the wrong way. Not only had he tried to hit on her, he was always telling her what to do with her money. It was hers, wasn't it? Didn't her father leave everything to her? She could do what she damn-well pleased. And if it wasn't for those hateful Board of Directors and the obnoxious Mr. Fletcher, she could do as she pleased.

"Thank you, Cindy." At least that's what she thought her name was. She'd completely lost count of the array of secretaries that swung in and out of her door. She expected a lot from her staff and if you couldn't cut it, you were out. Simple.

She pressed down the flashing red light, drew in a breath and blew out a bored, "Hello."

"Tristan, we need to talk."

"About what now?"

"The development project of course."

She rolled her eyes. "What's the problem this time?"

"I need to present a financial report to the Board at the end of the month and I need to go over some figures with you."

"Fine. Can you be here in an hour? If not we will have to make it another time. My schedule is very tight today." She had a hair and nail appointment and one with her masseuse. Then she needed to dart over to her designer and see if her outfit was ready for Friday night. She wanted to look extra special for Blake, whether or not he brought his frumpy— at least that's what she imagined—wife.

"An hour is pretty tight, Tristan, but I'll be there."

"Good." She hung up the phone without another word.

Tristan leaned back in her imported red-leather high-backed chair and swiveled it until she faced the panoramic window that looked out onto the skyline of Manhattan.

Everyone thought she was no more than a spoiled, airheaded woman who would never be anywhere had it not been for her father and his money. She smiled slowly. They had no idea who they were dealing with. Tristan Montgomery may be a lot of things, but stupid and naive were not on her list of attributes. Playing the dumb, oversexed heiress suited her purposes fine. Her father, God rest his soul, taught her well and she lived by his words: "Never let them see your true hand and, above all, trust no one."

Her eyes tightened ever so slightly as she gazed outward onto a world that she could write her own check for.

She reached for the phone and dialed the private number. It rang three times before the familiar voice answered.

"Buy ten more," she said, then hung up the phone. She lifted her chin defiantly. No, Tristan Montgomery was no fool.

Savannah juggled the box, her purse, tote and a shopping bag of groceries as she tried to get her front door open. To top it off she was dripping wet, unable to manage her load and hold up an umbrella as she'd darted down the street from her car to her town house.

She finally got the door open and shoved it closed with her hip. Her purse and tote landed on the hall table before she went to the kitchen to deposit the groceries.

It was barely five o'clock. Richard was feeling generous after a good day in court and sent everyone home early. Perfect for her. She knew Blake wouldn't be home before seven, which would give her plenty of time to go over the information she'd gotten at the library, review the catalog and her products and still have dinner ready by the time hubby walked through the door.

Quickly she got out of her wet clothes and changed into a tank top and a pair of butter-soft sweatpants. Then went to the kitchen to season two steaks and put them in the oven.

Once that was out of the way, she headed to the bedroom, sat down on the side of the bed and opened the box. Inside was the standard pink carryall case. With a bit of apprehensive excitement she flipped the faux gold latch and lifted the lid.

Everything looked innocent enough—at least to those who didn't know better. She lifted the two ounce bottle of body oil which, when opened, was actually a tranquilizer, along with the matching bottle of bubble bath. Of course, one had to be careful with the latter as you didn't want your suspect to drown in the tub.

Savannah got up from the side of the bed and crossed the room to her dresser. She opened the bottom drawer and fished out the folder containing the TLC catalog tucked beneath her sweaters. She brought it back to the bed and flipped it open.

She picked up the silver cylindrical tube from the case then scanned the pages of the catalog until she found the matching image with a description. She screwed off the top and emptied the contents out on the bed—burglary tools. There were picks for a variety of locks, putty to make key impressions and a small case to seal the putty. She returned the items to the tube. In what appeared to be a makeup case, beneath the pressed powder were several black flat disks. When adhered to any surface, they would serve as tracking devices that could be picked up on the GPS system of her cell phone and her car. The smaller disks were listening devices that could be placed inconspicuously just about anywhere that conversation took place. The case that contained the blush had a secret compartment, as well. When the blush was lifted out of its well, there was a tiny circular piece of metal.

Savannah flipped through the catalog to be sure it was what she thought. This was actually an upgraded listening and recording device that could be inserted in a telephone. She smiled.

In a separate compartment was her toss away cell phone. She already had her digital camera with a powerful zoom lens, small enough to tuck away in a pocket.

There was also a bottle of spray perfume that was actually mace, as well as dusting power that was used to dust for fingerprints along with its own dual-purpose makeup brush.

She expertly assembled a gun from the inconspicuous metal pieces in the case. She lifted the .22 in her palm, raised it and pointed. Satisfied, she returned all the items to their compartments, closed the case and locked it, returned the catalog to the bottom drawer and went to start dinner. By the time she had all four burners going on the stove and steak grilling in the oven, the front door opened and slammed shut.

Savannah grinned as she stirred the pot of mixed vegetables. Her man was home. Maybe tonight she could interest her hubby in a game of poker. Strip, of course, and of course she intended to lose each hand. It made Blake feel like he was invincible and it made her feel totally wicked.

Blake hung up his tan trench coat in the hall closet and set his briefcase inside, then shut the door. He dropped a copy of the *Wall Street Journal* on top of the table. Sounds and scents came from the kitchen, but he hesitated before going to greet his wife. He glanced at the headline in the sidebar then on the front page of the paper. *Montgomery Enterprise Inks Historic Deal with Blake Fields, Architects, PPC.*

He should be elated. His name and his company was showcased in one of the most elite papers in the country. It was what happened after the paper hit the newsstands that disturbed him. He'd handled it as best he could. At least he thought he did. It was getting sticky and so much rode on every piece of the puzzle fitting perfectly. And his conscience was the piece that just wouldn't seem to fit.

"Blake, is that you?" Savannah called out from the kitchen.

He heard her soft footsteps approach and drew

himself up, putting on his game face. "Hey, babe," he said as she came from the kitchen to where he stood.

A warm smile lit up her eyes, and his heart knocked hard in his chest. Blake loved Savannah with all his heart. He'd do everything within his power not to hurt her.

She walked up to him and lifted her head for a kiss. Blake took her in his arms, kissed her lips, the tip of her nose and her eyelids, then held her close. He shut his eyes and chanted deep in his heart how much she meant to him.

Savannah eased back and tilted her head up to look at him. A soft frown creased between her brows. She stroked his cheek compelling him to look at her.

"What is it?" she gently asked, reading him like an old family recipe.

He ran his hand slowly up and down the gentle sway of her back.

"Nothing, baby, just tired." The right corner of his mouth curved slightly upward. He brushed a wisp of hair away from her forehead. "How was your day?" He put his arm around her shoulders as they walked into the living room.

"The usual hustle and bustle. Richard did well in court today so he let the troops off early." At least that much of her day was true, she thought.

"I'm sure he owes his courtroom success to you as always." He plopped down onto the couch, stretched his legs out in front of him and loosened his burgundy colored tie.

Savannah sat opposite him, braced her arms on her thighs and leaned forward. "Do you think I'm wasting my time and talents at the firm?"

Blake drew in a slow breath. "I don't think you're wasting your time, but I do think you've grown comfortable. You can do that job with your eyes closed. You have a thirst for law and all things legal. I know you would whiz through law school if you decided it was what you wanted to do. But you have to want to do it."

Savannah was quiet for a moment. Being an attorney had been her dream since she was a teen and served on the debate and tort teams in high school. She had loved participating in mock trials. In all the years that she'd been on the team in high school and then college, she'd only lost one case as a defense attorney. But then she met Blake and her dreams for preparing her opening and closing remarks took a backseat to being a wife and one day mother.

She loved her job. Sure, she knew she could run rings around both of the partners if she set her mind to it. But if she went back to law school and then took the bar, her biological clock would barely be ticking. Besides she wouldn't be very threatening in the court room with a big belly and a "glow."

"Why are you asking this now? Or should I say again?" Blake asked.

"I've been thinking about it more, I guess. And Mia and Dani swear I'm wasting my time as a paralegal being worked to death." A faint smile dusted her face. "And if I went back to school, got my law degree and passed the bar, I could hang out my own shingle."

"You could. Is that what you want?"

Savannah got up and came to sit next to him. "You know what I want," she said, her voice laced with fleeting hope.

Blake pulled her close. "If it's going to happen it will, baby." He kissed the top of her head. "Stop worrying."

Savannah pressed her head against Blake's chest and drew in a long slow breath. Her heart jumped. She could swear under oath that she smelled perfume on his shirt.

Chapter 9

Savannah stood in front of her island counter, staring at the trays of food. She couldn't seem to move. For the last few minutes, since Blake had excused himself to take an early shower, she felt as if she were moving in slow motion.

She kept telling herself that she was simply imagining things, that her mind was in overdrive because of her assignment and Blake's possible involvement. Yet, her heart said something totally different.

How close do you have to be to someone to get their scent all over you? Her instincts went on alert when she greeted him in the hallway. It was not so much that he held her—something that he always did—it was the *way* he held her.

No! Just stop it. She trusted her husband. He'd never given her a reason not to.

"Earth to Savannah."

She jumped and looked toward the archway of the kitchen. Blake was grinning at her and running a towel over his damp air. His chest was bare and chiseled, his loose-fitting drawstring pajama bottoms hanging low on his hips. He came toward her and she felt her clit twitch the way it always did whenever he looked at her like that—whenever *he* looked like that.

Savannah swallowed back the doubt, pushed the impossible thoughts out of her head and walked toward her husband. She draped her arms around his neck and entwined her fingers.

"Ready to eat?"

"That's a loaded question." He ran his warm lips along the column of her neck.

Savannah shivered with delight. Her eyes drifted shut while she pressed closer to Blake. The clean scent of soap and water wafted beneath her nose. Her senses jerked and her earlier doubts rushed to the surface.

"Why don't we put everything on trays and take it into the bedroom?" Blake suggested.

Savannah swallowed and pulled in a slow breath. "Sure." She stepped out of his arms. "Wanna get out the trays?" She moved away.

"Savannah, is something wrong?" He put his hand on her shoulder and turned her around. She looked everywhere but in his eyes. "You've been acting kinda weird since I came home."

Her gaze bumped against his. "I smelled perfume on your shirt," she blurted out.

He sputtered a nervous laugh. "Perfume?"

She folded her arms and stared at her husband—waiting.

The afternoon flashed through his head in a nano-second. He couldn't explain. He didn't understand it himself.

"You're kidding, right?" was his comeback. "How in the world would perfume get on my shirt?"

"That's what I want to know."

Blake slowly shook his head in denial. "I think Richard is working you too hard and your imagination is getting the best of you." He stepped up to her and lifted her chin so that he could look right into her eyes. "The only woman I let get that close to me is you." His gaze danced over her face before settling on her eyes. "Only you," he said softly. He pulled her to him. "Come here." He held her tightly. "I love you, Savannah, only you." He pressed his face into her hair, felt her heart pound against his chest. He shut his eyes and said a silent prayer that the events of the day would stay buried and not rear their ugly head. He didn't know what he would do with his life if Savannah were hurt by his stupidity. He wouldn't let that happen. That's all there was to it.

Blake stepped back, holding Savannah at arm's length. He put a smile on his face. "So, we're good?"

She nodded.

"No more imagining things?"

She pushed out a laugh. "I guess I was being silly."

"You…never." He kissed the top of her head. "I'm starved." He turned away and walked across the kitchen to the cabinets and took out two lap trays and the dishes.

They worked side by side filling their plates.

"How about some wine with dinner?" Blake suggested.

"Sure. I'll get it."

"And I'll get us all set up." He took the two trays, balancing them like an experienced waiter and walked into the bedroom.

Savannah sighed heavily as she watched him walk away. She knew her husband loved her. But that never stopped a man from straying. She also knew if she kept dwelling on it, things would turn ugly. He'd never given her a reason not to trust him and she wasn't going to start losing faith in her man or her marriage now.

Savannah went to the cabinet and took out a bottle of merlot, then filled the ice bucket with ice and stuck the bottle inside. She drew in a long breath of resolve. Blake and Savannah forever, she reminded herself and headed to the bedroom to join her husband.

Blake had dimmed the lights, lit scented candles and turned down the bed. He'd popped a Kem CD in the player and *their* song, "Love Calls," was on. They'd played the *Kemistry* CD so many times that the original had worn out and they'd had to buy another one.

Savannah smiled. "Now, this is what I call intimate dining." She crossed the room and set the ice bucket down on the nightstand. She pulled her top up and over her head and tossed it to the side. Her pants came next. Her body warmed when she saw Blake's eyes darken with lust.

"You are so incredibly beautiful. More so than when I married you."

She stepped up to him. "Do you really mean that?"

"Every word." He kissed her lips then ran his tongue lightly along the contour of her mouth. "Hmm," he hummed deep in his throat. He snaked his arm around her bare waist and pulled her flush against him.

Savannah felt his erection press against her stomach. Her heart thundered.

"If we keep this up we'll never get through dinner," she whispered against his mouth.

"You're probably right." He ran his fingers along her spine before releasing her.

The settled themselves on the bed, relaxing against the overstuffed pillows, listening to music while making light conversation.

"Did I tell you that we've been invited to a dinner party on Friday night?"

Savannah chewed thoughtfully on her succulent

steak, the seasoned juices flowing over her lips and tongue. "Yeah, I think so. What time?"

"Eight."

"I'll make sure that Richard doesn't pull one of his traumas so that I can get out of the office early. Is this a dressy thing?"

"I have no idea. You're the fashionista in the fam, so you'll have to decide on outfits."

Savannah giggled. As quiet as it was kept, her very successful businessman husband, who looked like a cover model when he put on clothes, actually hated to get dressed up. He was most comfortable in a pair of jeans, an old white T-shirt and bare feet. Blake attributed it all to his early years of growing up on the West Coast in L.A. and spending his days and nights on the beach. She took pleasure in shopping for him and putting his outfits together. Blake had no idea how a patterned tie could go with a pinstriped shirt or why red and burgundy spelled power or that he could never have enough starched white shirts.

"I'll take care of it," she said. She lifted her tray from her lap and put it on the nightstand next to her side of the bed then wiped her mouth with the cloth napkin. "Want some more wine?"

"Sure." He held up his glass while she poured.

"So tell me, how is it working with Tristan Montgomery?"

A line of wine spilled over his lips and dribbled down his chin. Savannah grabbed a napkin and wiped the spill.

"Maybe I didn't need more wine," he said, sputtering a laugh while dabbing at his chest with the napkin.

That bad feeling snaked through her again. She glanced at Blake but he didn't meet her gaze. He set his glass down.

"She's your typical spoiled princess," he said with a slight shrug. "Wants everything her way and now."

"Oh," was all she could say.

"Why do you ask?"

"Just wondering, that's all. I've seen her face in the papers and magazines, mostly gossip columns. She's really quite beautiful."

"Hmm."

"I guess I'll see for myself on Friday, huh?"

"Yeah…you will." He reached for his glass of wine and took a long slow sip. He wasn't looking forward to Friday, but there was no way he could get out of it.

Chapter 10

"You what?" Mia squealed into the phone.

"Yes, perfume," Savannah said in a hushed voice.

"Aw, hell naw, not Blake. Girl, are you sure?"

Savannah frowned. "Pretty sure."

"Being pretty sure isn't enough to start thinking your man is cheating on you. What did he say when you asked him about it, 'cause I know you did."

"He denied it, said I must be overworked, stuff like that."

"And why don't you believe him?"

Savannah sighed heavily. "He…just the way he was acting."

"Acting like how? Guilty?"

"No, not exactly." She shook her head. "I can't put

it into words. All I can say is that I had a bad feeling and that there was something he wasn't telling me."

"Savannah, that man loves the ground you walk on. I've known Blake for a while and I've seen the way he looks at you when you aren't looking. He loves you, girl."

Savannah's eyes filled. She sniffed hard. "I know," she said, her voice wobbling. "I'm just being silly. Maybe it's PMS or something."

"Probably so. You know how hormones can make you half crazy." She chuckled. "So don't go getting yourself all twisted in a knot, okay? Go eat some chocolate. It always works for me."

Savannah sniffed and chuckled. "Okay. Look, I gotta go. Thanks for listening."

"Anytime. That's what friends are for. Talk to you later in the week. And I definitely want all the details from the little gathering at Ms. Montgomery's."

"Will do. 'Bye."

Savannah slowly hung up the phone. Mia was right. She dabbed at her eyes with a tissue from the box on her desk. She needed to let it go and trust her husband. And she would.

Blake sat at his drafting table working on some sketches for a possible job renovating an abandoned hospital into affordable housing units. The space was, of course, mammoth, but it would take some real creative genius to rid the environment of what it once was.

He started to toss his tie over his shoulder and out of the way as he always did when he was at work and sketching, when he realized that, much to Savannah's chagrin and his delight, it was a jeans and T-shirt day for him. He grinned. He had no outside meetings and was not expecting any clients to visit. He was free! He adjusted his banker's lamp and started to whistle as he looked at the hospital specs and began formulating a design.

Blake worked steadily for about an hour, the visions in his mind coming to life on his sketch pad. An old tune by Miles Davis wailed softly in the background. He was in his element. This is what he lived for—creating, making people's dreams come true.

A knot suddenly formed in his gut. Everyone except for Savannah. He straightened. His gaze danced around the room, bouncing off his desk, his wall of honors, his tools of the trade. He knew how desperately Savannah wanted a child and so did he. But the fates seemed to be against them. Savannah would make an incredible mother, he knew that. And it killed him every month when he saw the look of hurt and disappointment in her eyes. They'd purchased so many pregnancy kits that they could own stock.

He sighed heavily and put down his drafting pen. He succeeded in every other area of his life except the one that mattered most. It had been six years with no luck. Maybe they should consider adopting, he thought, but knew that Savannah would feel even more like a failure if he brought it up. It was the one area of their otherwise idyllic lives that was left unfulfilled and he had no idea what to do about it.

All of the doctors and specialists they'd seen had concurred that they were both healthy and they could find no cause as to why they could not conceive. Be patient they all said. Be patient. But he knew as well as Savannah that the clock was ticking.

The ringing of his phone tugged him away from the turn of his thoughts. He pulled himself up from the stool and went to his desk.

"Yes," he said, pressing down on the flashing intercom light.

"Ms. Montgomery is on line two," Jasmine said.

"Tell her I'm busy in a meeting."

"I did. She insists on speaking with you. She said it's urgent."

Blake pushed out a breath of annoyance as their last encounter flashed through his head. "Fine. I'll take it."

He plunked down in his chair behind his desk, took a moment to compose himself then snatched up the phone.

"Yes, Ms. Montgomery, what can I do for you?"

Her tinkling laughter ran through the line. "Blake, I was sure we'd gotten to first base—or at least a first-name basis. Ms. Montgomery sounds so old. And after the other day…"

Blake cleared his throat. "Tristan, what can I do for you?"

"That's so much better, don't you think?" She

didn't wait for a response. "I'm in your area and it's nearly lunchtime. I'd like you to meet me at the Bistro in say twenty minutes."

"I'm really busy. I hadn't planned on going out for lunch. As a matter of fact, Jasmine just ordered my lunch from the deli downstairs."

"Tell her to eat it. I'll be there in twenty. I do hope to see you there, Blake." She hung up before he could blink.

"Dammit!" He slammed down the phone and ran his hand roughly over his face. This was the last thing he needed. Tristan was getting totally out of hand and he was at a serious crossroads as to what to do about it. The one thing he had done about it so far was lie to his wife.

Savannah had been right when she said she smelled perfume on his shirt. His heart nearly stopped when she said it. But he should have known that Tristan would find a way to leave her mark.

Once again, she'd come to the office unexpected. Jasmine was out to lunch and the front office was open game for Tristan. She actually came into his office without knocking, catching him completely off guard.

"Blake, I hope you don't mind that I just barged in. There was no one out front," she'd said, her version of an apology. She shut the door behind her.

Blake sat upright in his chair. "Come in. What can I do for you today? We didn't have a meeting scheduled."

"No. Just an impromptu visit." She slinked across the room until she reached his desk. She sat on its edge, her tight skirt hiking up nearly to her hips.

Blake swallowed as he tore his gaze away from the buttery smooth thigh. She crossed her legs at the knee, and Blake swore he caught of glimpse of something hot pink.

Tristan leaned over, displaying a teasing view of cleavage as she adjusted his tie and before he knew what was happening, she kissed him. Her tongue was in his mouth and her fingers gripped his neck, holding him in place.

It could have been a second but it seemed to last an eternity before he gained enough of his senses to peel her away.

He wiped his mouth with the back of his hand. Her fire-red lipstick imprinted itself. He pushed back from his seat. Her eyes gleamed. She ran her tongue across her lips in a slow, sensual dance.

"Just as I thought," she said, her voice thick and vibrating. "Sweet and experienced."

"You need to leave. Now."

She hopped down from the edge of his desk and walked right up to him. Her breasts pressed hard up against his chest. He could see the flecks of light brown in her eyes. Her breath was hot and sweet.

Tristan took his hands and wrapped them around her waist. She pressed her pelvis up against him.

"I want you, Blake Fields. And it's my intention to have you. One way or the other."

She stepped back, let the heat of her eyes run a stream of fire up and down his body.

"This isn't going to work. I'll have my lawyers contact yours about rescinding the contract."

Tristan tossed her head back and laughed. "You mean to tell me you would lose out on the biggest land deal this town has seen in decades simply because a very desirable, beautiful, rich woman wants to go to bed with you?" She laughed again. "Trust me. I may seem like nothing more than a sex-starved socialite, but my lawyers aren't. If you even think about breaking this deal, the only thing you'll be drawing from that moment on are sketches from inside a jail cell for breach of contract and anything else my lawyers can think of. I'll take everything, your house, your business, your sacred marriage. By the time I get finished ripping your life to shreds you'll pray to let me make love to you to take the pain away."

She smiled so sweetly one would have thought she'd just wished him a happy birthday. She picked up her purse from the desk and turned toward the door.

"Think about it," she said, before opening the door and walking out, shutting it softly behind her.

For several moments he stood there in stunned disbelief. She'd essentially blackmailed him. He could still taste her on his lips, in his mouth and feel her hands on his body. What had he gotten himself into? Better yet, how was he going to find a way out without ruining everything he cared about?

All those thoughts ran through his head as he walked the three blocks to Bistro.

When he arrived he spotted her immediately. She was sitting at the outdoor table beneath an umbrella, wide, dark shades shielded her eyes. She took off her glasses when he stood above her.

"What is this about, Tristan?"

"You could say hello."

He jaw clenched. He didn't respond.

"I see we're still a bit testy. Please have a seat while we wait for our table."

Grudgingly, Blake sat down.

Tristan leaned forward, slid her hand beneath the table and placed it on his knee. "Admit it. You enjoyed it as much as I did. What could be more exciting than something forbidden?"

Danielle and her crew were in the van on their way to a photo shoot. They were already late and midtown traffic was horrendous.

"Take the next right, Adam," Dani called out from the backseat. She stared out the passenger window and her heart jumped up into her throat. The van slowed as it moved into the turning lane at the red light. She must be seeing things. "Wait! I need to get out."

"No time for potty breaks. We're already late. I'll have you there in five minutes," Adam said.

Instinct kicked in and she did what she was trained to do—she started shooting. Her high-speed camera snapped in rapid-fire succession.

The van roared off and away.

"What are you getting so snap happy about back there?" Lauren, her lighting assistant, asked.

Dani swallowed. "Nothing. Just testing the equipment." She prayed that it was nothing.

Chapter 11

By the time Danielle walked through the doors of her loft apartment in the West Village it was nearing midnight, yet the streets below were still alive with activity. The city that never sleeps, she thought absently. Under normal circumstances she would hop in the shower, wrap herself up in her favorite fluffy robe, sip a glass of white wine and hit the sack. This wasn't normal circumstances.

It had taken all of her concentration to stay focused on the photo shoot. Several times Adam had to get her attention because her thoughts had drifted off to what she'd seen on Amsterdam Avenue—her best friend's husband nestled up with the notorious Tristan Montgomery.

She knew Tristan from way back in the early days

of her photography career. She'd started off working freelance for some of the rags, snatching what pictures she could until she finally landed a reputable gig with *Fashion Daily*. One of her first assignments had been to attend Fashion Week and not only capture the photos of the supermodels but the fashion aficionados that attended. Tristan Montgomery was front and center. She attended the event with one man but left with another.

There was something about Tristan that totally fascinated Dani. She wasn't sure if it was her incredible beauty, the charisma that she wielded as easily as she took a breath or the fact that she had yet to reach thirty years old and she was one of the wealthiest and most powerful single females in America according to *Forbes* magazine.

Dani began to capture as many images as she could of the striking socialite, from random shopping trips on Fifth Avenue, jogging in Central Park with her Yorkie, to her sunning on her yacht in the Virgin Islands, movie premieres and political dinners. Her portfolio of Tristan Montgomery was thick and eclectic.

She stood in her dark room, the roll of film in her hand. If she developed the roll and her worst fears were true, what would she do? She tossed the roll on the table and returned to her bedroom.

"Are you sure?" Mia asked rubbing her eyes and yawning simultaneously. She squinted at the illuminated numbers on the digital bedside clock but couldn't quite make them out.

"Dammit, girl, you're the one who can't see! Yes, I'm sure. Do you think I would have gotten you out of your sleep at 2:00 a.m. if I wasn't sure?"

Mia groaned, turned partially on her side and sat up. She turned on the light. She pressed her face close to the neon numbers. Yep, Dani was right. It was 2:00 a.m.

"Okay, okay, I'm awake. Now, tell me what happened again?"

Dani sucked her teeth before proceeding to tell her who and what she'd seen earlier in the day.

Mia sputtered an expletive only fit for sailors.

"My sentiments exactly," Dani said. "So what are you going to do with the pictures?"

"That's why I called you. I'm torn. I mean, I'm Savannah's friend and if she saw my man screwing around with another woman, I would want her to tell me."

"It could be anything, maybe she was wiping lint off his pants." But the longer Mia thought about it the dumber it sounded and the more she was convinced it wasn't the case at all. Especially not after the conversation that she had with Savannah the other day, which she now told Dani about.

For several moments they sat on either end of the phone in silence.

"What are we going to do?" they suddenly said jointly.

A collective breath pushed through the phone lines.

"I don't know," echoed in the morning air.

"I have friends at Bistro," Mia said. "Let me make a call in the morning. See if he made the reservation or if she did."

"How will that help?"

"How should I know? But maybe it will tell us something before we go to Savannah—if we go to Savannah."

The following afternoon during her lunch break, Mia took a cab across town to Bistro, deciding on a personal visit as opposed to a phone call. She smiled and waved at the familiar faces of the staff and headed toward the back office. She knocked lightly on the door.

"Come in," came the slightly accented voice.

Mia opened the door and stepped inside the tight, cramped office of Jean Dubois. He stood with a broad smile on his flat face when he saw her.

"Mia! My favorite customer. Are you here to bring me more business?"

"Actually I'm here for a favor." She explained what she needed.

"Our guest list is private," he said slowly, glancing at her above his half-frame wire-rimmed glasses. "But for you I will make an exception. Can you at least tell me why you need our guest list?"

"It's personal."

He gave a short nod and reached for his phone. "Jules, will you bring me our reservation list from yesterday. Yes, thank you." He hung up the phone.

Moments later Mia was walking out of Bistro with a copy of the reservation list. It didn't take long for her to spot the name she was looking for. She hailed a cab and headed back to her office.

Slowly Mia sat down behind her desk, staring at the list. With a heavy heart she picked up her phone and dialed Dani on her cell.

Dani picked up on the second ring. She listened silently to what Mia had to say. After hanging up there was only one thing she could do. She went to her darkroom.

Now she could add these, she thought, watching the damning photographs materialize in the solution. She took her long tweezers and lifted the wet paper from the tub of chemicals.

A part of her had wanted to be wrong. She wanted to look at the pictures and see how silly she'd been.

Her heart and her hopes sank. Now what was she going to do? What were they going to do?

Chapter 12

Savannah left the office early. She wanted to have plenty of time to get ready for the dinner party at Tristan Montgomery's place. More important, she wanted to get home long before her husband so that she could be sure to tuck away her tools of the trade that she would need on her assignment.

Heading straight to her bedroom, she went to her walk-in closet and pulled down her TLC case and opened it up on the bed. She took out the listening devices, the recorder for the phone, and the mini digital camera. Just as a precaution she took out the two-ounce body lotion that had a separate compartment filled with a sedative—one never knew when it would come in handy. She looked at the pieces needed to assemble her gun. Hmm, not tonight, she thought.

She put the items in her black beaded purse. If anyone were to open it all they would see was a vain woman's array of makeup items. She smiled and closed the purse then put it on top of the dresser. Now for a quick shower then a tour through her closet.

"What time do you plan to get there tonight?" Steven asked Blake as they walked together to the employee garage.

"I figure around nine. She said it starts at eight, but I don't want her to have too much time to zero in on me."

"She's still giving you fever?" Steven chuckled.

"Worse."

Steven stopped short. "What do you mean?"

Blake shook his head slightly. "I can handle it." At least he hoped he could. He'd just be happy when this night was over, and prayed that Tristan would behave herself.

"Is there something that you're not telling me? Because if it affects this project I should know about it."

They approached Blake's silver Lexus first. He stopped and turned to his friend. "You have to swear not to say anything," he began.

Steven's smooth brown features crinkled. "What the hell is going on, man?"

Blake blew out a breath then slowly began to tell

Steven what had occurred between him and Tristan and about her veiled threats.

Steven whistled through his teeth. "Damn. I don't even know what to say. Seems there should be somebody we can go to."

"But who? It would only make things worse, I'm sure. I'll figure it out."

"Do you think she would really pull the plug on the project if you don't sleep with her?"

"At this point I think Tristan Montgomery is capable of anything." He pressed the icon on his keychain and the car alarm deactivated, the locks opened and the powerful engine hummed to life. "See you tonight." He opened the door and slid onto the plush leather seat behind the wheel.

Steven leaned down by the driver's-side door. "My advice, my brother, keep Savannah glued to your hip. Your wife is no joke. If you can't keep the wolf away, Savannah can."

Blake had to chuckle. "I think you're right on that one." He shut the door. Steven stepped back as Blake rolled out of his parking space.

Steven waved and walked to his behemoth black Hummer several spaces away. Some guys have all the luck, he thought, or not.

When Blake arrived home, Savannah was just getting out of the shower. He tossed his keys on top of the dresser right next to Savannah's purse.

She stepped out of the master bath, wrapped in a towel just as Blake was coming out of his shirt.

When he saw her standing in the doorway, the light from the bathroom forming a halo around her and the steam from the shower wafting behind her, she truly was a vision. His heart banged in his chest and the soothing warmth of slinking down into a hot bath began to envelop him.

God, he loved this woman.

Her eyes brightened and she smiled. His insides ached.

"Hey," she said softly. "I didn't hear you come in."

"Hey, yourself." His voice was low and intimate. He crossed the room to where she stood and something came over him so powerful it was as if he'd lost all control and was guided only by desire.

"Blake?" Her eyes widened in question. But it was never answered. At least not in words.

Blake took her mouth in a searing kiss, no build up, hot from the moment their lips met. He moaned deep in his belly, felt it rise up to his throat turning into a growl.

He snaked his fingers through her short pixie hair, pulled her head closer to his, sealing their lips. His tongue slid into her mouth, danced and dueled with hers as unadulterated lust raged through him. He backed her up against the wall, pinned her there with the weight of his muscled body and somehow managed to unbelt, unbutton and unzip his pants letting them pool at his feet. He kicked them away.

Blake's erection was so fiercely hard, so on fire that he knew if he didn't bury it deep inside her wetness soon he would combust. He pulled the towel away from her and tossed it to the floor next to his discarded pants.

His mouth left hers and snaked along her throat to the swell of her breasts that seemed to pulse of their own accord.

"Blake...baby..." she said, but still got no verbal response. Savannah's fingertips gripped his shoulders when his mouth encircled her right nipple and he teased it with the motion of his tongue. Her head lolled back, her legs trembled. He grabbed her full behind and lifted her off the floor. She wrapped her legs around his waist.

Their rapid breathing sounded like gushes of minigeysers filling the torrid air.

Savannah's slick, wet opening pressed against him. A light-headedness rushed through Blake when the sensitive tip of his penis found her.

He surged upward. Savannah cried out, a sound of exquisite delight to his ears. Blake pushed deep inside her and then remained motionless for a moment, relishing the pure pleasure of their union. Then the muscles of her insides gripped him, sucked him in deeper and he lost his natural mind.

Suddenly Savannah was light as air when Blake began lifting her up and down on his erection as if she were no heavier than a loaf of bread. Stars exploded behind her eyes. The sensations were so intense that she forgot to breathe, to think.

Blake called out to God and everything holy as he loved up his wife with all that he had. Without breaking contact he walked with her to their bed, locked her beneath him, raised her legs above his shoulders then spread them as far as they would go.

"Look at me," he urged in a deep groan.

Savannah's eyes flicked open. Her heart stammered in her chest. She'd never seen that look of raw, almost savage hunger in his eyes before. It was as frightening as it was a sensual turn on.

Staring down into her sparkling eyes, Blake moved in and out of her, keeping her totally immobile as he took his pleasure.

They both began to tremble, murmur incomprehensible words of love as the power of what was happening between them became almost more than either of them could stand.

With a strength born out of desperate need, Savannah managed to raise her hips even higher, then down, back up again. She used the muscles inside her walls to jerk him.

Blake cried out to the heavens.

"Give it to me," she demanded. "All of you."

Blake got up on his knees, letting her legs stretch up toward his head.

"Like this?" he hissed as he pushed in and out of her, slow and hard.

Savannah whimpered. "More. More."

"How 'bout this?" He rotated his hips and he dove inside her again.

Her entire body began to shudder beginning at her toes, shimmying up her legs and thighs. Her breasts filled, her nipples stood on end. The world seemed to come to a grinding, crashing halt. The scream erupted from her soul as her orgasm roared through her, vibrated in the air and raced through Blake's veins. He wound his hips again and again hitting that spot deep inside her over and over. His body suddenly went rigid as if he'd been shot with an electric charge as the uncontrolled grip and release of her wet walls sucked the life out of him. Every single drop.

Blake collapsed on top of her, his entire body trembling as he felt his penis continue to throb until he was sure he would go out of his mind with pleasure.

Savannah held him tightly against her, feeling the rapid-fire beating of their hearts, their hot breath beating in the air.

By degrees their pulses slowed and their heartbeats returned to a normal rhythm.

With much reluctance, Blake peeled himself away from Savannah and flipped over onto his back then turned on his side and drew Savannah close. "I love you," he whispered against her hair.

"I love you, too." She closed her eyes allowing the afterglow to flow through her.

"I think you may need another shower," he teased.

Savannah laughed lightly. "Yes, I think so. And you'll need one, too."

He spooned closer and cupped her breast in his palm, its fullness overflowing over his fingers.

"Don't start," she warned. "Or we'll never get out of here."

"Maybe that's not such a bad idea," he offered, seeing a possible way out of what could be a touch-and-go evening.

Savannah's heart bumped. "Don't be silly. Although I'd love to spend the rest of the night with you, this is a great opportunity for you. You said so yourself." She hoped she sounded more encouraging than desperate. This was her best chance and she didn't want to blow getting inside Tristan Montgomery's house.

Blake heaved a sigh. "You're right," he conceded, kissing the back of her neck. "You wanna go first or should I?"

"You first." She flipped around to face him. Her gaze skimmed over his handsome face. "That was really special," she said softly.

His eyes crinkled in the corners when he smiled. "Only for you, baby."

Savannah pecked him on the lips. Whatever doubts she may have had lingering in her heart and mind were dispelled by the sincerity in his voice and in his eyes.

"Go get ready," she said.

Blake kissed her one last time and got up from the bed.

Savannah lay back against the thick damp pillows. She folded her hands across her stomach and looked up at the ceiling then around the room at the turbulence they'd caused. Since the beginning of their relationship, she and Blake had always had traffic-stopping lovemaking sessions. But this one was for the record books. She still tingled from deep inside. How she was going to manage to concentrate on being social tonight while handling her business and not think about getting her husband back between the sheets was a mystery to her.

But, multitasking was her middle name, she thought, sitting up. But first things first, find that drop-dead outfit.

Chapter 13

Blake held Savannah's hand as she descended the steps of their town house. She glanced up to see a black Lincoln Town Car equipped with a driver waiting for them at the curb. She turned to Blake. Her brows rose in question.

"I forgot to mention that Tristan sent a car for us. It's at our disposal for the night."

"Oh," was all she could mutter. This Tristan was pulling out all the stops, she thought. If this was the prelude for the evening, they were in store for a treat. She took her husband's arm.

"My name is William," the driver said with a slight bow of his head. He opened the door and helped Savannah inside. "Ms. Montgomery has a full set up for you in the car. Please enjoy."

Blake got in beside his wife and William shut the door behind them. They both looked at each other and giggled. The luxurious interior came complete with piped in music, a phone, internet access, full bar, chilled appetizers of cocktail shrimp, smoked salmon, pâté and an assortment of crackers and dips, a sunroof, and a soundproof partition in case they wanted some privacy.

"Does she treat all of her architects this way?" Savannah asked, testing out the GPA system.

"Got me." Blake reached for a shrimp.

Savannah opened her mouth to allow Blake to pop a shrimp into it. She chewed thoughtfully. Maybe she was simply being paranoid considering what she planned to do when she arrived at Chez Montgomery, she thought cattily. But that unsettled feeling was creeping up again. Each time she put her husband and Tristan Montgomery's name together her stomach would do a nosedive. She wanted to chalk it up to the job at hand but her woman's intuition and a wife's instincts had her feeling much differently.

"Is Steven coming?" Savannah finally asked to take her mind off her disturbing thoughts.

"Yes, he said he was coming. I'm curious to see who he will have on his arm this time. I can't remember ever going out with Steven and seeing the same woman twice." He chuckled and went for another shrimp.

"Do you ever wish you were single?" she asked out of the blue.

Blake choked, coughing until water began to run out of his eyes. Savannah banged his back with one hand, grabbed a bottle of water with the other, stuck the bottle between her knees and twisted the top off.

"Here, drink this." She tilted the bottle to his head. He took a gurgling swallow, coughed some more.

Blake drew in a long lungful of much needed air, sputtering a lingering cough and took another swig of water. "Whew! Thought I was a goner there for a minute."

Savannah took one of the linen napkins from the tray and dribbled it with water then patted his face. "Feeling better?"

"Yeah, much," he said. He shook his head. "Shrimp must have gone down the wrong way."

Savannah looked at him askance. "Probably so. Told you about wolfing down food." She put on a smile.

"I was starving, especially after earlier this evening. You drained me." He leaned over and kissed her forehead. "Thanks for saving me from myself." He chuckled.

"Anytime."

Blake adjusted his tie, wiped his face with the damp napkin then relaxed against the smooth leather. "This is the life, isn't it baby? Just think, another job like this development and we can live exactly like this—chauffeurs, penthouses, beach houses, brand-new cars right off the lot and enough money for a thunderstorm, forget a rainy day." He chuckled then draped his arm around her shoulder and pulled her closer. "I want to do that for you," he said, his voice sounding urgent. "I want you to have everything, and whatever it takes I'm going to make sure that you do."

Alarms jangled in her head. She turned in his arm to look in his eyes. "Blake, I don't need all of the trappings. I would be happy with you in a hut—with lights and gas, of course—but I don't want all of this. All I want is you and a family. That's it."

He ran a finger slowly across her bottom lip until she trembled. "That's why I love you. And that's why I'm going to make sure that you have the life that you deserve."

She stared at him for a moment before turning away, knowing that there was no point in debating or arguing the point, at least not now. She gazed out the window. Yellow cabs darted in and out of traffic, horns blared and the distant wail of an ambulance siren could be heard in the distance. Pedestrians from the barely dressed to Broadway fabulous combed the streets. All one incredible sight to behold yet none of it was connected, each element was all part of the landscape but totally unrelated to each other. In between it all, the bright lights of the Manhattan skyscrapers, all-night eateries and nightclubs flashed like warning beacons. When had they fallen off the same page? When had they stopped wanting the same things?

The limo crossed Fifth Avenue and the visual ambiance was almost immediate. Gone were the throngs of people, noise and businesses entreating customers. This was the East side of Manhattan. And as the limo glided along Park Avenue the life of the rich and famous became plainly obvious. This was old money, original New York money earned from bootlegging, shipping, oil and cars. This was the land of Rockefellers, Fords, Astors, Huttons, Hiltons and Trumps—the upper stratosphere of wealth, a land where a luxury apartment could easily run eight to ten thousand dollars per month. Where nannies abounded, and purebred puppies had playdates.

The intercom chirped. Blake leaned forward and pressed a white button.

"We'll be arriving in approximately three minutes," William informed them.

Savannah and Blake turned to each other and stifled giggles.

Savannah cleared her throat. "Thank you, William." She covered her mouth to hold back her laughter.

In precisely three minutes the limo rolled to a stop in front of Tristan Montgomery's posh Sutton Place digs. The stately three-story town house looked like every other one of its ilk within the quiet enclave. But, as Savannah knew firsthand, looks were deceiving.

William came around and opened the door, helping Savannah alight from the car.

"I'll be at your disposal for the evening." He

handed them a miniature walkie-talkie. "Call whenever you are ready." He tipped his head and returned to his seat.

Savannah slipped her hand through the crook in Blake's arm and walked toward the entrance. Muted sounds could be heard coming from the other side of the door. Blake rang a bell that neither of them could hear. Moments later, like something right out of a Joan Crawford movie, a tuxedoed butler opened the door.

"Welcome and good evening. Your names, please?"

"Blake and Savannah Fields," Blake offered.

A tight smile tugged his mouth. "Please, come in. The guests are in the sitting room."

The gentle sounds of something soothing played in the rarified air. Chandeliers that sparkled like diamonds hung from the cathedral ceiling. To the right, a wall to wall window looked out upon The East River.

Savannah's heels clicked against the white marble floor in concert to the ping of champagne glasses and tinkling laughter coming from in front of them.

They were led a short distance and before them the sitting room, which was as big as their entire home, opened before them. Diamonds, platinum, emeralds and white gold blinged and popped like paparazzi blubs.

There were about forty guests milling about the lush space. A dozen or more waist-high tubular tables were set up around the room, draped in white linen, some surrounded by guests nibbling on hors d'oeuvres generously being distributed by more waiters and waitresses than a five-star restaurant.

"Is that 'the Donald'?" Savannah whispered behind her hand.

"Yeah, I think so. And that's the guy from *60 Minutes*."

There were other familiar faces from newspapers, television and film, huddling in comfortable lounge chairs or milling about at the bar or tables.

At least she was dressed for the part, Savannah thought. Her Chanel cocktail dress was a perfect fit for this high-heeled crowd.

"Blake! There you are."

They turned to the voice behind them.

Stunning was the first word that entered Savannah's mind when she laid eyes on Tristan Montgomery. She was taller than Savannah had imagined—at least five foot ten, curvy yet slender at the same time, a goddess's body. Everything around her seemed to flow—from her catwalk to her shoulder-length hair to the nearly sheer, wide-legged white evening pants that she wore. Her skin was flawless, the color of warm honey. But it was her eyes that were most arresting, perfectly shaped almonds with thick lashes that shadowed the secrets beneath. Her mouth was full with what men would call "kissable lips." Diamonds hung from her tiny lobes, embraced her right wrist and dotted her long neck.

"Did my driver pick you up on time?"

"Yes, and thanks again."

She tossed back her head, revealing the long lines of her throat. "Don't be silly. How many times do I have to remind you how special you are? And special people deserve special treatment." She said all of this with her hand trailing up and down Blake's arm.

Then as if she'd been given her cue, she seemed to notice Savannah for the first time. She turned a discerning eye on the wife of the man she coveted. She put on her best smile, flashing milky white, perfectly straight teeth.

"I am so rude. You must be Sarah." She extended her hand.

"This is my wife, *Savannah*," Blake quickly corrected. "Sweetheart, this is Tristan Montgomery."

Tristan's free hand flew to her ample bosom in mock embarrassment. "Oh, please excuse me Savannah, I am so horrible with names. I'm sure Blake could verify that." She laughed. "I can't remember one of my assistant's names from the other. Welcome to my little gathering. Please make yourself comfortable. Dinner will be served in about twenty minutes. I'm only waiting on the Secretary General." She shook her head sadly. "He only lives right down the street and he's never on time. Oh, please excuse me for just a moment. I must say hello to the congressman. Blake, why don't you come with me? I want to introduce you." She snatched him away before either he or Savannah could blink.

Tristan floated away with her husband, leaving her distinctive scent behind. The same scent she'd smelled on her husband's clothing.

Her stomach knotted and ugly images formed in her head. The room seemed to disappear and she was standing in its center alone, confused and angry. She looked across the room and Tristan was holding on to Blake as if he was *her* man. They looked like a couple.

Suddenly she felt ill. She turned. Her stomach lurched to her throat.

"Are you all right, miss?" a tiny waitress asked.

"Ladies' room," was all she could get out.

"Right down the hall on your left."

As she darted out of the room with as much composure as she could summon, she silently prayed that she wouldn't make a spectacle of herself before she reached the bathroom. *And, Lord, please don't let there be a line.*

Mercifully, the bathroom was empty. She rushed in and locked the door and immediately turned on the cold water full blast. She took handfuls, cupping the water to her mouth then patted her head.

Drawing in ragged breaths, she slowly lifted her head and looked in the mirror.

Truth looked right back at her.

Blake was having an affair with Tristan Montgomery. The nausea was slowly becoming replaced with a pain that was inexplicable. Could hearts actually break?

Her eyes burned with tears of anguish and fury. How long had it been going on? Did he come here? Terrible, dark thoughts raced through her mind.

She needed to confront him. Plain and simple. Ask him outright if he was sleeping with another woman. What if he said yes? What in heaven's name would she do? Did he love her? Would he leave her for Tristan?

Oh, God! She leaned over the sink, drawing in long, deep breaths, trying to slow her racing heart and the pounding in her temples.

She knew if she asked Blake, he would deny it. He would deny it as easily as he'd denied the perfume on his shirt.

Savannah glanced at her purse sitting on the edge of the sink. Everything she needed to discover the truth was right inside. She opened her purse and took out the compact that held the listening devices. She held it up in her hand. Her expression became resolute. She was here to do a job for TLC, uncover the truth behind Montgomery Enterprises. As she stepped out of the bathroom, scanning the spaces for the perfect hiding places, she wondered if what she was about to do was for the good of the assignment or her marriage.

Chapter 14

The rest of the night was a blur to Savannah. All of her concentration was focused on setting the devices and not strangling her husband and his lover. She vaguely heard Tristan as she went on and on about the legacy of Sutton Place and all the who's who that had resided there over the years.

"They recently finished filming a movie with that gorgeous Denzel Washington. I tried to get him to come tonight but he's on the coast," Tristan was saying. "This would be of interest to you, Blake," she trilled on, "the famous architect I.M. Pei lived here, as well. Isn't that wonderful. Not to mention that Marilyn Monroe and her then husband, Arthur Miller, were former residents."

Savannah nodded and smiled. She'd managed to

"accidentally" stumble into Tristan's bedroom and plant a device above a Picasso painting before the maid found her. There was one near the front door, tucked beneath the table and another right here in the "sitting room."

"With the kind of money and notoriety that Blake is going to receive from this redevelopment job, you two may want to think about getting a place here, as well." She smiled at Blake.

Said the spider to the fly, Savannah thought.

"We're happy where we are on Sugar Hill," Savannah said, without gritting her teeth. "The house has been in the family for decades."

Blake put his arm around Savannah's waist and drew her close. "Yes, we have a beautiful home that we love very much. Something to pass down to our kids one day." He looked down lovingly at Savannah and she wondered if he was vying for best actor or if he really meant it.

"Don't mean to interrupt, folks," Steven said, joining the trio, "but Karen and I are going to be heading home." He turned to Tristan and stretched out his hand, which she took. "Great party. Thanks for having us."

"Yes, thank you," his date, Karen, said.

Steven turned to Blake and patted his back. "See you in the office on Monday." He leaned over and kissed Savannah's cheek. "Great to see you as always." He leaned close to her ear and whispered, "Don't let her rattle you." He stepped back, took his date by the hand. "'Night, everyone." He waved and walked out.

"We probably need to be going, as well," Blake said.

"Oh, no. So early? The night is still young."

Blake chuckled. "Savannah and I have plans for tomorrow."

Tristan turned to Savannah. "If you want to go home early and get some rest, I can get William to drive you. There are still a few people I want Blake to meet." She took Blake's arm as if she were actually going to snatch him away.

"I don't think so," Savannah said. "One thing my mother always taught me, you come in with a man, you leave with him." Her hard gaze locked with Tristan's.

For a tense moment, nothing was said. Tristan laughed. "You have a wise mother." She blew out a breath. "Well, if you must leave, I'll stop by the office on Monday. There are a few things I want to go over with you."

"Fine. Thanks for a great evening."

"Pleasure to meet you, Savannah. You have a wonderful husband, but I'm sure you know that."

Savannah took Blake's hand. "Yes, I do. Good night and enjoy the rest of your evening."

By the time they reached the front door, Savannah was shaking all over. Anger replaced the blood in her veins and it raced through her like a tidal wave.

"Enjoy yourself?" Blake asked once they were settled inside the limo.

"Great time," she bit out.

Blake turned to her with a frown on his face. "Are you all right? You're as stiff as a board."

"I feel a headache coming on, that's all. Must have been the wine." She turned her head to look out the window to keep from looking at him.

Blake pressed back into the seat. "Are you sure that's it—a headache?"

"That's what I said, didn't I? Why would I lie to you?" Her throat knotted.

Blake threw up his hands in surrender. "Okay, okay. Sorry I asked."

They both moved to their respective corners of the car—and later that night in bed, as well.

When Savannah awoke the following morning, she found Blake's side of the bed empty. She turned onto her back and stared up at the ceiling. Last night was the first time in their six years of marriage that she had not fallen asleep in her husband's arms. Her heart lurched in her chest as the previous evening ran through her head in full color.

Savannah still could not believe that Tristan would be so bold and brazen as to drape herself all over Blake as if she didn't even exist. What was worse was that Blake didn't seem to mind. Her jaw tightened. She guessed he wouldn't.

Footsteps approaching the bedroom door drew her attention. She glanced toward it.

"Good morning, sleepyhead. You were resting so peacefully I didn't want to disturb you." He approached the bed and sat down next to her.

"Feeling better this morning? How's your headache?"

She pushed herself up into a sitting position and drew the sheet up to her chin then realized she had nothing to cover up as she'd slept with a nightgown on, something she hadn't done since the first night of their honeymoon. She wondered if Blake even noticed—or cared.

"Good morning," she murmured. "Headache's fine."

"Great. I promised Gwynne we would be there around one."

Blake's younger sister, Gwynne, had recently given birth to a beautiful baby girl a bit more than a month ago. Blake hadn't seen his niece since she was brought home from the hospital and had been promising Gwynne that he'd come out and see them both.

As much as she loved Gwynne and her husband, Alex, seeing a loving family with a brand-new baby was something she just couldn't handle today.

"For some reason I'm really tired," she said, unable to meet his eyes. "I know I'm not up to a car ride all the way to Philadelphia today. Please give my love to Gwynne and Alex and kisses for Mikayla."

She got out of bed and headed for the bathroom. Blake grabbed her by the shoulder and turned her around.

"You want to tell me what the hell is going on with you? You've been treating me like I've got something you can catch ever since last night. You think I didn't notice the granny gown you went to bed in? What's up? Talk to me."

She looked into his eyes and saw the hurt and concern hovering there waiting for answers.

It was on her lips but she could not say the words or ask the question. The fear of his answer was greater than her desire to know.

"Nothing. Just out of sorts, that's all." She gently touched his arm and sparks, as always, ran through her. "I'm sorry." She went into the bathroom, shutting the door behind her.

When she emerged a half hour later, bathed and wrapped in her favorite sky-blue terry cloth robe, Blake was standing at the dresser putting his wallet in the front pocket of his jeans. He turned toward her.

"I'm going to head out," he said almost to himself. "I should be back before it gets too late. If I decide to stay over I'll give you a call." He didn't wait for her response. He walked out and moments later she heard the front door shut.

That's when the tears came, silent, burning and painful. She curled up on the bed and wept.

Chapter 15

Dani and Mia pulled up in front of Savannah's house. Danielle put the SUV in Park.

"You really think we should do this?" Mia asked, suddenly not so sure of their bright idea.

"Look, Savannah is our girl. If Blake is messing around on her, she deserves to know. Wouldn't you want to know?"

Mia's brows bunched together for a minute. "Yeah, I guess. But this kind of thing always turns out badly. I don't want this to ruin our friendship. You know the old saying about shooting the messenger."

Dani cut her gaze in Mia's direction then rolled her eyes. "Let's go. I'd rather she be pissed off at us than to see her on the eleven o'clock news with a jacket over her face while reporters ask her why she ran over her husband a dozen times in the parking lot."

Mia grimaced at the image. "You're probably right."

They got out and marched up the steps to the front door. Dani rang the bell.

"Maybe she's not home," Mia said after several moments.

Dani glanced down the street and pointed. "There's her car over there."

Mia followed Dani's outstretched finger. "I don't see Blake's Lexus. Maybe they're together."

Dani rang the bell again, pressing hard and long.

From the other side of the door they heard a faint voice ask who was there.

Dani and Mia looked at each other, concern etched on their faces.

"Savannah, it's me and Mia. Open up, girl. Got us standing out here like vacuum salespeople."

"Don't feel like company."

Dani knocked on the door. "Savannah. Open the door! You're scaring me. You know I'll call the damned po po if you don't."

Several moments passed before they heard the locks disengaged. The door slowly opened. Savannah stepped aside and let her girlfriends in.

"Why is it so damned dark in here?" Dani demanded to know.

"Look you wanted to come in so now you're in.

Don't start bitching." Savannah stormed off toward the kitchen.

Dani's brows rose to her hairline.

"Maybe we should have left her alone," Mia whispered.

"Aw, hell, naw. Something is up and she's gonna tell me before I leave outta here today. And put your damned glasses on. Can't you see she's a mess?" She followed Savannah into the kitchen, pulled out a chair from beneath the table and sat down.

Savannah had her face buried in the interior of the refrigerator.

"You're gonna talk to us, Anna. We're your girls. Whatever it is…"

Mia slowly took a seat, as well. "Three heads and shoulders are better than one, honey."

Savannah wiped her face with the sleeve of her robe. She drew in a shuddering breath. She knew she couldn't stay in the fridge for the rest of the afternoon and she also knew that Dani was the most stubborn person on the planet. She would sit there until doomsday.

Slowly she turned around.

Both Mia and Dani's mouths opened in silent exclamations of shock. Savannah might never grace the cover of *Essence* or *Glamour* magazine for looks, but she was still a good-looking woman. This Savannah Fields, however, neither of them recognized. The whites of her eyes were red and her lids were so swollen she looked as if she'd done twelve rounds with the champ.

Dani rose from her seat. "What the hell is going on?" She rushed around the table to where Savannah stood. She lifted Savannah's chin to force her to focus. "Did he hit you? 'Cause, I swear, if he…"

Savannah shook her head back and forth. "No. No, nothing like that." She drew in a breath. "I wish he would have. It would have been less painful." She moved away from Dani and went to sit down at the table.

Seeing the pain and anguish on her friend's face, forced Mia to shake away any reservations she may have had about getting all up in Savannah's business.

"You need to tell us what's going on. Right now," Mia said. "Where's Blake?"

"He went out. To his sister's house in Philly."

"Have you eaten anything?" Mia asked.

"Not hungry."

"Well, I am. I'm going to fix us something and then we are going to talk."

Dani went to the side counter and turned on the radio. Then she opened the kitchen window and the blinds. Soft music and the warmth of the afternoon sun floated into the room. Within moments the atmosphere softened and the tenseness in Savannah's chest began to ease.

Mia was whipping out pots, defrosting meat in the microwave and chopping up green onions and tomatoes. She found several packs of shredded cheeses in the vegetable bin and took those out along with a package of soft taco shells.

Before long the kitchen was filled with the mouthwatering aroma of grilling ground beef sautéed in spices.

Dani got out dishes and glasses and set the table. "How about some wine?" she asked.

Savannah nodded. Dani headed off to the living room and checked the liquor cabinet. She found a bottle of red wine, filled the ice bucket with ice and stuck the bottle in the ice to chill.

Mia finished up with the beans and rice then shredded some lettuce and mashed three avocados. She took a large platter from the cabinet and put it on the counter. She gently warmed the taco shells then placed them on the tray. In one mixing bowl she added the beans and rice, in another was her special guacamole dip, then the shredded cheeses, lettuce and tomatoes.

She balanced the tray and set it down on the center of the table. In less than thirty minutes she'd created a small feast.

"Black bean soup would have been perfect, but it needs time to simmer," Mia murmured.

Mia was certainly the cook in the trio. She could make something out of nothing even without her glasses. She'd confessed to them once that her childhood dream was to be a chef. The closest she'd come, however, was being an advocate for all the restaurants and cafes in the city.

"Well, eat up," she said, reaching for a taco and quickly beginning to fill it to overflowing.

The ladies dug in, then began filling their glasses with the rich red wine. Before long, Savannah actually began to smile as she listened to Dani talk about her latest "sexcapade" with a model.

"Dani, you are crazy," Mia said, with a chuckle. "That man ain't even a man, he's still a boy. What twenty-five?"

"But," Mia said, holding up a finger for emphasis. "What he lacks in experience he makes up for in enthusiasm."

The trio cracked up laughing.

"And where did you meet this underage Adonis?" Savannah asked, uttering her first words since she agreed to the wine.

"I was doing a photo shoot at the Pause for Men day spa on 135th Street for a *Men's Health* magazine spread. They're doing an article on workout attire for men. He was one of the guys at the spa. We exchanged numbers and the rest was…incredible." A wicked grin stretched across her generous mouth.

Mia shook her head and chuckled then turned to Savannah. "Speaking of men. We've politely danced around you for a couple of hours now, Anna. You can't tell us there's nothing wrong."

Savannah stared into two pairs of concerned eyes. If nothing else she knew she had the support and love of her girlfriends. They may get on each other's nerves from time to time but when the dust settled it was the three of them against the world. She reached for her glass of wine and held it out to Mia for a refill then took a long swallow. She put the glass down but kept her hand wrapped around it as if it was some secret source of strength.

With great effort she spilled out the story about Blake and Tristan. Everything she felt and all that she saw. She did, however, leave out the tiny little detail about her working for TLC.

Mia and Dani looked at each other once Savannah was done. Mia gave an imperceptible shake of her head, no.

"What can we do to help?" Dani asked taking her cue from Mia.

Savannah lowered her head. "I wish I knew. Right now I'm still trying to process it all."

"What if you're wrong?" Mia asked, even as she doubted her own question.

"You need to talk to Blake. Put your feelings on the table."

"And what if he lies to me? What then?" Her gaze pleaded for an answer that she could handle.

"It could all be nothing. Blake is one fine brother. Any woman in her right mind would be attracted to him—including Tristan Montgomery," Dani said.

"Exactly. And it doesn't mean he feels the same way about her." Mia leaned forward and took Savannah's hand. "Blake loves the ground you walk on."

A glimmer of a smile tugged at Savannah's mouth.

"How do you feel about Blake?" Mia gently asked.

The knot grew in Savannah's throat. "He's my… soul, my life. I can't imagine going through my days without him." Tears shimmered in her eyes.

"Then fight for your husband and your marriage," Dani said, slapping her palm on the table. "Don't you dare roll over and play dead."

"That's *your* man and Tristan Montgomery needs to know that."

They were right, Savannah realized, looking from one determined face to the other, and she knew exactly what she was going to do next.

Chapter 16

How she got through the rest of the weekend while playing the contrite, dutiful wife, was a minor miracle in Savannah's mind. She was visibly relieved when she opened her eyes on Monday morning and prepared for work.

By the time Blake had returned Saturday evening from visiting with his sister, she'd fixed a dinner fit for a king. Scented candles flickered throughout the house, soft music played in the background and she greeted him in a black lace thong and nothing else.

As she made wild, uninhibited love to her husband, in the back of her mind she thought that at the very least she'd wear him out so bad he wouldn't have the energy for anyone else. Sunday, as usual, had been a breeze as Blake assumed his position on the couch.

"Good morning, Richard," Savannah chimed as she walked into the office kitchen.

"Hi. You're mighty chipper this morning. Have a good weekend?" He poured a cup of coffee and added enough sugar to go into shock.

Savannah watched and grimaced. "Can't complain. And you?" She went to the fridge in search of some OJ.

"Went sailing with the family out on Sag Harbor."

Richard was a frustrated sailor trapped in a lawyer's body. Every chance he got, he was on the water in his boat.

Savannah poured a tall glass of juice. "Well, I'd better get busy. I have those briefs of yours to prepare."

Richard checked his watch. "I have a discovery hearing to attend at ten. Hopefully it won't take too long. We can go over the brief when I get back."

"I'll be ready." She took her glass and headed to her desk. Besides preparing a brief she had other things on her agenda.

Savannah worked feverishly for two hours. Finally the brief was completed, checked and rechecked. She printed out all of the supporting documents and put everything in a folder just as Richard returned from court. She held up the folder with a triumphant grin.

Richard took the folder. "Gotta hand it to you,

Savannah, you are the best. I'll take a look and we can review, in say, about a half hour."

Savannah stole a quick glance at the overhead clock. Eleven. "Sure."

He tapped the folder against the desk then walked away to his office. The instant he was out of earshot, Savannah picked up the phone and dialed. Her heart hammered in her chest.

The phone rang twice before it was picked up. "Montgomery Enterprises."

"Good morning. I was hoping to speak to Ms. Montgomery."

"I'm sorry, Ms. Montgomery is busy. I'll be happy to take a message."

"I'm sure she'll want to speak to me. I'm Mrs. Fields, wife of Blake Fields, the architect on the Brooklyn project."

"Please hold. I'll see if Ms. Montgomery can be disturbed."

Savannah tugged on her bottom lip with her teeth as she waited for what seemed an eternity.

"Sarah!" Tristan's voice trilled through the line.

"Savannah. Hello, Ms. Montgomery."

"Oh, please excuse me. Why can't I remember names? What can I do for you?"

"I wanted to personally call you and tell you what a wonderful time I had at your gathering on Friday."

"That wasn't necessary. But thank you for calling."

"You have such a beautiful home." Savannah nervously tapped her foot. "And I felt like royalty the entire night. I simply never knew what famous face was going to show up next. You seem to know everyone who's anyone." Savannah laughed lightly.

"I do have wonderful friends."

Savannah could hear the smile in her voice and the slow shift in her formal tone.

"I'm happy that you enjoyed yourself enough to make a personal call. Not many people do that."

"I have to blame it on my upbringing."

"Well, if there's nothing else. I have a full day ahead of me. As a matter of fact, I'm supposed to see your husband later."

"Actually I wanted to ask you…um, what is the name of that fabulous perfume you were wearing?"

"Oh… Do you like it?"

"Love it. It's so…unique."

"To be truthful, I have it specially prepared."

"You're kidding." Her foot tapped faster.

"If you really like it, I'd be happy to give you the information to the guy I use."

"Would you? Oh, you are truly a jewel. I was wondering, Blake has said such fabulous things about you and your business, I was wondering… I mean, I know it may be an imposition, but I was hoping I could stop by your office and look around. He can't stop talking about the decor and I've really been thinking about redecorating our town house. And your taste is impeccable." She held her breath, knew how utterly stupid it sounded but she was relying on Tristan's vanity.

"Well, since you put it that way. Sure, why not? How about next week?"

"I was thinking this afternoon. Say lunchtime? One-thirty? I was going to be in your area."

Tristan blew out a breath. "I...suppose that would be fine. I can't spend much time. As I said I have an appointment today."

"I totally understand. I would simply love to get some ideas and...surprise Blake."

"Fine. Come by."

Zero for common sense and point one for vanity. "Thank you so much. I'll see you soon."

When she hung up the phone her hands were shaking. She checked the clock. She had a little more than an hour to get it together. She grabbed her purse and darted into Richard's office.

"Richard, sorry for busting in, but something has come up. I need to run out and I may not be back."

He swept his reading glasses from the bridge of his nose and looked across at her from his seated position behind his desk.

"Is everything all right? Something I can do?"

Savannah held up her hand. "No, I'm fine. Just something I need to take care of right away and it may take longer than a couple of hours, that's all. I'll be here first thing in the morning and we can go over the brief then if you have any questions."

"Sure…okay," he answered slowly. "See you tomorrow."

"Thanks." She spun away and rushed out. By the time she got to her car it was nearly noon. If she could beat traffic she could do what she needed to do and get to Tristan's in time.

Her first stop was Neiman Marcus on Fifth Avenue. She went straight to the designer floor. She knew exactly what she was looking for. She'd seen the dress in a catalog and fell in love with it. It was totally out of her price range but she didn't care.

After about twenty minutes, she found the dress, paid for it and quickly changed in the dressing room along with her new shoes and matching purse. The last thing to do was to transfer her surveillance devices from her old purse to her new one. She took one last look in the triple mirror.

When she emerged, she was the African-American version of Audrey Hepburn from *Breakfast at Tiffany's*. Her discarded clothing was tucked away in her Neiman Marcus bag. She checked her watch—twelve forty-five. She headed for the makeup counter, for a complete free makeover with the purchase of select products, of course.

At one-ten Savannah was strolling out, redone from head to toe. She had twenty minutes to get across town to Montgomery Enterprises.

Savannah pulled up in front of Trump Tower, where Montgomery Enterprises was housed. A valet met her car at the curb.

"How long will you be, ma'am?"

Savannah grabbed her purse, left her keys in the ignition and stepped out. "No more than an hour." She glanced upward at the towering building of glass and steel then walked through the revolving doors.

Montgomery Enterprises was located on the fortieth floor. She stepped off the elevator into what could be considered no less than a spectacular reception area. White dominated the space, punctuated by glass tables, crystal cut bowls, strategically placed mirrors, a horseshoe-shaped glass reception desk and bursts of color from exotic tropical blooms set in tubular glass vases. She felt as if she should take off her shoes as her heels sank into the plush white carpet.

Savannah proceeded to the front desk.

"Good afternoon. Welcome to ME. How may I help you?"

"I'm here to see Ms. Montgomery. My name is Savannah Fields."

"Yes, Ms. Montgomery is expecting you. Why don't you have a seat for a moment?"

Savannah gave a short nod and turned to take a seat on the long, sleek white leather sofa.

Moments later a young woman who looked like she should be on the cover of Vogue approached Savannah.

"Mrs. Fields?"

Savannah looked up from perusing a magazine. "Yes…"

"Ms. Montgomery will see you now. If you will follow me."

Savannah's heart thumped in her chest. She put on her best smile, picked up her purse and followed the ingenue down the wide corridor.

Each of the offices she passed had glass fronts. It was almost eerie in that she felt that each of the employees was on some sort of display and that privacy was not an option at Montgomery Enterprises.

The stopped at the first office that was not glass enclosed. Instead it had a thick, maple door with embossed gold. The young woman knocked lightly and turned the knob.

The door opened onto what was no less than paradise. Whereas all of what she'd seen so far had given a sleek almost sterile illusion, Tristan's space burst with color; from tropical fish in an enormous tank that covered one wall to the muted lighting and deep burgundy carpeting. Tristan was seated behind a huge desk that matched the door. Flowers bloomed on tabletops and covered the sill from end to end. This was certainly not what Savannah expected. A portrait of Tristan and a man Savannah assumed was her father graced one wall. A forty-two-inch television took up another. Leather furnishings matched the rich-colored carpet to perfection.

Tristan acknowledged Savannah's presence with a raised index finger as she finished up her phone conversation. She placed the phone on the cradle.

"Mrs. Fields. Sorry for the wait. I was tying up

some loose ends and I'm sure you know how those can be." Her smile missed her eyes. She stood. "Please have a seat." She came from behind her desk and sat opposite Savannah in an armchair. "So, what do you think so far about what you've seen?" she asked, getting straight to the business at hand.

"Stunning. This office space is incredible," she said with sincerity.

"Would you believe I did it all myself?"

Savannah's brows rose in surprise. "Really?"

Tristan's smile was filled with pride. "Actually I attended Fashion Institute of Technology right here in New York. My major was interior design. My father, of course, thought it just a frivolous activity and demanded that I take business courses, as well. When he died, I redid the entire office to suit me." She chuckled. "He's probably spinning in his grave as we speak."

She folded her hands on top of her desk. A diamond flashed on her right hand. "So, I can have someone show you around. I'm not really sure how office decor would fit with a town house." She gazed at her curiously.

"After being in your home, I had to see what your work space looked like. I thought that I'd somehow be able to take ideas from both." That sounded pretty good. "And as I said, Blake can't stop raving about it. Maybe I can even make some suggestions to my boss about updating our offices." She smiled.

Tristan gave a slight shrug of her left shoulder. "I

have a meeting in about five minutes. I'll have one of the assistants show you around."

"That would be perfect. I can't thank you enough."

Tristan stood, gathered some folders from her desk and locked her drawer. "You can wait here. Someone will be in shortly. Make yourself comfortable." She came from behind her desk. Savannah stood up and extended her hand.

"I really appreciate this."

Tristan shook her hand, looked her hard in the eye. "Anything for Blake."

Savannah's heart stood still for an instant then raced. Tristan turned and walked out.

Savannah stood rock still. It wasn't so much what Tristan said, it was *how* she said it and the look of blatant predatory gleam in her eyes. Savannah drew in a breath.

"An eye for an eye" as the Good Book says. And hell hath no fury like a woman fighting to save her marriage. She glanced quickly around, her mission clear. She took what she needed from her purse and moved expertly around the office. Everything she'd ever learned about surveillance rushed to the forefront of her thoughts, fighting for space against the images of Blake and Tristan. She worked with a single-minded purpose—get Tristan Montgomery and save her marriage.

By the time the young woman who'd escorted her to Tristan's office came to take her on the tour, Savannah had successfully planted two listening devices in Tristan's office and had taken a seat. One was hidden in a plant directly behind her desk, the other tucked beneath the center conference table. She'd also installed a mini video camera that was no bigger than a penny—and nearly as flat as a piece of paper—right on the frame of the portrait of Tristan and her father. The black dot blended perfectly with the frame.

"If you're ready, I'll be happy to show you around," the woman said with the same smile as before.

"Thank you." Savannah rose. "You have no idea how much I appreciate this."

"No problem." The woman headed for the door.

"Oh, one second. I'm sorry." Savannah pulled out her BlackBerry, which had been specially configured. Feigning checking for messages, she located the right code, pressed Send and activated the devices hidden in the office. Now she would be able to access any activity from her BlackBerry and from her laptop.

She popped her BlackBerry into her purse, and beamed a smile. "Ready!"

Chapter 17

Blake wasn't looking forward to his meeting with Tristan. Since their last private encounter he'd been successful at keeping her at bay. Knowing Tristan, however, he knew it wouldn't last long. At some point he knew there would be a showdown.

His intercom buzzed. "Yes?"

"Ms. Montgomery is here."

"Show her to the conference room. Thanks."

He drew in a long breath of resolve. This was business. He intended to keep it that way. He grabbed his jacket from the back of his chair and slipped it on then headed for the conference room. Steven stopped him in the hallway.

"Hey, man, I was on my way to your office."

"Why? We have a meeting with Tristan."

"Yeah, I know. That's why I was coming to see you. I just got a call from my brother's wife, Monica. Carl was in a pretty bad car accident. I need to get to the hospital."

Blake grabbed Steven's shoulder and squeezed. "Man, I'm sorry. Did she say how he was?"

"Monica was so hysterical I barely made out where they'd taken him. Finally figured out she was saying South Orange General in New Jersey."

Blake eyed his friend. Steven was the coolest guy he knew, nothing rattled him. But he could see how badly shaken he was. Carl was Steven's baby brother and they were really close.

"Listen, go. Call me the minute you hear something and if there's anything I can do you let me know."

Steven nodded numbly. "Thanks. Listen, I wish I could be there in that meeting…"

"Don't worry about me. I can handle it. Go."

Steven gave a short nod and jogged to the elevator. Blake uttered a silent prayer that Carl would be just fine then headed off to meet the next disaster waiting to happen.

Blake continued down the corridor then turned right at the fork in the hallway and walked down to the conference room. He opened the door ready to do battle but found the room empty. He stepped all the way in and looked around. Not a sign of Tristan. She'd been there. Her scent was still in the air.

He walked to the phone and dialed from the desk. "Jasmine, where is Ms. Montgomery?"

"In the conference room."

"No, she's not."

"Maybe she went to the restroom."

"Did she come alone?"

"Yes, sir."

"Thank you, Jasmine." He hung up the phone. He was getting a bad feeling.

Fifteen minutes passed and no Tristan. Finally he left and returned to his office, the whole incident pissing him off more than making him curious.

He threw open the door of his office and there was Tristan sitting behind his desk with her feet propped up.

"I thought you'd never get here."

He kept the door open. "We had a meeting in the conference room." He stepped farther into the room.

She brought her legs to the floor and spun the chair away from the desk and stood. Slowly she approached him.

"I thought this would be cozier."

"I don't do cozy, Tristan."

"Really?"

In a single motion she popped open the snaps of her lemon yellow faux-suede dress and let it fall to the floor.

"What the hell…" His head spun toward the open door. Voices drew close. His mind raced through all the scenarios if someone should walk by and see her standing there half naked. Instinct and self preservation made him shut the door.

Tristan smiled seductively and took a step closer. Blake held up his palm. "Don't."

She grabbed his hand and took one of his fingers into her mouth.

He tugged his hand away. "This has got to stop." He glared at her. "Get dressed and get out of my office." He turned to leave. She rushed and placed herself between him and the door. Her body was flush up against him.

"You know you want me," she whispered. Her chest heaved in and out. "I want you and I always have from the first moment I saw you." She snatched a handful of his shirt in her fist. "Your wife will never have to know."

Her scent was all around him. Her lips a breath away from his.

She reached between them and unsnapped the front of her bra. Her breasts spilled out.

Blake groaned deep in his throat. Savannah's face wafted before him.

He grabbed Tristan by her shoulders and forcibly moved her out of the way. He yanked the door open and glared at her.

"The next time I walk into my office, I don't want to find you here. And the hell with your company, the deal and anything else you want to toss at me. You're not worth it."

He slammed the door and stormed down the hallway to the men's room. Thankfully it was empty. He went to the sink and splashed cold water on his face. His heart was pumping like crazy. He braced his palms on the sink and drew in long deep breaths. Fury pounded in his temples.

Blake ran a hand across his face. He knew Tristan was bold but never did he expect her to pull something like that. Suppose someone would have walked in. His jaw clenched.

Tomorrow he would set up a meeting with his lawyers and see if there was any way he could break the contract. His shoulders suddenly sagged. What about the company? His employees? The future of his business?

He looked at his reflection in the mirror. No matter what was at stake, he'd never be able to face himself or Savannah if he slept with Tristan. Never.

He straightened his shirt and walked out. He went directly to the front desk.

"Did Ms. Montgomery leave?" he asked Jasmine.

"Yes, a few minutes ago. Is everything okay? She was furious. She looked like she was crying."

Blake blinked back his surprise. "I have no idea. Maybe she got an upsetting phone call. Listen, I'm heading home."

"Did Steven tell you about his brother?"

"Yes. I'm going to see if I can get any more details. If I hear anything before the end of the day, I'll call so that you can inform the staff."

Jasmine nodded her head.

Blake returned to his office, grabbed his briefcase, turned off his computer and headed out. He needed to see Savannah.

Savannah got out of her dress and tossed it on the bed, then kicked off her shoes. Blake wouldn't be home for a couple of hours. That would give her plenty of time to check the devices.

She sat on the edge of the bed and pulled her laptop to her, booted it up and waited. After logging in, she went to the TLC database and punched in her codes and turned up her speakers. After several keystrokes she saw the audio grid appear on her screen with an indication that it was location one, Tristan's home.

Her pulse rate accelerated. She could hear the housekeepers talking. A smile bloomed. She'd done it. She set the audio to Record, then entered the codes necessary to access audio and video from Tristan's office. After several moments, a grainy picture of Tristan's office appeared on her screen. The room, from what Savannah could tell, was empty. She adjusted the sound quality and set the audio to Record.

She sat back and took a shaky breath. There was no telling what she would see or hear in the coming days, but her gut instinct told her it would be well worth the wait.

Now that everything was set, she synched her PDA to the activated signals. This would give her access to anything that came through whenever she was away from her laptop.

She shut down her computer and put it away. The last thing she needed at this point was to be careless and have Blake stumble across what she was doing.

Her stomach tightened. Blake. She tried to push to the back of her mind images of him and Tristan. She didn't want what she felt to be true. One way or the other she would find out—her way.

She returned her laptop to the upper shelf of her closet then went to take a shower.

Chapter 18

Blake arrived at Savannah's office, the need to see and speak with his wife overpowering. On the drive over he'd decided that he was going to tell Savannah everything—the kiss, the threats and Tristan's performance today in his office. Together they would decide what to do.

He pushed through the glass doors and ran into Richard.

"Blake. This is a surprise. What brings you here?"

"I wanted to surprise Savannah."

"Oh." He frowned. "Savannah left several hours ago. Said something came up and she darted out. Is everything all right?"

Blake was stumped for a moment. "I… Did she say what it was?"

"No, she didn't."

"Thanks." He flashed a sheepish grin. "I guess the surprise is on me. I'll catch her at home. Take it easy, Richard."

"Yeah, you, too," he said to Blake's retreating back.

The minute he got into his car he called Savannah on her cell phone. After several rings it went straight to voice mail. He left a short message asking her to call him then disconnected the call.

For a few minutes he sat in the car trying to think what could have come up that had her dashing out of the office. He put the car in gear and headed home.

Savannah stepped out of the steamy bathroom, feeling a bit better. After she'd activated all the listening devices she'd suddenly felt dirty—peeking into someone else's personal life. It was such a violation of privacy. But then she thought about her assignment and her marriage. Feeling a little dirty was worth it and nothing that a little hot water and soap wouldn't cure.

She was just putting on her robe when the phone rang. Caller ID indicated that it was her mother.

"Hey, Mom."

"Did I ever tell you how much I dislike caller ID?" was her response.

Savannah laughed. "It has its perks. How are you?"

"Fine."

"I called your office and the secretary said you left early. Is everything okay?"

"Everything is fine, Mom."

"Did I ever tell you that as much as I dislike caller ID, I dislike you lying to me even more?"

Savannah pushed out a breath and strolled back into the bathroom. She'd wanted to spill what had been weighing so heavily on her heart to someone. She'd hinted at it with the girls and their response was not what she'd wanted to hear.

"What is it, Savannah? The assignment? Blake? Are you ill?"

There was a long pause before she finally responded. "A combination of all three," she confessed.

"Talk to me, sweetheart."

Savannah sat on the side of the tub and slowly began to tell her mother what had happened; the blatant lie that Blake told, how she was still torn about the assignment that could possibly implicate Blake, her fear of losing him to Tristan.

Claudia listened with an open heart and an open mind. She knew her daughter. Savannah was loyal to a fault, but when she felt slighted or betrayed she could be vengeful. She'd been like that since she was a little girl. She'd seen Savannah cut off her friends for the slightest infraction of trust. And she knew that as much as Savannah loved Blake she would slice him off at the knees if she discovered what she believed to be true. But Claudia also knew that one of Savannah's biggest faults was her sometimes lack of confidence in herself, not so much her abilities, but her looks. Savannah always felt she didn't measure up in the looks department when compared with other women. And if Tristan Montgomery even slightly resembled her photographs, Savannah was probably tied in knots.

"Honey, you listen and you listen to me good. Blake loves you. I'm sorry that the very first assignment from the Cartel had to involve him. But, no matter what, you must not reveal anything about the organization to him. Ever."

"I know that but—"

"No buts. Do your job and believe in your husband. I'm sure there is an explanation for the perfume."

"But he lied to me. How am I supposed to deal with that? How can I trust him after that or believe anything he has to say?"

"He very well may have had a reason. And you can sort it all out when the job is finished."

"But suppose…"

"Get all of the ugly pictures out of your head and stay focused. What have you found out so far?"

"I've set the listening devices in her home and office…."

Blake stood on the other side of the bathroom door, frozen.

"I have a little more than a week to collect the evidence I need before the groundbreaking."

He couldn't make sense of what she was saying. Listening devices? The groundbreaking?

He caught a glimpse of the dress on the bed. He walked over and picked it up. The tag was still inside but he could tell it had been worn. What the hell was going on?

"I've got to go. I'll keep you posted. Love you, too." She turned to leave the bathroom and stopped cold.

Tristan stormed into her town house. Fury boiled in her veins. How dare he turn her down? Who in the hell did he think he was? He was nobody, that's who he was.

She tossed her purse on the hall table and stomped into her bedroom. Suddenly, she didn't feel so tough anymore. She was hurt, humiliated. Hot tears burned her eyes. She plopped down on her bed just as her phone rang.

She snatched up the phone. "Yes?"

"Hey, Tristan. It's Cynthia."

Tristan drew herself up. Cynthia Harrington was her closest friend and biggest competitor. Since they were kids growing up on Long Island they had been in constant competition with each other, from clothes to cars to men—always trying to outdo the other.

"Hi, Cynthia. How are you?"

"Good. Calling to see what you're up to and to get all the juicy details on Mr. Fields."

Tristan squeezed her eyes shut. She'd never hear

the end of it if she told Cynthia the truth—that Blake had turned down her advances.

"Everything is going according to plan and right on schedule."

"Really? Tell, tell. How and when?"

Tristan wove a tale fit for the raciest romance novel up to and including her fabricated session in Blake's office hours earlier.

"What! You seduced him right in his own office?"

"Right on the desk, the floor." She laughed. "It was fabulous. He was fabulous. Just like I knew he'd be."

"I have to hand it to you, when you set your sights on something it's a done deal. So now what? What about his wife?"

"It's like I told him, she never has to know. And she won't. Unless I decide otherwise." She sputtered a nasty chuckle.

They talked some more and Tristan finally begged off, complaining of needing to sit in a hot tub to massage her aching body after being with Blake.

She hung up the phone, disgusted with her lie but more disgusted that it wasn't true.

Chapter 19

"Blake...I didn't hear you come in." She pulled her robe closed.

He stared at her for a moment. "Left work early. I stopped by your job."

Her heart thumped.

"Ran into Richard. He said something came up and you rushed out."

"Uh, yes." She forced a smile and brushed by him.

"So...what happened?"

She kept her back to him, noticed the flashing light on her PDA that was sitting on the nightstand.

"I... Mia and I are planning a surprise party for Dani. I had some running around to do. That's all."

"Really? That's the reason for the dress?"

Her eyes darted to the dress still on the bed. Inwardly, she groaned. "Yes. I went to Neiman Marcus and bought it today. It's going to be a dressy affair."

"And what are you ladies celebrating?"

"She, uh, just landed a major new client and we wanted to celebrate. Just the girls. You know."

She finally turned to him. "What made you come up to my office?"

It was on the tip of his tongue to tell her everything, the turmoil he felt, the decisions he wasn't sure if he could make. But suddenly, he didn't know who she was.

"Had an urge to see you, that's all. And I wanted to tell you about Steven. His brother was in an accident."

Her eyes widened in alarm. "Oh, no. Is Carl okay?"

"I'm not sure." He crossed the room. "I'm going to call Steven shortly and find out." He walked to his dresser then turned to face her. "You want to tell me what's really going on, Savannah?"

"I don't know what you mean."

"How about starting with listening devices?" His gaze zeroed in on her. She didn't flinch.

Savannah felt her stomach drop to her knees. Dammit. She had to think fast. "If you must know… and I really shouldn't be telling you this…it's an ugly divorce case that Richard has me working on."

He leaned against the dresser and stared at her. "Richard has you working on a case and planting listening devices?" he asked, his voice laced with disbelief.

She planted her hands on her hips. "Yes. Why is that so hard to believe?"

"Since when does Billings and Tate handle divorces and why in heavens name would they have *you* planting devices instead of a P.I.?"

She swallowed. "I asked to do it," she said, the lie flowing as smooth as melted butter. "And we do handle divorces…indirectly. This client is a major corporate executive. He wants to get something on his wife to ensure that she won't take his company."

Blake slung his hands into his pockets. He gave a short shake of his head, not knowing whether to swallow the story whole or to laugh.

"So now you're what…some kind of spy?"

Her eye twitched. "Of course not! I convinced Richard that I could get close enough without being someone that she would suspect."

Blake held up his hand. "Enough! Okay. Why are you lying to me? I heard you. You can tell whoever it was on the phone the truth but not me?"

No matter what, you must never reveal what we do. The warning rang in her head.

She spun away. "You're right. I am lying." She walked out of the room. Blake was hot on her heels.

"Savannah. Who is it that you love?"

She nearly tripped over her own feet.

"I heard you tell whoever you were talking to that

you loved them, too. Is that the reason for the new dress, for leaving work early, for lying to my face?"

She whirled around. "How dare you?" Her chest heaved in and out. She glared at him. *Don't do it, Savannah,* came the warning. Her thoughts raced. Maybe it would do him some good to feel as crappy as she'd been feeling lately. "Think whatever you want, Blake. If you believe that something is going on, then…then maybe we don't have what I thought we did." She brushed by him and headed back to the bedroom. She rifled through her closet and drawers in search of something to put on.

"What are you doing?"

"Getting out of here," she snapped, pulling on a pair of jeans. She tugged a T-shirt over her head.

"Going to meet him!"

She snatched a look at him, stormed past him and snatched her PDA up from the nightstand.

"Don't walk out of here, Savannah. We need to talk."

"Not when you're in this frame of mind." She had to get out of there.

"If you leave, Savannah, I won't be here when you get back."

She halted her steps for an instant. She'd make this right when everything was done, when she had the information she needed. And either she and Blake would weather the storm, or they wouldn't.

"That's your choice, Blake." She picked up her purse and car keys and walked out.

By the time she reached her car and got behind the wheel she was shaking like a leaf. What in the world had she done? What if she was totally wrong about Blake and Tristan? She'd jeopardized her marriage.

But then she thought about his lie—the perfume on his shirt, the same perfume that Tristan wore. If he would lie about something that, what other stories would he tell her? She still gripped her PDA. She looked at it, opened the file and stuck in her headset. Her head began to spin. The contents of her stomach rose to her throat. What she heard pulled the last brick of foundation right out from under her.

Blake was beside himself. What had just happened? Had Savannah walked out on him, on their marriage? Was she really involved with someone else?

Nothing made sense. The only thing that did was going after her and settling this once and for all. He should never have let her leave. He dashed out of the house and ran down the stairs just as Savannah's SUV tore off from the curb.

Chapter 20

Mia was just settling in front of the television when her downstairs doorbell rang. She took off her glasses, pulled herself up from the couch and went to her intercom.

"Who?"

"It's me," a weak voice answered.

Mia frowned and buzzed the door. She was waiting for Savannah when she came upstairs.

"Anna, what is it?"

Savannah walked by her like a ghost.

Mia shut the door and followed Savannah inside. "What's wrong?"

Savannah turned to her friend and Mia's mouth dropped open. She rushed to her and cupped her face in her hands. Her eyes ran over Savannah's face. "What happened?" She bit out the two words.

Savannah's shoulders began to shake and the tears rolled down her cheeks in an unending stream. Her body shuddered and the wretched pain of her sobs pierced Mia's heart. She wrapped Savannah in her arms and held her close, whispering soothing words of comfort.

"Let it out. It's okay."

Savannah held on as an overboard passenger hangs on to a life raft.

Mia ushered Savannah into the living room and eased her down into a chair, never letting her go.

Savannah cried until she had nothing left but dry heaving sobs.

Mia had no idea what was wrong, but she knew it was bad. She'd never seen Savannah like this. They'd always wept on each other's shoulders at one time or the other, but never like this, never this kind of anguish. Everything in her wanted to make Savannah talk, but she knew it would be fruitless until Savannah was ready. Mia being Mia did as she always did during a crisis…

"I'm going to fix us something to nibble on. We'll relax, break out a bottle of wine and…"

Savannah lifted her head from Mia's shoulder. Her wide dark eyes filled with hurt. "I left him, Mia. I walked out on Blake, on my marriage."

Mia couldn't respond. She thought of the restaurant, of Dani's photographs, Savannah's story about the perfume. Still, she couldn't believe it had come to this.

"Anna, honey, I'm going to call Dani. Okay?"

Savannah nodded.

Mia got up and went to the phone. When Dani answered Mia could instantly tell that she was otherwise engaged.

"Dani, kick him to the curb," she said instead of hello. "Anna needs us. It's bad. Come to my place, now."

By the time Dani arrived Savannah's sobs had dissipated to silent whimpers. Mia scrunched her face in confusion, looking to Mia for information.

Mia eased up from the couch and pulled Dani into the kitchen.

"What the hell is going on? What happened to her?" Dani hissed through her teeth so as not to be overheard.

"She hasn't said a word other than 'I left him.'"

"What? She left Blake?" her voice snapped in stunned disbelief.

"That's all she said. I was waiting for you before I started asking any questions so that she wouldn't have to go through it more than once."

Dani's head cocked to one side, her right brow arched and her hand went straight to her hip. "I swear, if that man hurt her, I don't care how fine he is, it's gonna be me and him."

Mia put her hand on Dani's shoulder. "We don't

know what happened, so relax until we do. I don't need you going in there in one of your rages."

Dani was infamous for "going off" as she put it. Her tough-girl attitude came from her years of growing up in one of the toughest projects in Brooklyn, walking the treacherous streets to school and circumnavigating the dangerous stairwells of her building. She'd made it out in one piece but many of her childhood friends did not, having succumbed to drugs, gangs, jail or worse. She promised herself that if she ever made it out she would create a world of beauty all around her, which led to her profession as a fashion photographer. She never wanted to see anything ugly again. Nonetheless, old habits die hard and she may have left the projects behind but it was still in her blood.

Dani rolled her eyes. "Okay. I'll be cool. But—" she wagged a warning finger "—if Savannah even breathes that he hurt her…"

Mia took her arm. "Come on. And just relax, hear her out."

They returned to the living room. Savannah looked at her friends with swollen eyes. She could tell by Dani's stance that she was ready to do battle and Mia would go along for the ride. Savannah inhaled deeply.

"Since we're all here," she began, "I guess I should tell you what's going on, huh?"

"Whenever you feel like talking, sweetie," Mia said gently.

Dani sat on one side of Savannah and Mia on the other.

"I'm going to tell you something that I've been sworn not to divulge to anyone. It's going to sound crazy, but just hear me out."

They both frowned.

Savannah drew in a breath and slowly laid out her incredible story from the time she was recruited by her mother up to her listening to the recording. When she was finished nearly an hour later, a pin could be heard falling onto Mia's thick carpet.

"Wait…let me get this straight," Mia finally said. "You work for some kind of secret agency and you were assigned to spy on Tristan Montgomery?"

Savannah nodded.

"And while you're spying you find out about her and Blake?" Dani asked.

Savannah nodded again. She tugged on her bottom lip with her teeth, suddenly uncertain whether she should have told them anything. But these were her dearest friends. They would never betray her.

"Damn," Dani whispered.

"Double damn," Mia added. "Honey, I'm so sorry. I don't even know what to say."

"I know what to say," Dani said. "Brother needs a beat down and sister girl, too!"

"That's not going to solve anything," Mia said.

"Maybe not, but it would make me feel better."

Savannah gave a weak smile. "I appreciate the sentiment, but Mia is right."

"I want to get back to this secret-agent thing," Dani said. "I'm still trying to wrap my mind around it."

"I've been part of the Cartel for about a year now. This was my first assignment."

Mia shook her head slowly. "Unreal." She paused and looked at Savannah. "So, uh, other than listening equipment, what other tricks of the trade do you have?"

"A PDA that links to computers, tracking devices, software programs to tap into secure Web sites and e-mails, mini video cameras…a gun."

Their eyes widened. "Get out!" they said in unison.

Savannah slowly nodded. "But now I'm wishing I didn't have any of it. This was the biggest mistake I've ever made."

Dani slipped her arm around Savannah's shoulder. "Look, I'm all for kicking a no good man to the curb, but as much as this rubs me the wrong way, I have my doubts."

"Doubts! Were you not listening to Savannah and what she heard on the tape?"

"I know, I know," Dani said, "but I'm a photographer."

"No kidding," Mia cut in.

"Just hear me out. My business is making something out of nothing. I know all about doctoring photos to create a specific impression."

"What are you getting at?" Savannah asked, with an inkling of hope in her voice.

"I'm just saying that life has taught me that most things are not what they seem."

"But I heard it," Savannah insisted.

"Or you heard what she wanted you to hear. What if Blake is totally the innocent one here and Ms. Girl was just running off at the mouth with her friend?"

"But the perfume? What about that?" Savannah asked.

"That could be anything. Maybe she was all up against him and he didn't know how to tell you."

"I can't believe I'm hearing this from you," Mia said, sincerely surprised. "A minute ago you were ready for a beat down."

Dani grinned. "That was my hothead talking." She turned to face Savannah. "The truth is, I honestly believe that Blake loves you. I don't think he would risk his marriage over a fling. There has to be something else to it."

"Like what?"

Dani was quiet for a moment. "Like I don't know…but something."

"So what are you suggesting?" Mia asked.

Dani looked from Mia to Savannah. "I was thinking that even though you said you had the resources of the Cartel at your service, if, and I say if, Blake is up to something it's not a situation that you would want strangers to find out about. Right? Not even your mother."

Savannah's brows drew together. "True," she admitted.

"That's why I think that you should let me and Mia be part of the 'auxiliary' cartel...."

Chapter 21

He'd waited long enough. It had been nearly three hours since Savannah had stormed out of the house. His first instinct was to go after her, but then thought it best to let her cool off. She should be icy cold by now and the waiting and not knowing were making him crazy.

In all the years of their marriage nothing like this had ever happened. Sure, they'd had their share of disagreements, as any married couple did. But they'd never walked out on each other, never shut down communication.

If he was honest with himself, he knew that he was the source of the problem between them now. It was his own conscience that caused him to accuse Savannah. She didn't deserve that.

Sitting here wasn't getting the job done. He had to find her, tell her how sorry he was and then try to explain.

He went to the dresser and snatched up his car keys. The only places he could think of were either Dani's or Mia's house or Savannah's mother's. He certainly didn't want to show up on Claudia's doorstep, looking for Savannah. He'd never hear the end of it, no matter how things turned out.

Just as he was heading out of the bedroom, he heard the front door open. He rushed out.

Savannah walked in, looking a little frayed around the edges and her eyes spoke volumes. She'd been crying.

"Baby, listen, I'm sorry." Slowly he approached, unsure of her reaction.

Her eyes held his. "So am I." She pushed out a breath. "We need to talk." She put down her purse and came toward him. She looked up at him, trying to see beyond the idealized image she had of him— her knight in shining armor. "I'm going to ask you something, and I need you to tell me the truth, Blake, no matter what."

His heart thumped. "Of course."

"Do you love me? I mean, really love me?" Her gaze bore into him.

"Savannah…" He clasped her shoulders. "I've always loved you." His eyes ran over her face, taking in every detail. "I love you now and tomorrow and the day after, for as long as I can see my future I will love you." He pulled her to him. "I'm in love with you, from the depths of my soul."

Savannah sunk into his embrace, listened to the beating of his heart that pulsed in perfect rhythm with her own, felt the depth of his feelings for her in every breath he took. Whatever happened between him and Tristan, she could not believe it was of his doing. She understood that now as never before.

She tilted her head back and looked at him, the anguish in his eyes, the questions there pierced her heart. She desperately wanted to tell him what she'd been assigned to do. But still, she couldn't. Not yet.

"Then tell me why Tristan's perfume was all over your clothes," she said in a soft, even tone.

Slowly, Blake nodded his head. "She came to my office as she usually does, unexpected." He stepped back and released her, slid his hands into his pants pockets. He leaned against the wall, looking suddenly young and terribly vulnerable.

Savannah held her breath and waited.

He recounted to her what had transpired. She watched every expression that drifted across his face; from stunned surprise to disgust.

"It just came out of nowhere. She kissed me."

A knot formed in Savannah chest. "Did…you kiss her back?"

His brows flicked. "It happened so fast I don't even know." He looked straight at her. "I may have. That's the thing that's been eating at me. She was all over me like a heat wave."

Savannah drew in a breath. "So...what happened?"

"I put her out."

Savannah turned away and went to sit on the side of the bed.

"There's more."

Her head shot up toward him. The air seemed to get sucked out of her lungs. Please, God, no...

"Today we had another meeting, a scheduled one." He shifted his weight from one leg to the other. "Steve and I were supposed to meet with her together so that there wouldn't be any more incidents."

"Steve knows?"

Blake nodded.

Savannah shook her head. The old boy's network, she mused. "Go ahead, I'm listening."

"Well, just before we were getting ready to meet, Steven stopped me in the hallway to tell me about Carl." He swallowed. "So I went in to meet her alone."

Savannah's hands clenched.

"When I got to the conference room she wasn't there. I waited. After about fifteen minutes I figured she left." He paused. "She hadn't. When I went back to my office, she was there."

Telling his wife what happened next was the hardest thing he'd ever had to do, but he needed to get it out, all of it.

Savannah listened in shock. This woman was that bold, that brazen as to out and out seduce her husband in his own office! Her husband! She continued to listen, seething inside. All she wanted to do at that very moment was to snatch Tristan by her hair.

"She's threatened to pull the project away from the company if I don't sleep with her," he finally said, his chest deflating once the words were finally out.

"She what?"

Blake nodded. "She's said it more than once. I told her to go ahead. She swore she would ruin me, ruin the company."

"Why didn't you tell me? You've been dealing with this alone."

"I thought she was bluffing until today."

Savannah's mind was running in circles. This woman so desperately wanted her husband that she was threatening to ruin his business to get her way. If she was capable of that, then she was capable of anything.

"We can't let that happen," she was finally able to say. "You worked too hard. Everyone did. She's not going to ruin that for you, for any of them."

He looked at her with a half smirk. "Great minds think alike." He finally dared to sit next to her. "I didn't want any of this to touch you. But there would have been no way to keep it from you if she went through with her threat. Money and power can do just about anything. If she set her mind to it, I may never be able to work again and I have a staff with families to think about."

"I may as well tell you now," she said.

"What? Don't tell me Richard has been making moves on you?" he said half joking.

Savannah snickered. "No. Nothing like that. I—uh, went to see Tristan today."

His neck jerked back. "Why?"

"Insecurity."

"Insecurity? What are you talking about?"

She glanced over her shoulder toward the dress on the bed. "That was the reason for the dress. I wanted her to see me as fabulous as she is." She swallowed. "Ever since I met her at the party and realized she wore the same perfume I'd smelled on you and then you denied it…I felt…hurt and confused and I thought that I might lose you to her."

"Savannah, baby, you can't lose me. It's not possible." He took her hand. "And why in the world would you feel insecure?"

She pushed up from the bed. "I've always felt that way," she said almost to herself. "Especially around beautiful women." She turned to face him. "I know I'm no beauty queen, I never have been." She held up her hand as he opened his mouth. "I know, I'm beautiful to you. But, the truth is, I'm short. I can get overweight just thinking about food and if I didn't go to the salon every week I could be a cover model for *Fright Digest*. But, as I always tell myself, I clean up good." She sputtered a self-deprecating laugh. "But up against someone like Tristan, who is naturally beautiful, rich and powerful, I felt totally inadequate. And I wanted to at least level the playing field when I went to see her." She lowered her head focusing on the pattern of the rug. "And I thought there was something going on between you, and it was killing me inside."

The next thing she knew her feet were off the floor and she was up in Blake's muscular arms. He cradled her against him and walked to the bed, putting her down like a fine piece of china. He leaned over her.

He unbuttoned her blouse and peeled it away. Her breasts, rapidly, rose and fell. He slid her drawstring sweatpants down over her hips and pulled them off. He reached behind her and unhooked her bra, pulled it off and tossed it on the floor. His dark, hungry gaze ran up and down her body, setting every inch on fire.

Then suddenly he took her hands and pulled her to her feet. "Come." He took her across the room, opened the closet and stood her in front of the full-length mirror, with him behind her.

"You want to know what I see when I look at you?"

She pressed her lips together to keep from crying.

"I see silky smooth brown skin that feels like satin beneath my fingertips. I see warmth and heat and sparkle in your brown eyes and a hint of mischief. I love the way they turn slightly up at the end and the sweep of your brows that crinkle when you're deep in thought. And your mouth, it's full and rich and so very kissable. Your high cheekbones speak to your ancestry and make me remember from where we came." His hands trailed down to her waist and held her. "I can put my hands around your waist and feel my fingers curve out to your delicious hips. And those thighs, they're strong and tight and hug me when I make love with you." His hands rose upward and cupped the weight of her breasts in his palms. "These are a work of art, perfect in every way," he whispered.

He turned her around to face him and saw the tears sparkling in her eyes. "Yeah, you're not tall enough to be a runway model, but you're just right for me. You make me feel powerful and strong and longing to protect you." He tilted her face up with the tip of his fingers. "But most of all what I see is your spirit, the joy and fullness of it that reaches out and embraces everyone and everything. Love may be blind, but I see you, Savannah Fields. I see all of you, inside and out and I love every bit of you, from the bottom of your tiny feet to the crown of your head. All of you, everyday, always."

The tears came in a steady stream, hanging on the corners of her mouth before falling onto Blake's hand. He wiped them away with the pads of his thumbs.

"I want you to finally see yourself as I see you," he said with so much tenderness a new wave of tears fell down to her cheeks. "And I promise no more secrets between us, no matter what. We're a team."

A pang of guilt mixed with the pangs of love she felt for Blake. She desperately wanted to tell him everything. But she couldn't. She wrapped her arms around him, held him as tight as she could, never wanting to let him go, let the ugliness of the world get in between them.

In unison, reading each other's need they moved toward the bed. They lay next to each other, touching, sharing featherlight kisses, heating their bodies by leaping degrees. Savannah moaned against Blake's mouth.

He turned her onto her back, suckled her neck until he could feel her entire body shudder. He whispered hot words of love and desire deep into her ear while his hands electrified her skin.

Every place he touched caught on fire. Her pulse sounded like a tidal wave in her ears.

Blake pushed his hand between their bodies, found her center wet and pulsing. Savannah squirmed, pushed her pelvis against his hand.

One finger slid inside of her. Savannah whimpered.

"Blake," she cried out in a rush of air.

"I know," he said in a hushed voice before easing deep inside her. "I love you, too."

As she lay curled next to her husband, comforted by the security of his embrace she felt a hard knot of guilt. Sex and lies. They'd become all tangled together. Still, much of what she told Blake was true. She'd left out only part of the reason *why* she went to see Tristan. She was more determined than ever to get the goods on her. And now she had the help of her two best friends.

Chapter 22

Blake jumped up with a start about an hour later. He'd never gotten around to calling Steven to check on Carl. He cursed under his breath and eased out of bed trying not to disturb Savannah. He tiptoed out of the bedroom and went up front to use the phone.

After several rings Steven picked up his cell.

"Hey, man, I know it's late," Blake said. "It's been a crazy day. How is Carl?"

"The doctors say he's going to be fine. He has a concussion, a broken leg and a cracked rib."

Blake leaned against the fridge and expelled a breath of relief. "That's great news. It could have been worse. I know you must be feeling a hundred percent better."

"Definitely." He yawned. "We're just getting in

from the hospital. He'll be in about a week and then they plan to send him home. I'm gonna take a few days off and stay here with my sister-in-law. Seems like no matter what the docs say she's still worried. I don't want her to be alone and with the kids, too."

"Hey, no problem, do what you have to for your family, just keep me posted."

"Hang on a sec. Let me grab a beer then you can tell me how the meeting went."

Blake hung on and decided to raid the fridge while he waited.

Savannah felt and heard Blake leave the bedroom. She got out of bed and went to the door. He was on the phone in the kitchen. More than likely he was talking with Steve, she surmised. If that was the case that would give her a few minutes to check the recordings from Tristan's office and home. Steve and Blake were notorious for lengthy conversations.

She got her PDA and her headset from her purse then returned to the bed. After turning it on, she surfed to the secure Web site and keyed in her code which would upload the recorded files that she needed. The two-inch screen displayed an audio box in full color complete with sound levels. She put on her headset and within minutes was listening to conversations in Tristan's office. Most were basic business conversations, a call to what sounded like her hairstylist, another to her masseuse.

Savannah rolled her eyes as she listened to the

drivel and wondered how in the world this woman could run a major empire when the bulk of her time was taken up with hair and nail appointments, massages and trying to seduce other women's husbands. She was just about to turn it off, when she hit pay dirt. She turned up the volume and listened intently.

"I don't give a damn about the regulations, Larry. I told you what needed to be done with the project. I'm not going to have some paper-pushing lackey tell me when I can build, where and on what. Make it go away. This has got to go on schedule as planned. The groundbreaking is next week."

"Tristan, at some point this is going to be discovered. And when it does all hell is going to break loose."

"All the more reason why you need to make it go away. Pay them whatever it takes, but this project starts on time. Too much is riding on it."

"I'll see what can be done."

"Don't see, do. Goodbye, Larry, and don't call back unless you have good news."

The call disconnected. Who was Larry, and what did Tristan want to go away?

Savannah glanced up and saw Blake's shadow moving toward the bedroom. She quickly took off the earbuds and popped the PDA in the nightstand drawer just as he walked in.

He grinned when he saw her. "You're up." He took another bite of his overstuffed turkey sandwich.

Savannah smiled and slowly shook her head in amazement. Blake was blessed with a metabolism that burned off food almost as soon as he ate it. He could gobble down anything he wanted day or night and still stayed lean and muscular. She was sure his once or twice a week workout helped, but nothing beats good genes. ·

He ambled over to the bed. "I didn't mean to wake you." He held out the sandwich toward her. "Want a bite?"

Her stomach yelled yes. But she knew better. "No, thanks. I'll get some water."

"I talked to Steve."

She placed a hand on his forearm. "How is Carl?"

He relayed the conversation.

"Thank God for that."

"He's going to take some time off and stay out there at least until Carl comes home, maybe a bit longer."

Savannah nodded. "Are you going to be able to manage the office and the projects without him?"

"Yeah, we worked it all out over the phone. He has his laptop and his BlackBerry. We'll stay in touch. If necessary with can video-teleconference any major meeting." The corner of his mouth quirked up into a grin. "Technology. Humph." He chewed on the last of his sandwich. "You can do just about anything these days with all the gadgets."

No kidding, Savannah thought as Blake slid back in bed. No kidding.

* * *

"So how are we going to do this?" Dani asked Mia as she munched on a croissant with jelly.

They were seated inside their favorite coffee and bagel spot down in Tribeca a few blocks from the Borough of Manhattan Community College, off Chambers Street. Even though this little eatery was in the heart of where the World Trade Center once stood, miraculously it hadn't sustained a scratch during the 9/11 attack. If anything, once life in lower Manhattan returned to seminormal, it had become even more of an attraction. It was additionally convenient for both Dani and Mia as their respective offices were walking distance in either direction. At any given time one star or the other would saunter into the shop trying to blend in with the crowd. But Dani's eagle photographic eye always caught them all. Kevin Bacon, De Niro, Spike, the author Bernice McFadden, Gwyneth Paltrow, even Brad and Angie have popped in with their brood in tow.

But the one day that had them both on the floor, practically under the table, was when Denzel Washington strolled in with a black baseball cap pulled down low over his brow, baggy jeans, sneakers and wearing a black windbreaker. He may have gone totally unnoticed but Dani could spot that signature Denzel walk in the dark and blindfolded. But by the time they'd both pulled themselves together he was gliding out of the door. They still laughed about how they'd sat there with their mouths hanging open unable to move.

Mia lifted the cup of green tea to her lips and took a sip. "Well, Savannah has Tristan covered. So any funny business and she'll be the first to know."

"Uh-huh."

"So I think our focus should be on the location. And watching Tristan's comings and goings, who she's with, stuff like that."

"I can take care of that. You handle the location."

Mia agreed. "I'm going to check into everyone involved with the project. You've got Tristan's movements covered and Savannah takes care of video and audio."

"Between the three of us we'll be able to nail her." Dani slapped her palm on the table, causing a few heads to turn in their direction. She cut her eyes from side to side. "Sorry," she muttered. "One thing we left out. Tristan's friend, the chick she was talking to on the phone."

"What about her?"

"We need to find out who she is, where she hangs out. Maybe Ms. Montgomery confided more than a few lies to her." She raised her brows to make her point.

Mia slowly nodded her head in agreement. "I'll take care of it."

"Good." Dani checked her watch. "I've got to run. I have a photo shoot in midtown at noon. I need to meet my crew in like twenty minutes." She scrambled out of the booth, grabbed her backpack and snatched up her car keys from the table. She bent down and planted a quick kiss on Mia's cheek. "See you later. Double 0."

Mia giggled at the James Bond reference and swatted Dani's arm. "Guess I'm paying, huh?"

"Guess so." Dani hummed to herself as she dashed out.

Mia took her purse from beside her, fished around inside and took out her eyeglass case, took a quick look around and slipped on her glasses. She flipped open her electronic address book.

In the years that she'd been in the event-planning business, she'd made it her duty and the duty of everyone that worked for her to take names and numbers, from busboys to corporate CEOs. Her list was legendary in the business. Everyone knew that if you wanted to find someone, Mia Turner had the number.

She scrolled through her database and found the info for Desmond Reynolds. Desi, as his friends called him, of which Mia was a close one. He knew everything there was to know about New York City history. She wanted to find out all that she could about the construction site in Brooklyn. She highlighted his name and all his info came up from his private cell number to his shoe size. She scrolled for his number then punched it into her BlackBerry.

"You've reached my voice mail. What a shame. However, leave me a message with your name and number and if I choose, I'll call you back. Ciao."

"Hey, Desi. This is Mia Turner. I really need to pick your brain and soon. Give me a call as soon as possible. It's important." She left both her cell phone and home number before hanging up.

She'd packed up her gadgets and tucked her glasses away, just as her BlackBerry chimed. Desi's name and number showed in the illuminated display.

"Thanks for getting back so quickly," she said in greeting.

"Anything for you, doll. Now, what can I do to enlighten your day?"

"Well…"

Chapter 23

Savannah arrived at her office feeling much better than she had the day before. She knew she'd broken the cardinal rule of the Ladies Cartel by divulging its existence and purpose to Dani and Mia, but what they'd said as she'd bared her soul hit a chord with her. Would she rather have some outsider looking into her husband and Tristan, or her best friends? She chose friendship over protocol.

What was most troubling, which she hadn't voiced out loud, was the fact that when she was given the assignment Jean had to know who Blake was and that he was her husband.

That fact alone she knew was the ultimate test of her loyalty to the Cartel. But it also gave her even more impetus to clear her husband of any wrongdoing and prove to the Cartel that she could be trusted with any assignment—well, almost trusted.

Savannah tucked her newest Kate Spade purse in her bottom desk drawer, spun her chair toward her computer screen and powered it up.

Each member of the trio had their assignments. Hers was to tap into Tristan's computer.

While her computer loaded her programs, she took out her PDA and connected it to her Black-Berry, then she opened her e-mail program. On her PDA she scrolled to the files and found the one she needed. It was a Trojan file that, when sent to an un-suspecting recipient would trace and record every keystroke that was made.

Savannah typed her thank-you note to Tristan.

Dear, Ms. Montgomery,
I can't thank you enough for allowing me to visit your offices. Just as Blake said, it is fab-ulous. I will certainly be speaking with my boss about upgrading our office space. I am truly inspired.
All best,
Savannah Fields

Normally, it should read "all the best," but the tracking code was embedded in those two words, innocuous enough to be ignored as no more than a typo.

Savannah drew in a breath as she re-read the note.

Satisfied, she hit Send from her PDA which sent the signal to the BlackBerry. In an instant her display showed that her message had been sent. Now all she had to do was wait.

"I need a little more light on her face," Dani instructed as she peered through the lens of her camera.

This particular shoot was for one of her big corporate clients—Bergdorf Goodman. She was shooting their winter catalog, which was a feat in and of itself since it was the height of summer in the city and the models were layered down in fur coats, boots and scarves. It was a herculean task to keep the barely there, waiflike models from passing out from heat exhaustion. Her interns had to continually ply them with water.

By two o'clock they called it quits with a check-in time for 10:00 a.m. the following morning.

"Great day today," Nick Touro said as he slung his bag of equipment over his shoulder.

Nick had been with Danielle's International— the name for her business—for a little more than six months. In that time they'd become more than business associates. None of her employees knew they were seeing each other, they made sure of that, which was fine with her. What did tug at her conscience was that she hadn't told the girls and she wasn't sure if it was because of her uncertainty about where the relationship was heading or because Nick was white.

Sure, she had some Hispanic blood in her veins on her maternal grandmother's side which accounted for her golden brown complexion and silky ink-black hair. But her dad was black through and through, so therefore she was, as well.

She lived in a black world, grew up with all the stigmas and pressures associated with being a person of color. If anything, because of her mixed heritage and outward looks, it made her more militant, more pro black as if she needed to validate her blackness. The fact that she had fallen for a white guy totally messed with her head and shook up the very foundation upon which she built her life.

Dani stole a look at Nick as they trudged out of the fake winter studio, and her heart thumped just a little in her chest.

What would the girls think? she wondered.

He turned eyes so inky black they were almost purple in her direction. A dimple dented his left cheek.

"How about dinner later? I was thinking of going to the Lenox Lounge afterward. The Danny Mixon trio is playing tonight."

Dani laughed inwardly. Nick Touro was the blackest white boy she knew. He was more into every phase of black music than she ever was and had a collection that would rival Motown. His favorite food was ribs dripping in sauce with spicy collards and a heaping helping of potato salad. They spent many a Friday or Saturday night at Brothers restaurant on

Seventh Avenue South where they specialized in his favorite foods. Sometimes she felt like a discredit to her race when Nick would discuss the politics of Cornell West or Michael Eric Dyson or the inner workings of apartheid in South Africa and the chilling similarities in the States. She felt compelled to bone up on her history here and abroad.

"Then I was hoping I could entreat you to stay at my place tonight. I bought this new massage oil that I'm dying to try out on you," he said as they stood on the corner of Houston Street.

That was the other thing. Sex. Lord, just thinking about sex with Nick made her entire body go on full alert. He held nothing back and took her to sexual heights that you only read about in romance novels. Maybe white men can't jump but this one sure knew how to put it down.

A hot flush raced from her center and flooded her cheeks.

Nick grinned. "Am I embarrassing you?"

"No. Why?" She stammered.

"Because your cheeks are red."

"Oh." She waved her hand to toss the comment aside. "Just hot, that's all."

Nick winked. "That's the way I like you," he said in a whisper.

Perspiration trickled down the center of her back.

"So how about it?" he asked. "We'll make a night of it." His dark eyes bored into her.

"Sure. Love it. What time?"

"I'll pick you up around six. We'll eat then head back uptown then to my place."

Dani smiled, feeling giddy and girlish. "Can't wait," she said, and meant it.

Nick bent down just a bit and kissed her lightly on the lips. "See you later," he said against her mouth.

Her eyes fluttered open. "See ya."

Nick started off down the street toward the train station en route to Gold's Gym, which he frequented at least three times per week.

She'd have to tell the girls about Nick pretty soon. She knew she couldn't keep how she felt to herself much longer without bursting.

Dani turned and headed toward the garage where her Edge was parked. She checked her watch. Two forty-five. That would give her a few hours to do a bit of eye-spy work on Ms. Tristan Montgomery.

Tristan was crankier than usual when she returned to her office from an off-site meeting.

What had transpired between her and Blake in his office still stabbed deeply at her ego and her womanhood.

She breezed by the receptionists and staffers without a word or even to acknowledge their greetings. Her mind was on Blake Fields and had been since she met him.

Thoughts of Blake plagued her dreams both day and night. She couldn't get him out of her mind, and the desire to make love to him was sometimes so overwhelming that she found herself sneaking off from meetings to find a place to release her pent-up urges. Erotic images of the two of them would wake her from her sleep and she'd find herself trembling and moaning from the orgasm that dreams of Blake would evoke.

It was making her crazy. It drove her to pull that stunt in his office. She'd never been so humiliated in her life or felt that desperate.

Tristan entered her office and shut the door. She drew the blinds over the glass front of her office that faced the corridor. Sighing heavily she took off her suit jacket and dropped it across the couch then went to her desk. Pushing her honey brown hair over her shoulder she turned on her computer and started off by checking her e-mail.

She had forty new messages. She went through each one, replied to the ones that required her immediate attention, forwarded others to her assistant, deleted most and left the others for another time.

She came to one whose e-mail address—sf@billingstate.com—she didn't immediately recognize. She frowned for a moment but since it had no attachments she figured it was safe. She clicked it open, but it took several seconds for the message to appear.

She couldn't have been more surprised or annoyed, she couldn't tell which. It was a note from Savannah, the one thing that stood in the way of her and Blake.

Tristan read the very gracious note, picturing Savannah in her mind and wondered what Blake saw in her. Everything about Savannah was ordinary, from her height to her hairdo. She just couldn't understand Blake's fascination or, more important, his loyal devotion.

Was that love? Was that what it made you do? Was it so powerful that it would make you risk anything to keep it safe?

Tristan didn't know what that was. What it felt like for someone to feel that way about her. But she wanted it. She wanted to know and experience it. And she wanted it with Blake. Somehow she'd find a way to make him want her just as desperately.

She clicked off Savannah's e-mail without answering.

Her intercom buzzed. She rolled her eyes at the flashing light before responding.

"Yes."

"Mr. Washington is on two."

"Thank you." She picked up the line. "Yes, Larry. Only good news I hope."

"Yes, I'll be over in about a half hour. We'll do a late lunch and talk."

"I'll make reservations at Cipriani's."

"That's why I love dining with you. See you soon."

Tristan hung up, feeling shades better. At least one of her headaches was being dealt with. There was no way that this project could be stopped. Everything was riding on it.

She returned to her e-mail screen and sent a quick note to her driver that he was needed shortly and to be out front in ten minutes.

Then she sent off an e-mail to one of her financiers—Jeffrey Corbin of the Corbin Group.

Dear, Jeff.
Just a quick note to let you know that everything is still on schedule. All of the glitches have been worked out and it's full steam ahead. We're both going to be very happy and very rich.
Best, T.

Dani pulled up in front of Trump Tower and was instantly pounced upon by bellhops and valets.

"I'm just waiting for someone," she said, leaning toward her passenger-side window.

"You can't wait here, ma'am. You're going to have to move down toward the corner or I'd be happy to park your car for you."

She had to think fast. If she pulled too far away she wouldn't be able to see Tristan if she left the building. If she parked her car she'd never get it in time to follow her.

"Please, miss, you're going to have to move your vehicle."

She was just about to call Savannah and check to see if her camera was on Tristan when she spotted her coming out of the building with a man in a gray suit. Tristan put on her shades, walked to the curb just as a black town car pulled up right in front of her. The duo ducked inside.

"Never mind. I guess I'd better go," she said to the flustered valet.

She eased off into traffic and followed the car. Once they were about a block away her cell phone chirped. She pressed her hands-free set.

"Hello?"

"Dani, it's Savannah. I found out that Tristan is meeting Larry and they're going to Cipriani's."

"I'm right behind her car," Dani said with a note of pride in her voice. "At least knowing where they're going will make following them easier in case I lose them."

"Great. See if you can get a picture of this guy. Okay?"

"That's the plan. Hey, call Mia. I'm sure she knows the head somebody in charge over there. See if she can get me a table."

"I'll call you right back."

Dani had watched enough episodes of *Law & Order* to know not to get too close. But just on the off chance that they changed their minds about the restaurant, she didn't want to lag too far behind.

Her cell chirped again.

"Hello?"

"I don't know how she does it, but she got you a reservation."

Dani beamed. She'd been dying to go to Cipriani's.

"Thanks. I'll keep you posted." She disconnected the call and a few moments later the car glided to a stop in front of the famed restaurant.

Dani aimed her telephoto lens at the car and began snapping as the gentleman exited the car and helped Tristan to her feet. She caught him at several angles before they entered the restaurant.

She pulled up front and a valet came and opened her door.

"Welcome to Cipriani's."

"Thank you." She stepped out as regally as the rest of the high-heeled, high-browed guests, glad that she was always attired to go anywhere at any time. She pulled her two-foot silk, leopard-print scarf out of her purse and draped it around her neck, letting it fall over each shoulder. Her black safari shirt dress was perfect with her black peep-toe, sling backed pumps. She slung her black and beige designer signature purse over her shoulder, slid on her black shades and strolled inside looking every bit like a super model.

A hostess greeted her at the door.

"Welcome. The name on your reservation, please?"

"Danielle Holloway."

The hostess tapped some keys on her computer screen then smiled up at Dani.

"Right this way."

Dani scanned the semidark interior looking for signs of Tristan and company. She spotted them up ahead in a booth separated from the one next to it with beveled glass.

The hostess led Dani right past Tristan's table.

"Um, would it be all right if I sat here?" Dani asked pointing to the empty booth opposite Tristan's.

The hostess turned. "Those are for more than one person."

"When the reservation was made the restaurant was informed that it would be for two people."

The young woman looked put out for a minute. "I'm sure there…"

"Mia Turner made my reservation." Hopefully Mia's name carried as much weight with the Indians as it did with the chiefs.

The woman's blue eyes widened in delight and a smile stretched across her thin lips.

"Miss Turner! Why didn't you say so? If she took care of you I'm sure it's fine."

Dayum, Dani thought. It does work.

The hostess doubled backed to the empty booth and helped Dani into her seat. "As soon as your other party arrives, I'll have them seated. Please tell Miss Turner hello for me and that I still love that scarf she sent for my birthday."

Dani smiled. "I'll be sure to tell her." She peered at her name tag. "Jillian."

Once she was gone, Dani opened her menu. Fortunately in a restaurant like this the noise level was more of a hum as opposed to real noise. Dani sat right next to the glass in hopes of catching tidbits of conversation.

With Tristan out of the office and away from home there wasn't much she could do except to wait.

Richard strolled over to her desk. She only hoped that he wasn't in trauma mode.

"Hey, Richard."

"Hi. I need you to go over to the county clerk's office in Brooklyn and pull what you can on this address." He handed her a sheet of paper with a map and a property grid. The address he needed verified was circled in red.

"We're going to need the history of this place—all the owners from as far back as you can dig."

"Okay, what's the case about?"

"Seems that there's been some major discrepancies about who the true owners of the property are. Our clients said that they own it, that it was deeded to them by their great grandmother and they've only discovered the deed. However, the current owners say they have the deed. It is a prime piece of property in Westchester. The value of the house alone is well over three million and that's not including the land value."

"Wow. I'll get right on it. Find out what I can."

"I'm sure it will take the rest of the day, so bring in whatever you find in the morning." He paused. "By the way, is everything all right with you and

Blake? He came here looking for you after you left the other day."

She nodded. "Yes, fine. We just got our signals crossed."

Richard looked at her for a moment.

She reached for her purse in the bottom drawer. "I'm, uh, going to head out now. See how much I can accomplish before they close shop for the day."

"Fine, and thanks, Savannah."

"Not a problem." She gathered her things, thankful for the distraction of an assignment to get her mind off of her "other assignment."

After circling the block surrounding the county clerk's office looking for a parking space, she finally gave up and parked in one of the overpriced lots.

Hurrying up the granite steps into the building entrance her cell phone rang. It was Mia.

"I'm not sure what all of this means," she began without even a hello. "But I got some information from my friend Desi. It seems that those rail yards where the development is being constructed have a very interesting history…"

Savannah's thoughts were spinning by the time she found the right office to begin her research. If what Desi found out was true, not only were they sitting on a land mine, but the conspiracy to keep it quiet ran all the way up the ladder of local government, maybe higher.

Her temples pounded. She was more certain than ever that Blake knew nothing about this. She couldn't imagine that he would have signed on if he had the full story.

The thing now was to prove it and to prove that Tristan Montgomery was complicit in the cover-up.

As she sat in front of the microfiche machine tracing the history of the land in Westchester something suddenly occurred to her.

If someone desperately wanted land that could bring them millions in revenue, how far would they go to make sure that happened?

The case she was working on for Richard was the perfect example. People will do anything for money and money-producing land only sweetened the pot.

Savannah took copious notes. One thing that she always prided herself on was her ability to sift through the fluff of legal documents and get to the facts. In a bit more than an hour she'd gone as far back as 1910 to discover the original owners and traced the progression of the deed right up until the present day. She smiled. Satisfied. Richard would be pleased and so would their client. They had a very nice case against the offenders who'd apparently moved into the home when it became abandoned, rehabbed it and dummied up the ownership documents. There was nothing in the files to indicate that the offenders were the true owners of the building.

She slipped all of the copies and the notes she'd made into a folder just as a wizened clerk came around to say that they were closing in twenty minutes.

Savannah tapped him on the shoulder as he passed.

"Excuse me. I know it's getting late but I hope you can help me. I'm trying to find out the early history of the rail yards in downtown Brooklyn."

His face became a mass of wrinkles as he seemed to be trying to pull information out of the air.

"Well, you have two choices," he began in slow motion. "You can come back tomorrow or you can go across the street to Borough Hall and check with Topography. Gives you layouts, addresses, history." He bobbed his head as he spoke.

"Thanks. Thank you so much." She hurried out and darted across the street.

By the time she left Borough Hall, her heart and her mind were racing. She was so close to the ugly truth she could taste the sourness in her mouth. Her next stop was the Central Library on Grand Army Plaza. She needed all the history she could find. Digging up facts was her specialty and she was damned good at it.

Chapter 24

Blake decided to come home early and surprise Savannah by having dinner ready and a nice bubble bath waiting, and something very sexy for her to lounge around in.

He'd stopped at the market on his way home and picked up fresh shrimp and scallops along with two pounds of mussels—one of Savannah's favorites. A bottle of cooking wine, angel-hair pasta, Italian bread and condiments rounded out his purchases.

Blake dropped the bags off in the kitchen then went directly to their bedroom to get out of his work clothes.

He took a quick shower, put on a pair of shorts and a T-shirt, then looked for the perfect outfit for his wife. Had he thought about it early enough he would have picked her up something new. But the truth was Savannah had more enticing little outfits than a department store. Shopping for lingerie was her personal fetish—and he loved it.

He chuckled to himself as he looked in the treasure chest. Some of the pieces still had price tags on them. He shook his head. It almost felt decadent going through her undies. Although they'd been married for years, he couldn't remember ever going in her drawers. Just as he thought he'd found the perfect set—a firebrand red, no more than sets of strings with frills—he noticed her Tender Loving Care carrying case buried under the layers of lingerie.

He started to close the drawer but curiosity coursed through his fingertips. He started to lift it out, just as the phone rang. He crossed the room and picked up the phone on the nightstand.

"Hello?"

"Blake, how are you?"

He gripped the phone. "I'm fine thank you. Why are you calling me at home?"

"I wanted to apologize about the other day in your office. What I did was truly out of line. Your secretary said you left early and—"

"Fine. Thanks for the apology. I've got to go."

"Blake, please…wait. I'm right in front of your house. I wanted to bring you a peace offering."

His chest tightened. In front of his house! "Look, it's not necessary."

"I know, but I want to. I'll sit right here all night

if I have to." She laughed lightly. "I simply want to look you in the eye and say I'm sorry."

Blake rushed out of the bedroom and went up front then pulled back the curtain. There she was, waving to him from the window of her Town Car.

He slapped his palm against his forehead and let loose a string of curses. This was going to stop once and for all.

Dani pulled up across the street from Savannah and Blake's town house. She couldn't believe the nerve of this heifer. Worse, was Blake expecting her, thinking that Savannah was still at work?

When Tristan got out of the car and headed for the house, Dani's first reaction was to jump out and tackle the home wrecker to the ground. But she had on her good shoes and she'd just had her nails done—or it would have been on and poppin'.

Instead she called Mia.

"What?"

"Exactly. She's here, live and in living color. Wait. Blake is coming to the door." She whipped out her camera and started shooting.

"Dani! Dani!" Mia yelled into the phone. "What's going on?"

Dani put down the camera. "Looks like Blake is pissed. I'm going over there."

"No! She doesn't need to see you—just in case.

You're on surveillance, remember? See and not be seen."

"Damn!" Dani tapped her foot with impatience. "Wait, looks like she's leaving and she doesn't look like a happy camper."

"Blake has been redeemed," Mia murmured, relieved.

Dani checked the clock on the dash. It was after six. Nick would be waiting. He was always on time. "Look, I gotta go. I have a date tonight and I'm already late."

"Another date? Same guy?"

"Maybe."

"What kind of answer is that?"

"The only one you're getting at the moment. Listen, let's all meet tomorrow after work at The Shop."

"Let's do an early breakfast instead."

"Fine. Whatever. You call Savannah and confirm. I overheard some stuff today at the restaurant and maybe between the three of us we can make some sense out of it."

"See you tomorrow. Enjoy your date."

"Thanks. I intend to."

Dani pulled off from the curb and used speed dial to call Nick. He picked up his cell on the second ring.

"I know. You're running late," he answered good naturedly.

Dani smiled. "Yeah, just a little. Where are you?"

"Camped out in front of your door, like a lovestruck Romeo, while listening to Wendy Williams, they're playing that interview that she did with Whitney a couple of years ago." He chuckled. "What a mess."

Dang, she didn't even listen to Wendy. "I'll be there in about twenty minutes."

"No problem. I'll be here."

"See you soon." She disconnected the call and realized how much she wanted to see him.

When Savannah walked into her home about eight that evening, she'd already gotten the 4-1-1 from Mia and Dani about Tristan's visit to her house. If she'd had any qualms about crossing the line into Tristan's life before—all bets were off now.

She turned the key in the door and stepped in. Blake was on the couch looking as if he had news about Armageddon.

Savannah slowly put her purse down on the hall table and walked over to him.

"Blake, what is it?" She'd have to wait for him to tell her what she already knew. And he'd better tell her.

He glanced up at her. "We need to talk." He reached for her hand and eased her down beside him.

Please tell me the truth, she silently prayed.

"I was getting ready to surprise you with dinner and a hot bubble bath when Tristan Montgomery showed up—unannounced," he quickly added.

Savannah's eyes widened and her mouth dropped open. She leaped up from the chair and shot Blake a death gaze. "Don't even tell me she came into my house," she said, biting out every word for emphasis.

"No, she didn't, I made sure of that."

Savannah let the air out of her chest, smiling inside at her stellar performance.

"I'm contacting my attorney in the morning to see what my options are in terms of breaking this contract." He reached for her and pulled her down onto his lap. "I don't intend to spend the next two to three years that it's going to take to complete this job, under her thumb. I don't like being threatened. I'd rather lose the contract and deal with the loss than to ruin our life. Some things just aren't worth it. And I'm definitely not going to allow her to mess with my marriage. I don't give a damn how much money she has or what she can do to me." He paused and looked deep into her eyes. "Us, is the important thing, you and me."

Savannah's heart thundered with happiness. "We'll find a way to get through this." She stroked his cheek and rested her head against his chest.

"I know. I just have to figure out what I'm going to tell the crew."

"There will be other jobs, Blake."

"Let's hope so."

They sat wrapped around each other for several moments.

"Wow, the reason I came home early was to surprise you with dinner. I think I better get started."

"We'll do it together. Let me get changed." She

kissed him lightly on the lips, stood then looked down at him. "Don't worry, okay? Everything is going to work out."

"From your lips…" he said, trying to put some cheer in his voice. He knew that if Tristan was as vindictive as she put on, the next job for his company could be a long time coming.

Savannah walked off to the bedroom and stopped short. Her TLC case was on the bed. A cold sweat broke out on her forehead. Her head snapped toward the open door. Had he been in the case? Why was it out? Her thoughts ran at lightning speed. Even if he did open it, there was no way he could figure out what each of the items really was. Could he?

"Sorry, I was hunting for something sexy for you to wear during dinner."

She nearly jumped out of her skin. She slowly turned with a placid look on her face. "And you thought you'd find it in my cosmetics case?" she said, teasing, hoping that the tremors in her voice were only in her head.

Blake stepped in the room. "No." He looked embarrassed. "I found it when I was looking for an outfit for you." He frowned. "What's in there anyway, that you would keep it buried in the bottom of the drawer—top secrets?" He chuckled.

Her throat was suddenly as dry as sand. "Don't be silly. Top secrets." She laughed. "Yes, darling, the secrets to eternal beauty." She reached for the case and walked to her dresser and put it back. She shoved the drawer shut then turned to Blake with a smile plastered on her face. Her heart was beating so fast she could barely breathe.

Blake looked at her curiously. "You're sweating. Want me to turn on the air?"

She swallowed. "Uh, no. I'm going to take a quick shower. Don't want to catch a chill."

"I'll get dinner started. I'd wanted to have a bubble bath ready for you but…"

"It's the thought that counts. I'll be out to help in a few minutes." She snatched up her robe from the foot of the bed and hustled off to the bathroom.

Once the door was shut she finally breathed. Blake was no fool. If he'd opened the case, which apparently he hadn't, it wouldn't have taken him too long to figure out that the cosmetics had no cosmetic value. Fortunately for the casual observer everything looked fine. There were a few authentic items in the case, but for the most part…

She'd have to be more careful in the future.

Savannah was the last to arrive at The Shop. Mia and Dani had secured a table in the back.

"Sorry I'm late—long night," she said, sliding into her seat.

"Long night as in good, or long night as in long?" Mia asked.

Savannah grinned thinking about the exquisite loving Blake had put on her the night before. She was still tingling. "Long as in good—if you must know," she said with a wicked grin.

The trio laughed.

"Dang, seems like everyone had a hot evening except for me," Mia complained.

Savannah looked at Dani who had her eyes focused on her cup of tea. Savannah loudly cleared her throat. "And who was it?" she asked Dani.

"Just a guy."

"Yeah, just a guy that she's been on more than one date with," Mia added.

Dani looked at her and rolled her eyes. "Don't hate."

"Why not?" Mia said, biting into her bagel. "Anna has Blake and you have your mystery man. Who do I have?"

"Anyway," Dani said, dismissing Mia's blatant inquiry. "We're not here to discuss our love lives or lack thereof." She gave Mia a pointed look. Mia huffed. "We have real business to discuss."

"So, what did you two find out?" Savannah asked. She put her folder on the table.

"Well, it seems that Tristan and this Larry fellow—her attorney—are definitely in it together," Dani began. "There's been a lot of money changing hands since way before this deal for the development was signed." She looked from one to the other. "She is well connected and has friends in very high places—the decision makers. And apparently, from what I could overhear, Larry has worked the contracts to protect Tristan. But the city council and the zoning commission are all involved up to their eyeballs."

"With all the gentrification going on in the area," Mia added, "and everyone gobbling up the prime real estate it was all about profit. None of them cared what happened to the people or the land as long as they got their cut." She opened a small notebook where she'd taken down the information that Desi had given her.

Savannah's lips pinched into a tight line when she read it. "Then it is true. Everything I found out yesterday and your information, Mia, and your take on the conversation, Dani, points to a major conspiracy not just to the people who have been displaced but to an entire heritage."

They all nodded in silent agreement.

Dani spoke up first. "So what are you going to do now? I can't imagine that anyone involved is going to let you go public with the information."

Savannah pushed out a long breath. "The groundbreaking is in three days. I'm going to compile all of the information that we have into one document and present it to Jean." She sighed. "She'll have to take it from there."

"Do you plan to tell Blake?" Mia asked.

"I may have to. I don't want him to be totally blindsided. This is bound to hit the news."

"Yeah, but how are you going to tell him you found out?" Dani asked.

"I'll think of something. It may be a moot point. He plans to talk to his attorney today to see how he can break the contract. If he does then I don't have to worry about it."

She checked her watch. "I have to get to the office." She looked from one face to the other. "Thanks, for everything. For being in my corner, for keeping this secret and for…just being my girls." She smiled warmly.

"Hey, if you can't share sex, lies and intrigue with your best friends, who can you share it with?" Dani joked.

"You're right about that." She stood and the room swayed. She gripped the edge of the table.

"You okay?" Mia asked, jumping to her feet.

Savannah shut her eyes for a minute and drew in a breath. "Yeah, fine. Lack of sleep and no food."

"Here, take the rest of my bagel," Dani offered. "Eat it in the car."

"Thanks." She took it from Dani and took a tentative bite. Her head and stomach slowly settled. "I'll talk to you guys later."

Dani and Mia watched her leave.

"Savannah lives on no sleep and lack of food when she's on a project for that crazy job of hers." She looked Dani in the eyes. "Are you thinking what I'm thinking?"

Dani slowly nodded her head and grinned. "Maybe we'll be aunties after all."

* * *

Blake sat opposite Frank Lloyd, the corporate attorney, in the conference room.

"This contract is airtight, Blake. I have to tell you that if you break it, she can sue you for everything you have and then some. You'll be ruined, financially and professionally. Is there no way you can see your way around dealing with Montgomery Enterprises?"

"No." He shook his head. "There has to be some clause, some loophole that I can slip through to get out of this without getting burned too badly."

"You would have to prove sexual harassment and that she threatened you. And at this point it's your word against hers. And I have to tell you, it would be a helluva case to try to prove in court."

Blake's shoulders slumped. Slowly he rose from his seat, chewing on his bottom lip as he thought of his options, which were zero to none.

"Have you talked to Steven about this?"

"He had a family crisis," he said absently.

"Is there anyone who can corroborate your allegations against Ms. Montgomery?"

Blake blew out a breath. "No."

Frank shut the folder. "If you want to proceed, I can put in the paperwork, but I'm warning you it will get ugly and you will be the one who will suffer. She'll find another developer and you will be finished."

Blake slung his hands into the pockets of his khakis. "I'll think of something and get back to you."

Frank gathered his things and stood. "You don't have much time."

"I know, I know."

"Call me. And whatever you decide, I'll take care of it."

"Thanks."

After Frank left, Blake placed a call to Steven. It was only fair that he told his business partner that they would soon be out of business unless a miracle happened.

Chapter 25

By the time Savannah arrived at her office she was feeling much better. She couldn't remember the last time she'd gotten light-headed. All the stress and pressure of the past couple of weeks were beginning to take their toll. That and having to keep secrets from Blake.

The moment she was settled at her desk, Richard showed up.

"So what did you find out?"

"Plenty," she said, reaching for her bag. She pulled out her notes on the house in Westchester. "I'll get them all typed up and have it to you in about an hour."

"How does it look for our clients?"

"According to everything that I've found out, our clients will be very happy landowners."

Richard grinned. "Now, that's the kind of news I like to hear. I knew I could depend on you. Thanks, as always."

"My pleasure."

He turned to leave. "Bring the info in when you're done so we can go over it together."

"Sure," she called out.

Her phone rang.

"Billings and Tate, Savannah speaking."

"Hey, sweetheart, it's Mom."

"Hi, Mom."

"How is everything going?"

"Turned out to be a little bit more than I bargained for, but I'm just about to wrap everything up."

"How are things with you and Blake?"

"Great."

"You're not just saying that to shut me up, are you?"

"Shut *you* up! Never." She laughed. "But seriously, things are fine between me and Blake."

"Good." She paused. "I thought we could meet for lunch. I was going to do some shopping and I'll be in your neck of the woods."

"I'd like that. How about one?"

"Perfect. Can I meet you in the lobby of your building?"

"Sure. I'll see you at one."

"Goodbye, sweetheart. I'll see you soon."

"'Bye, Mom."

Savannah slowly hung up the phone. Spending an hour with her mom might be just the medicine she needed. Her mom, always pragmatic, would have the best advice on how she should proceed. After all Claudia was a card-carrying member of the Cartel. Savannah grinned and shook her head. Who would have ever thought it?

In the meantime, she needed to compile her information for Richard. But before she did she needed to listen to the recordings from Tristan's home and office. There wasn't a moment to check the night before and just maybe there was something she could use.

She pulled out her PDA, put on her headset and scrolled to her audio program. While it went through the registry process, she turned on her computer and began putting together the draft of information for Richard. Finally the program was fully loaded and the audio began.

The first set of conversations was in Tristan's home. Nothing of major interest. Then, just when she was getting bored, Tristan made a call to her girlfriend.

"...I went to his office and got practically naked in front of him and he wouldn't bite," Tristan was saying.

"Girl, are you out of your mind? Suppose a secretary or somebody had come in?"

"I didn't care. I just wanted him."

"Maybe you need to just give up and move on.

The man is apparently in love with his wife and the only reason why you want him is because he belongs to someone else."

"That's not true! Well, maybe a little. But from the first time I saw his profile in *Black Enterprise* magazine I set my sights on him. I could have chosen dozens of other architectural developers, but I chose him."

"Now you need to un-choose him. It's not working. At least not the way you want it to."

"You know I don't give up. I have him backed into a corner."

"What are you talking about now?"

"I told him plain and simple that if he doesn't satisfy my carnal needs, I'd ruin him." She laughed. "And you know I will."

Bingo!

Her friend chuckled. "Tristan, you are a mess. You need your head examined."

"No, what I need is a taste of what Mrs. Fields gets every night."

"What if you go through all of this and he's lousy in bed? Looks are deceiving, you know."

Tristan laughed. "Trust me, I know a good man when I see one. It's like picking out shoes. You know the ones you want and even if they don't fit perfectly, they still look good with that outfit. You simply work them into shape."

"Yeah, well, you tell me how it fits—if you ever find out."

"Oh, I will. Blake is not going to let his entire business go down the toilet over something as simple as a long roll in the sack."

"If you say so. I gotta go, hubby just came home and we have dinner reservations. I'll talk to you soon."

"'Bye."

The call disconnected. Savannah's emotions vacillated between outright fury and vindication. She finally had what she needed to nail that wench and get Blake off the hook. The trick now was how she was going to use the information without Blake finding out what she'd been up to.

Maybe her mom would have some answers. She saved the audio recording on a portable flash drive. It certainly wouldn't do to lose this tasty bit of information. She popped the flash drive into its case and put it in her purse.

One o'clock couldn't get here fast enough.

They were seated in an outdoor café across the street from Lincoln Center. The day was gorgeous, with a warm breeze and clear blue skies, and the view of the center with its magnificent fountain could almost make Savannah forget all the things that weighed so heavily on her mind.

Savannah was ravenous. Her stomach growled and grumbled as she studied the menu. Everything looked good and she felt as if she could eat it all.

"I feel as if I haven't seen you in forever," Claudia said, setting her dark shades on the table.

As always Claudia was totally en vogue. Her two-piece designer suit in pale peach was stunning on her. And of course, her nails and hair were done to perfection. Savannah felt almost dowdy in her tailored gray business suit.

"I know it has been a while since we've had a chance to talk."

Claudia glanced up at the waitress who approached their table. "I'll have a bottle of spring water, a glass with no ice and a piece of lemon. And for my meal I'll have the seared salmon salad." She handed her menu to the waitress.

Savannah wanted the steak and potatoes but thought about the pounds. "Make that two." She handed over her menu, as well.

Claudia tilted her head to the side and looked at her daughter. "Your eyes are sparkling and your skin looks beautiful."

"Really? I hadn't noticed."

Claudia didn't comment further but steered the conversation to the matters at hand. "So, tell me how the case is coming along."

"There's so much to tell, I hardly know where to begin."

"Just give me the highlights and I'll fill in the blanks."

Savannah pushed out a long breath and leaned forward, lowering her voice. "Well..."

By the time Savannah had finished telling her mother everything that had gone on since she took the case, they'd completed their meal and the waitress was presenting the check.

Claudia's light brown eyes were cinched into tight slits. "I can't believe the nerve of that woman. And now Blake has to pay the cost." She roughly shook her head. "At least with all the details you have about the construction site, Jean can take care of that. Not a brick will be laid without a full and complete investigation. It's just sick what people are capable of." She rubbed her mouth with the napkin then zeroed in on Savannah. "Your issue is this woman and your husband. If he pulls out before Jean can launch a halt, Tristan will do what she's threatened. That much I'm sure of. It's your marriage that I'm concerned about."

"I have the tape out of her own mouth saying how she tried to seduce him and blackmail him into complying. I just don't know how I can use the information without Blake finding out."

Claudia mulled it over. "Listen, forget about the job, and forget about politics. Think about this as one woman up against another. If the assignment wasn't involved and some woman was trying to take your husband, what would you do?"

"I would be in her face with what I knew."

Claudia slapped her palm on the table. "Exactly. You're going to take that recording and march yourself up to her office and let her hear what you have on her."

"She's going to want to know how I found out."

"Do you really care what she wants to know? The facts are the facts. Lay them on the table and dare her to bluff her way out of it. You have the trump card."

A surge of excitement rushed through Savannah. Of course, this went beyond some shady land dealings. This was her marriage. This was her man. And if Tristan wanted to fight dirty, so could she.

She focused on her mother's steady gaze, a slow grin moved across her mouth. "I'll let you know what happened." She started to get up from the table. "Thanks, Mom." She leaned down and kissed her soft cheek, then put forty dollars on the table. "Advice on you, lunch on me. Talk to you soon." She turned to leave.

"Oh, and Savannah…"

She stopped. "Yes?"

"Make an appointment with your doctor."

Savannah frowned. "Why?"

"Just do it."

Savannah shrugged it off and hurried back to her office. She'd have to come up with some excuse to see Tristan again, but she'd think of something. And she'd have to make it quick, she didn't want Blake to lose his company before she could play her cards. She'd just have to come up with some excuse when she got back to the office as to why she had to leave early—again.

But first things first. She needed to make sure that

Blake hadn't done anything crazy. She called him from her cell phone on her way back to her office.

"Hi, Savannah, Blake is out of the office for the rest of the day," his secretary said. "You should probably be able to reach him on his cell."

"Did he say where he was going?"

"No, only that he had some business to take care of out of the office and he wouldn't be back."

"Okay, thanks. If he should call before I reach him, please tell him to call me. It's important."

"Sure thing."

"Thanks." She quickly disconnected and put in Blake's cell-phone number. It rang and rang then went to voice mail. She left a quick message to call her and hung up. Where in the world was he and why wasn't he answering his phone?

Chapter 26

Blake thought about hashing it all out with Steven on the phone but this was something they needed to discuss face-to-face. They'd built the business together and he had every right to know exactly what was going on and what they were on the precipice of losing.

Maybe by some miracle, Steve could see some way out of it that he couldn't.

Traffic leading into and through the Holland Tunnel was hellacious. He'd been sitting inside the tunnel for fifteen minutes. It was apparent that there had to be an accident or something up ahead. He put the car in Neutral and waited, growing increasingly impatient, although there was nothing he could do about it. To make matters worse he couldn't even listen to the radio. All he got was static. He should have listened to Savannah when she'd told him long ago to pack some CDs in the car. At this rate it would be nightfall by the time he arrived in New Jersey.

He should have called her before he left so that she wouldn't worry and to update her on his plans. He picked up his cell phone and saw the icon for no signal. He tossed it onto the passenger seat. Figures.

Finally the traffic began to creep forward. Another twenty minutes and he finally hit daylight. He surged ahead, not wanting to waste any more time. He'd call Savannah once he finally reached Steve's sister's house.

Savannah returned to her office still mulling over what story she needed to come up with to leave early and get to Tristan's office before the end of the day. She'd been listening in on Tristan's office conversations on her walk back to her office and knew that Tristan would be there at least until six.

Just as she stepped off the elevator she ran smack into Richard.

"Oh, Savannah. Glad I ran into you," he joked. "I'm heading out to Westchester to meet with the client and bring them up to date on what you found out."

"Great. Uh…"

"And for doing such a great job, why don't you take the rest of the afternoon off? Things are pretty quiet and I don't need you for anything right now."

"Wow, thanks."

"Sure." He stepped onto the elevator. "See you in the morning."

The elevator doors swooshed shut.

Savannah grinned. That couldn't have worked out better if she'd planned it herself. She hurried to her desk, shut down her computer and collected her things.

Moments later she was pulling out of the employee parking lot and heading to Tristan's office. On the way over, she tried Blake on his cell one more time. Finally he picked up.

"Hey, did you get my message?"

"No, I was stuck in the tunnel. What's up?"

"The tunnel?"

"Yeah, I'm on my way to see Steven. I met with Frank this morning and he doesn't see how I can get out of this contract without losing my shirt. I want to talk to Steven about it."

"You haven't said anything to Tristan yet, have you?" Her heart pounded.

"No. I didn't think it would be fair to not talk to Steven first."

She released a sigh. "Well, you two discuss it. I'm sure something will work out."

"I hope so, babe, just not sure what. Anyway, I'll see you at home later tonight."

"Drive safe."

"Thanks. Love you."

"Love you, too." Savannah disconnected the call.

Well, at least she had some time to put her own plan into action. Trump Tower loomed ahead.

She turned her car over to the valet and hurried inside. She had the tape recording of Tristan's late-night conversation in her purse. Two could play at this dirty game.

"I need to see Ms. Montgomery," she said to the receptionist, which was a different woman since the last time she was there.

"Do you have an appointment?"

"No. But it's important. Can you please tell her that Mrs. Fields is here and it's about the rail-yard project?"

"I'm really sorry, but she's in meetings all afternoon. If you want to leave a message I'll be sure to get it to her as soon as she's done."

Savannah braced her palms on the desk and leaned forward. "Tell her I want to see her now. If not, the information I have will be on the news instead of in her hands. Got it?"

The woman flicked backward. Without taking her eyes off Savannah, she pressed a button on the phone and talked through her headset.

"Sorry to disturb you, Ms. Montgomery, but there is a Mrs. Fields here to see you and she says it's urgent.

"I know, ma'am, I told her. She said—" she lowered her voice "—either she gives the information to you or the press."

"Yes, ma'am." She pursed her lips before speaking. "She said you can wait here. She'll be out shortly."

"Thank you."

Savannah turned on her heel and took a seat on the white leather sofa, tapping her foot while she waited.

About ten minutes later, Tristan strutted down the corridor to Savannah. She was stunned once again by Tristan's beauty, but she wasn't going to get distracted by looks or let her own insecurities rear their ugly heads. This was war.

She stood.

"What is this about?" Tristan demanded, pinning Savannah with a hard gaze.

"I think it best if we talk in private. Unless you want your staff to overhear what I have to say."

Tristan's jaw clenched. She whirled away and headed toward her office. Savannah followed.

"You have two minutes and then I'm calling security." She folded her arms and stared at Savannah.

Savannah went into her purse and took out the tape recorder. She placed it on the table.

"What the hell is this?"

"Listen, and you'll find out."

Savannah pressed Play.

Within moments, Tristan's voice, clear as a bell, could be heard detailing her escapade to her friend.

Tristan's cool features went frigid. Her eyes widened. She glared at Savannah.

"What the hell? Where did you get that?"

"It really doesn't matter where I got it. The point is I have it. And if you even think about messing with my husband again, or his business, this little baby will be all over the six-o'clock news. I'm sure it won't sit well with your board members or all of your big-shot friends."

Tristan's chest heaved in and out. "What do you want?" she finally said.

"I want you to stay the hell away from my husband. Period. And if you think for a New York minute that I'm bluffing, try me."

Tristan slowly lowered herself into her chair. Finally she looked at Savannah. "Fine. Now, give me the tape."

Savannah tossed her head back and laughed. "I may not travel in high society, but I'm not a fool. This is my insurance. You do your part and I'll do mine. But if I even think in my sleep that you have him on your mind, I will make this tape public. Do we understand each other?"

Tristan's nostrils flared. "Yes. Now, please leave."

"With pleasure." She snatched up the recorder and walked out.

As she walked down the corridor to the elevator she had the heart-pounding feeling that at any second security was going to snatch her up and make her disappear. She didn't breathe easy until she'd gotten outside, behind the wheel of her car and was halfway home.

The first thing she did when she arrived was to

make copies of every piece of evidence that she had. There were barely two days left before the ground-breaking. She needed to have all her ducks in a row when she presented her information to Jean.

She called her mother.

"How did it go?"

"It couldn't have gone better."

"Great," Claudia cheered. "I'm proud of you. At least you have her in a holding pattern until Jean can work things on her end."

"That's the reason why I called. I was hoping you could come by for an hour or so before Blake gets here and help me put all of this information together. You've done this before and I could use your help. I don't want anything to be overlooked or not have all that I need to present a strong case."

"I can be there in about twenty minutes."

"Great. Blake is in New Jersey. I don't expect him back until later on tonight."

"See you in a few."

With that bit of business out of the way, Savannah finally sighed in a moment of relief. It was all coming together. Blake would be able to keep his business, the building would cease and a full investigation launched and, best of all, her marriage was as solid as a rock.

Savannah darted into the kitchen and hunted around in the fridge for some quick leftovers. She was starving. She found a pot of black beans and rice and some fried chicken. She put it all into a bowl and popped it in the microwave. The three-minute warm-up time seemed to take an eternity. Her head started to spin. She went to the table and sat down.

Maybe she did need to see a doctor. She'd been feeling weird all day. Once all of this was over she was sure she'd feel better. If not she would take her mother's advice and make an appointment.

The bell chimed on the microwave and in minutes, she'd devoured the plate of food, just as the doorbell rang.

"Your mouth is greasy," Claudia said as she came through the door.

"Oh, I just finished eating some fried chicken." She wiped the corners of her mouth with her fingers.

Claudia breezed inside. "Where do you have everything?"

"In the bedroom."

"Bring it all out here. That way we can hear Blake when he comes in."

"Good idea." She went to the bedroom and retrieved all of the information and the tapes she'd made.

For the next hour they organized all of the data.

"They are going to want to see a list of everyone who may be involved, along with dates and times that this information was gathered. That's just to insure that nothing has been doctored."

Savannah nodded, and culled through her paperwork and the data on her PDA and BlackBerry. She plugged the PDA into her laptop and connected that to the printer and it spit out the list and timetable.

The last piece of damning evidence was what she'd received from the library and the Topography office.

"It totally blows my mind that no one has said anything about this," Savannah said.

"If the right people were paid enough money why would they talk?"

"I guess you're right. Funny, Jean wanted me to investigate Tristan for what she thought was substandard contracting and under the table payments. But this…" She shook her head.

"It's going to make the news. And of course, you can never tell anyone of your involvement."

"I know."

Claudia brushed her daughter's hair with her hand. "You did good, Savannah. Real good."

Savannah smiled like a proud child. "Thanks. So many things got in the middle of this. I really didn't think I would pull it off."

"But you did. And you are going to make history."

"Yeah, even if I can't take the credit for it."

"But you'll know it in your heart and generations will be thanking you for it. Now, you need to transfer all of the data into one location and burn it onto a CD. Make two copies. One for Jean and one for safekeeping."

"Right. I'll do that now."

"Then you need to call Jean and let her know what you have. I'm sure she'll want to see you right away."

They'd taken care of all the details and Savannah had placed a high-priority call to Jean. She and her mother were just settling down for a glass of wine when Blake came through the door.

Savannah got up to greet him. She wrapped her arms around his waist and kissed him long and slow on his lips.

"Hmm, and what did I do to deserve that?" His eyes sparkled. He pulled her close.

"Love me," she whispered.

"That's the easy part." He dipped his head to take her mouth again when Claudia loudly cleared her throat.

Blake's head popped up. "Claudia. I didn't know you were here."

"Apparently," she said with a chuckle. "I was just leaving. Came to see about my daughter." She picked up her purse from the coffee table and walked toward the door.

Blake pecked her on the cheek. "Sure you don't want to stay?"

She looked wickedly from one to the other. "And mess up the good time you two are planning to have? I don't think so, sweetheart."

Heat rushed to Savannah's face. She never would get over how blunt her mother could be when it came to sex.

"I'll talk to you soon, Savannah."

"'Night, Mom. Thanks for stopping by."

Claudia wagged a finger at her son-in-law. "And you, young man, need to check the premises before you go jumping on your wife." She laughed and walked out.

"Whew, your mom…" He let the comment hang in the air.

Savannah held up her hand. "I know, don't say it." She took his hand and led him inside.

They settled down on the couch.

"So what happened with Steven?"

Blake draped his arm across the back of the couch and played in her hair. "He agrees with me. We'll take the hit and hope to beat it in court."

She swallowed. "Do you trust me?"

His brow knitted. "Of course. Why?"

She tugged on her bottom lip with her teeth. "If I ask you not to say anything to Tristan for at least two days and not ask me any questions, would you do it?"

"Savannah, what's going on? The groundbreaking is day after tomorrow. I need to disconnect myself and my company from the project before then. Maybe if you tell me why—"

"Please just trust me. Okay, not two days. Wait until tomorrow evening. Please."

"It would really help your case 'counselor' if you told me why."

She put a finger to his lips. "No questions."

He heaved a sigh. "Okay. No questions and I'll

wait until tomorrow, end of business. No later. I'll have to prepare a press release to send to the media by then."

"Fair enough."

"I'd feel a lot better if I knew why I was holding off on the announcement."

"Trust me, everything will be fine. Hungry?"

He rubbed his stomach. "I could use some food."

Savannah chuckled. "I'll see what I can whip together. I'm pretty hungry myself," she said, and wondered why. She'd eaten less than two hours earlier.

While Savannah was in the kitchen she heard her cell phone. "Honey, could you answer that for me?" she yelled out.

A moment later he came into the kitchen mouthing, "Jean." He handed her the phone.

"Thanks."

Blake stood there.

"It's the head of TLC, probably wants to talk to me about my next order," she said, pressing the phone to her chest.

He opened the fridge and took out an apple then went to the sink and washed it off. "Don't mind me, I'm going. I'll let you ladies talk about your secret beauty products." He chuckled, took a bite from the apple and returned to the living room.

Shortly Savannah heard the television. He was watching CNN.

"Hello, Jean, sorry for the wait."

"I got your message. I need you to bring all of the documents to me right away."

"Now?"

"Yes. We don't have any time to waste."

"But I can't leave. My husband's home. What am I going to tell him? I have the information on a CD. I can e-mail it to you."

"No. the file is too large. I'll send a messenger. It will be someone that you know. Give the package to them."

"Okay."

"And, Savannah…"

"Yes?"

"If this all pans out…well, we'll see. Good night. I'll be in touch."

Savannah hung up and she could almost hear the James Bond theme song playing in the background.

She stepped out into the living room. Blake was engrossed in the news and didn't notice her. She went straight into the bedroom, took the envelope out of her carryall and brought it with her back to the kitchen. In the event that she needed some kind of excuse to go out and meet the driver, she'd just say she was taking out the garbage.

In the meantime, she still needed to fix something for dinner. She stood staring inside the refrigerator totally unable to decide. So many things were running through her head at once she couldn't think clearly.

Frustrated she trooped back into the living room and plopped down next to Blake.

"How about if we order in? I can't figure out what to fix."

"Fine with me. What are you in the mood for?"

"Mexican?"

"Cool. Get me whatever you're having," he said, surfing over to a tennis game.

She pushed up from the couch and went to get the menu from the kitchen drawer just as the door-bell rang.

Savannah's heart pounded in her chest. A wave of heat suddenly rushed through her and the room swayed. She grabbed on to the counter.

"I'll get it!" Blake called out. "Are you expecting anyone?"

She drew in deep breaths to clear her head. "Huh?"

"Never mind. I got it."

Savannah shook her head and moved toward the door. It was probably whomever Jean sent. Gosh, what was wrong with her? She stepped out into the foyer, just as Blake was closing the door.

"Mom?"

"Hi. Silly me. I left my envelope with my TLC orders." She gave Savannah a pointed look.

"Oh…yes, you sure did. I noticed it in the kitchen. I'll get it for you."

Claudia followed Savannah.

"Jean sent *you?*" Savannah said under her breath.

"Yep. Surprised?"

"Nothing surprises me anymore." She took the envelope from the top of the fridge. "That's everything."

"You have your copies?"

"Yes."

"Good. I'm sure you'll be hearing from Jean the minute she goes through everything." She headed for the door. "Good night again, Blake."

"'Night," he called out from his spot on the couch.

"Talk to you tomorrow," Claudia said. "Be prepared for the fireworks, and I do mean in the bedroom. I saw that look in Blake's eyes." She winked and walked out.

Savannah pinched her lips together and shut the door behind her mother. There was just no telling what Claudia might say.

"Did Mom get everything?"

"Mmm, hmm." She sat down next to Blake.

"So what did you order for dinner?"

"I didn't. I'll do it now." She started to get up.

Blake caught her wrist. "Are you okay? You look flushed or something."

"I'm okay. Just tired, I guess, and it's catching up with me."

"Let's eat. Then I'll give you an all over body massage. How's that sound?"

Savannah cuddled next to him. "Sounds wonderful." She yawned.

"You order, I'll run you a hot bath. Okay."

She nodded and yawned again. Blake pushed up from the couch and handed her the phone. "You want me to put anything special in the water?"

She looked up at him with a crooked smile. "Yeah, you."

"Don't have to ask me twice."

Savannah rested her head against the back of the couch and shut her eyes. By this time tomorrow this would all be over and she could stop lying to her husband and sneaking around. At least for now. Her stomach growled. She dialed the restaurant and placed the order. Maybe she was going to have to stop taking those vitamins.

She went into the bedroom and was greeted by the scent of mango coming from the master bath. She poked her head in the open doorway.

Blake was sitting on the edge of the tub testing the water. He looked up. "Hey, gorgeous. Bath is almost ready."

She came inside and drew in a long deep breath inhaling the sweet steam then looked down at him. She slowly unbuttoned her blouse and tossed it to the floor. Her skirt followed.

"Still planning to join me?" she said, unsnapping her bra. She dropped it on the growing pile.

Blake's eyes darkened. He stood. "You want to do the honors?"

The corner of Savannah's mouth curved upward. "With pleasure…"

Chapter 27

The following morning as Savannah and Blake were preparing for work, the news played in the background.

Savannah was sitting on the side of the bed when the *Today Show* was interrupted with a special bulletin.

The scene flashed to downtown Brooklyn.

"Blake. Isn't that the construction site?"

He stopped buttoning his shirt and focused on the television.

"We're here at the construction site that was scheduled for the groundbreaking tomorrow. But according to reports, that's not going to happen. The city was given official notice this morning to cease any work in this area. It seems that information received by the Department of Design and Construction late last night indicates that this is holy ground—an ancient African burial site."

Savannah's pulse was racing as she listened.

Blake's head snapped in Savannah's direction. She hoped she looked shocked.

"Sources close to the investigation have informed us that Tristan Montgomery of Montgomery Enterprises, the entity that financed and pushed through the development, was well aware of what she was building on and that certain city officials knew, as well. We have been unable to reach Ms. Montgomery for comment."

"Whoa." Blake dropped down beside Savannah on the bed.

"This location was touted to be the one to revitalize downtown Brooklyn. It took several years to get approval for building and to move out hundreds of families in the surrounding area. This is a major blow to Montgomery Enterprises, and with allegations of cover-ups and coercion, this is something that is not likely to go away soon. This is Geri Castle in downtown Brooklyn. Back to you, Matt."

"African burial grounds," Blake said in awe. Slowly he shook his head. "How could she have known and still want to build?"

"Money was obviously more important than the preservation of our history," Savannah said with distaste.

"I wonder how they finally found out?"

Savannah shrugged. "Who knows? I'm just glad that they did. And I'm glad that you didn't have to cancel the contract. Now you're off the hook and you can move on." She took his hand. "See, I told you things would work themselves out."

He looked at her curiously. "You were pretty sure, weren't you?"

She averted her gaze. "I have faith—in you." She kissed him lightly on the lips. "I wonder what they are going to do with the area now."

"We won't know, I'm sure, until they do a thorough investigation. But to think that our ancestors are buried there."

"The same thing happened in Manhattan a few years back, remember?"

He nodded. "True. It's just when you think of slavery, you think of the South. We tend to forget that slavery had a history right here in New York."

"Exactly." She stood and put her arms around his waist. "I love you. So very much."

"What brought that on?"

"Just everything. It's been a crazy few weeks and we came through it. Together."

"I'm really sorry that I put you through all that madness with Tristan."

"It wasn't your fault."

"I never want you to doubt me."

"I don't."

His eyes danced over her face. "There's something about you that's different. I don't know what it is."

"Is it good or bad?"

"Good. You're glowing."

"I'm happy."

"Well, it shows." He kissed the tip of her nose. "I better get out of here. I know it's going to be crazy at the office and I can imagine the phone calls from the press."

"Okay, get going. Call me later if you get a chance."

"I will."

The minute Blake left for work, Savannah called the girls. Then she made an appointment with her doctor. She didn't want to say anything until she was sure, but the little stick turned blue.

"We did it," Dani said, as the trio sat around the table at The Shop.

"We sure did. And I hope that conniving woman gets what she deserves," Mia added.

"I couldn't have done it without the both of you. And I really appreciate you guys."

They raised their teacups and toasted.

"So what happens now?" Dani asked.

Savannah shrugged. "I guess they'll investigate. Tristan and some folks on the city council and the zoning board will probably be brought up on charges. This is a major scandal."

"How is Blake handling it all?" Mia asked.

"He was stunned to say the least. But I know he's glad it's over and he's in the clear."

"So what's our next assignment?" Dani asked with a grin.

"You two weren't even supposed to be involved. If they ever found out, I'd probably get kicked out of the Cartel."

"So we can be your double secret agents," Mia joked.

"Yeah, right. I think I'm going to take a break for a minute and recoup from this little adventure." She looked from one face to the other. "It was kind of exciting, though."

They giggled.

"Yeah, I can really get into this spy stuff," Mia said. "Covert ops."

They all cracked up laughing.

"Hey, I gotta run. Let's get together this weekend," Savannah said.

"Sure. And, there's someone I want you both to meet," Dani said.

Mia and Savannah looked at each other.

"So, uh, why don't we do brunch on Sunday at my place?"

"Sure," they said in unison.

"And bring Blake if you want."

"What about me?" Mia whined.

"You'll be the fifth wheel as usual," Dani teased.

Mia socked her in the arm. "Not funny."

"Well, you two duke it out. I gotta go. I'll bring Mom. She'll round out the playing field. See ya."

* * *

As Savannah headed off to work she passed a newsstand. The headlines were glaring and so very satisfying.

Montgomery Enterprises On The Brink Of Collapse. The New Enron. Federal Investigation.

Savannah smiled. She'd done good.

Chapter 28

"I'm only doing this because I love you," Blake said as they headed for the door. "You know Sunday is sports day. I'm supposed to be on the couch." He snatched her around the waist. "And you're supposed to be there with me." He kissed her, gently at first then let his tongue dance along the curve of her lips until he felt her shudder just a bit in his arms. Tentatively he eased back. "See, we could stay here and…"

"No, you promised. Besides I want everyone together."

"Okay fine. Just for you."

"Is Steve going to meet us there?"

"Yeah, I gave him the address. I still can't believe he's never met Mia."

"I think they'd be perfect for each other. Steve needs to settle down and Mia needs a good man."

"If you say so."

"I do. Now, come on and let's go. Everyone else is probably there already."

"Does Dani have ESPN?" he asked, trailing behind her.

Savannah glanced over her shoulder and rolled her eyes.

Just as Savannah predicted, they were the last ones to arrive. And she couldn't have been more surprised if Martin Luther King had been sitting in her living room.

She glided in on Blake's arm.

Dani hurried over. "Close your mouth," she whispered. "Let me introduce you." She took Savannah by the hand and led her over to meet Nick who was in deep conversation with Claudia.

"Nick, I want you to meet my other best friend, Savannah Fields, and her husband, Blake."

Nick stood up and shook Savannah's hand and then Blake's. "Dani talks about you all the time. Glad to finally meet you both."

"Thanks. So how long have you known Dani?" Savannah asked.

Blake nudged her.

Nick looked to Dani. "How long has it been, babe? Seems like only yesterday," he teased.

"Don't mind him," Dani cut in. She took Savannah by the hand. "Come with me in the kitchen, will ya?"

"So, what do you think?" Dani asked the instant they were alone.

"I think he's gorgeous, for starters. But it's not about what I think. What do you think?"

Dani looked vulnerable for the first time that Savannah could remember. "I think I'm in love with him." She looked at her friend. "And it's scary."

"Oh, Danielle." She wrapped her in a hug. "Love is scary. It's supposed to be. That's what makes it so exciting."

"Hey, can I get a hug?" Mia came into the kitchen. Dani sniffed back tears.

"We were talking about Dani's new man," Savannah offered. "Our girl is in love."

"Ain't he fine?" Mia said. "No wonder she's been keeping him under wraps."

"Is that the only reason?" Savannah asked gently.

"I…I wasn't sure what you guys would think. I wasn't even sure myself."

"None of that matters, girl. As long as he treats you right and treats us right, he can hang," Mia teased.

Dani chuckled. "Thanks, ya'll. That means a lot."

"And thanks for bringing Steve," Mia said. "He's another cutie pie and really nice."

"Steve's a great guy. He just needs a great woman," Savannah said.

"How ya'll gonna leave me in there with those men?" Claudia said, busting in.

"'Cause we know you could handle them, Mom."

"Well, I'm starving. When are we going to eat?"

"Right now. It's buffet so everyone can help themselves."

The group filed into the kitchen and heaped their plates with fried salmon patties, chicken fingers, yellow rice, salad and fresh fruit. Then they settled in the living room where the men had commandeered the television.

The doorbell rang.

"Oh, I'll get it," Claudia announced. She went to the door and all eyes followed her.

She returned with a dead ringer for a young and virile Billie Dee Williams.

"Everyone, I'd like you to meet my friend Bernard Hassel. Bernard, this is everyone."

Savannah stared at her mother dumbfounded.

"I thought we were more than friends," Bernard said in that same Billie Dee voice. Claudia giggled like a schoolgirl.

"Bernie, behave yourself. We don't want to give these young folks the wrong idea." She took him by the hand and led him to an available seat.

One by one introductions were made while Claudia went to fix Bernard a plate.

Laughter and chatter filled the air, as potent as the smell of all that good food. The atmosphere was filled with friendship, love and happiness.

"I have an announcement to make," Savannah shouted over the din. "Well, *we* have an announcement to make." She grabbed Blake's hand. "We're going to have a baby."

Dani and Mia jumped and squealed. "I knew it!" they said in unison.

"A mother knows," Claudia chimed in, beaming like a proud grandma. "I told you."

"Congratulations, man," Steven said, slapping Blake on the back. "You did it." He laughed.

"Very funny." Blake chuckled.

Nick came over and shook Blake's hand and kissed Savannah's cheek. "Congratulations."

"If it's a girl I hope she's as beautiful as your mother," Bernard offered, hugging Claudia.

Claudia looked up at him with adorning eyes.

"This calls for a toast," Dani announced.

Everyone grabbed a glass.

"To Anna and Blake."

"To love and happiness."

"Friendship."

"New beginnings."

"To shopping for baby clothes!"

"Cheers!"

"I had a great time today," Blake admitted to Savannah as they lay in bed together.

"So did I." She rested her head on his shoulder. "We're having a baby," she whispered in awe.

"I know." He stroked her arm. "I told you it would happen. You just have to have faith."

She tilted her face up to him. "Yeah, how about that."

Tenderly he kissed her, and held her like spun glass, suddenly afraid of hurting her.

"I won't break," she whispered.

"Are you sure…it's all right?"

"The doctor said I'm fine. I'm only six weeks. Ask me again in about seven months."

"In that case…" He eased the straps from her gown off her shoulders and kissed her right in the valley of her neck then let his tongue trail across her bare shoulder.

Savannah moaned softly, letting her fingers play along the muscles in his back.

His head drifted down to the swell of her breasts until his tongue flicked across the peak of her nipple.

Instinctively her body arched toward him. He took the nipple into his mouth and spent the next hour loving every inch of her body.

Savannah didn't think it was possible to feel this exquisite, to have so many incredible sensations rushing through her at once. Every inch of her was electrified. And when Blake finally entered her body she knew heaven.

Epilogue

"Thank you for coming in, Savannah," Jean said from behind her ornate desk.

"Sure." She took a seat.

"You did an incredible job on your first assignment and I wanted to congratulate you personally."

"Thank you. That means a great deal."

"I know it must have been difficult for you to have to investigate your own husband."

"You knew all along, didn't you?"

"Of course. It's why I chose you. I had to see if you had what it took."

"You could have been wrong."

Jean gave her a pointed look. "I'm never wrong." She flipped open a folder and briefly looked it over. "I have another assignment for you." She closed the folder and pushed it toward Savannah. "With the baby on the way, you may want to engage the services of…your friends."

Savannah smiled.

* * * * *

SEDUCTION AND LIES

Chapter 1

Danielle Holloway pranced into her kitchen wearing a pink thong adorned along the waistband with tiny rhinestones, and not much else. She pulled open the camel-colored wood cabinet above the sink and took out two plates. Cooking really wasn't her thing, but for Nick she was willing to make the effort—hopefully she wouldn't kill him in the process.

She opened the freezer and took out a box of Aunt Jemima frozen waffles and a box of frozen Jimmy Dean turkey sausage. She was pretty sure she had some syrup around somewhere.

"Need some help?" came the rough-textured voice behind her.

Slowly she turned around, her size-C breasts standing at attention.

Nick's dark blue, almost black, eyes rolled over her from head to toe. Dani watched his throat work up and down as his gaze caressed every inch of her, reminding her quite vividly of the night and half the morning they'd spent together.

What she felt for Nick Mateo scared her—badly. Sometimes when she was around him, she couldn't breathe, her thoughts would get scrambled and her heart would beat so fast she thought she'd faint. She thought about him when she should have been concentrating on a photo shoot or developing film. He made her laugh, and thoughts of being without him made her want to cry. She was in love for the first time in her adult life, and she was scared as hell. And to compound it all, Nick Mateo was white—at least legally. Well, kinda white. His mom was black, his dad Italian. She was half black and half Hispanic, which accounted for her waist-length, raven-black hair and honey-brown complexion. Both of them had to check "other" on all those applications. She had enough cultural issues to deal with on her own—and now his as well.

Nonetheless, together, Nick and Dani made a stunning couple. He, a subtle look-alike for a young Alec Baldwin, dark short hair, a sexy five-o'clock shadow and a body to die for. She, a striking beauty whose face could easily grace the pages of fashion magazines.

He sauntered toward her with a pearl-gray towel wrapped around his narrow hips and slid his muscular arms around her waist. He nuzzled her neck, and Dani's body warmed all over.

"I…was going to fix us something to eat," she said on a breath, inhaling his cool, clean scent from his recent shower. She tilted her head back to give him better access to that spot that made her weak in the knees.

He held her a little tighter. "I already have something to eat." He nibbled her neck and ran his hands along the curve of her spine. Dani moaned. "God, I can't get enough of you," he groaned. He drew in a long, hot breath and reluctantly stepped back. He looked deep into her eyes, down into her soul. "I'm in love with you—you better know that."

Dani's heart banged in her chest. "Me, too." It was as close as she had come to saying the *L* word.

"I'll settle for that," he said, knowing the emotional struggle Dani was having wrestling with her feelings. Admitting that she could be vulnerable enough to turn her heart and soul over to someone else was something she wasn't ready to handle. He was willing to give her as much time as she needed. He knew what was in her heart. He could see it when she looked at him, when she moaned his name as he made love to her, when she laughed at his stupid jokes and told him about her life and her deepest fears. They had no secrets between them, and that was why he knew this relationship was going to work, whether or not she ever said the *L* word.

Danielle kissed him on the lips, tasting the minty

toothpaste. "So are you going to be a help or a hindrance in the kitchen?"

He peeked over her shoulder to see what was on the menu. He turned up his nose. "How 'bout I fix us breakfast?"

A sunshiny smile bloomed across her face. "Sure."

Nick shook his head and chuckled. "You didn't have to give in so quickly, ya know. Let me put on some clothes—pickings are kinda thin in the fridge, if I remember correctly." He kissed her on the tip of her nose, turned and went into the bedroom to get dressed.

"Whataman," she murmured.

Savannah Fields woke up on Sunday morning and barely made it to the bathroom. She was only in her first trimester, and morning sickness was kicking her butt—*day and night.*

"You okay, baby?" Blake called from the other side of the bathroom door.

Savannah splashed cold water on her face, leaned over the sink and drew in long, slow breaths in the hopes of controlling the rocking and rolling going on in her stomach. How could something that would ultimately be so precious make you feel like you wanted to die?

"I'm…fine," she was finally able to say. "Be out in a minute."

Slowly she raised her head and gazed at her reflection in the mirror. The doctor assured her that the morning sickness would stop after three months. She still had one to go. She gripped the side of the sink as another wave of nausea swept through her belly and made her head spin.

Savannah moaned. How was she going to be able to fulfill her latest undercover assignment if she could barely hold her head up? She was going to need help.

Jean Armstrong, the head of The Ladies Cartel—affectionately known as TLC—had called her into the Cartel offices at the brownstone on 135th Street in Harlem three weeks earlier to congratulate her on the successful completion of her last assignment, which was to uncover a suspected land fraud deal in downtown Brooklyn. What Savannah had uncovered was not only a major scam but also the fact that the development was going to be built on top of an ancient African burial ground. It had been a difficult assignment, and not so much because it was her first but because her husband, Blake, was the contractor on the deal and she was bound by her oath to the Cartel not to reveal what she was doing to anyone—and that included her husband.

Her investigation had also led her to believe that her husband, her soul mate, was not only involved in the unscrupulous land deal but also was having an affair with the woman who was behind it all, millionaire heiress Tristan Montgomery. Savannah needed the help of her two best friends, Danielle Holloway and Nia Turner, to prove otherwise, and they did.

Unfortunately, Savannah had broken a major rule of The Ladies Cartel by involving anyone who was not a sworn member. Fortunately for her, it had turned out well, and Jean reminded her how lucky she was when she gave her this latest assignment.

Savannah flushed the toilet and rinsed out her mouth. At least her head had stopped spinning.

One thing she knew for certain was that she was going to have to break some more rules if she was to get the next job accomplished. She could certainly use the skills of the Cartel members, but she knew she could trust Dani and Nia more than any other two people on earth.

Blake knocked on the door. "Savannah, are you okay?"

"Coming." Gingerly she made her way to the door and opened it.

Blake was standing on the other side with a distraught look on his ruggedly handsome face. She smiled wanly.

He put his arm around her shoulder. "Can I get you anything?"

"Yeah, a time machine. Speed this process up by about seven months."

Blake grinned and kissed the top of her head, and led her back to the bed. "If I could, you know I would, baby."

She waved off the bed. "I think I need to move around. I want to meet the girls for a late lunch."

"You sure you're up to it?"

She nodded. "Yeah, some ginger ale and a few crackers, and I'll be good as new." She left his embrace and went into the kitchen. Moments later she could hear the blare and roar of a basketball game coming from the living-room television set.

Must be Sunday, she mused, smiling as she popped open a can of ice-cold ginger ale and took a long, refreshing swallow. Sunday was game day in the Fields' household. Blake carved out his position on the couch and watched games all day long, nonstop, even if they were on videotape, which gave Savannah the perfect opportunity to hang out with the girls. And today they needed an emergency meeting.

While Nick was at the local grocer, Dani took a quick shower and straightened up the bedroom. As she sat on the edge of the bed, applying the Victoria's Secret brand of lotion that Nick loved, her phone rang.

She turned behind her, reached across the bed and picked up the phone from the nightstand. Lying on her stomach, she answered.

"Hello?"

"Hey, Dani, it's me, Savannah."

"Hey, girl, how ya feeling?"

"Don't ask."

"You're a better woman than me."

"Listen, I was hoping the three of us could get together this afternoon."

"Hmm, what time? Me and Nick were getting ready to fix something to eat."

"You mean, Nick is fixing something to eat."

Dani giggled. "Don't hate."

"How about four at The Shop? Maybe by then my stomach will have settled down to a quiet roar."

The digital clock on the nightstand illuminated eleven.

"Sounds good. Did you call Nia?"

"No, not yet. Would you mind? It's going to take me a while to get myself together as it is, and I don't need Nia slowing me down by needing all the details of a simple late lunch."

The friends laughed. Of the trio, Nia Turner was the organizer—to a fault. As head of her own events management business, she was a stickler for planning each and every move. Although it was an outrageously annoying habit, her obsession with order and detail always ultimately paid off.

"Sure. I'll do that as soon as we finish. What's up, anyway? Just need to get out?"

"Actually it's a little more than that." She lowered her voice and got off the side of the bed to make sure Blake was still parked securely in front of the television. She closed the bedroom door. "I have another assignment, and I need yours and Nia's help."

Nia Turner had been up since daybreak. She fixed a spectacular breakfast for her and Steve—homemade Belgian waffles; egg-white omelets filled with mushrooms, tomatoes, green peppers and cheddar cheese; fresh orange juice and an incredible Turkish coffee that she'd received from one of her corporate clients as a thank-you gift.

Of the trio it had always been efficient Nia who hadn't had a man in her life. Savannah had Blake and before Danielle finally starting playing house with Nick, she always had men to keep her warm and well tuned.

Nia had always known about Steve Long: she'd seen him from a distance from time to time, since he and Savannah's husband, Blake, were tight buddies and business partners. But they'd never spent any time together, and it had never occurred to Nia to do so. It wasn't until she'd planned a get-together, with Steve being an invited guest, that they both realized what they'd been missing. They'd been an item ever since, and Nia couldn't have been happier.

Steve left shortly after breakfast for a game of tennis, and Nia decided to get a jump start on the week. She went into her immaculate office, where not a paper clip was out of place, and settled down for a few hours of planning. She had several corporate clients that were planning major conferences as well as restaurant locations that she needed to set up for more intimate meetings.

She turned on her seventeen-inch flat-screen computer and quickly clicked on her color-coded spreadsheet program; then she opened up another program window, this one with a grid of Manhattan.

Just as she started plugging in information, her phone rang. It was Dani.

"Hey, girl, what's up?" Nia kept her attention on the screen while she talked to Dani on speaker.

"I hate that damned speakerphone! Makes me sound like I'm underwater."

"Oh, don't be silly."

"Can you please just stop doing what you're doing and pay attention to me for a minute?"

"You know, you sound like a whiny five-year-old," Nia said, taking the call off speaker. "Better now?"

"Much," Dani said with a huff.

"So what is it? You're breaking my flow."

"Savannah just called. She wants us to get together around four at The Shop."

Nia frowned. That was not on her agenda for the day. She'd have to rearrange things to make that happen. If there was one thing that worked Nia's nerves more than anything, it was surprises that knocked off her schedule and her plans.

"Well, okay. I'll have to shift around a few things. Why today? Did she say what it was about? Our get-togethers are always planned in advance..."

"Dang, Nia. This *is* the best advance notice we can give. Five damned hours. Now do whatever it is that you do to get yourself in gear, and we'll see you there at four."

Nia huffed with indignation. "You don't have to be nasty... I was just saying..."

She almost sounded hurt, Dani thought. "I'm sorry. Didn't mean to snap. You know my mouth sometimes. Anyway, Savannah said it was important." She paused. "She needs our help."

Nia knew exactly what that meant.

Chapter 2

For four o'clock on a Sunday, The Shop, located in the West Village, was pretty crowded. The hum of conversation interspersed with bits of laughter floated over the pulse of some nondescript listening music.

Although she'd complained about the disruption in her day, Nia was, of course, the first to arrive and had secured their favorite booth in the back. She was sipping on a mimosa when Dani walked in looking like a supermodel, followed moments later by Savannah, whose petite frame was getting plumper by the day.

"Movin' kinda slow there, sis," Dani teased, as Savannah lowered herself into the seat next to Nia.

Savannah put her purse on her lap and took off her sunglasses, setting them on the table. "Don't make fun. It ain't funny," she grumbled over a half smile.

Nia put her arm around Savannah's shoulder and pulled her in for a short hug. "At least you look cute."

That much was true. Much like Danielle, Savannah loved to dress, and being pregnant only upped the ante. She was determined that the worse she felt, the better she would look. No expense was spared when it came to her wardrobe.

Today, she wore a bolero sweater, cuffed at the elbow, in a sea-moss green that sparkled in the sunlight, over an empire shirt in the same color, with tight accordion pleats that fell just to the waistband of her designer jeans, and a pair of emerald-green ankle boots in butter-soft suede.

"Thanks. And thanks for coming."

"No problem," the duo murmured.

Dani flipped open a menu. "So whatsup?"

Savannah leaned forward. Dani and Nia drew closer.

"I got another assignment."

"We figured as much," Dani said. "So how can we help?"

"I got major grief from Jean about pulling you two in the last time around. But because everything turned out so well, she sort of gave me a pass to 'use my resources.' Anyway, I've been feeling so crappy I know I can't handle this alone at all."

"The suspense is killing me already. What is it?" Dani asked.

"Well, it's identity theft."

"Whoa." Nia reared back, then lowered her voice. "For real? Like the kind of identity theft that's been on the news lately?"

Savannah nodded. "Apparently there is a major ring operating right here in New York."

Dani leaned in. "Why aren't the cops or the FBI or somebody handling this?"

"They are. But it goes a little deeper than that. This thing is extremely sensitive due to the nature of the people involved, so Jean was called in by a friend of hers in the Bureau."

"This is pretty major," Nia said.

"There's more." Savannah folded her hands. "This is where it gets kind of James Bond-y. There are some folks that have come to Jean...on a personal level. People who can't go to the police or the FBI and who are in the same boat." She looked from one friend to the other, making sure they got her meaning. Their eyes brightened in understanding.

"Illegals?" Dani asked.

"No. Just folks who can't be scrutinized by the authorities. They can't risk this showing up in the media."

Nia flopped back against the leather seat. "How much time do you have?"

"A few weeks. A month at best."

"That's going to be a problem on my end. I'm out

of town for the next two weeks setting up several conventions, one in Atlanta the other in D.C. I leave tomorrow afternoon. Of course I'll do what I can— any contacts and resources that I can provide…"

"Count me in," Dani said. "Do you think I'll get to use a gun this time?" Her eyes sparkled with hope.

Both Savannah and Nia looked at her and shook their heads.

"I would hope not," Savannah said.

Dani sucked her teeth in disappointment. "Figures."

"However, this time I'm not taking any chances. This is major and we can't afford to screw this up." She zeroed in on Danielle. "I'm going to make sure I have clearance to bring you in. You're going to have to meet Jean."

A big grin dashed across Danielle's mocha-colored face. "The head chick in charge! Well, all righty then. That's what I'm talking about."

"What about me?" Nia whined.

"Since you won't be directly involved, I don't think it's necessary."

"Damn." She finished off her drink and slunk down in her seat, pouting.

The waitress finally came over. "Sorry, ladies. It's crazy busy. Can I get you anything?"

They flipped open their menus and one by one gave their orders.

"Now that we have that out of the way, how have

you both been doing?" Savannah asked, sipping a glass of water.

"I finally know what always keeps a smile on the two of your faces," Nia said.

"Oh, really?" Dani said with a raised brow. "And what might that be?"

"Having a fine, sexy man to wake up to every morning." She flashed a wicked grin and a wink.

Savannah and Dani laughed.

"So you've discovered the secret of sublime happiness," Savannah said.

Nia bobbed her head. "Yes, chile," she said, emphasizing each word. "Steven is absolutely a dream come true. And to think we've known each other for years and never took it further than hello." She looked off wistfully. "It's just so wonderful. I mean, I've never really had anyone that made me feel good all…the…time. Know what I mean?" She looked from one to the other. Well, there was someone once, but she'd never told her friends about him then and with good reason. And with everything going so right in her life with Steven there was no point in bringing it up now. It was old news and best that it stay buried in the past.

"I know exactly what you mean," Dani offered. "And you know me, Ms. Love 'em and Leave 'em. I think I've been whipped, my sistahs."

Savannah and Nia applauded.

"We never thought we'd see the day," Savannah said.

"Me, either. Nick has totally taken me by surprise.

It's like those romance novels where the heroine gets swept off her feet and lands flat on her back, ready and raring to go," she added in her typical ribald fashion.

The trio broke up laughing.

"Some days," Savannah offered, "it's still hard for me to believe that me and Blake are still so crazy in love and still hungry for each other."

"Even with the loaf in the oven?" Dani asked.

Savannah's eyes widened. "Girl, it's even worse. When I'm not sick, I'm horny as hell! Can't wait for the man to get home from work! Hormones are in overdrive or something. And Blake, Lawd, he never felt so good!"

Dani started fanning herself and Nia quickly followed suit.

Their meals arrived, and they continued swapping stories of their scorching love lives.

Outside the restaurant, the three women hugged.

"Have a safe trip, Nia," Savannah said. "And I'll be in touch if I can use your help."

"Yeah, take care, sis." Dani kissed her cheek. "What is Steven going to do while you're gone?"

"Miss me." She rocked her head to the side. "I intend to wear the brother out before I leave. Make sure it holds him over until I get back."

"Now that's gangsta," Dani teased.

"See you guys in two weeks." Nia waved as she headed down the street to where her car was parked.

Savannah turned to face Danielle. "Let me know when you have some free time. I'm going to call Jean in the morning and try to set up a meeting as soon as possible."

"You know me. I'm my own boss. My schedule is pretty light this week with photo shoots. I have a couple of location shots, but that's it."

"Great. So as soon as I get it set up, I will give you a call."

"Sounds good."

"Thanks, Dani, I really appreciate this."

"Hey, that's what superspy friends are for, right?" she teased.

"Yeah, exactly."

When Danielle returned to her apartment, it was empty. She was surprised that Nick wasn't there. He hadn't mentioned he was going out.

She tossed her purse on the table in the hall and deposited her keys in the glass bowl right next to it before heading to the kitchen for an ice-cold beer.

She took her beer and went to the so-called second bedroom, which served as her office/darkroom. There should be a law against false advertising, she thought, as she flipped on the light. When she'd read the ad for the "spacious two-bedroom apartment" some five years ago, she was expecting spacious. Well, the "second bedroom" was about eight feet long and five feet wide. The only person who could sleep in there was a midget. If you put a full-size bed in the room you'd have to walk over it to get in and out! So she'd converted it to a tiny office space with a flat-screen computer, a small desk and her photography equipment, which was stored in the closet. With a few shelves mounted on the wall, it actually became a functional space.

Danielle had a photo shoot scheduled for the following morning and wanted to go over the shot schedule. There were five models involved in the shoot for a new designer who was launching a line for the fall. They were going to set up in the Central Park Zoo so that the caged animals could serve as a backdrop.

The weather for the next day was set to be in the high seventies, which would make for a very uncomfortable day for the models and the crew.

She went down her list of supplies for the day, making sure to include two cases of water and an ice cooler.

The front door opened and shut, and the sound of male voices filled the front room.

Danielle pushed her papers aside and went to the front room.

"Hey, hon," Danielle greeted Nick, as she strolled up to him in the living room and kissed him lightly on the lips. She turned to their guest. "Bernard…"

"Good to see you again, Danielle."

She'd met Bernard Hassell several weeks earlier at a get-together at Nia's house. Bernard was a dead ringer for Billy Dee Williams and the current love interest of Claudia, Savannah's mother.

"You, too, Bernard." Her brow wrinkled ever so slightly. "Where did you two hook up?"

"At the gym," Nick said. "Well, as I was going to the gym. Bernard was walking by on his way to this new spot, Pause for Men. He invited me to join him." Nick grinned. "The place is fabulous. Full spa, exercise rooms, saunas—the works—and a health-food cafe."

Bernard hooked his thumb over his shoulder toward Nick. "I think Pause just got a new member." He chuckled lightly.

Dani eyed Bernard. "Wow, no wonder you stay in such great shape," she teased.

Bernard grinned and made a slight bow. "I'll take that as a compliment."

"Can I offer you something to drink?" she asked, moving toward the kitchen.

"We were gonna grab a couple of beers and catch the end of the game," Nick said, pecking her cheek. "How was the afternoon with the girls?"

"Fine," she answered absentmindedly, trying to wrap her mind around the odd matchup of her man with one old enough to be his dad. "Well, I'll leave you boys to your games. Good to see you again, Bernard," she said before returning to her office.

Once inside, she closed the door behind her and dialed Nia on her cell.

"Hey, Dani, whatsup?"

Danielle cut a quick glance toward the closed door, then spoke in a harsh whisper. "Guess who's here?"

"What? Why are you whispering?"

"Put your damned glasses on so you can hear me!"

"Not funny. Abuse I don't need," Nia said haughtily. "Now, speak up."

Danielle blew out an exasperated breath. "Bernard is here."

"Who?"

"Bernard! Claudia's Bernard."

"Savannah's mom, Claudia?"

"Yes!" she hissed.

"Why? Did something happen to Claudia?"

"No. He's hanging out with Nick, of all things. They met at some spa." She shook her head in bewilderment.

"Soooo…the problem is…?"

"Don't you think it's odd? I mean, Bernard is… older."

Nia laughed. "Guys aren't like women, D. They bond over all sorts of stuff, sports, video games. Age isn't an issue with them."

"Hmm, I guess…"

"Besides, didn't you say Nick lost his dad when he was a teen?"

"Yes."

"Maybe Bernie's like a substitute or something."

"You're probably right. I'm making something out of nothing."

"Bet they're watching a game and drinking beer."

Danielle giggled. "Exactly."

"See what I mean? Anyway, relax. I need to pack. And don't forget if you and Savannah need my help…"

"I know, sis. Thanks."

"Good luck. I mean that."

"Thanks. Safe travels."

"Safe spying."

That was what she should be focused on, Danielle reasoned as she disconnected the call—working her first undercover assignment.

She couldn't wait to meet Jean.

The sounds of male laughter drifted into the bedroom. Even with Nia's wise words about male bonding, she still couldn't shake her misgivings about Bernard. It was nothing that she could actually put her finger on. He was nice enough and obviously Claudia cared about him. But he simply seemed too good to be true: handsome, smooth talking, well put-together for a man of his age, and he seemed to have plenty of time on his hands. What did he do for a living? How could he afford a fancy spa like the one they were talking about, and where did he come from, anyway? She was probably overanalyzing, seeing ghosts in the closet when there weren't any. She pushed her wayward thoughts about Bernard Hassell to the back of her mind, at least for the time being. She had more pressing matters to concentrate on. Her first assignment. She grinned with anticipation.

Chapter 3

It was three nerve-racking days before Savannah heard from Jean with a date for the meeting.

"Do I look okay?" Danielle asked for the tenth time in as many minutes as they drove to the Cartel brownstone.

"Dani, I swear, if you ask me just one more time…"

"I want to make a good impression."

"You'll be fine. And when have you not made a good impression?" She paused, frowned slightly. "Well, there was that time in the restaurant in Chelsea when your name wasn't on the reservation list, and the time you got into a shouting match with that model's agent during a photo shoot, and the time…"

Danielle held up her hand. "All right, all right! I'll behave. I get it." She huffed and folded her arms.

"What I'm trying to say, sweetie, is you always *look* fabulous, but you simply have to keep your temper in check and be, uh, more diplomatic."

Of the trio, Danielle was notorious for flying off the handle at the drop of a hat, and it didn't take much for her to feel slighted. But most of her flare-ups occurred when she felt one of her friends was being mistreated or the people she expected to fall in line, such as staff, support people and…well, the general public, didn't live up to what *she* expected of them. But if you ever wanted anyone in the trenches with you, it was definitely Danielle. She would go down swinging and still look incredible.

"I want to make a good impression," Danielle finally said, looking uncharacteristically uncertain. She tugged on her bottom lip with her teeth.

"You'll be fine." Savannah reached across the gears and squeezed Danielle's hand. "I promise."

Danielle looked into Savannah's eyes and saw the confidence there. She drew in a long breath. "Thanks."

"Here we are."

Danielle peeked out the window at the very stately four-story brownstone, which looked like all the other well-taken-care-of homes on the restored block. "This is it?"

Savannah chuckled. "What did you expect? The

Batcave?" She unfastened her seat belt and got out. "Come on."

Danielle followed Savannah to the ground-floor entrance of the house.

"See that house across the street?" Savannah said, lifting her chin toward the house.

"You mean, where that F-I-N-E man is going in followed by another one?"

"Yes, it's a day spa for men."

"Get out."

"Yep, run by four women, best friends."

"What? Wait a minute. Is it called Pause for Men?"

"Yeah, why?" She pressed the bell. A chime echoed gently in the background.

"Uh, nothing. I think I heard about it somewhere." That sounded like the same spa that Bernard had taken Nick to, she thought. She'd have to make sure, and if it was, hopefully she wouldn't have to come to headquarters too often. That could get pretty sticky. And she certainly wasn't about to mention anything to Savannah to give her or Jean a reason not to give her this assignment.

The door opened. Savannah recognized Margaret, the woman the Cartel had honored the previous month for having been responsible for shutting down a senior retirement home in Brooklyn that had been abusing the seniors.

"Hi. We're here to see Jean."

"Come in. Come in. Good to see you again, Sa-

vannah," the middle-aged Cartel member said with
a warm smile. Tiny laugh lines fanned out from the
corners of her blue eyes.

"Margaret, this is Danielle Holloway."

Margaret stared at her for a long moment then
turned to Savannah. "Looks like she has what
it takes." She winked. "It's all in the eyes. Make
yourselves comfortable a moment. I'll let Jean know
you're here."

"Thanks, Margaret," Savannah said with a light
laugh.

"That was weird," Danielle said under her breath.
"Did you see how she looked at me?"

Savannah waved her hand in dismissal. "That's
one of the top agents. She's been with the Cartel
since the beginning, and she's Jean's right hand. Definitely someone you want on your side, and if she
says you've got what it takes, then you've got it."

"If you say so," Danielle murmured, glancing up
at the twelve-foot ceiling and the incredible crystal
chandelier that looked like something out of a holi-
day movie. She slowly strolled around the massive
room and took in the decor.

Antique furnishings dotted the enormous room.
Sunshine spilled across the sparkling parquet floors
from eight-foot-long windows treated with sheer
white curtains billowing ever so gently from the light
breeze. An oak mantle with a massive fireplace was
the centerpiece of the room, reminiscent of the great
party days of old Harlem.

Margaret appeared in the doorway as silently as she'd left. "Jean is ready for you," she said.

She led them upstairs, turned right at the top of the landing and walked down a long hallway that was lined on either side with photographs of Cartel members. Danielle caught a glimpse of Savannah's mother, Claudia, and just before Margaret tapped on the partially opened door, Danielle saw a picture of a smiling Savannah.

Wow, it's like going to the White House or somewhere prestigious and seeing the rows of presidents hanging on the walls, she thought, then she wondered if her picture would wind up there one day.

Margaret opened the door, stepped aside and let Savannah and Danielle pass. "Good luck," she whispered to Danielle before closing the door behind her.

The room was dimly lit by an antique lamp on a desk behind which Jean sat. Outdoor sunshine was blocked by the heavy brocade drapes, in sharp contrast to the floor below.

"Ladies." Jean took off her pink-framed glasses and stood. "Thank you for coming. Please have a seat." Her radiant red hair fell in soft waves around her delicate face to brush her shoulders.

Danielle noticed that her skin was almost translucent as a trickle of perspiration shimmied down the center of her own spine even though the air-conditioning was running at optimum level. She took a seat opposite Jean and next to Savannah. She crossed her ankles and drew in a long, calming breath, then put on her best smile.

"How are you feeling these days, Savannah?"

Savannah gently patted her barely noticeable baby bump. "If I can get past these first three months, I just might survive."

Jean offered a lukewarm smile. "Children." Her right brow flicked reflexively. "They never factored into my life—always busy traveling, getting from one assignment to the next." She sighed. "Now it's too late."

"I'm sorry," Savannah offered.

"Oh, don't be," she said with a wave of her hand. "I'd make a terrible mother. I don't have a nurturing bone in my body." She turned her attention to Danielle. "Ms. Holloway." She said it in such a way that it hung in the air, more like an accusation than a greeting.

Danielle swallowed and offered a tight-lipped smile, feeling as if she'd been caught with her top off in the boys' locker room with the captain of the basketball team. "It's good to meet you."

"I'm sure that Savannah told you this is completely against protocol. This is not how we recruit members." She tossed Savannah a sharp look, and Savannah adjusted her behind in her seat. "However, because Savannah did such an excellent job on her first assignment and was recruited by her mother, whom I hold in the highest regard…" She drew in a breath, then on the exhale said, "I've decided after much deliberation and consultation, to consider your admittance."

Danielle felt her lungs fill with air and realized that she'd been holding her breath. She almost broke out in laughter, she was so relieved.

"However, you have no skills. You haven't been trained. Ideally I should be using one of our more seasoned members, but I wanted Savannah for this job. Obviously she can't handle it now, and because you and Nia Turner were so integral to resolving the land fraud deal, I think that you would be a perfect substitute."

"Thank you." I *think*.

"You're going to have to take a crash course. We don't have much time to get you up to speed. You will need to master in two weeks what would normally take two to three months. If I'm satisfied with your progress at the end of the training, you'll get your kit and be briefed on the details of the assignment."

"Is she always like that?" Danielle asked once they were safely inside Savannah's car.

Savannah grinned. "Like what?"

"So…distant, no-nonsense and…cold." She fastened her seat belt.

"In her position, I think you have to be. She has a lot of responsibility."

"You think she has a man in her life?"

"You would ask something like that," she said, laughing. "Why?"

"Just figured if she had a man, it would loosen the lines around her mouth."

Savannah cracked up. "Girl, you are terrible."

"Just honest. Anyway," she continued as Savannah pulled off, "what does this training entail?"

"Well…"

It was nearly nine by the time Danielle got home. She'd told Nick that she was going with Savannah after work to look at cribs.

"Hey, babe," Nick said from the archway of the kitchen. He brushed a damp lock of hair away from his forehead and stepped out, a towel wrapped around his waist. His torso was a series of hard ripples, his slightly tanned skin glistening with water where the towel had missed. His eyes sparkled and crinkled at the corners when he smiled, which was often.

Danielle's heart sputtered in her chest, and that butterfly feeling in the center of her stomach went on a rampage. Just looking at Nick and having him look at her with such love and lust in his eyes made her weak all over.

She tossed her bag on the counter and slowly approached him. He leaned against the frame of the door. She stood right in front of him, barely a breath away, and pressed the palms of her hands against his chest.

Nick lowered his head, brushed her fluttering eyelids with his lips.

Danielle felt the heat tap out a rhythm between her thighs.

Nick snaked an arm around her waist, his other hand cupped the back of her head. His mouth dragged down her upturned face, planting kisses until he reached her lips; then he took her mouth in movie close-up fashion, slow, soft and sure.

Danielle's body vibrated. She sighed into his mouth as his tongue played with hers.

Nick pulled her tightly against him. Dani groaned, feeling the bulge of his erection press firmly against her stomach.

He lifted his mouth from Danielle's. Her eyes remained slightly parted, then fluttered open. Nick's lips curved upward.

"And how was your day?" he teased, stroking her back.

Danielle pressed her head against his chest. "It just got better, but I need to get settled."

"No problem. I fixed dinner. Come on out when you're ready."

She tilted her head back, looked into his inky dark eyes and lost herself in the light that danced in their depths.

"I...I'm crazy about you," she whispered over the sudden tightness in her throat.

For a nanosecond she caught the flash of disappointment that passed across his gorgeous face and dimmed his eyes. Then it was gone, and that half smile that always made her melt was in place.

"I know." His gaze locked with hers, seeing beyond her words.

Danielle tugged in a breath. "I'll be out in a few." She picked up her purse from the hall table and walked toward their bedroom. She plopped down on the side of bed and took off her shoes.

A sense of exhilaration rippled through her. She had her first assignment—well, almost—and she couldn't wait to get started with her training. Two weeks, humph, she could handle it. Piece of cake.

She got up from the bed and began to take off her clothes. Walking into the bathroom and turning on the shower, she wondered how she was going to handle Nick, especially if he was going to the spa right across the street. Geez, how freaky was that?

Not only did she and Nick live together, but they also worked together as fashion photographers. Their days were busy, often grueling yet at the same time exciting. They loved what they did and were as passionate about their work as they were about each other. The adrenaline rush that they felt all day while shooting those perfect shots, getting the lighting just right to frame the model, spilled over into the bedroom, where they strove for the perfection that would run them all day as they watched the other work— Nick getting turned on watching Danielle style the set, then get behind the lens to capture the moment, or Dani as she looked on while Nick, now behind the camera, coaxed and cooed at the models to bring out that special something that would pop on film.

Maybe that was what made their lovemaking so intense, so passionate and earth-shaking, Danielle thought, as she stepped under the rush of water. The need that built up between them all day exploded at night.

She knew their relationship was more than great sex. There were feelings involved. Nick was in love with her. She knew it, she felt it, he admitted it.

She also knew that she had deep feelings for Nick. She felt it deep in her soul. It was probably love—something she admitted hesitantly to Savannah and Nia but never to Nick. She couldn't. If she did, it would become real—and if it was real, it could hurt her and she could lose again.

Danielle lathered her body with her favorite mango body wash, running her hands over her smooth skin. They settled for a moment over her flat stomach.

Life once bloomed there. Once. Not even Savannah or Nia knew. She never spoke about it. Too painful. Because, of course, if she said it out loud, it would be real and that devastating reality she wouldn't deal with.

So she kept that dark part of her life buried so deep beneath the surface that she hardly thought about it, especially because she could cover it all up with beauty, excitement, work—and now Nick Mateo.

Danielle stepped out of the shower stall and wrapped herself in a thick, pearl-gray towel. Before leaving, she caught a glimpse of herself in the foggy mirror. The ethereal image evoked a sense of illusion—something or someone being there but not quite. That was her. That was her life.

She opened the door and the cool rush of air blew in, dissolving the steam. Her image cleared. The hazy edges evaporated. There she stood, the way the world saw and knew her. She looked away.

"You and Savannah find a crib?" Nick asked before he lifted a forkful of penne pasta swathed in primavera sauce to his mouth.

"Crib?" For a moment, Danielle had no clue what he was talking about.

"Yeah, you said you two were going crib shopping."

"Oh." She laughed, hoping to cover her gaff. "Yes, uh, we looked around. There were a couple that she really liked." She kept her gaze focused on her mixed-green salad.

Nick angled his head a bit to the right. "Are you okay? You seem out of it since you got home."

She forced herself to look at him, and her heart hammered in her chest as the lie flowed smoothly from her lips. She shrugged, then reached across the small table and covered his hand. "You know the kind of day we had, and then all that walking around from store to store this evening. I don't know how Savannah does it, but I'm beat. That's all."

Nick stared at her a moment.

"For real," she insisted with a smile.

"Okay." He paused. "If something was wrong, you'd tell me, right?"

"Of course."

It was the first lie and, like scalding water it burned her tongue, and she knew it was only the first of many.

"Are you all set for your shoot tomorrow?" she asked, switching to a neutral topic.

"Yeah." He dipped his bread in the sauce and took a bite. "I'm going to the site early to check on the final details."

"If I can finish in time with my meeting with Michael Preston, I'll stop by. I'm determined to get the account to photograph the ads for his new line."

Nick chuckled. "I love when you get that little bass in your voice and that kick-ass look in your eye."

"Very funny," she said, failing at sounding offended.

"It's one of the things I love about you, Dani, that fierce determination, knowing what you want and going after it."

Her gaze dragged over the planes and valleys of his face. That determination that he spoke of was instilled in her as a child growing up in a mixed-heritage household, filling out countless applications and checking "other" for ethnicity, never wanting to negate one parent's heritage for the other and living a life walking that fine line. All of that made her determined to be somebody on her own, independent of tags and labels.

Often she believed that stubborn streak of independence kept her from allowing anyone to get too close, beneath the surface, only to discover that she was no more than a confused girl who was searching for her identity.

She reached over and with the tip of her finger wiped a spot of sauce from the corner of Nick's mouth.

He took her hand and kissed her fingertips, and she silently hoped that when the investigation was all over he would still want to hold her hand.

Chapter 4

If she could land the Michael Preston account, it would take her business to the next level, Danielle thought, as she entered the building on Seventh Avenue—also known as Fashion Avenue. And she was dressed for the part. Her ebony hair flowed in gentle waves around her face. Her five-foot nine-inch frame was the perfect showpiece for the body-hugging, sleeveless, black cotton T-shirt, covered with a belted, hip-length jacket in a riot of orange, gold and muted green, over skinny black jeans that hugged her hips and defined her long legs.

Danielle gripped the handle of her oversize black leather portfolio and stabbed the button for the elevator. Impatiently she tapped her foot, encased in black alligator sling backs with three-inch heels. The finishing touch was her Sean John designer shades, which gave her a hint of mystery. More times than she could count, she'd been mistaken for the song-stress Alicia Keys, and although she'd had several opportunities to profit from the mistake, she never had.

The elevator bell dinged and the stainless-steel doors soundlessly slid open. She stepped on with two other riders.

Preston's offices were on the thirty-fifth floor of the glass and steel tower. She watched the numbers light up as they ascended.

"Love that jacket," the woman standing next to her said.

Danielle turned. "Thanks."

"Anyone ever tell you look like Alicia Keys?"

Danielle gave a slight smile. "Every now and then."

The woman reached into her purse and pulled out a business card. "If you're ever interested in mod-eling work, give me a call. I do a whole thing with celebrity look-alikes."

Danielle took the card just as the doors opened on her floor. "Thanks." She stepped off.

"Call me. I'd love to work with you."

Danielle took a quick look at the woman before the doors closed. She walked away, shaking her head in amusement, and stuck the card in her jacket pocket.

She strode down the corridor toward the glass doors with the Michael Preston logo on them. She drew in a breath and pressed the buzzer.

"Yes?" came the voice through the intercom from the fashionista sitting at the desk on the other side of the glass door.

"Danielle Holloway to see Mr. Preston."

The lock buzzed and the door slowly swooshed inward. She entered a space that could only be described as classy. Sleek elegance in simple black and white. Bursting blooms of exotic plants showcased in glass bowls sat majestically on low tables. The stark white walls were adorned with near life-size photographs of models wearing Michael's creations. The frames matched the walls so perfectly that the images seemed to float. It was a powerful optical illusion.

A stunning young woman who couldn't have been more than twenty greeted her. She was pencil thin with startling blue eyes and a mane of strawberry-blond hair that fell straight as a board down the center of her back, held away from her heart-shaped face with a tortoiseshell headband.

"Good morning." She stuck out her hand, which Danielle shook. Her thin lips tinged in dramatic fuchsia widened to reveal a brilliantly perfect smile. "My name is Tasha, Michael's assistant. If you'll follow me, we can get started."

We?

Danielle followed Tasha and the scent of patchouli

that wafted around her down a short carpeted hallway, turning right along another that was three times the length of the first. Behind either side of the glass walls, designers were busy at work, their creations in various stages of construction.

Tasha led her to the end of the hallway and opened a heavy inlaid wooden door with Conference Room etched in gold on the front. She stepped aside to let Danielle enter.

Danielle expected to see Michael sitting behind a desk, but he wasn't.

"Please have a seat, I'm eager to see some of your work."

Trying not to show her confusion, which bordered on annoyance, Danielle laid her portfolio on a table that could easily seat twenty, and she unzipped it.

"Uh, is Mr. Preston going to be joining us?"

Tasha gave a little laugh. "Michael is out of town. But not to worry. If I like what I see, he likes what I see."

Danielle blew out a silent breath. *This chick wasn't old enough to know the difference between commercial photography and Photoshop.*

"Actually, I'm a fan of yours," Tasha said, as she sat down and began reviewing Danielle's work.

"Really?" The knot in her stomach loosened.

"I've studied your work at Parsons and The New School for Design in my advertising and marketing classes."

Her brows rose in surprise. "I had no idea."

"You have a very distinct style, Ms. Holloway. I could pick your shots out from a crowd any day."

"I hope that's a good thing."

There was that little laugh again. "I think so."

Tasha closed the book before she was even half-way finished. Not a good sign, Danielle thought.

"I'd like to take you on a tour of the design floor—get your impressions—and then we can wrap up in my office."

A little more than an hour and a half later, Danielle was sitting behind the wheel of her Navigator with a retainer check in her hand for ten thousand dollars.

Her head was still spinning. She'd actually landed the account. She was to be the official photographer for the Michael Preston fall collection.

Her photographs would be on his Web site, in his catalogs and all of his promotional material. They'd wind up in every fashion magazine across the country and in Europe.

She didn't even care why they needed a new photographer. All she knew was that she had finally taken her business to the next level.

This called for some serious celebrating. Under normal circumstances Nia would offer to whip up one of her fabulous meals at her house, since she was the only one of the trio who could really cook. But because she was out of town, Danielle and Nick would have to go out.

She reached for her cell phone to call Nick and

give him the good news when the phone chirped in her hand, indicating she had a message waiting. She dialed into her voice mail.

It was Savannah. Danielle's training was to start tonight. She was to come to the TLC headquarters at eight.

Well, that put a wrinkle in things, Danielle thought as she put the SUV in gear and drove off.

Chapter 5

Danielle pulled up to the photo shoot site in mid-town Manhattan. As usual, the area had its curious onlookers, but for the most part New Yorkers, who are used to seeing just about anything and everybody, pretty much took a peek and went on their way.

She tossed her parking permit on her dashboard, grabbed her equipment from the passenger seat and hopped out. She ducked under the tape that separated the set from the pedestrians and weaved in and out of the crew until she reached Nick's side.

"How's it going?" she whispered in his ear, causing him to jump in surprise.

Nick turned to her, a smile blooming on his face. He leaned down for a quick kiss. "You made it.

Things are cool here. The usual drama. Let's take ten," he shouted. "So tell me what happened." He slid his arm around her waist and ushered her away from the crowd.

"Wellll." She dragged the word out. "I got it!" She jumped up and down doing a happy dance.

Nick swept her up in his arms and spun her around, drawing the wide-eyed stares of passersby. "Oh, baby—I'm so happy for you!" He kissed her lips.

"Happy for *us*. This is a package deal. It's you and me babe. And I have a ten-thousand-dollar check to prove it."

"Whoa, this is definitely cause for celebration." He pulled her close. "What do you want to do? You name it."

Her heart began to pound. "Well, how about we, uh, plan something for the weekend. Just the two of us."

He gave a slight shrug. "Sure. I didn't think you would want to wait that long."

"We have a crazy week ahead of us and it will be the perfect way to end it." She stroked his jaw.

"Whatever you want," he said halfheartedly.

"Good." She pecked him on the lips. "Now bring me up to speed with the shoot," she said, smoothly switching into business mode.

Danielle followed Nick back over to the set, half listening to him as she tried to think of an excuse for why she would be away for the evening.

* * *

"So what are you going to tell him?" Savannah asked.

Danielle turned her back to the people on the set and cradled her phone a bit closer. "I have no idea. Any suggestions? What did you tell Blake during your training?"

"For one thing, Blake and I didn't work together, and he was so accustomed to me working overtime at the law firm that I never really had to come up with an explanation."

"Great," she said with a sigh. "I've already used the shopping-for-cribs excuse."

"Dani!" one of her crew members called out.

She turned in the direction of the voice.

"We need you over here."

"Be right there," she shouted over the noise of traffic. "Gotta go," she said to Savannah. "If you think of anything, call me."

"Will do."

Danielle disconnected the call, stuck her Black-Berry in the case on her hip and joined her team.

The photo shoot was an ad campaign for Lincoln Center's fall season. The bevy of models were attired in gorgeous evening gowns from the Vera Wang collection. They had to shoot them from a variety of angles: getting in and out of cars, walking through the plaza and of course the establishing shot in front of the fountain. The shoot itself was easy. The hard part was keeping would-be passersby from straying into the shots. After five long hours, they called it a wrap for the day.

* * *

"I figured as long as you didn't want to go out and celebrate we could celebrate, at home," Nick said to Danielle as they packed up their equipment. "Nice home-cooked meal, some champagne, and then I'll make love to you like I've been hungry to do all day." He winked at her.

"Sounds perfect." She screwed her lens cap on her camera and put it in its case, then hoisted it up on her shoulder by the strap.

"You could sound a little more enthusiastic."

"Sorry. Just a little headache."

"Hmm, we have some Tylenol at home, but if you can't wait, we can stop and get something."

She waved off his offer. "No. I'll be okay. Just the sun, the work and all the excitement. I'll be fine."

Nick stared at her a moment, then took her by the shoulders and turned her to face him. "You want to tell me what's going on with you?"

"I don't know what you mean."

"I mean, the way you're acting. Like… I don't know, like you're hiding something."

She made a face. "Hiding something," she echoed. "Don't be silly."

"Hey, whatever. When the real Danielle Holloway gets back, let me know. I'm going to the gym." He walked off toward his car, got behind the wheel and drove off.

Danielle's shoulders slumped as if the air had been let out of her. She couldn't go on lying to Nick, but what choice did she have? Maybe this whole TLC thing wasn't for her after all. Yet it was something she felt compelled to do from deep down inside. It wasn't the case itself. It was about proving to herself that she could be so much more than just a pretty face, someone's girlfriend, good in bed. It would provide personal satisfaction to take on something challenging, something that didn't come easily to her, like everything else in her life. She'd always gotten a pass because of how she looked. Most times it had nothing to do with her ability. And a part of her always felt inadequate as a result. This was different. She knew that it would challenge her relationship with Nick. But it was a risk she needed to take—for herself.

She waved goodbye to her crew and the models and headed to her ride. Then it hit her. Nick was going to the gym. She knew his routine. He would go home, drop off his equipment, change into his exercise gear, then head out. He'd be gone at least three hours. She checked her watch. It was six forty-five. If she played it right, she could be home from her meeting before Nick got back from the gym.

She hopped behind the wheel of her vehicle, pulled out her BlackBerry and dialed Savannah.

"I have a real short window," she said, checking before pulling out into traffic. "Nick is going to the gym."

"Great."

"How long do you think this will take?"

"No more than an hour. It's basically orientation, signing confidentiality papers, getting contact info and the CD with TLC information on it."

Danielle blew out a breath. "Okay. I can manage that."

"Call me later and let me know how it went."

"I will."

Danielle disconnected the call and headed across town. Hopefully, Nick had gone to his own gym down in the West Village and not Pause for Men.

The last of the rush-hour traffic extended Danielle's half-hour drive to nearly an hour. It was all the residual effects of the U.N. Summit, which had tied the city in knots for almost a week.

She eased onto 135th Street in Harlem, on the lookout for any signs of Nick's car. She pulled the Navigator around the corner and parked. It was only seven forty. She hoped Ms. Jean "Rules and Regulations" Wallington-Armstrong didn't mind her being early.

She approached the corner and stopped dead in her tracks. Bernard Hassell was crossing the street in the direction of Pause for Men. His back was almost to her, but if he turned his head, she'd be right in his line of vision. She took several steps backward, ducked around the corner and watched him from the side of the building until he'd gone inside.

Her heart was pounding so hard in her chest that she could barely breathe. For a moment she shut her eyes and shook her head. This was crazy, she thought, before easing around the corner. She hurried to the building, intermittently checking the house across the street. At the downstairs door she rang the bell, and the few seconds that ticked by seemed like an eternity.

"Good evening, Ms. Holloway. Nice to see you again," Margaret said. "Jean is waiting for you. Go right up. Do you remember the way?" she asked, stepping aside to let Danielle in.

"Yes, I'm pretty sure I remember. Are you here… full-time?" Danielle asked as they entered the foyer.

"You could say that. With all that's going on in the world, solving its problems is a full-time job." She stopped at the bottom of the staircase. Danielle turned to her. "Good luck," Margaret said with a wise smile. "You'll be fine." She turned and walked away.

I sure as hell hope so, Danielle thought as she walked upstairs.

When Danielle approached the door, she could hear Jean talking to someone. She didn't hear anyone else and realized she was on the phone. For an instant she debated about announcing herself or listening for a minute. Her curiosity won out.

"…I understand that. Is there really a reason to get Homeland Security involved? I see. You know I'll help in any way that I can on the local level. You do understand that the people I'm working for on this case cannot be involved. It's the reason why I was hired. Of course. Keep me posted and I'll do the same."

What the hell was that about? Danielle wondered. She stepped up to the door and knocked.

"Come in."

She entered as Jean was hanging up the phone.

"Close the door, please."

Danielle did as she was asked, crossed the room and sat down.

"This shouldn't take long," Jean said, a line of worry bunching her brows together. She went to a file cabinet on the far side of the room and took out a thick folder, then brought it to her desk. She flipped the folder open and put on her pink-framed glasses.

"We've completed our background check on you, Danielle, and for the most part everything came back fine." She extracted several photographs and pushed them across the table.

It was a series of pictures of her with Savannah and Nia at The Shop, her and Nick several weeks ago on one of their evening walks, her getting into her SUV, and even a photograph from that morning of her visit to Michael Preston's studio.

Her eyes flashed at Jean. "You've been following me?"

"Of course." She pushed another document across the table. It was her credit report and another series of papers detailing her entire life, everything from where she lived to the schools she'd attended, her parents' information and the loan from the bank to get her business operational.

"It's very easy to find out anything you want

about someone. It's the business we're in. And of course we had to be sure that your lifestyle and your associations wouldn't hamper your ability to do this job. I'm sure you understand."

Danielle didn't know what she understood or what she thought. She felt so violated that she was speechless.

"Any questions?"

Danielle blinked. "No," she murmured.

"Good." She opened her desk drawer and took out a very legal-looking document and passed it to Danielle. "Please look this over, and if you agree, I'll need your signature."

It was pretty much what Savannah described: a confidentiality statement in addition to a clause that stated if she were caught, the Cartel would do what they could from behind the scenes, but they would never acknowledge her association with them. Her temples began to pound.

If she was caught. Ugly images filled her head, first of old, dank warehouses with her inside—tied to a chair and being interrogated by men in dark clothes and indistinguishable features—filled her head, then of a two-bunk cell that she shared with a woman whose nickname was Big Bertha and, finally, being thrown from a speeding car onto some desolate road, where she'd be left for the vultures—man or beast.

She stared at the words until they blurred. Her and her big mouth. She could have said she was busy, too.

She wouldn't have been lying. But, noooo, she had to volunteer and even asked for a gun. God, Savannah was her dearest friend, and she would do anything in the world for her, but this… Identity theft sounded mundane on the surface, but what if it wasn't?

What had she gotten herself into?

"Is there a problem?"

Jean's strident voice snapped the final thread that connected Danielle the woman she was to Danielle the woman she was crossing the threshold to becoming. If she signed her name, there was no turning back. For a moment she hung suspended, unsure whether to leap across or crawl back to the other side.

Danielle glanced at Jean, who was rolling a silver pen between her thin fingers—or was it a stake?—and she could swear she saw the word *coward* reflected in Jean's emerald-green eyes. But it was her own face.

Jean abruptly stood. "We can't use anyone in the Cartel who is unsure of themselves, Ms. Holloway. Too much is at stake, and it's apparent that this is not for you."

…that's one of the things I love about you, your fierce determination. Nick's words ejected her out of the abyss of doubt to which she'd momentarily sunk. This was about proving something to herself, to remove all the inward doubts that she harbored about her own validity.

She reached for the pen on the desk and signed with a flourish, then pushed the papers back across the desk. She pinned Jean with a withering stare of her own. "That's where you're wrong."

Was that an inkling of a smile taunting Jean's barely there lips?

Jean put the form back in the folder, then looked at Danielle. "I'm assigning you to Margaret, who will give you a full history on the organization. She will set your schedule and monitor your progress. You're going to have to be trained in how to use all of the surveillance equipment. Once Margaret is satisfied, the details of your assignment will be given to you. I cannot impress upon you enough that under no circumstance are you to ever divulge anything about TLC to anyone—that includes Nick Mateo." She paused. "Are we clear?"

"Yes."

"Good." She stood. "Margaret will give you the information that you need on your way out."

Danielle got up. "Thank you." She turned to leave.

Jean watched her as she walked out and hoped that she hadn't made a mistake. The truth was, their resources were stretched thin. If she'd had her way, she would have gotten someone else. But she'd made promises and she had to fulfill them.

Margaret was waiting for Danielle in the main room on the parlor floor.

"That wasn't so bad, now, was it?" she asked with that secret gleam in her eyes.

Danielle drew in a breath. "I guess that depends on what you call bad." She forced a nervous smile.

"Come with me. I have some things to go over with you."

* * *

A little more than an hour later, Danielle was walking out of the door of the Cartel headquarters and surreptitiously heading toward her car, keeping a corner of an eye out for any signs of Bernard Hassell.

Once behind the wheel she breathed a sigh of relief. The time on the dash read eight forty-five. If she hurried, she knew she would beat Nick home; maybe she would order something fancy from a local restaurant for dinner and use her feminine wiles to make up to him for being so unreceptive earlier.

She turned the key in the ignition in concert with a sharp knock on her window that jerked her an inch off her seat.

Oh, damn! She turned down the window. "Nick."

Chapter 6

Savannah pushed open the door to her town house and couldn't wait to get out of her shoes. Even though she was only in her first trimester and tried to remember to put her feet up whenever she could during the day, they were still swollen. Not badly, but enough to be just a little uncomfortable. Her one nightmare about this pregnancy was that with her being a petite five foot three that she would blow up to whale size and have to wear ugly balloon clothes and special shoes, instead of the jazzy designer maternity outfits she'd spent a zillion dollars on. She carried her shoes in one hand and her purse in the other, padding barefoot to her bedroom.

She took off her suit jacket and tossed it on the bed. Her shirt, bra and panties shortly followed.

"Whew, that feels good."

Savannah plopped down on the side of the bed and massaged her feet and wished that Danielle was around. A week earlier she'd given her the best foot massage.

She sighed and wondered how Danielle was making out with her assignment. She felt responsible for however it turned out, since she had recommended Dani to Jean in the first place.

Had Savannah not been in her current condition, the case would have been hers, and she felt a little left out of the action. She loved the fact that she was finally pregnant after trying for so long, but her friends, her mother and even her workaholic boss, Richard, treated her like spun glass.

She squeezed her toes between her fingers. Sometimes what she wanted to do was jump out and tell them that less than a month earlier she'd been a superspy, taking down a major foundation!

She yawned loudly and rubbed her tummy. She really did want to help Dani the way she'd helped her. But the truth was all she could concentrate on for the most part was sleep, sex and sustenance—and not necessarily in that order, she thought with a smile.

Slowly she pushed herself up and caught a glimpse of her slightly rounding form in the mirror that hung on the closet door. She turned from side to side, admiring the added plumpness of her behind and the fullness of her breasts.

The bedroom door pushed open. Savannah turned.

Blake's dark eyes darkened even more. His so very kissable mouth moved into a slow smile. He closed the door and moved toward his wife.

"Damn, baby," he said in a low growl. "You could make a man crazy coming home to look at you like this."

Savannah's body heated. Her heart pounded. "Like what?" she said, her voice laced with a desire for the man in front of her that never seemed to leave.

Blake moved closer, tugging at his tie. "Lush, sexy as all hell, beautiful." He was right on her now, the cotton fabric of his shirt brushing against her very tender nipples, sending jolts of electricity rushing through her. His fingertips trailed across her baby bump. "And filled with our child." He lowered his head and kissed her so tenderly, Savannah felt like weeping. "I love you so much," he uttered against her mouth.

Savannah was on fire and knew that if her husband didn't make love to her right then and there, she was going to implode. Her fingers fumbled with the buttons of his shirt. He tugged it off while she unfastened his thin leather belt and unzipped him.

They moved in unison to their bed, with Savannah landing on top of him. He cupped her breasts, their fullness overflowing in his hands. Savannah moaned, spread her thighs on either side of him, bent her knees and positioned herself over his erection, which was throbbing against her.

She slid down on him, her wet heat enveloping him like a glove.

"Ohhhh," Blake cried out. His eyes squeezed shut. He grabbed her behind and pushed upward.

Savannah tossed her head back as a strangled cry gurgled up from her throat. The indescribable sensations that pulsed through every fiber of her being each time Blake moved inside her made her head spin. She felt outside herself, as if she were floating on a bed of pleasure and her body was a receptacle for delight.

She rotated her hips, then thrust her pelvis forward. The tendons in Blake's neck stretched tautly. He looked into her eyes, his breath rushing through his partially opened mouth. He rose up, took the tip of her left nipple between his lips and teased it with the tip of his tongue then grazed it with his teeth. Savannah began to tremble, from the balls of her feet, up the backs of her thighs, to pulse in the rise and fall of her behind, grip her spine and shake it.

"Come on, baby," Blake urged in a voice coated in lust. "Bring it." He grabbed her tightly by the hips so that she was unable to move, only able to take what he gave her—slow, deep, rotating thrusts that had her whimpering and shuddering. Tears of sublime pleasure sprang from her eyes.

"That's how we like it, right, baby?" he moaned.

"Yessss," she said through her teeth. She snatched his hands away and pressed them against her breasts as she took them to unbelievable heights with quick swirls of her lower body to meet his every push and pull.

Their incomprehensible sounds of pleasure filled the room, taking them higher and higher until they both exploded like rockets on the Fourth of July.

Savannah collapsed on top of Blake, both of them breathing hard and ragged.

Blake cuddled with her close to him, gently stroking her back, whispering his love for her in her ear and she whispering it back.

Life didn't get better than this. If only every couple could be as happy as she and Blake, Savannah thought as she felt herself drifting off into the sleep of the satiated—just as the phone rang.

Savannah buried her head deeper into Blake's chest, but it didn't stop the ringing. Blake stretched his long arm across the bed and snatched up the phone.

"Hello?" he said, sounding sleepy. "Hey, Mom. Yeah, uh, she's right here."

Savannah flipped onto her back, mouthed "sorry" to her husband and took the phone.

"Mom. Hi." She listened for a few minutes, her eyes widening, followed by a frown. "Are you kidding me?"

Blake propped himself up on his elbow and looked with concern at Savannah.

"I… I don't know what to say. I mean…if you're happy, that's what's important. Sure. Okay, I'll talk to you tomorrow." Dreamlike, she hung up the phone and turned to Blake. "Mom and Bernard are getting married, and she wants me to help plan the wedding."

"I was hoping to see you," Danielle said, thinking fast. Her heart was banging so hard in her chest that she knew Nick could hear it.

"Really? What made you come over here instead of to my regular spot at Gold's Gym?"

"You said how much you liked this place. I just took a wild guess."

He looked at her for a long moment, as if trying to see something behind her words. "Lucky guess." He grinned and the line of tension between them snapped. "Look, I'm sorry about earlier."

"Me, too." She unbuckled her seat belt and got out. She stood in front of him, reached up and stroked his face. "Are you going to be long?"

"About an hour." He paused. "But I can come home now if you want."

Danielle smiled. "I'd like that," she said softly.

He kissed her lips and ran his hand along her hair that hung down her back. "See you at home."

Danielle got back into her Navigator and watched as Nick walked off to his Trailblazer. She let out a long breath of relief, realizing she was shaking all over, and gripped the steering wheel and stared off into space. She was going to have to be supercareful if she was to get through this without getting caught.

* * *

Danielle and Nick arrived at the same time and parked behind each other on the narrow street. Nick set the alarm on his vehicle and met up with Danielle at the top of the stairs to their apartment.

"I was really surprised to see you," he said, unlocking the front door. "For a minute I thought you were following me or something...or meeting someone."

She almost choked on that one.

Nick stepped aside to let her in and followed her up the steps. She kept her gaze focused on her feet.

"I felt bad and silly for being such a witch this afternoon. Especially when you were only being sweet." She glanced over her shoulder. "Like you always are."

She opened the door to their second-floor apartment, tossed her bag on the table in the foyer and turned to Nick, stopping him in his tracks.

Her eyes moved across his face. "I'm glad I found you," she said softly.

Nick slid his arms around her waist. "Tonight or in general?" he teased.

"Both."

"I'm glad I found you, too, Dani." He drew in a breath. "You're everything I want in every way." He pushed a loose strand of hair away from her face. "You know that?"

She looked up into his eyes. "Yes, I do." She rested her head on his chest and listened for a moment to the comforting beat of his heart. Why couldn't she totally commit to this man? she asked herself for the countless time.

Nick leaned back. "We got some great shots today before you arrived."

"Let's take a look while we fix something to eat. I'm suddenly ravenous."

"You mean, while I fix something to eat, don't you?"

She made a face and poked him in the arm. "Whatever."

Nick chuckled. "Come on."

Huddled together on their king-size bed, with a steaming plate of homemade chicken fajitas next to them, they reviewed the day's shoot on Nick's twenty-one-inch Mac.

"These are fantastic," Danielle muttered over a mouthful of food. "Stephanie is incredible to work with. Wow, look at the way the light hits her accessories," she said, pointing to a shot of the model near the water fountain with the rush of Manhattan traffic in the background.

"And she knows exactly how to play up each piece without taking away from herself," Nick added.

"That's why she gets the megabucks," Danielle said drolly.

"Speaking of megabucks…" He hopped off the bed and left the room. Moments later he returned with two long-stemmed wineglasses and a bottle of champagne.

Danielle's eyes widened in delight. "What are you doing? And where did you find champagne?" she asked over her laughter.

He sauntered toward her and winked. "I always have a surprise up my sleeve. Well…actually," he hedged, "this was a gift from Nia when we went to her party a few months back."

"Ohhhh, right. I'd forgotten all about it."

"So had I." He sat on the side of the bed and after several attempts popped the cork with a flourish. The bubbling brew rushed to the top and spilled down the sides of the bottle neck.

They giggled as the champagne splashed over Nick's fingers and he stuck his head beneath the flow to catch it on his tongue.

Danielle held out her glass and he filled it. The bubbles tickled her nose, but the expensive champagne went down like silk.

"Mmmm, good stuff," she said.

Nick placed the bottle on the nightstand. He raised his glass. "To the new 'it' girl in the photography world." He touched his glass to hers.

"To *our* continued success," she said. "I couldn't have done it without you." She leaned forward and kissed him.

Nick took her glass from her hand and set it on the table next to the bed. He gazed into her eyes as he unbuttoned her blouse and slipped it from her shoulders. "Do you want this?" he asked, dropping featherlike kisses along the crests of her breasts.

Danielle's body shuddered. "Yes," she whispered.

He lowered one strap of her bra and then the other before pushing it down below the swell of her breasts so that they rose even higher.

"You're so beautiful," he said, his tone growing thick with desire.

"You make me feel beautiful all the time."

"I never want you to forget how much I adore you, Dani," he said in a ragged voice and eased her back against the thick pillows.

She draped her hands behind his head and urged him toward her mouth. His kiss was sweet, tender and possessive all at once, and Danielle lost herself in the bliss of it, giving him everything he gave her.

Their tongues danced the waltz, slow and sure; then they dueled in a tango and whined with the rhythm of the Caribbean.

She tugged at the hem of his gray T-shirt, and Nick needed no further coaxing. He pulled it over his head and tossed it on the floor.

Danielle's heart banged against her chest, and the bud between her thighs thickened and pulsed. Just looking at Nick's body was the ultimate turn-on. His devout exercise regime had rewarded him with the body of a god. His arms were like steel, and whenever he wrapped them around her, she knew she was safe and protected. His chest was defined and rock hard, and it led down to a six-pack-like stomach that would make Mr. America weep in shame.

Through a series of maneuvers, they discarded the rest of their clothing and rolled around on the bed, laughing and finding places on each other's body to nibble, stroke and kiss until Danielle found herself pinned beneath Nick's weight.

"Don't move," he ordered, before inching his way down her body, starting at the pulse beat in her throat. He suckled her there until she began to squirm with pleasure. "Don't move," he said again. His tongue flicked across the tip of her hardened nipple, and a moan pushed through her lips. She grabbed a handful of sheet as he continued to lick and draw her nipple into his mouth, slowly and firmly.

Her stomach muscles fluttered and the inside of her thighs trembled. She gripped the sheets tighter as he neared her belly button and took a little dip.

Nick's strong fingers stroked her hips and thighs before pushing her legs apart.

"You sure you want this?" he asked, taunting her.

She couldn't speak. Her body was on fire. She nodded vigorously.

"I'll take that as a yes."

His thumb brushed across her wet, swollen pearl, and her hips instinctively rose in response.

"Naughty girl," he said, before grabbing her hips in a viselike grip and pinning her to the mattress.

His expert tongue and lush lips separated her wet folds and played her like a master violinist, each stroke, flick, lick more intense than the other. He drew the bud tenderly into his mouth and sucked on it until her cries filled the room in sweet agony.

Her head thrashed back and forth as bolts of electricity ran up and down her legs. She wanted to buck up against him, to push her essence even farther into his waiting mouth, but she couldn't move—and that reality only intensified her need and the experience.

Tears squeezed from the corners of her closed eyes when suddenly Nick released his grip on her and draped her legs over his neck, cupping her lush rear in his palms, and he went at her like a man hungry for dessert.

Danielle's thoughts spun while jolt after jolt of pleasure surged through her veins, and just as she was on the brink of release, Nick stopped. Her eyes shot open; her breath caught and held in her throat as she was suddenly filled with the hard thickness of him.

They both groaned in unison at the contact as Nick slid deep into her pulsing walls.

Nick held her like a bundled baby, crooning softly in her ear, professing his love and need for her as their bodies rose in ecstasy.

Danielle felt electrified as her limbs stiffened, her toes curled and her hips arched, thrusting hard and fast against each of Nick's downward strokes.

Then, like a volcanic eruption, she came, the sublime pleasure spewing from her lips in a rush of incoherent sounds of release that pushed Nick over the edge to fill her to her core with all the love he felt for her.

They lay together, still linked, their breathing exhaling in short erratic bursts while their heart rate slowed almost in unison.

"Congratulations," Nick murmured before sucking on her bottom lip, a glint of delight in his eyes.

Danielle giggled. "I think the congratulations should go to you, sir. That was quite a performance."

"Aw, shucks." He grinned. "Yeah, well, I *was* pretty good, if I have to say so myself."

She pinched his bare butt. He feigned a yelp and rolled off her and onto his back.

"You weren't half bad either," he said, still teasing her.

Danielle rolled her eyes, then snuggled against him. She draped her arm across his hard belly and nestled her head between his neck and shoulder.

"I was thinking that maybe we could take a weekend off and get away somewhere," Nick said.

Danielle tensed. "Hmm, sounds good."

"How 'bout next weekend?"

Her thoughts raced. "Well, let's see how things start off with this new account. There's no telling what is going to be required until we get that under wraps."

Nick blew out a breath, and Danielle fully expected him to reject the delay.

"You're probably right," he conceded. "Plus we

still have the catalog work for JCPenney and the new shots for Ford Models."

She shut her eyes with relief. "True. So as soon as we can see some daylight, okay?"

"Sure." He rolled onto his side to face her. "As long as I get to spend some alone time with you." He kissed her shoulder. "I'm going to get some of the prints ready." He got off the bed.

"Okay," she said with a drawn-out sigh. "I'll just lie right here."

Nick laughed. "You do that." He wagged his finger. "Then you'll be well rested when I get back."

Once she was alone, she closed her eyes and all of her near misses for the day flashed behind her lids. She knew that Nick would be a while in their workroom, so she took the opportunity to check out the TLC video on her laptop.

The thirty-minute infomercial narrated by Jean Armstrong told of the beginnings of TLC and the reason why an organization that could function under the radar was necessary. They could go places that the police and government officials couldn't. She told of building the Cartel from former CIA and Homeland Security agents. All women, all highly skilled, all above suspicion. But Jean had envisioned an even more covert way to infiltrate the unsuspecting: train ordinary women who had innate, savvy and useful skills.

There were several links detailing many of the assignments that had been fulfilled since the organization's inception five years earlier, as well as short demonstrations of the tools of the trade: recording and listening devices, fingerprint tools, telephoto lens cameras and guns. All of which came in every TLC member's handy little makeup case.

Overall, it gave Danielle a sense of belonging to something greater than herself, and she felt the loyalty among the women whose stories were detailed on the presentation.

Throughout her childhood she'd never felt that she belonged anywhere. She'd spent much of her life trying to fit in. Her mixed heritage had been a burden that constantly reared its ugly head in a world that held appearance in the highest esteem.

She remembered going to family gatherings on her mother's side of the family, which was Hispanic. Her father never went, and it wasn't until one afternoon that she found out why. She was sitting in the kitchen with her grandmother helping to prepare the standard rice and beans for dinner. Danielle adored her grandmother, and loved the times she spent with her, hanging on her every word. If her grandma said so, then it was so, as far as Danielle was concerned.

"You are such a beautiful girl," her grandmother had said as she poured a cup of coconut juice into the pot. "You take after your mother." She placed the cover on the pot and turned to her granddaughter. "Thank God for that." She shook her head.

"What do you mean, Ma Ma?"

Her grandmother turned to her, her sharp features

pulled taut by the salt-and-pepper bun that she religiously wore like a badge of honor.

She wagged a finger at Danielle. "I told your mother not to marry that man. He wasn't good enough for her. But she wouldn't listen."

"I don't understand."

"Mixing," she said as if that would explain everything.

Danielle looked at her, curiously waiting for an explanation.

"Your father, he is not one of us. Black." She spat the word out as if it would poison her if she didn't get rid of it quickly.

Danielle was blindsided by confusion.

"You could have turned out looking just like him. Black. With a big nose, thick lips and knotty hair." She breathed in relief. "But thank God—" she made a sign of the cross "—you didn't. I can't imagine what your life would have been like if you had." She went to the counter and began cutting up tomatoes for her special salsa. "Remember this if you remember nothing else, never marry anyone darker than a paper bag. If you do, I warn you, he will not be welcome in this family," she said with a haughty lift of her pointed chin.

The startling declaration from her grandmother had rocked Danielle to her core. She knew that she was different, that her mother and father were different from each other. It had never occurred to her that those differences had affected how the family viewed them, her grandmother in particular.

But those words stuck with Danielle and she began to see things that she hadn't seen before, or at least hadn't paid attention to. There was a time when she was out with her father in the supermarket. Her father had taken her hand and a woman strode right up to him and asked what he was doing with that little girl. He explained that she was his daughter. The woman looked from one to the other in blatant disbelief.

When she was out with her father they always got strange looks, but until that conversation with her grandmother, Danielle had never really noticed.

Then there were those rare occasions when they went to Atlanta to visit her father's family. Her cousins would always tease her, pull her long hair and insist that she thought she was better than them. Invariably she wound up playing by herself. When her mother would ask her about it, she'd simply say that was what she wanted to do.

When her father would ask her to accompany him somewhere she began making excuses not to go.

As she moved into her teens and her natural beauty intensified, the distance between her and her father widened. She would look at him and feel ashamed.

Memories from her childhood haunted her, and there were many nights she lay awake next to Nick and wondered if what she felt for him was real or just easy.

Danielle heard Nick move from the workroom to the kitchen just as the CD was coming to an end.

She popped out the CD and closed the cover of her laptop just as Nick walked back into the room. The success of TLC hinged on its secrecy. It was a rule that was not to be broken.

"I thought you were resting." He tugged his T-shirt over his head and walked toward her.

"I was just making some notes for tomorrow." She forced a smile and palmed the CD, pushing the thoughts of her past into the background.

"What's that?"

"What?"

He jutted his chin in the direction of the CD. "That. In your hand."

"Oh, just a CD." She shrugged, hopped off the bed and dropped it in her purse.

She turned toward him. "Finished with the photos?"

"Yeah," he said absentmindedly. He slowly shook his head, then looked directly at her. "Are you seeing someone else?"

Chapter 7

"He actually asked you if you were seeing some-one?" Savannah asked in disbelief. She lifted the cup of iced herb tea to her lips and took a sip.

"Yes. Would I make up something like that?" She took a long swallow of her mango and pineapple smoothie.

She'd called Savannah first thing in the morning after Nick had gone off to set up the shoot and had asked to meet at The Shop.

"What did you tell him?" She buttered her wheat toast.

"The truth! He kept insisting that I've been act-ing strange lately, and he's getting the feeling that he doesn't know who I am anymore. If it's like this now, what's going to happen once I get involved in the assignment—whatever the hell it is."

"Take it easy. Everything is going to be fine."

"I don't want to ruin my relationship over this. I haven't even started yet and it's already putting a strain on us."

"You won't have to. Nick is a great guy. He's not going to leave you." She paused for a moment. "Do you want to back out...because if you do, I'm sure Jean can find someone else."

"No." She reminded herself of all the reasons why she needed to do this. "When have you ever known me to back out of anything?"

"Are you sure?"

She hesitated for a moment. "Yes," she said on a long breath.

Savannah reached across the table and covered Danielle's hand. She looked into her friend's troubled eyes. "The only thing I can suggest, girlfriend, is to make it up to that man every chance you get."

Danielle half smiled at the innuendo.

"I have some stunning news myself."

"What?"

"My mother is getting married."

Danielle's dark brows shot upward. "Get. Outta. Here," she said, defining each word. "To Bernard?"

Savannah nodded slowly and took a bite of her toast. "I was so stunned I'm not sure I even congratulated her. She's only known him a couple of months. It's crazy."

"Wow" was all Danielle could manage. She had yet to tell Savannah about Bernard and Nick attending the spa right across the street from the Cartel. That was a sticky little problem she would work out on her own. "Hey, your mom has plenty of sense. I'm sure she's in love with him," she offered.

"I guess," Savannah said, sounding unconvinced. "If the tables were turned, she'd have me on *Oprah* for some kind of counseling."

They laughed. Yes, that was something Claudia Martin would certainly do. When it came to her daughter, she was the definition of a lioness protecting her cub.

"Be happy for her, sweetie. Your dad has been dead a long time, and your mother has been alone."

"I know. I'm sure that's one of the reasons why she got involved with the Cartel in the first place— to fill those days and hours. It's just…I don't want her to be hurt. I mean, how much do we know about him anyway, other than the fact that he looks and sounds like Billy Dee Williams?"

Danielle twisted her lips. "That's true. But again, Claudia is a savvy woman. She'll be fine." She checked her watch. "Ouch, I gotta go before I have more explaining to do."

Savannah finished her tea. "Me, too."

They left the money on the table for their mini-breakfast and stood.

"When do you start your training?" Savannah asked as they walked outside.

"I got the CD and went over it again this morning while Nick was in the shower. I start this evening."

"Great. You need a cover story for Nick?"

"We're not actually speaking at the moment. So I don't think I'll need one. He said he was going to stay at his apartment tonight."

Savannah could see the cloud of sadness around Danielle's eyes. "I didn't know he still had his place."

"Yeah. Even though he has most of his stuff at my place and we're together every night, he never gave up his spot in the Village." She laughed without humor. "Guess it was a good move on his part, huh?"

"It may seem awful at the moment, but let it work in your favor. Know what I mean."

"True. Well, let me get going." She kissed Savannah's cheek. "Oh, I forgot to tell you. I got the Michael Preston account. I'll be photographing his entire fall line."

Savannah's mouth opened to a perfect *O*. "Girl! Why didn't you tell me? Now that *is* major news." She grabbed Danielle in a quick hug. "Congratulations."

Danielle smiled a real smile for the first time that morning. "I'm excited."

"You should be. We must celebrate. As soon as Nia gets back."

"Definitely."

"Okay, gotta run. Love ya, girl, and don't worry."

Danielle finger-waved as Savannah got in her car.

She turned in the opposite direction and walked the half block to reach hers.

She would find a way to make this all work, she decided as she got into her vehicle. She would do her job, manage the Preston account, do her Cartel thing, win back her man and fry up some bacon while she was at it.

Danielle smiled to herself as she put the SUV in gear. *After all, I am woman,* she thought, before dramatically slipping on her designer shades and pulling out into traffic. *Hear me roar.*

All things considered, the day on location went by relatively smoothly. Nick was polite and professional, if a little indifferent.

Danielle caught him looking at her several times when he thought she wasn't watching, and she caught the look of longing and maybe a bit of sadness around his indigo eyes.

As much as she wanted to go over to him, wrap him in her arms and tell him how sorry she was, she knew it would be a bad move on her part. They would make up, he'd come back to her place and it would ruin her night of training.

So, as much as it hurt her, she played the indifferent role as well.

"Good day today," Nick said as they packed up their gear.

"Yes, very." She kept her eyes focused on her camera as she placed it in the case.

"So, uh, I guess I'll see you tomorrow."

"Today's a wrap, remember?"

"Oh…right."

She watched his throat bob up and down as if the words were stuck there.

She hoisted her carryall on her right shoulder. "Guess I'll see you…next week."

"Yeah…I guess," he said, his voice barely above a whisper.

She turned to leave, her eyes burning and her heart pounding. A part of her wanted him to come after her, tell her he was coming home. The other part of her dreaded it, knowing what it would mean. She lifted her head a notch higher and walked to her vehicle.

Danielle arrived at the brownstone without incident and spent the next two hours with Margaret learning the intricacies of the surveillance equipment. Cameras were not an issue, so they were able to bypass that lesson.

Margaret had her set up the magnetic listening devices in several of the rooms. Then Margaret went to see how well they'd been placed and how good the transmission was.

"You catch on very quickly," Margaret said as she placed the dime-size receiver back in the box.

"Thanks."

"You may or may not need to use these, but it's always an excellent skill to have." Margaret opened another compartment in the makeup case and took out what looked like a manicure set. In actuality, it was burglary tools.

For the next half hour, Margaret showed her how to open different types of locks without detection on a set of doors that were installed for that purpose down in the basement of the brownstone.

"It's all about touch," Margaret said as Danielle worked the razor-thin tools in the lock. "Concentrate and remember to press your fingertips around the lock. You can feel the tumblers move. Very similar to breaking into a safe," she said matter-of-factly.

Danielle stole a glance over her shoulder and looked at Margaret's serene expression, waiting for her to say she was only kidding. But she could tell by the even set of her lips that she wasn't. She turned back to the task at hand, and several moments later the door clicked open.

Danielle stood, turned to Margaret and beamed in delight.

"Excellent. A few more tries and you can get it under a minute. That's the goal," she added with a wag of her finger. "One last thing before we end the lesson for today." She led Danielle back upstairs to the computer center on the top floor of the four-story building.

Danielle was blown away when Margaret opened the door to a room filled with the latest in computer technology. There was a digital map of the world on the wall with pulsating green lights highlighting different locations. Several women wearing headsets with microphones attached sat in front of large computer screens. The hum of electronics buzzed in the air. It looked like a room right out of a *Mission: Impossible* movie.

"This is the nerve center of the Cartel," Margaret explained as she gave her a short tour. "We can track any of our members, contact them at any time and keep a pinpoint on all of the ongoing cases anywhere around the world right from this room. In addition, any tracking device put on a vehicle or an individual is monitored from this room. It's soundproof and all of the computers are programmed to self-destruct the information contained on the hard drives should that become necessary."

Danielle was impressed.

"Our spyware is developed here as well." She pointed to a woman who looked to be no more than twenty-five. "Jasmine is one of the techies who designed the 'hello dolly' virus that shut down Regency Airlines three years ago. Disastrous for the airline, but it was quite brilliant. She spent about a year in jail, but the government felt she would be much more effective working for us than for them." She walked over to Jasmine and introduced her to Danielle.

"She is our newest recruit but is on a fast-track training regime. I need you to show her how to install one of the keystroke viruses on the computer and how to connect her audio and video recorders to come up on her PDA and her personal computer."

"Sure thing. Have a seat."

"I'll see you in about an hour," Margaret said and left.

Jasmine was not only brilliant but also funny, and she had Danielle cracking up about some of the antics she'd pulled on the computer.

"Where did you learn all this stuff?" Danielle asked as she plugged in her PDA to the computer with a USB cable.

"I think I was born with a love for gadgets," she said, pushing her thin, wire-framed glasses farther up the bridge of her narrow nose. "I've been taking things apart for as long as I can remember. Electronics fascinate me."

Danielle looked at the screen on her PDA and was thrilled to find a live video of the inside of the very room they were in.

Jasmine grinned. "I think you've got it."

Danielle bobbed her head in delighted agreement.

On the drive home she went over all the things she'd learned in one evening. She was sure there was much more to it, but at least she had the basics. She'd do more reading at home and watch the second CD that she'd gotten from Margaret on her way out.

At least she could stay busy and keep her mind occupied and off Nick.

The mere mention of his name in her thoughts made the muscles in her stomach clench. She missed him already, and it could only get worse before it got better.

When she walked into her apartment, the familiar sound of Nick's off-key singing and the scent of something scrumptious in the air were missing.

A wave of sadness washed over her. Since she'd allowed herself to believe that she actually deserved a happy relationship, she'd let Nick into her heart, her spirit. That was something she'd avoided for much too long of a time, and for reasons that she didn't want to even think about.

She had relationship issues, she knew that. How could she truly love anyone else when she didn't love herself? Sure, she went through the motions with the men she'd met. Most, if not all, were always attracted to how she looked. She'd become so jaded by it that she treated men the same way. Good looks and great sex—that was all she needed or wanted. But Nick's love and patience were slowly beginning to climb over the walls she'd erected around her emotions. And that scared her. It had been so long since the wall went up that she had no idea what was on the other side anymore, or if there was anything worth finding. And that was why this assignment was so important to her, even at the risk of damaging her relationship with Nick. She had something to prove to herself, that she was so much more than an image. And Nick's words of adoration and support were not enough. She must discover it for herself if she was to ever be the woman that he deserved.

Slowly she walked through the empty apartment. She could almost feel his presence, smell his scent. She went into the bedroom, tossed her things on the bed and followed right behind them.

What if he didn't come back? she thought, the rush of misery running over her like an unwanted icy shower. There had to be a quick way out of this mess she'd gotten herself into. The truth of the matter was, she wanted her cake and she wanted to eat it, too.

The phone rang, jerking her up from the bed. She scrambled across the mattress. If it was Nick, she was going to tell him to come home—no matter what. Maybe she'd even say the *L* word if that was what it took.

She snatched up the receiver and calmed herself because she didn't want to sound too eager. "Hello?" Her heart pounded.

"Danielle, please."

Her spirits shrank to a level right below the bottom of the soles of her shoes.

"Speaking."

"This is Jean Armstrong."

Danielle sat up straight on the bed. "Yes, Ms. Armstrong." She cleared her throat.

"I just concluded my meeting with Margaret and Jasmine. I understand that you did extremely well."

"Thank you."

"Better than any new recruit we've seen in quite some time."

Her brows rose. "Really?"

"As a result I'd like you to stop by tomorrow and pick up your kit. You will be given the instructions about your assignment at that time. Come whenever it's convenient for you."

"Are you saying that I don't have to do any more training?"

"At some point you will, but for the purposes of this assignment you have a very good handle on what you will need to get it done. You see, dear, what we rely on more than technology from our Cartel members are determination and ingenuity. You have both."

"Thank you. That means a great deal."

"Tomorrow, then. Welcome to the Cartel."

"Thanks."

"Oh, and by the way, Danielle, it was a brave thing you did to allow Nick to go back to his apartment. Not many women would be willing to risk that. Actually, it was the deciding factor in allowing you to join us."

"W-what," she sputtered. "How could you know that?"

"Believe me, my dear, I know everything. And always remember that Cartel members don't have a label on their foreheads. They look just like me and you. That's the whole point, isn't it? Rest well. And not to worry, he'll be back."

The next thing Danielle knew the dial tone was humming in her ear. Dreamlike, she hung up the phone.

How could she know those things? Was one of her photography team members part of the Cartel? One of the models? Did Savannah say something to Jean?

She didn't know whether to be furious or scared out of her thong. It was beyond creepy that someone could know those kinds of intimate details about a person without their knowledge. But like Jean said, that was the whole point.

Slowly the threads of excitement began to wind their way through her veins. However complex the assignment, she would handle it, and since Jean seemed to know everything, Nick would be back as well.

She only hoped, on that note, that it wouldn't be the one time Jean was wrong.

Chapter 8

Nick was seated at the juice bar at the Pause for Men day spa when Bernard slid onto the stool beside him. He clapped him on the back.

"Had a good workout?"

Nick angled his head to the left. "Yeah, pretty good."

Bernard signaled to the waitress, who came and took his order for a veggie burger and a shake. "So how are you liking this place so far?"

"I like it a lot. You couldn't ask for more. The workout rooms are top-notch, customer service is great and you can't beat the food for the price."

Bernard chuckled. "So do you think you want to join, or are you going to live out your guest privileges?"

Nick lowered his head and grinned. "Yeah, I plan to sign up. Actually I was going to do that today. The way things are going in my life I'm going to need all the destressing I can get—or afford."

"Something wrong? Maybe I can help. You look like you could use a friend or an ear. I'm pretty good at both." He gave the young man an encouraging smile.

Nick drew in a breath. When was the last time he'd expressed his feelings or his insecurities to anyone until he'd met Danielle? It had been so long since he'd had a man-to-man talk that he wasn't sure he knew how. But there was something about Bernard that made him feel safe and comfortable, as if they'd known each other for years.

He angled his body toward Bernard. His words came out halting, as if he were testing out the language for the first time.

"I guess I've always been pretty much a loner. I can't admit to having a best male buddy, just acquaintances, guys I hang out with from time to time." He swallowed, pausing for a moment in thought. "My best friend was my dad. When he died, I was only fourteen."

"I'm sorry," Bernard murmured.

Nick continued as if he didn't hear him. "We were together...when it happened." He stared off into space. His heart started racing like it always did when he thought about that day. "He took me to a baseball game at Shea Stadium. When we got back home, we were tossing the ball back and forth to each other. I missed one of his throws and—" his voice thickened "—it went into the street. Stupid me, I went running after it. I never even heard him yell for me to look out. The next thing I knew, I was thrown onto the sidewalk and my dad was in the middle of the street nearly half a block away. The car that missed me hit him." He took a swallow of his smoothie to keep Bernard from seeing the tears that were burning his eyes. "I don't think my mother ever forgave me. She never came right out and said that it was my fault, but I could see it in her eyes every time she looked at me. I moved out the day after high-school graduation.

"I've never allowed myself those kinds of attachments again. And I know that a lot of how I feel about myself stems from back then. After he died, I didn't know where I fit. I look like my dad, with his strong Italian features, dark hair and eyes and swarthy complexion. So I identified with him, even though my mother's African-American blood runs through my veins, too." He turned his head toward Bernard. "I was lost, just going through the motions until I met Danielle. And now I think she's seeing someone else." He finished off his drink.

"Why would you think that?"

"All the signs are there."

"It could be a lot of things. That's pretty extreme, don't you think? I mean, I've only met her a couple of times, but when I see her look at you, I can't imagine that she looks at anyone else like that."

Nick sputtered a derisive chuckle. "Thanks for the ego boost."

"I wasn't trying to boost your ego, son, I'm just telling you what I see. Take it from one who knows, the woman is in love with you."

"That's where you're wrong. She can barely get the words to frame in her head, least of all say them," he said, the hurt and disappointment tainting his voice.

"It's not about the words. It's about what's in here." He tapped his chest.

Nick laced his fingers together on top of the counter and studied his knuckles. "I never told Dani any of that stuff," he said, so quietly Bernard almost missed it.

"Why don't you talk to her about how you feel? The same way you told me. I think you would be surprised."

"Maybe." He drew himself up, forcing a bright expression on his face. "If you want to get me to sign up with this joint, you'd better catch me now," he said, pushing the conversation and the past into the back of his mind.

Just then the waitress returned with his food.

"I'm sorry. Can you hang on to that for me for a bit—keep it warm? I'll be right back."

"Sure, Bernie."

"Thanks, doll."

"No problem."

Bernard cocked his head toward the registration counter. "Come on, I'll introduce you to the owners. There are only three of them now. One of the original owners, Barbara Allen, moved down south with her new husband."

They stepped up to the horseshoe-shaped desk. "Evenin', ladies," Bernard said to the trio, who had gathered at the counter which was their routine at the end of each evening.

The three were as different as apples, oranges and grapes, Nick observed. One was a stunning petite beauty, barely reaching the shoulders of the other two; one could give Tyra Banks a run for her money; the third reminded him of Angela Bassett, with her wide, open smile and dancing eyes.

"Hey, Bernie," Ann Marie greeted him, followed by Elizabeth and Stephanie.

"I wanted you ladies to meet a new recruit, Nick Mateo."

The Tyra Banks runner-up stuck out her hand. "Stephanie Moore. I'm *supposed* to be the publicist promoting the spa, but it looks like Bernie is after my job." She laughed good-naturedly and winked at Bernard.

Then it was the tiny dynamo. "Ann Marie Dennis, Girl Friday, and the one responsible for securing this building. In my other life I do real estate, so if you're ever in the market, be sure to let me know," she said, with what Nick noticed as a slight Caribbean accent.

"Elizabeth Lewis. I'm the general manager. I actually live on the top floor."

"Yes, she luck out and catch de man who fixin' up de whole damn place," Ann Marie said, laying on her accent hot and heavy. She pursed her lips in feigned annoyance. "Me have to go all the way home to me man. All she 'ave to do is run upstairs. Ya call dat fair?"

The trio chuckled.

Nick couldn't help but laugh.

"Don't hate, as the kids would say," Elizabeth said calmly.

"Anyway," Stephanie cut in. "Don't mind them. It's an everyday thing with those two. So how can I help you?"

"I *think* I want to sign up for membership," Nick said over the remnants of his laughter.

"The more the merrier," Ann Marie said. "Well, folks, I'm heading home to Sterling. See you tomorrow." She turned to Nick. "Nice to meet you. I'm sure you'll enjoy being here. And any friend of Bernard's is a friend of ours." She wagged her fingers and sauntered off, and it was then that Nick noticed that she had on at least three-inch heels and was still no bigger than a minute.

"I'll leave you to take care of your business. I'll be in the café when you're done," Bernie said.

"Sure." He took a seat in one of the leather pedestal chairs, while Stephanie took out some of the brochures and Elizabeth pulled out the paperwork.

* * *

"Wanna grab a beer?" Bernard asked as he and Nick left Pause for Men.

Did he really want to go home to a tiny, empty apartment and lie awake, staring at the ceiling, for the rest of the night?

"Sure. Why not?"

"Great. If you don't mind walking a few blocks, we can go to the Lenox Lounge."

"Sounds great. I haven't been there since—" His thought skidded to a stop. The last time he was there was with Danielle. "—in a while," he finished.

As they strolled through Harlem, the sights and sounds of the famous district surrounded them. Even though many of the historical spots such as Small's Paradise, Copelands, Sugar Hill and other after-hours locales and restaurants were long gone, there was still a pulse, a vitality that one could feel in the air.

They pushed through the doors of the Lenox Lounge and were surprised to find the place packed on a weeknight. Inching their way to the end of the bar, they squeezed in.

The barmaid came down to meet them. "What'll you have?"

"Two beers. Whatever you have on tap," Bernard shouted over the noise of voices and music. The aroma of fried chicken wafted in the air. "What's going on tonight? It's pretty crowded."

"New singer, Dawne. Young sister from Brooklyn. Sounds like a young Aretha. We've been promoting her all week." She expertly filled two mugs to the brim and placed them on the counter. "Four bucks each."

Nick went into his pocket.

Bernard stopped him with a hand on his wrist. "I got it."

"Thanks."

They took their beers to the back room, just as the first set was getting started. As promised, the little powerhouse was a young Aretha in the making who earned the respect and rousing applause of the audience.

By the time they left nearly two hours later, Nick was in a much better frame of mind. They strolled back to their cars, talking about a little bit of everything along the way.

Bernard told Nick about his growing-up years in St. Albans, in Queens, New York, and Nick shared more of his life in Staten Island before moving to Manhattan.

"Hey, I hope you'll come to my wedding," Bernard said.

"Wedding?" Nick asked, stopping in front of his car.

Bernard grinned. "Yeah, I popped the question to Claudia, and she said yes."

Nick stuck out his hand, which Bernard heartily shook. He was beaming like a kid on Christmas.

"Congratulations. I had no idea."

"It's all kind of new. She told Savannah last night."

Nick grinned. "Claudia is a great lady. You're a lucky man."

"When you find someone you love, you can't let them get away. You may not be as lucky the next time." He clapped Nick on the shoulder. "See you at the gym. Thanks for hanging out with an old man." He walked away.

Nick got in his vehicle and sat there for a few minutes, going over his evening with Bernard. He glanced at the time on the digital dash. It was nearly eleven thirty. He put the car in gear and slowly headed home.

Nick took his key out of his pocket and stuck it in the lock. As he'd expected, the apartment was quiet. He tucked his backpack in the hall closet and headed toward the bedroom.

He gently sat down on the side of the bed and leaned over and brushed a lock of hair away from Danielle's face. She stirred. Her eyes fluttered open, and she jerked partially upward and gasped in alarm.

"Shhh. It's me, baby." He leaned down and kissed the top of her head, and she all but crawled into his arms.

He squeezed her to him, stroking her back, and

she held on as if she feared he would vanish like a dream upon awakening.

"I'm sorry," they said in unison, then laughed.

"I'm giving up my apartment tomorrow," he whispered in her ear. "I don't ever want there to be anywhere else I come home to but to you."

Danielle's heart swelled with emotion. Tears of relief and joy slipped from behind her closed lids.

"I don't want you to be anywhere else but here," she whispered.

"Are you sure?"

"I've never been more sure of anything in my life." She slid over in the bed and lifted the covers back.

Nick kicked off his shoes and spooned with her in the bed, not even bothering to get out of his clothes.

Danielle felt the warmth of his breath on her neck, the comfort of his arms around her, the security of the steady beat of his heart, and she knew that somehow things would be all right. She would do whatever she must to ensure it.

And then she felt Nick's hands begin to slowly explore her body, and the rush of anticipation began to fill her. Jean's closing words came to mind. *He'll be back.*

Jean was right, but it was now up to her to make certain that she didn't do anything to make him leave ever again.

She turned onto her back, cupped his face in her

palms. "Let me show you how much I missed you," she said in a husky whisper.

"Whatever you say, baby."

She unzipped him and went to work.

Chapter 9

"Who was at the door?" Danielle asked the following morning as she stepped out of the bathroom.

"Oh, a messenger dropped off a box for you. I left it in the living room. Were you expecting a package?" Nick was busy staring at the computer screen and munching on a blueberry muffin.

"Hmm, no. Don't think so." She wrapped her wet hair in a towel and tightened the belt around her robe, then padded barefoot across the hardwood floors to the living room.

"Your breakfast is in the oven," he called out.

"Thanks!"

She saw the box right away, perched atop the hall table. Unable to imagine what it could be, she frowned, then checked for a name and didn't see one. She took the box over to the couch and began digging it open. Once the top was finally pulled off, her heart thumped. She stole a glance over her shoulder. Gingerly, she took the package out. It was the TLC Bath and Body carrying case.

She was so excited that she nearly squealed in anticipation. With a turn of the catch, the box opened. To the untrained eye the contents were no more sinister than eye shadows, makeup brushes, minidisks of lip gloss, body washes, oils and lotions. But she knew better. Each item had a dual purpose. She lifted the top layer of the case and nestled beneath was the outline of where a .22 would fit.

She'd have to find a secure place to put it. There was no way that she was going to give Nick an opportunity to sample the massage oil that worked like chloroform!

Danielle smiled in triumph. She was now an official member of the Cartel. She ran her hands over the contents.

"So what was it?" Nick said, coming up behind her.

She sucked in a quick breath. "Oh, Savannah convinced me to join Tender Loving Care with her and her mother. It's like Avon." She smiled up at him.

He shook his head and chuckled. "Women and their products. Sure you're going to have time?"

"Well, they have meetings periodically, and you sell at your leisure."

Nick shrugged. "Have fun. I'll be in the workroom. I want to put the contact sheets together."

"Okay."

He stopped and said over his shoulder, "By the way, you can be my Avon Lady anytime."

She laughed, feeling warm all over just thinking about all the naughty things they had done the night before. Her body still tingled. Nick did things with ice cubes that should be illegal. Her still-swollen bud pulsed in agreement. She took the case with the intention of putting it on the top shelf of her closet, when the phone rang. She picked it up in the bedroom.

"Hello?"

"You should have received a package," the now familiar voice said.

"Yes, just a little while ago."

"You'll need to come to the brownstone today and get your assignment. Can you be here by noon?"

Danielle stole a quick glance at the digital clock. "Yes, sure."

"I'll see you at noon. I was right, wasn't I?"

"Right?"

"Yes, about him coming back."

The call disconnected.

Danielle left Nick at the apartment, busily working on the contact sheets from the photo shoots. She headed over to the brownstone. It took the recollection of all of her driver-education classes to keep her from breaking the speed limit. She made it uptown in ten minutes; then it took her another ten minutes to find a parking space.

She took a quick look at the spa across the street. Several men were coming in and out, but thankfully none of them were Bernard. That whole thing with Bernard and Nick, and now Bernard was marrying Claudia—it was all a little much. Nick told her that he'd spent the evening with the man. Bernard just seemed to be everywhere with everyone.

She wasn't sure why it bothered her so much. It just did. She rang the ground-floor bell and was expecting to see Margaret answer the door as usual, but to her surprise it was Claudia.

She greeted Danielle with a big hug. "Hello, sweetheart. Come on in. Congratulations," she added and gently squeezed her arm. "Welcome to the family."

"Thanks. I hear congratulations are in order for you," she said, looking Claudia over and seeing that she was as fashionable as ever in an aqua-blue shirt-dress, with a split along the left side, complemented by a pair of cream sling-backs. And her short, sleek haircut was perfect as always.

Claudia beamed. "Isn't it exciting! I am so happy."

Danielle leaned down and brushed her cheek with a light kiss. "You deserve it."

Claudia's exuberant expression slowly evaporated. She lowered her gaze. "Anna doesn't think so."

"Of course she does. Why would you say that?"

"I know my daughter. I could hear it in her voice."

Danielle took a short breath. How could she tell her that she had her own reservations about Bernard? He seemed to be too good to be true, everyone's best friend. "Savannah will come around. She loves you and wants you to be happy." She hugged Claudia around her shoulders. "You'll see."

Claudia pressed her lips together and nodded. "Well, come on. You don't want to keep Jean waiting."

"Will I see you before I go?"

"I'll be down in the front room working on some reports."

"Okay. And, Claudia, don't worry about Savannah. Promise?"

"Promise," she said, not at all convincingly.

Danielle tapped on Jean's door.

"Come in, Danielle."

This lady really gave her the willies. She came in and closed the door behind her.

"Please have a seat. We have a lot to go over, and I want you to be clear about everything before you leave."

"This is the envelope that was given to Savannah. As you can see, it still has the seal on it. The reason being that once the envelope is opened, the information dissolves within the hour."

Danielle wanted to laugh. It sounded like something Mr. Phelps would say to one of his *Mission: Im-*

possible agents. But she was sure that Jean wouldn't appreciate the humor.

"I'm not sure how much Savannah may or may not have told you, but the assignment is to infiltrate an elite identity theft ring. They have amassed a fortune by taking over the lives of unsuspecting people. They've gained property, bank accounts, credit cards. We know that their base is in New York, but we need them to lead us to the ringleaders." She paused, folded her hands and looked Danielle hard in the eyes. "There's one catch. This assignment is twofold, the government's half and ours."

"Ours?"

"Several of the victims have come to me personally. They…can't go to the authorities. They can't afford to have their backgrounds investigated should this hit the news. Am I clear?"

"Y-yes."

"Good." She slid the envelope across the table. "The list is inside, with all of the information you need to get started." She went into her desk drawer and pulled out a shiny new PDA. It looked simple enough, but Danielle knew that it would be her lifeline. Jean passed the PDA to Danielle. "The Cartel is at your disposal. I'll expect regular updates. Be sure to review the CD that came with your kit."

"I did, but I will again," she said.

"Any questions?"

"I thought TLC worked within the law. Why are

you working with people who don't want to prosecute?"

Jean lifted her chin. "Sometimes in this business we have to do things…that are not sanctioned. And sometimes we do things for friends." She held Danielle's gaze. "If you have any reservations, now is the time to tell me."

Danielle looked at the envelope and the PDA, then at Jean. She thought about Nick.

"I can do this," she said finally.

"Good." Jean stood up. "Good luck."

"Thank you." She got up, took the envelope and PDA and put them in her oversize purse, then turned and walked out.

When she got down to the first floor, Claudia was in the sitting room, going over a stack of papers. She looked up when Danielle crossed the doorway.

"All done?"

"Yep." She joined Claudia on the antique lounge chair. Now that she'd officially gotten the assignment, she felt she could broach the question that had been plaguing her. "Claudia, I have to ask you… I mean, I know that Bernard goes to the spa across the street. He's somehow teamed up with Nick. How do you keep him from finding out about this place?"

Claudia's glance darted away for an instant. "Bernard is very understanding. And I keep up with his schedule and plan my activities accordingly."

Danielle absorbed the information. "I guess it will be a bit easier now," Danielle said, "but when I was leaving here the other night, I ran right into Nick, and I'd seen Bernard earlier. I was a nervous wreck."

"I know, Savannah told me. You'll simply have to be careful, Dani. They must never know."

Danielle nodded. "Well, thanks for the advice. I need to get going. Nick will be wondering what happened to me."

"You take care, sweetheart," Claudia said, walking Danielle to the door. "And you know if you need anything, I'm here to help in any way that I can."

"Thanks." She gave a shaky smile. "I'm going to need it."

Danielle headed back home, eager to review the contents of the envelope. Identity theft, she thought. Of all the assignments to get, she landed the one thing she'd been battling with her entire life—*identity.*

Although hers hadn't been "stolen," she'd always battled with who she was. But even more pressing in her mind was who the people were who couldn't go to the police.

Curiosity was gnawing at her, but she knew that she had a short window to review the material before the ink dissolved. She couldn't risk pulling over and tearing the envelope open before she was someplace private and quiet.

Then she thought about the library on 136th Street. She could have all the privacy and quiet she needed. She made the turn and drove toward Adam Clayton Powell Jr. Boulevard and 136th Street.

She parked in the lot across the street and hopped out. Once inside, she found one of the computer tables that also had Internet access. Her privacy was afforded by the two short partitions on either side of the desk where she sat.

Her fingers shook as she took the envelope from her bag. She looked around, took a deep breath and lifted the seal. Slowly she pulled the pages out of the envelope.

For the next hour she went over the material. Each of the eight pages highlighted the victims, providing details of all their personal information and the degree to which they'd been violated. The names weren't familiar, but the level to which they'd been taken advantage of was mind-boggling.

Their computers had been hacked and all of their personal information accessed: passwords, banking information and credit-card numbers. In two of the cases, victims reported that though they'd never been to the Caribbean or to Europe, there were massive charges to their credit cards to prove they'd traveled there, along with airline manifest lists showing that they'd been on flights they'd never taken. Which meant that not only their finances were accessed, but also *who* they were. Somewhere, these people were actually posing as the victims, complete with driver's licenses, birth certificates and passports.

Danielle keyed all the victims' names into her

PDA, along with contact information, then saved it with a pass code, as she'd been instructed. Although all the information in her PDA was encrypted, it didn't hurt to take that one extra step, Jasmine had advised during her training.

The most disturbing were the victims who refused to go to the authorities. And when it registered who they were, Danielle immediately knew why.

One was Doris and Richard Matlock. He was the CEO of Empress Oil, one of the largest distributors of oil in the United States, with connections in the Middle East.

The other was Leslie Davenport, head of the Davenport Foundation, which was responsible for overseeing more than fifty charity and nonprofit organizations in New York.

Danielle leaned back in the chair, stunned. This was major. When she'd read stories about identity theft, she'd never comprehended the magnitude of how it could devastate people's lives. It was disturbing that people wanted to hide the fact that they'd been duped.

She put those pages aside and began to go over the information that had been gathered to date. It was clear that the central headquarters was headed by someone inside New York City and that there were several levels of people involved—from the top man or woman to the actual thieves themselves. It was also clear that at some point the victims must have come in contact with the thieves either in their daily lives or through business.

There was a short list of possible places to start. Whoever was behind this was highly skilled technologically and could move in and out of elite circles without being questioned. What struck her as most chilling was that these people, whoever they were, actually masqueraded as the victims in public places and were able to get away with it.

She made some additional notes in her PDA, then continued to read the backup information.

There was a paragraph about a man who'd been on the watch list for about six months, but they could never tie him to anything. They believed he was high up in the chain of command and were certain that the name he was using was false. *Bernard Hassell*.

Danielle stopped breathing. She blinked several times, rubbed her eyes and read the name again. It had to be wrong, she thought, as her head began to pound. "There must be a million Bernard Hassells," she sputtered nervously.

She read on and the information gave her a link to a photograph. With shaky fingers she picked up her PDA and after several attempts was able to finally key in the link information. Her heart pounded and her stomach rose and fell as she waited for the image to appear. She was sure that there was some kind of mistake and her own vivid imagination was simply in overdrive. To think that the Bernard she knew and the one in this file were the same person was ridiculous.

The image began to unfold on the sixteen-inch-wide screen.

Danielle's loud gasp turned several curious heads in her direction. The last thing she needed was to draw attention to herself. She focused on the images and information on the screen.

She covered her mouth in shocked disbelief. Bernard Hassell, Claudia's fiancé, Savannah's potential stepfather and now Nick's new buddy, stared back at her.

Chapter 10

Danielle sat there unable to move. She sat there for so long—staring at the image and trying to slow down her racing thoughts—that when she pulled herself together, she noticed that the ink on the pages was beginning to lighten. The first page was already blank.

She didn't even care. She felt ill. What was she going to do? How in good conscience could she not tell Claudia? Or Savannah or Nick?

But what if the information was wrong? she reasoned. That was possible. Maybe it only appeared that Bernard was someone involved. Innocent people are implicated in things all the time.

Her gut told her something else entirely. And that

was that Jean Armstrong didn't make mistakes—not a mistake like this one—which meant that she already knew about Claudia and Bernard…like she knew about everything.

What really made her stomach turn was the fact that Jean had planned to give this assignment to Savannah. How was she supposed to handle this information when it related to her own mother?

My God, Jean, what kind of bitch are you?

Anger flushed through her system. Now they were messing with her friends, her surrogate family. That made it all very personal.

She snatched up the now blank pages, stuffed them into her bag, turned off her PDA and dropped it inside as well. All she could see was red, and she knew she needed to get to her car and calm down so that she could think and work out a plan.

The trouble was, as much as Jean told her that the Cartel resources were available to her and she could always use one of the members for assistance, that, too, was a bunch of crap. How? How could she possibly bring in any of the members on something so sensitive? She'd never want any of them to know that Claudia was involved with someone who was being investigated in a major series of crimes.

After sliding into the driver's seat, she slammed her fist against the steering wheel, but she was so angry she barely registered the shock of pain that jetted up her arm.

Danielle lowered her head onto the wheel and took

in long, deep breaths. She had to be clearheaded. She couldn't overreact and allow her feelings to make mistakes for her.

She looked up. First things first—go home to her man. Then she'd take one step at a time.

When she got back to her apartment, Nick was on his way out.

"Hey, babe. I'm heading out for a few." He slung his knapsack over his right shoulder. He turned and actually focused on her. His brow wrinkled. "You okay? You look like you ate something bad." He walked over to her.

"I'm fine." She smiled. "I was hoping we could spend the afternoon together," she said, feeling the need to be with and hold on to something real.

"Wow. I figured you'd be gone for a while. I decided to get a jump on the JCPenney project. I'm going with Mark to scout out some locations." He cupped her chin. "I promise, I'll be back as soon as I can." He leaned down and kissed her, giving her just a little bit of tongue.

Danielle suddenly clung to him, wrapping her arms tightly around his neck. She buried her face in the hollow of his neck and inhaled his scent.

"I swear, I won't be more than two hours," he said lightly. He leaned back, looked down at her and lifted her chin with the tip of his finger. His eyes ran back and forth across her face. "Then I'm all yours, okay?"

She nodded, not daring to speak over the knot in her throat.

"Be back before you know it." He pecked her lips one last time, then headed out.

Danielle released a long, heavy sigh and aimlessly wandered through the apartment, trying to line up her thoughts. She finally plopped down on the living-room couch, her long legs splayed out in front of her. She folded her arms across her stomach and stared across the room at a piece of art by Budson, an Atlanta-based artist, that hung on the far wall.

It was the photograph of a man and woman intertwined on what looked like a couch. But their bodies were so intricately coupled that it was hard to determine where one began and the other ended.

How appropriate that she would have a picture where the identities in the portrait were marred by illusion.

There'd been moments on the drive home that she'd begun to believe she was the wrong person for this assignment. But in examining the portrait and her life, she thought, who better than she to uncover those who pretend to be something they aren't?

Hadn't she been pretending all her life, allowing her looks—her silky hair and exotic features—to gain her access to people and places she wouldn't have otherwise had access to? It was so much easier in life to go through the open doors rather than having to knock them down. She'd never had to stand up for a cause in her life. She didn't have to. Those ugly things in the world didn't apply to her. She was above it all, moving through life in that privileged circle of acceptance. She'd gotten so good at it that she'd forgotten she wasn't really one of the chosen ones. That was until she looked at a family portrait, the picture of her father, dark as a moonless night and her mother light as a brand-new day, with ink-colored hair that met the rise of her behind.

For years the stares from strangers made her secretly ashamed of her father's blackness, his coarse hair, wide nose and thick lips. And she hated the taunts her classmates tossed at her about her father's strong ethnic features.

Every guy she'd dated since high school had been white or Hispanic or a light-skinned black with "good hair." All practices and beliefs that had been unconsciously ingrained in her from her grandmother—things she'd been unable to shake all these years.

That was the ugliness that stalked her thoughts and emotions day in and day out. She rested her head back against the cushion of the couch and closed her eyes. It was the shadow that hovered around her heart when it came to Nick and her feelings for him.

Was she with him because he fit the image she'd imposed on herself years ago, or did she really care for him? Or worse, did she care for him only because of his appearance and not for who he was?

She hadn't seen her parents in years, and she felt the always present ache in her heart. Only her closest friends—Nia and Savannah—even knew who her parents were.

In college, the girls had always teased her about her choice in men, dating only the white or pretty boys. But to this day, neither Nia nor Savannah knew the terror that lurked in her heart about one day settling down and having a child that looked like her dad. A child who would grow up in a world that valued looks over substance. A child who would be teased by classmates and would begin to devalue themselves, and the vicious cycle would continue.

She'd never forget the time she was walking into the apartment building where they lived when she was about twelve. The downstairs neighbors were in the hallway talking when she came in from school.

"Hi, Mrs. Walker, Ms. Daisy."

"Hi. Looking beautiful as always," Mrs. Walker said.

"Had a good day at school?" Ms. Daisy asked.

"Yep." She started up the steps and was on the next landing putting her key in the door to her apartment when their voices floated up to her.

"Her father is going to have some time keeping the boys away when she gets to dating age," Danielle heard Mrs. Walker say.

"All he has to do is show that ugly black face and scare them away!"

They laughed as if that was the best joke.

"I swear that child's mama must have been drunk when she laid down with that man."

"Chile is lucky she looks like her mama…"

And she had been "lucky" that she looked like her mother. It had given her a free pass in life. She never had to do much more than smile. Even her business was an outgrowth of all the self-hatred that she had about herself and who she was. What did she choose for a career? Photographing beautiful people and beautiful clothes, creating images that no one could ever live up to.

Knowing that about herself made her sick. She might be able to deceive others but never herself. The truth was evident each time she looked in the mirror. She was a fake. Just like the people she had to go after. She had to do this. She had to, not only for the victims but for herself.

Danielle sniffed hard and realized she was crying. She swiped away at the tears with the back of her hand just as the phone rang, and went to the kitchen to get it. She cleared her throat.

"Hello."

"You could sound more enthused to hear from me!"

Danielle's sour mood quickly elevated.

"Nia! Girl, how are you? Are you home?"

"On my way. I just landed at JFK. We're pulling up to the gate."

Suddenly Danielle felt as if she would burst into tears. "It's so good to hear your voice," she said, even as hers cracked with emotion.

"Dani, what's wrong? I know you didn't miss me that much."

Nia was always able to read her like a book. She sniffed. "Just can't wait to see you." She paused. "I need someone to talk to." Tears spilled down her cheeks.

"I have a car waiting for me. I'm going to swing by your place on the way home. It sounds like you need one of my famous meals."

Danielle laughed lightly through her tears. "Thanks."

"Give Savannah a call and tell her to meet us when she gets off work."

"No!"

"Why? What's up? Did you and Anna have a falling out?"

Danielle swallowed. "No. It's nothing like that. It's—it's just the things I need to say to you. I can't have Savannah hear them."

"Oh" was all Nia could initially manage. "Whatever it is, we'll work it out, sweetie. Promise. Now put on something fierce and I'll see you soon."

"Thanks, Nia."

"Hey, what are friends for?"

The call disconnected.

Exactly, Danielle thought. What are friends for if not to have each other's back? She'd work this out. One way or the other.

Chapter 11

On the ride from Danielle's apartment to Nia's co-op, Nia filled Danielle's ear with tales from her trip, the exciting people she'd met and the killer client list she'd built.

Nia Turner's success was hinged on who she knew. And in New York, Nia knew everyone. As an event planner for major corporations and moneybag clients, she had to know the best restaurants, chefs, vacation spots, airlines, designers—everyone who was anyone and all of their assistants. Nia was on a first-name basis with virtually every secretary in the city. It always pays to get in good with the secretaries and personal assistants, she'd often said. They know everything and will be the ones to get you behind closed doors when no one else can.

Nothing could have been more true. Nia's connections had garnered the trio the prime tables in restaurants, best seats at premieres and countless free trips to exotic resorts and spas.

She may be a bit anal at times with her quirks about perfection and time, Danielle thought, but she more than made up for it with her giving nature.

"Wow, it's good to be home," Nia enthused once the key turned the lock and the door swung open. She dropped her bags in the hallway and strolled through her space, spinning around in a circle—for a moment Danielle thought Nia might do that Mary Tyler Moore move and throw her hat up in the air.

Instead, Nia collapsed into a champagne-colored armchair and kicked off her shoes.

"I'm not sure what's in the fridge. Steve isn't much of a cook or shopper," she said with a soft smile framing her full mouth.

"Did you call him to let him know you were back?"

"Yep. He said he would try to get home early. He and Blake were working on a new project, and they had a late meeting set up." She angled her head to the side. "You wanna talk or you wanna eat?"

Danielle smiled. "Both."

Nia pushed herself up from the chair and grabbed Danielle's hand. "Come on and tell me all about it."

As Danielle washed romaine lettuce and diced cucumbers and tomatoes, Nia seasoned a fresh piece of salmon to get it ready for baking.

Danielle talked as she worked, bringing Nia up-to-the-minute information on what she'd been assigned to do, and the ambivalence she felt in doing it.

"Dayum," Nia murmured. "This would kill Claudia—if it's true," she qualified.

"I know. But like I've been saying, there's been something bugging me about Bernard since the day he showed up at my apartment with Nick."

"Right. I remember." She turned and glanced at Danielle over her shoulder. "Sorry I just tossed your concerns off."

Danielle waved off the apology. "No need to apologize. You didn't know and neither did I. But now we do."

"Wow, suppose Bernard is trying to get close to Nick to steal his identity or yours."

Danielle chuckled at that. "I think he would really be pissed off if he did. I have about ten dollars more than zero."

"Chile, please. I know you are doing well."

"I know, but not the kind of *well* that these people are interested in. You should see the list and what's been taken from them. Scary."

Nia put the tray with the salmon in the oven, rinsed her hands and joined Danielle at the kitchen table. She dried her hands on a paper towel, rolled it into a ball and set it on the center of the table.

"So what's your plan?" Nia asked.

"I'm figuring the first thing I need to do is work

with what I know. And the only one that I know in this scenario is Bernard."

"Makes sense," Nia said. She played with the rolled-up paper towel for a moment, hoping that, given some breathing room, Danielle would spill the rest on her own. Several moments passed. "Okay, now that we have all that nasty spy business out of the way, you want to tell me what's really bothering you? I could hear it in your voice, and I know it's not about the case, especially if you didn't want Savannah to be here."

Danielle glanced away; she didn't want Nia to see the self-hatred that hung in her eyes or the guilt that colored her life.

"Whatever it is, talking about it will help. It always does," she said gently. "Did something happen between you and Savannah?"

Danielle shook her head. "No. Nothing like that." She swallowed, her throat feeling thick and tight. She reached for the glass of spring water and took a long swallow. Slowly she lowered the glass.

"There are things…that you don't know about me, things that I'm ashamed of."

"Ashamed of? Like what? We all have something about ourselves that we don't like. How bad could it be?"

"Ashamed of who I am," she said in a monotone. She looked straight at Nia.

Nia frowned in confusion. "What do you mean?"

Danielle looked away, beyond Nia, back to a time

in her life that she'd never wanted to revisit but which had tainted every move she'd made ever since.

She was a senior in college and madly in love with Michael Fleming, a grad student in the art department. Michael was one of the beautiful people. Everything about him was perfect, from the shape of his eyes and the sweep of his thick brows to the body of Adonis and the pinch of cinnamon on his skin, giving him the appearance of a year-round tan. Not only was Michael heavenly to look at, but he was wealthy to boot. His father, Jackson Fleming, made his mint with hotels, running one of the most successful privately owned hotel chains in the country. He started out with a ten-room motel in Silver Springs, Maryland, which grew to fifteen hotels and resorts throughout the United States. Fleming Hotel and Resorts were synonymous with class and money.

As the only child, Michael would inherit it all as long as he toed daddy's line: went to school, got his master's and brought home the perfect wife to carry on the Fleming legacy.

Danielle was completely captivated by Michael. He took her places she'd only dreamed of, such as a spur-of-the-moment weekend in Paris, skiing in Aspen or dinner on his father's yacht. And they would always end their evenings making love.

Michael was as gifted in bed as he was in looks and stature. She'd been with a few men before him but none who could satisfy her. All along she'd been faking it, not wanting to hurt anyone's feelings, but with Michael it was real and so damned good she knew she was addicted. She couldn't get enough of him, and they made love every chance they got.

Michael was exceptionally virile one particular night. They'd just come home from an art gallery opening when they tumbled into Danielle's tiny one-bedroom apartment in lower Manhattan, better known as Alphabet City. Danielle lived on Avenue C in a five-story walk-up. She was on the third floor.

She turned the key in the lock, and the instant the door opened, Michael swept her up in his arms and took her to the bedroom. He plopped her down on the bed even as he was taking off his pristine white shirt, tossing it to the floor.

Danielle scrambled out of her peasant skirt and shirred blouse, her heart puttering like crazy from seeing the hot look in his eyes.

Before she knew what was happening, Michael was all over her. There didn't seem to be a spot on her body that he didn't pay homage to.

The force of his entry pinned her to the mattress and trapped the strangled cry of exquisite pleasure in her throat. He rode her like a man who'd lost his way in the dark, had been starved, afraid, lonely and had suddenly seen daylight—and everything he'd ever wanted was only a stroke away—and he moved toward it as hard and as fast as he could.

Danielle felt the incredible hardness of him fill every square inch of her, and she knew that at any moment Michael would find his release and she wanted to be there with him.

He grabbed her, wrapping his arms around her body. She locked her ankles behind his back, sealing them together.

Michael's heartbeat slammed against Danielle's breasts. The veins in his neck bulged as sweat dripped from his forehead down the valley of her chest.

He groaned, so deep and hard as he pushed inside her to the hilt.

"Marry me," he said on a ragged breath.

Danielle's mind spun.

He pounded into her again. "Marry...me."

Her body was on fire. She was searing with wet, hot need. His thrusts sent shards of electricity racing through her limbs, short-circuiting her brain.

"Say yes," he demanded. He ground his hips against her, and an explosion of lights erupted behind her eyelids. Her body shook as wave after wave of satisfaction coursed through her. "Say it," he urged as he leaned down, took a nipple into his mouth and pushed her completely over the edge.

"Yes!" she screamed at the moment that Michael emptied himself into her.

"Did you mean that?" she asked a bit later as they lay entwined with each other on the damp and twisted sheets.

He pushed her hair away from her face and looked into her uncertain eyes.

"Of course I meant it. I love you. I'm crazy about you and I want to spend the rest of my life with you." He brushed her slightly swollen lips with the tip of his thumb. "Do you feel the same way about me?"

She nodded vigorously, too overcome to speak. This was more than she could have ever hoped to have happen to her. Michael Fleming was considered one of the greatest catches of his generation. And he was hers. She was going to be Mrs. Michael Fleming. It must be a dream.

For the next two weeks, whenever they had free time, they were shopping for the perfect engagement ring. They finally found what they were looking for in a specialty diamond shop on Fifth Avenue in Manhattan. It was a marquis diamond surrounded by eight baguettes and set in platinum.

"Oh, Michael, it's incredible."

"Just like you." He kissed her tenderly. "We'll take it," Michael said to the dealer before taking her mouth again.

"This feels like some kind of dream," she whispered.

"If it is, I never want to wake up."

But she did wake up, much sooner than she would have wanted.

She'd met Michael's parents on several occasions; now it was her turn to introduce her parents to them. In the days leading up to the lunch she'd planned for her parents and Michael's parents, she'd wondered why she'd never discussed her parentage and her own mixed ethnicity with Michael. It just wasn't something that came up in everyday conversation. She should have and could have avoided the humiliation that ensued.

But she hadn't, and now here she was in the middle of Cipriani's, with the wall of politeness so thick that none of the six people sitting at the table could speak for fear of saying what was really on their minds and causing the thin thread of civility to snap.

When Michael's mother was introduced to Danielle's father, her mouth dropped open. From some deep reserve of upbringing, she forced a smile, and maneuvered herself in such a way that she sat down before she had to shake his outstretched hand.

Mr. Fleming cleared his throat after the waiter came and placed the menus on the table. "So where did you two meet?"

Danielle's mother spoke up. "We both worked for the board of education."

"Maintenance?" Mrs. Fleming asked. "I mean, not teachers."

"I'm a science teacher and my wife teaches math."

"How interesting," Mrs. Fleming said. "Affirmative action is such a wonderful thing. Isn't it, dear," she said to her husband.

Inwardly, Danielle grew smaller and smaller, imagining what was going through Mr. and Mrs. Fleming's minds, seeing the pain on her mother's and father's faces and not caring. All she wanted was for the afternoon to be over.

"I'm going to, uh, spend the night with my folks out on Long Island tonight," Michael said, pulling her aside after the excruciatingly long two-hour lunch. His parents had already said their goodbyes, paid the check and were outside. But not before pulling Michael off to the side to speak with him privately.

Danielle's heart was in her throat. She gripped his hands, her diamond flashing in the afternoon sun. "Michael…"

"I have to go. I'll call you later on tonight." He turned without another word and walked out.

"He seems like a very nice young man," her mother said, slowly rising from her seat.

Danielle turned to her mother and father, simple, ordinary, decent people whom she knew loved her without question and she wished that they would disappear.

"I've got to get home. I have a test in the morning." She couldn't look them in the eye.

"They seem like nice enough people," her father said, speaking for the first time in a while. "But they are the kind of people who look at you from the outside. It wouldn't matter what you were made of. And I'm sorry to say, their son is no different."

"What do you know? What do you know about anything?" She leaped up from her seat, knocking a teacup to the floor. "I hate you. Both of you. You've ruined everything." She spun away and ran out into the street and kept on running until she was out of breath and soaking wet with perspiration. She stopped on a corner, hailed a cab and went home, fully expecting a message from Michael.

"But he didn't call," Danielle said, still trapped in time. "Not that night or the next. I didn't hear from him for about a week. Finally I couldn't take it anymore and went looking for him in every classroom on his campus. I finally found him, and he acted like he didn't know me."

"Talk to me, Mike. This is me, Danielle, the woman you swore to love, the woman you gave this to," she had pleaded. She held out her hand, and the diamond sparkled in the sunlight.

"It's best if we…don't see each other, Danielle," he said coldly, as if he were reading a laundry list of chores.

The world seemed to stand still. What he said didn't make any sense. "What…are you saying?" She grabbed his arm. "You love me! What do you mean? We're supposed to get married."

"Don't do this, Dani." He tried to pull away.

"Do what? Ask you to explain why you're doing this? Tell me, dammit!"

"Fine! There's no way that I can marry you and take the chance on…on having a child that…looks like your father."

The air was sucked out of her lungs. The pulse in her temples pounded, blurring her vision. When the world around her came back into focus, Michael was halfway across campus.

"Dani, I'm so sorry." Nia reached across the table to cover her hand. "He was a bastard. It's his loss."

Tears fell in a steady stream down her face. She swiped them away with the back of her hand but they were immediately replaced.

"About a month later I found out I was pregnant."

Nia squeezed her hand a bit tighter.

"I don't know if it was fate or fortune. Before I could digest what I was going to do, I had a miscarriage."

Nia was speechless. This was an entire era of her friend's life that she knew nothing about.

Danielle sniffed hard. "It was one thing for me to endure harsh criticism and ugly words about my parents from other people, but for them to be voiced by someone I believed myself to be in love with only validated the ugliness of it all."

"Dani, that was a long time ago. You're all grown up, a different person."

"That's just it, I'm not different. At least I'm not sure if I am. That day did something to me. It stole a piece of me. I haven't dared allowed myself to feel that way again about anyone. I didn't want to take the chance…"

"Until Nick?"

Danielle nodded. "But what terrifies me is I don't know if the way I feel about him is real or if it's simply easy because of how he looks—the pretty boy—the image I've worked out in my mind that is right for me. And what if he met my parents? It would kill me if he reacted the way Michael did. I couldn't take it."

Nia suddenly stood and Danielle was sure she'd gone too far, opened up a door that couldn't be closed. Now she'd lost her friend.

Nia crossed the room and went to the sink. She kept her back to Danielle.

"Dani, all of us have crap about ourselves that we don't like. We do things in life that we are not proud of." She turned to face her and leaned back against the sink as she spoke. "But what separates us from the four-legged creatures is our conscience and our ability to think things through and change the things that are wrong.

"Nick loves you. And I believe that you love him, too—for all the right reasons. But at some point you are going to have to let go of the past so that you can live for the now and move into the future. You'll never know the kind of man Nick is or the kind of woman you are until you give him the chance to show you. You've got to trust his love for you, or you'll never find happiness with him or anyone."

Danielle's smile was wobbly at best. "For someone who just found Mr. Right, you sure have a lot of good advice."

"I've been practicing."

By the time Danielle returned to her apartment, she was feeling much better. Nia had a way of turning lemons into lemonade, even if the lemons were rotten.

As much as she dreaded the inevitable, at some point she was going to have to be totally honest with Nick about everything. Well…almost everything.

She sauntered in, full of purpose, and was secretly glad that Nick hadn't gotten back yet. The scouting must have taken longer than he thought. She headed for the bedroom and was going to use her time alone to do some investigating. But she had no intention of being caught off guard when Nick could walk through the door at any moment. She called him on his cell phone. It rang three times before he picked up.

"Hey, babe. Actually we finished up about an hour ago," Nick said. "But I decided to run over to the gym. And guess who I ran into? Bernard. So we're gonna hang out for a bit and then I'll be home. See you soon. Okay?"

He stuck his cell back in its case on his hip, smiling as he did so.

"That must have been your lady love," Bernard said, coming up to Nick, a towel draped around his neck. He mopped his face with the tail of the towel.

"That transparent, huh?"

"It's a vibe and a look in the eye. Nothing wrong with that. Let's other ladies know that you're taken. Cuts down on a lot of drama," he said with a chuckle.

"Yeah, you're probably right."

They walked toward the treadmill.

"Have you and Claudia set a date yet?"

"I'd prefer sooner rather than later, something small and intimate. But Claudia is not hearing that. She wants the whole package."

"Well, from what I hear, weddings are all about the women anyway. The guys are just told where to show up and when."

Both men laughed.

"You're absolutely right," Bernard said.

"You ever been married before?" Nick asked.

"No."

"Any reason?"

Bernard turned on his machine, and the track beneath his feet began to move. Nick followed suit.

"Never found the right woman who could deal with my long hours and weeks of being away from home."

"Oh." Nick pushed up the dial to heighten the incline. "I don't think I've ever asked you what you do...or did." He blew out slowly through his mouth and inhaled deeply.

"Army, for a lot of years."

"Really," he said, beginning to feel the burn in his upper thighs. "How many?"

"I retired after twenty-five years," he said, still not breaking a sweat.

"Long time. You into anything now?"

Bernard turned his head to look at Nick. "Pretty much whatever I want."

Nick chuckled. "What a life."

* * *

Although Nia could not "officially" be involved, she'd promised Danielle she'd make some discreet inquiries regarding Bernard. It would be up to Danielle, however, to get some basics.

Her kit came equipped with hacking software that Jasmine had gleefully showed her how to use. She went to the closet and took the kit down from the top shelf.

Taking it to the bed, she opened the top and took out an innocuous-looking compact. She opened it and pried behind the mirror to reveal a small computer disk. The disk contained six hacking programs that would gain her access to the three major credit-card companies, Department of Health, phone company, Department of Motor Vehicles, Social Security Administration and Internal Revenue Service.

She put the disk into her laptop. First she accessed the Department of Health database, entered Bernard's approximate age and keyed in his name. The list was too long to even bother with. From there she tried the phone company, and as bizarre as it was, there wasn't one listing in Manhattan for Bernard Hassell. He didn't even show up in the unlisted directory. Maybe he used only a cell phone, like many people did these days. But it was still curious. She tried the credit-card companies, the IRS and the Department of Motor Vehicles. Either she came up blank, more often than not, or the profiles didn't match.

Frustrated, Danielle ejected the disk and returned it to its hiding place. She was going to need more concrete information to go on in order to narrow her search. But the more she thought about it, the more concerned she became. Something wasn't right.

Bernard wasn't the only piece of the puzzle, however. There were the victims she needed to concentrate on to find out who had stolen their identities.

She began by plugging the names, one by one, into the PDA while waiting for the Wi-Fi to connect with the main terminal at the brownstone. Within moments she had access to their computers.

She made notes and planned to give the list to Nia to see if she knew or had knowledge of anyone on it.

Danielle shut down the computer and turned off the PDA. At least now she didn't feel so helpless. She was doing something. Somehow she had to get behind the wall that Bernard Hassell had built around himself. There had to be an opening somewhere. What she needed was some inside information. And since she couldn't very well ask the astute Claudia, the next likely candidate was Nick.

Chapter 12

"So you and Bernard are getting to be pretty good friends," Danielle mentioned casually as they sat on the couch watching Jay Leno on *The Tonight Show.*

"He's a really decent guy," Nick said. "I like him."

"He must be nice for Claudia to decide to marry him."

"True," he said absentmindedly then tossed his head back and laughed at one of Jay's barbs about dumb criminals.

"Where is he from?"

"Who?"

"Bernard."

"Oh, uh, I think he told me he was originally from D.C."

She filed that bit of information away. "Is he working now or retired?"

He played with a lock of her hair while he listened to the rest of the "Headlines." It was his favorite portion of the show.

Danielle gently nudged him in the ribs.

"Ouch, what did I do?"

"I'm talking to you, and you're not even paying me any attention."

"I'm sorry, what did you say?"

A commercial was on, so she had his full attention.

"I was asking you what Bernard does for a living or if he's retired?"

"Oh. Retired from the army. Did twenty-five years."

"Hmm, impressive." There had to be some information on him if he'd been in the army. "He lives in Manhattan, right?"

"Yeah. Why are you so interested in Bernard all of a sudden?"

Her stomach clenched. She shrugged. "No special interest. You know all of my friends, and since he seems to be one of yours now and is going to marry my best friend's mother, I want to get an idea of who he is. That's all."

"Well, I mean, he's a nice guy. Good listener, funny, likes sports and working out in the gym. What else is there?" He turned to her and grinned. "Satisfied, Sherlock?"

"Very funny." She settled down into his embrace and pretended to focus on the rest of the show, but her mind was a million miles away.

The following morning they were greeted by dark skies and torrents of rain. According to the forecast the rest of the day wouldn't be much better.

Nick was in the kitchen scrambling some eggs when Danielle joined him, her face still soft from sleep.

"Mornin'."

"Hi," she said over a yawn and plopped down at the table. "Smells good."

"Want me to fix you a plate?"

"No, coffee is good."

"Oh, I turned in my keys to my place yesterday and paid them for the last month's rent. So I guess you're stuck with me for real."

She laughed lightly in response. "Looks that way. But who's complaining." She winked at him.

As she sat there allowing her head to clear, she watched Nick as he worked. He was a wonderful man in every way. Any woman would be lucky to have him. He was handsome, sexy, an unselfish lover, funny and talented. Not to mention a great cook.

So she asked herself again, why couldn't she commit? Why couldn't she tell him that she loved him? Why? The question constantly reverberated in her head.

She knew Nick would move mountains to make

her happy. Was she willing to do the same? She sighed deeply. They'd only been a couple for less than a year, and had worked together for slightly longer than that.

She'd been reluctant to move out of the safety of a coworker relationship into a personal one. But Nick wouldn't be dissuaded.

"I knew you were the one for me the day you hired me," he'd confessed to her one night over dinner during the early days of their romance.

She grinned. "Is that so?"

"For real."

"How did you know?"

"When I stepped into the studio and caught a glimpse of you behind the camera doing your thing, something happened to me inside. I know it sounds corny but it's true. Then after I got to talk to you and you hired me on the team, it was eating me up inside to be so close to you and not be able to do anything about it."

"I've broken every rule in the 'employer's handbook' by going out with you."

"I know. You risked a lot. And I'm going to prove to you that you didn't make a mistake."

And he had. There wasn't a day that went by that Nick didn't try to show her how much he cared, from keeping their relationship out of the spotlight at work to fixing dinner, running her bath and most recently giving up his apartment.

He'd turned his heart and his life over to her, but

she didn't seem able to do the same. And as much as he loved her, she wasn't sure how long her lack of indecisiveness with regard to their relationship could go on without him deciding to leave.

He brought his plate of eggs to the table, then the pot of coffee. He filled her mug and sat down.

"I already called the crew to cancel for today. Even if the rain stops, there's no way we can get any decent shots."

She nodded in agreement and took a sip of her coffee. "It worked out anyway. I totally forgot I have an appointment at the Preston Studio this afternoon. I need to go over their schedule to coordinate the photography time."

"Well, while you're gone I'll get with the crew and the models to reschedule. We should have had a plan B in place for something just like this—an alternative indoor location."

"We usually do. I guess it just slipped under the radar."

"We'll plan better next time. Did you rest well?"

"Yes, I think so. Why?"

"You were mumbling in your sleep last night."

Her nerves tightened. "Really? Did I say anything interesting?"

"Got me. Sounded like you were talking about a *cartel*." He chuckled and she almost strangled on her coffee. "Must have been the aftereffects of something you watched on TV." He forked a mouthful of eggs and chewed slowly.

"Yeah, I guess," she muttered.

He finished his eggs and took his plate to the sink. "I'm going to get busy contacting folks and coordinating schedules." He ruffled her hair as he walked by her.

She felt light-headed. *Talking in her sleep.* She never knew she did that, but then again until you sleep with someone every night, who was going to tell you? What if she'd really said something damaging, incriminating? Oh, God. The coffee in her stomach burned.

Danielle arrived at the Michael Preston Studio shortly before two. This time Tasha was waiting for her at the reception desk. She stuck out her hand.

"Good to see you again. Horrible day out. You can drop your umbrella in the stand by the desk."

"Thanks." She took off her light raincoat and gently shook her umbrella before depositing it in the stand, then followed Tasha down the corridor.

"Come right in," she said, holding open the door to her office. "So how have you been?" She walked around the large desk that was covered in swatches of fabric and photographs.

"Busy," Danielle said. "But that's a good thing."

"Please excuse the mess and have a seat at the conference table. It will be much easier to work." Tasha opened a large file cabinet that was built into the wall and extracted an oversize portfolio and brought it to the table. She began flipping through the pages, talking as she did so.

"These are the models that we will use for the collection. But what I'd like you to do is meet with them and get a sense of who they are and how they work. Since everyone is so busy, scheduling is going to be a major undertaking. But I can have one of the assistants take care of that."

"Fine."

"I'm thinking it will take a couple of weeks to pull it all together before we can even get started. But I'm sure we should be ready with everyone in place no later than the second week in June. By that time all of the pieces will be completed."

Danielle was taking notes as Tasha spoke.

"I think I counted fifteen models. Is that right?"

Tasha grinned. "On the money. I'd like to take you on a tour of the showroom. The designers have been working nonstop to get everything ready. Many of the new items are available for viewing."

"Sure." She draped her jacket and purse across her arm and followed Tasha out.

The designs for the most part were typical Michael Preston, clean lines, all-American look. His new collection, however, was in bold colors with mix-and-match pieces that could easily go from a day at the office to a night on the town.

"I love what I'm seeing," Danielle said as they made the rounds through the studio.

"Michael wanted to go in a different direction for

the fall but still maintain his signature look. We're all very happy with the results."

"I'm sure the store buyers and the ladies will be as well. I know I can do some great things in shooting this line."

Tasha looked purposefully at Danielle. "That's why we hired you. We only want the best."

Danielle's ego had been suitably stroked by the time she left the showroom. She had her work cut out for her, but she had a great team, she thought as she stepped off the elevator and ran right into the woman she'd met a couple of days earlier.

"Alicia Keys!" the woman joked. "Back again, I see."

"I had a meeting."

"My offer still stands. The pay is great, easy hours."

"I don't think so," Danielle said, stepping around her.

"Well, if you change your mind, my office is on twenty."

Danielle pushed a smile across her mouth and walked to the exit.

What people won't do for money, she thought as she stepped out into the rain. She opened her umbrella and darted and dodged around the flow of human traffic until she reached the garage at the end of the street where her car was parked. And just before she went down the ramp, she glanced up the street and could have sworn she saw Bernard coming out of the building she'd just left.

She tried to get a better look, but there were too many people and umbrellas blocking her view. When her line of sight cleared, he was gone.

Danielle shook her head, trying to convince herself that she couldn't have seen Bernard and even if she had, there was no law that said he couldn't have business there as well.

She slowly descended the ramp, trying to re-create that fleeting moment, but as that woman from the elevator had said, everybody looks like somebody. She shook it off and went to retrieve her car.

Instead of going home, Danielle decided to stop by Nia's office in midtown. She'd just returned from a meeting when Danielle pulled up in front.

"Hey, girl. What a surprise." She buzzed her cheek. "Come on in. You know this is a bad hair day…for some of us," she quipped, having pulled her hair in a safe ponytail, unlike Danielle whose beautiful mane simply flowed full of waves in the dampness. "What brings you to my neck of the woods?" She shook out her umbrella and pushed through the glass door.

"I finished up my meeting at the Preston Studio and took a chance that you might be around."

"Well, come on back to my sanctuary and relax a minute. Grace, any messages?" she asked her assistant as she breezed by. "You remember Danielle, right?" she asked over her shoulder but didn't wait for an answer to either question.

"They're on your desk," Grace called out and waved to Danielle.

Nia opened the door to her office, which was a study in pure class. The winter-white walls were strategically adorned with African art. Low-slung chairs and hardwood tables dotted the glistening wood floors. A huge flat-screen television was mounted on one wall that faced a fabric couch covered in kente cloth and topped with thick throw pillows.

Her ground-floor office was connected to a forty-story condominium that boasted annual rents in the hundreds of thousands. On any given day you were sure to see several movie stars, models or politicians coming in and out. Nia's rent was outrageous, but the perks were worth it, she'd always said.

"So." Nia tossed her jacket onto the back of a chair. "Spill it. Something is definitely on your mind." She reached into her purse for her glasses, which she refused to wear in public.

Danielle told her about her sighting of Bernard.

Nia frowned, behind the thin frames and thick lenses. "It doesn't actually mean anything. I mean, it might not have even been him."

"I know. But I would bet money that it was." She leaned forward. "I know this is going to sound crazy, but I'm starting to think that maybe he's following me."

"Why in the world would you think that?"

"Maybe it's not just coincidence that he hooked up with Nick and showed up at my apartment, or was going to the spa when I was going to the brownstone, or that he turned up today."

"That is a lot of coincidences, but it doesn't really mean anything. Manhattan isn't half as big as we'd like to believe. I think you're just being paranoid."

"Probably." She was quiet for a minute.

"Have you found out any more information about him?"

Danielle brought her up to date on what she'd pried from Nick.

"I was hoping that maybe you could tap some of your resources and see if you can find out anything about him."

"No problem. I'll get started first thing in the morning. Somebody somewhere has to know something about this guy." Her eyes suddenly widened. "I have an idea. Why don't I arrange one of my little dinner parties…to celebrate Claudia and Bernard's engagement. It would get him out of the house and give you a chance to get in…"

Chapter 13

When Danielle arrived back at her apartment, Nick was on the couch watching a basketball game. She hung up her coat, kicked off her shoes and joined him.

"Hey, babe, how'd everything go today?"

She stretched out beside him, and he slid over to make room. She rested her head on his chest.

"Long and wet."

"Hmm, you really shouldn't put those two words together around me. Gives me all kinds of ideas," he teased, kissing her on top of her head.

"You're terrible." She playfully swatted his arm. "Who's winning?"

"Not New York," he said with disgust. "Lakers by fifteen. Two minutes left in the third."

"Want me to fix us something for dinner?"

"Uh, no." He chuckled when she swatted him again. "You asked."

"We can order in."

"Fine with me. Oh, Savannah called. She said to give her a call."

She hadn't spoken to Savannah in days. She couldn't. With what she knew or at least suspected, she couldn't talk to Savannah without her friend knowing that something was wrong. But she couldn't avoid her forever. And she didn't want to. She missed her friend.

She pushed up from the couch. "I'll call now before it starts getting late. Decide what you want and order the same for me."

"Idiot!" he roared. "Where'd you learn how to play, from your grandma?"

Danielle shook her head and walked into the bedroom. She'd tell him about Nia's dinner party plans after the game. Anything she said now wouldn't even register.

Sitting down on the side of the bed, she stared at the phone. Finally she snatched it up and dialed Savannah's number.

"Okay, girl, don't cuss me out. I know it's been a minute," Danielle said the moment Savannah answered.

"I was wondering what was going on. Nia was gone, you disappear. How are you?"

"Great." She brought her up to date on what had

been going on with the assignment, leaving out everything having to do with Bernard, and then told her about her meeting with Tasha.

"You have been busy. Is there any way I can help? You were in my corner when I had to deal with my first case."

"I think I'm okay. I'm running some checks on the people from the list." She lowered her voice. "Jasmine showed me how to have a search program run from the PDA while I'm doing other things. I set the search modes this morning. As soon as I can I'm going to check and see what came up."

"Great. But don't hesitate to ask if you need me."

"Oh, Nia is having a dinner party on Saturday to celebrate the engagement, but it's a surprise. So can you get your mom over there?"

"Sure, I'll tell her something. She's always happy to go to one of Nia's soirees."

"Something's wrong. I can hear it in your voice. What is it?"

Savannah blew out a breath through the phone. "You know how close me and my mother are?"

"Sure."

"Things have been really strained since she made her big announcement," she said with a hint of an edge to her voice.

Danielle totally understood Savannah's reservations. But hers were for entirely different reasons.

"As much as we don't want to accept it, Anna,

Claudia is a grown woman, perfectly capable of making her own decisions."

"I know. It's just that it's so soon. She barely knows the man."

"Unfortunately, sis, it's not our decision to make. It's Claudia's."

"I know. I've had her to myself for so long, and with the baby coming, I want my mom," she said in an exaggerated whine.

Danielle laughed. "Girl, you need to stop. How are you feeling, by the way?"

"Like I've gained ten pounds, which I did."

"How's Blake dealing with impending fatherhood and your extra pounds?"

"Blake is a dream. He says the nicest things even when my hormones are raging and I'm being a real bitch." She laughed. "And, girl…the sex is to die for. If I knew I could be this good, I would have made sure I got pregnant a long time ago!"

"You are a hot mess."

"Hot is the word. All the time. Anyway, it's good to hear your voice. I was beginning to feel like an orphan. No mother, no girlfriends…sniff, sniff."

Danielle cracked up. "You missed your calling on Broadway. I'll see you Saturday night."

"Looking forward to it."

Danielle hung up. Based on the roar coming from the living room, the game was still in full swing. She retrieved her PDA from her purse and powered it on.

Before she'd left for her meeting that morning,

she'd set up a search protocol on Bernard. She'd plugged in all the information she had to date. She couldn't wait to see what the results were. She'd also submitted his image to the facial recognition databank, by using a picture they'd all taken several months earlier at Nia's gathering. It wasn't great but should be good enough.

Within moments the pages began to load. Danielle scrolled and scrolled, her thoughts scrambling in disbelief and fear.

For all intents and purposes, Bernard Hassell didn't exist. There was no record of him anywhere, at all.

How was that possible? There had to be something wrong with the program.

But what if there wasn't?

Chapter 14

Danielle was in the shower, getting ready for the party and working out the plan in her head that she and Nia had discussed. It was risky. There was no question about it. But if she could pull it off, maybe she could finally get a lead.

The bathroom door opened and Nick came in. He slid open the shower door and stood there for a moment admiring Danielle before he got in and stood behind her.

"It's been all over the news," he crooned in her ear as he massaged her hips.

"What?" The word jerked out of her throat when his fingers slipped between her wet, slippery folds. She drew in a breath and shut her eyes.

"Water conservation. Everyone has to do their part."

She turned into his arms and faced him. "Is that what you heard?"

"Yep." He nibbled her neck, and she felt his erection press between her thighs.

She took his manhood in her palm and began massaging him in a slow up-and-down motion until he groaned with pleasure.

"We're going to be late," she whispered in his ear.

Steam enveloped them. The pulsing water cascaded around them.

"Looks that way."

He lifted her up and she wrapped her legs tightly around his waist—he pushed deep inside her.

Danielle put the finishing touches on her makeup while Nick finished getting dressed. "I promised Nia I would get there early to help." She spun toward him. "But someone distracted me," she added with a sly grin.

Nick chuckled. "Sorry," he singsonged, totally unapologetic. "Go on ahead and I'll meet you there."

"Thanks, sweetie." She pecked him on the lips. "Don't be too long," she said, hurrying out.

"I won't."

As she opened the door to leave, she heard the distinct sound of the television turning on and the roar of a basketball game in progress. She shook her head and laughed.

* * *

"You two always look like you have a secret," Nia said when she came to the door and greeted Nick.

Danielle, who was standing in earshot, blushed as she walked up to Nick, and images of what they'd done to each other in the shower flashed through her head.

"Come on in. Everyone is here," Danielle said, taking his hand.

Nick went straight to Savannah and wrapped her in a hug. "You look fabulous," he said, stepping back and taking a good look at her.

Savannah did a little curtsy. "Thank you."

"And how are you, proud papa to be?"

Blake grinned and beamed down at his wife. "Counting the days." He leaned forward and shook Nick's hand. "Long time, man. Good to see you."

"You, too. We have to stop waiting on Nia's dinner parties to hang out."

"For sure. As a matter of fact I have some tickets to the next Knicks game. She hates 'em," he added with a toss of his head in Savannah's direction.

"They're bound to be playing someone better than themselves, so why not?" Nick said with a chuckle.

The two men walked off to continue talking about sports.

Danielle asked about Claudia.

"She called a little while ago and said they were on their way."

A tingle of relief released the knot in her stomach. Everything hinged on Bernard's being there that night. Just then Steve Long, Nia's beau, came from the kitchen with a tray of finger food appetizers.

"Evenin' folks," he said. "This woman has had me chained to the stove all evening." He passed the tray around and greeted everyone amid bubbles of laughter.

Danielle had a minute to again question Nia. "Where are they?" she said in a whisper.

"On their way. Claudia said something had come up with Bernard at the last minute and they were running late."

"I don't want us to be in the middle of dinner when…"

The ringing doorbell cut her off in midsentence. Nia briefly clasped Danielle's wrist and squeezed lightly before heading for the door.

Squeals of laughter underscored by a gentle bass floated into the living room. Nia led the last of the guests inside.

"Sorry we're late," Claudia said, holding on to Bernard's hand.

"I hear congratulations are in order," Steve said, breaking out a bottle of champagne.

Nia followed him with a tray of champagne flutes and a bottle of sparkling cider for the mama-to-be.

"To Claudia and Bernard," Steve said, raising his glass.

"Claudia and Bernard!" the group chorused.

Glasses clinked all around.

Claudia looked up at Bernard with so much love in her eyes, and Danielle cringed because deep in her gut she knew that this man was not who he pretended to be.

Nia caught Danielle's eye while the guests were busy talking. Nia gave an almost imperceptible nod of her head.

"For those of you who don't know, this is a surprise engagement party," Danielle announced with a flourish.

"Oh, my goodness," Claudia said, covering her mouth with one hand and grabbing Bernard with her other. He swept her up in a hug.

Danielle slapped her palm against her forehead. "I need to run home. I forgot the gift."

"Oh, don't worry about it," Claudia said. "This is surprise enough," she said, beaming with delight.

"No, I wouldn't feel right, and I want you to have it on your special night. It won't take long. I'll be back before you know it."

Danielle rushed toward the door and darted out. She was in her car by the time Nick reached the top of the stairs. She pulled off without looking back.

Danielle checked the time on the dashboard. It was nine fifteen. It would take ten minutes to get there, do a quick five-minute search and ten minutes back. Her heart was racing like crazy.

Everything she needed was in her purse. She made a right turn at the next corner, got caught at a red light, then took a left. The house was on the next block. She checked the addresses on the right-hand side, slowed and parked two doors away.

Danielle grabbed her purse and took out the small makeup kit that held her burglary tools. She prayed that she would remember what Margaret had taught her and would not get herself arrested for breaking and entering.

Danielle looked both ways and jogged up the short flight of brick stairs to the front door. Her pulse was beating so hard and fast in her ears that she could barely hear the sounds around her.

Her hands shook as she took the pin and hook out of the case. She inserted them into the lock, pressing her free fingers against the door as she worked the tools. She felt the lock click open. A rush of air burst from her lungs. She stole a look behind her, then went inside.

She knew there had to be a computer there— somewhere. She needed to find it and get the information she needed.

A little more than five minutes later, she was locking the door behind her. She jogged down the stairs and hurried toward her car.

Then she stopped short.

"Nick."

Chapter 15

"Wh-what are you doing here?"

"I should be asking you that, Dani."

"You followed me?" she asked incredulously, trying to buy time.

"I tried to tell you that I would ride with you. Then I saw you go the wrong way to our house, so I followed you. Here."

Danielle looked everywhere but in Nick's accusing eyes. "I can't do this now." She made a move to get in her car. Nick grabbed her arm. Her gaze flew to where he held her.

"Don't walk away from me, Danielle. I want to know what's going on."

She looked right into his eyes. "Whatever you're thinking, you're wrong."

"You have no idea what I'm thinking!" he shouted, his voice echoing along the quiet street.

"You're right. I don't. But this isn't going to be solved on a street corner." She moved toward her car.

Nick hung his head. "Go ahead, leave." He turned and walked away.

"Nick! If you love me, you'll trust me."

He turned slowly toward her. "If you loved me, we wouldn't be here."

Something inside her seemed to break. She knew if she let him walk away he'd never come back, not this time. Everything was teetering on the edge, and a move in any direction would send it all crashing to the ground.

Nick opened the door to his car.

"I promise to explain everything. Please, you have to trust me." Her voice cracked with emotion. "Please."

Nick hesitated with his hand on the handle of the car door. "Make my excuses to your friends." He got in the car, and with Danielle watching he drove off.

Danielle didn't know what to expect when she came home from the party several hours later.

When she'd returned to the party with Claudia's gift which she'd stashed in the trunk earlier, she'd told the guests that Nick wasn't feeling well and had gone home. Only Nia guessed what really had transpired. Danielle hadn't explained much while they cleaned up the kitchen. Nia had tried to assure her that everything would work out.

But as she headed home that night and walked toward her bedroom, she wasn't too sure. She stepped inside—Nick was sitting in the dark on the edge of the bed.

"Nick, I—"

"Don't. I need you to listen, okay?" He spoke so quietly that she wasn't sure she'd heard him.

She stepped farther into the room but dared not get too close. Her heart thumped as she braced herself for the worst.

"When I met you, I thought…finally, the woman I'd been born to love. All the ugliness that was my life was wiped away when you smiled. The emptiness that I'd lived with since my dad died was filled with your presence. I wasn't lonely anymore. I felt that I'd found myself. I wasn't adrift. That was because of you." He turned toward her. "But now I don't know who I fell in love with. Maybe it was only my imagination. I wanted it so bad that I made you real. And if I don't know who you are, then maybe I don't know myself either."

Tears stung her eyes. She searched for the words to make it all okay, but she couldn't find them.

Nick pushed up from the bed and came toward her. "All I ever wanted was someone who was going to be as real with me as I was with them. I thought that's what we had. I was wrong."

"Please don't go," she whispered. "All I can say

is that…I'm working on something and right now I can't tell you about it."

He looked at her and shook his head. "Goodbye, Danielle." He walked toward the door, and that was when she noticed the suitcase.

She heard herself calling his name, knew that her feet were moving, running behind him. But like waking from a dream she realized that she was in the room alone and Nick was gone.

By morning Danielle's eyes were so red and swollen from crying all night that she could barely see. Worn out, frustrated and totally miserable, she stumbled into the kitchen to put on a pot of coffee. She had to pull herself together. There was a shoot scheduled for the afternoon, and she knew that Nick would be there. No way would she allow him to see the mess that she'd become in only a matter of hours.

As the coffee brewed, the events of the previous night ran through her head like a bad movie. The only saving grace was the information she'd gained on Bernard.

After breaking into his apartment, she'd located his computer in a small room in the back of the one-bedroom duplex.

She'd used a USB hookup to download his files onto a memory stick. While the information was being transferred, she had done a quick search of his bedroom. What she'd discovered still had her mind reeling, and she wasn't sure what to make of it—passports and driver's licenses with four different aliases. So who was Bernard Hassell?

With her coffee cup in hand, she returned to her bedroom and retrieved the memory stick from her purse. She plugged it into her laptop and massaged her temples with the tips of her fingers while she waited. Her head pounded from lack of sleep, and she'd cried so much that she was totally dehydrated.

But at least for a little while she could focus on someone else's issues instead of her own, for which she had no easy answers. She rubbed her eyes, took a long swallow of coffee and watched the information appear on the screen.

The more she read, the more disturbed she became. The ringing telephone drew her attention away from the damning information.

She reached across the bed, hesitating for a moment. What if it was Nick? What would she say? Would she have sense enough to find her voice this time and tell him what was in her heart?

Her shaky hand hovered over the receiver. It rang for the fourth time. If she waited for the next ring, it would be sent to their voice-mail service.

Danielle drew in a breath and snatched up the phone. "Hello?" Her heart pounded.

"Dani, it's Nia. I was calling to see if you were all right. I know that story you gave us about Nick last night was B.S. What happened? He darted out of here. You come back alone, looking like you'd been struck by lightning…"

Danielle leaned back against the thick down pillows, drew in a long breath and spilled the story about what she'd found in Bernard's apartment—including Nick's appearance in front of Bernard's house.

"Oh, dayum," Nia murmured. "What are you going to do?"

"I've been asking myself that question since I found out. But my own life is so screwed up that I can't even think straight."

They both sighed, deep in thought.

"I think it's time you told Savannah," Nia said.

"I've been thinking the same thing. Can you meet me at The Shop at noon?"

"I'll be there. And I'll give Savannah a call and tell her it's important and that she needs to take an early lunch."

"Thanks. See you in a few."

By the time Savannah arrived, a bit breathless, Danielle and Nia were already seated in their favorite booth.

"What's the big emergency?" she asked while taking her seat. She looked from one gloomy face to the other. "Somebody better tell me something. You're making me nervous."

Nia looked to Danielle and gave a short nod of her head.

Danielle pressed her lips together in concentration

and looked directly at Savannah. "It's a long story. But it's all related to the assignment and Bernard…."

"Oh…my…God," Savannah said between the fingers that covered her mouth when Danielle brought her story to a close. "I… My mother." Tears filled her eyes but they didn't fall. "I knew it. I knew something was wrong." She frowned, her dark eyes were like laser beams as they zeroed in on Danielle. "I'm going over there." She started up from her seat, and Nia grabbed her wrist.

"No, you're not! That's not an option." She turned to Danielle. "*You* need to confront him."

"What! Are you crazy? I don't want to wind up a statistic in the news—or worse, never make the headlines because I've simply vanished," she said, her voice rising in alarm.

"Look, you've verified the fact that he was in the service, but not as Bernard Hassell. Use that as leverage."

"I don't see how."

"Tell him that you will spill it all to Claudia," Savannah offered.

"What if he doesn't care and sees me as a threat to whatever it is he's up to?"

"What if he *does* care?" Nia said, always the romantic.

Danielle sighed heavily. "I don't know…"

"Do it somewhere safe," Savannah said.

"Like where?"

"Your place," Nia said.

"You have got to be kidding."

"No, seriously. You said that he and Nick were friends, right? Well, tell him you need to talk to him about Nick. Tell him Nick left and you're worried about him. And you need his advice."

Danielle thought about it. "Maybe it could work," she said slowly, not completely convinced.

"I'll be there as well—out of sight."

"Me, too," Savannah said.

"No, you won't!" the duo responded.

Savannah puffed and pouted, folding her arms over her growing baby bump.

"Okay," Danielle conceded. "If we can get to Bernard, or whoever he is, I know it's going to lead us to the people behind the identity theft operation."

"By the way," Nia said, "I've checked with everyone I know and everyone they know, and not a soul has ever heard of Bernard Hassell."

Chapter 16

Nick awoke with every bone in his body aching. His eyes squinted open and he turned, barely catching himself before falling off the couch.

He expelled an expletive as he hoisted himself back up and took a look around, trying to get his bearings. Nothing looked familiar. He pushed himself into a sitting position and the inside of his brain did a rapid 360-degree turn. His stomach lurched to his throat, and he was a gulp away from spewing its contents all over this rug that he didn't recognize.

"You're up."

Nick's hazy gaze moved in the direction of the voice. He squinted the image into focus. "Bernard?" he asked in confusion.

Bernard grinned and slowly approached. He handed him a glass of tomato juice and two aspirin. "Take these. You'll feel better—eventually."

Nick tossed down the aspirin, then ran his fingers through his spiky hair. "How did I get here, and what was I doing before I arrived?" His tongue felt like an old slipper.

"After you left the party, you never returned. I guess you must have spent the next few hours drinking at Bob & Lou's Bar and Lounge up on Amsterdam Avenue. The owner called me about three this morning. He said you told him to call. He found my name in your cell phone. I picked you up—literally—and brought you here. You kept insisting that you weren't going home."

Bernard took a seat opposite Nick. He leaned forward, bracing his arms on his thighs. "You want to tell me why you didn't want to go home?"

"It's complicated." He rubbed his brow. "Me and Dani…she's keeping things from me, lying, doing stuff that she can't explain, but she wants me to trust her. She begged me to trust her. But I can't, not anymore, not if she can't be honest with me."

Bernard was thoughtful for a moment, knowing that what he said next could affect Nick's relationship with Danielle for good.

"Sometimes, man, you gotta let go of all the things that ground you and step out on faith."

Nick glared at him.

"Do you believe in God?"

The question threw him. "Yeah, why?"

"You believe that there is a God even though you can't see God or hear God, right? You believe not because of anything concrete but because of what you feel in your mind and in your heart."

Nick's jaw clenched.

"Same thing with love, man. You can't see it or touch it, but you believe in it. You know it's real because you can feel it in your heart and in your head even if you can't explain it."

"What's that got to do with what Dani did?"

"Sometimes you just have to believe, son, simple as that. Give her a chance."

He stood. "I put some fresh towels in the bathroom. There's plenty of food in the fridge. Make yourself at home. I need to run out for about an hour."

Nick's thoughts were still plowing through what Bernard had said when a thought struck him. "My car? I think I drove." He looked up at Bernard. "Did I?"

Bernard grinned. "I'm going to pick up your car now. The bartender wisely kept your keys and gave them to me when I got there." He lifted them from his pocket and shook them in the air. "See you in a few."

"Thanks, man."

"Don't worry about it." He walked toward the door. "At least think about what I said. Sometimes, things aren't as apparent as they appear." He opened the door and walked out.

Nick slowly got up from the couch and walked to

the window. He watched Bernard drive off, and the events of the previous night began to come clear. He could see himself standing in front of the building, imagining the worst when he saw Danielle go inside. He could still hear her plead with him to "trust her."

His jaw clenched. He'd told Bernard everything except that where he'd followed Danielle wasn't to some random house, but *his*. He wondered what sage advice Bernard would offer if he had known that bit of information.

Chapter 17

Danielle went through the motions at the photo shoot, setting the scenes, coaxing the models and motivating her crew. Thank goodness for Mark. He was an excellent photographer and filled in on a moment's notice for Nick.

She'd expected Nick to be there. She'd expected that even if he pretended she didn't exist, she could at least see him and maybe he could tell by looking into her eyes how much she cared and how sorry she was for messing things up between them.

All through the night, through the tears, fits of anger and frustration, she silently prayed that if Nick just gave her one more chance, she would tell him she loved him. She would say the words from the bottom of her heart.

But as the hours ticked by, it became apparent that he wasn't coming and she grew more and more on edge. He'd never done that before. He'd never missed a session and surely never missed one and didn't call.

She flipped open her cell-phone case that hung on her hip. At least if she could hear his voice, she would know that he was okay.

Nick stepped out of the shower, running a towel over his wet hair. He was beginning to feel halfway human again. He was staring in the mirror, accessing his red-rimmed eyes, when the ringing of his cell phone pulled him in the direction of the living room, where he'd left his pile of clothes. He dug through his shirt and dress slacks and found it beneath his socks.

He flipped the front cover open. The familiar number registered on the screen. He stared at it, listened until the ringing stopped and then tossed the phone onto the couch.

The tightness in Danielle's throat was almost unbearable. She listened to Nick's recorded voice, the one that soothed her, teased her, whispered in her ear. She didn't bother to leave a message. She returned to the set and tried to concentrate but couldn't. Her thoughts kept shifting back to Nick. Maybe he was hurt, lying in a ditch somewhere. Maybe he was sick and needed someone to look after him. He could have been in an accident.

The ugly scenarios kept repeating and repeating

in her head on a continuous loop until she thought she'd scream—and she did.

"Break! Twenty minutes." Her breathing escalated with the anxiety that was making her crazy.

Gladys, one of her crew members, who handled the lights, asked her if she was sick, because she didn't look well, and Danielle nearly burst into tears. She knew she was on the verge of breaking, and that reality shook her up even more.

The fact that she had allowed her feelings for someone else to get the best of her, cloud her thoughts and confuse her judgment was way more than she was prepared to deal with.

Danielle Holloway was used to being in charge. She called the shots both in relationships and out. This whole thing with Nick was new and it was scary.

And to complicate matters further, she had the Cartel assignment to fulfill, and the more she found out, the worse things became.

She glanced up and saw Reggie, one of her cameramen, walking past her.

"Hey, Reggie."

He stopped and turned. Danielle approached him. "Listen, I need to take care of some things. Do you think you can handle the rest of the shoot for today? We have nineteen more cityscape shots and two indoors. Mark will guide you through what needs to be done."

"Sure," he said, seemingly thrilled by the chance.

"Just follow the shot sheet. Melody will keep the models in order."

"Not a problem, Dani. Thanks for the chance."

She nodded and hurried off toward her car before she could change her mind.

The "brain trust"—her, Nia and Savannah—had come up with the brilliant idea of having her confront Bernard using the ruse that she needed his advice on how to handle the mess between her and Nick.

But what she needed now was to know that he was all right. And the only person she could think of who could tell her was Bernard, or whatever his name was.

If something had happened to Nick because of her, she'd never forgive herself. She got behind the wheel of her vehicle, took her PDA out of her bag and pulled up everything she had on Bernard Hassell. Jasmine had finally been able to work her magic and come up with landline and cell-phone numbers for Bernard. Danielle wasn't sure how she'd missed it when she'd done her own search, but Jasmine was, after all, a true techie.

Danielle tried the cell first.

Bernard picked up on the second ring. "Hello, Danielle. I wondered how long it was going to take you to get to me."

Frowning, she jerked back from the voice on the phone. "What?"

"Meet me at the corner of West Fourth and Houston in twenty minutes." He disconnected the call.

Shit. Had Nick told him that she'd broken into his house? No. It didn't sound as if he was upset, more as if he was *expecting* her call. He *was* expecting her call. He'd said as much.

She shook her head in confusion and caught a glimpse of the dashboard clock. It was already after three. It would take her the full twenty minutes and then some to get to the Village from midtown at that time of day.

Danielle put the car in gear and eased into traffic. What if this was some kind of setup? If he'd been expecting her call, then he may know more about her than she realized.

One of the first things explained in the CD lessons was to always be aware of potential traps and going into situations when no one else knew where you were.

It wasn't likely he would try anything in broad daylight on a busy street corner, but the cold truth was that people disappeared off New York City streets every day. She didn't intend to be one of them.

Danielle got her cell and speed-dialed Nia's number. She quickly ran down the troubling conversation and told her where she was going—*just in case*.

"This doesn't sound good, Dani. Don't do anything stupid. I can meet you."

"No. Just stay available. If you don't hear from me in an hour, call Savannah. She'll know what to do. Gotta go."

The trip felt as if it were taking forever. She must

have hit every red light in lower Manhattan. By the time she arrived, her nerves were so frazzled that she was damp all over. She found a spot at a meter and parked.

Danielle looked around. The streets were full of activity. That was a good thing. The more people there were, the better she felt. She got out of the SUV, fed the meter and began walking toward the meeting place a block away and spotted Bernard leaning against a mailbox. He was casually dressed in a pair of khaki pants, brown loafers and a tan windbreaker.

She took a good look around before going any farther. Her trained photographic eye scouted out the stores, the entrance to the train station and the shortest distance back to her car. Drawing in a deep breath, she walked forward.

Bernard seemed to sense her and turned in her direction. It struck her again how much he resembled Billy Dee Williams. He could probably get plenty of work with that woman she'd met on the elevator.

Danielle lifted her chin, putting on a façade of bravado that eluded her.

Bernard actually smiled at her. "Glad you could make it. Let's walk and talk." He started off without waiting for her response. She picked up her pace. Her ponytail bounced with every step, and she was glad that she'd kept on her sneakers in case she needed to make a run for it. She caught up with him.

He made a right onto a short residential block

away from the heavy flow of traffic on West Fourth Street. Her throat grew dry.

"Where are we going?"

"I'm sure you must be concerned about Nick," he said rather than answer her question.

Her breath stuck in her chest. Was Nick a hostage? "Yes."

"He's fine. A little hungover but fine. He's at my place. You know where that is, don't you?"

She curled her hands into fists to keep them from shaking.

He pressed his hand against the small of her back and steered her around the corner. The sounds of vehicular and pedestrian noises grew faint. Her feet suddenly felt like lead.

"I know all about what you're doing," he said, stopping in front of an abandoned building.

Her eyes widened in alarm. She began to back away.

Bernard reached inside his jacket, and Danielle bolted for the corner, which seemed to get farther away with every step she took. Her car was now more than three blocks away. She hadn't run farther than to the bathroom in ages, she thought frantically. He, on the other hand, was in shape. He'd catch her before she made it to the corner. She could almost feel the heat of a bullet tearing through her back.

A heavy hand grabbed her shoulder, nearly spinning her around. She screamed.

"Cell phone, cell phone," he said, pushing it in front of her face. "Here, Jean wants to speak to you."

She was breathing so hard she was dizzy. It took several moments before what he said registered. She stared at him in disbelief. Nothing made sense.

He pushed the phone toward her. "Take it, Danielle. Jean will explain everything."

Slowly she reached for the phone and brought it to her ear without taking her eyes off Bernard. "Hello…"

Danielle listened in stunned silence as Jean explained that Bernard was working with her from the Office of Homeland Security and that information had been planted in her files about Bernard to test Danielle to see how strong her instincts were.

"Th-this was all part of a test!" She didn't know whether to laugh or cry. And she'd passed with flying colors, according to Jean, who was proud to officially declare Danielle a member of The Ladies Cartel. In addition to which Bernard would be her contact and her partner.

Danielle slumped back against a streetlamp and gazed at Bernard. She was waiting for Ashton Kutcher to jump out of a van and tell her that she'd been "punk'd."

"Sorry I had to be so mysterious, but we needed to know you had what it took to do the job."

Danielle drew in a long breath. "You've been watching me all along—and Nick?"

He nodded.

"You befriended him. He likes you. Is that all part of the plan?" She felt her anger begin to rise. It was one thing to screw around with her—she'd invited it by getting involved with the Cartel—but screwing around with Nick was a different story.

"It was in the beginning, but I like Nick. I really like him and he loves you…deeply." He looked right in her eyes. "And I think right about now he'd be willing to listen to you."

"Does Claudia know?" she asked as they walked back to the car.

Bernard turned to her and grinned. "Of course. It was her idea."

Danielle shook her head. This was all too much to process, but when she got it together, she was going to spill it all to the girls.

They reached where Bernard was parked, and she realized he was driving Nick's car.

"Long story," he said when he saw the question form on her lips. "Hop in. I'll take you to your car and explain on the way."

Chapter 18

Bernard opened the door to his small house and stepped aside to let Danielle pass.

Nick glanced up, then did a double take when he saw Danielle standing there looking a little lost and uncertain.

He got up from the couch but didn't come toward her.

Bernard cleared his throat. "Uh, I forgot...ice cream." He backed out of the door and left them alone.

Danielle clasped her hands in front of her.

Silence dragged out between them, then they both spoke at once.

"You first," Nick conceded, with a nervous laugh.

Danielle took a tentative step toward him.

"I'm so sorry, Nick. I should have told you in the beginning what was going on," she began. "Claudia is planning a surprise party for Bernard, and she needed to get a list of his friends without him knowing. We figured that during the party would be a perfect time, and I volunteered." She nearly choked on the lie she and Bernard had concocted in the car with Claudia's help.

Nick squeezed his eyes shut and shook his head. He threw his hands up in the air. "What? Why didn't you just tell me?"

"Because you can't keep a secret," she said with a sly grin.

"I can't keep a secret?" he asked, sounding mildly offended.

Danielle planted her right hand on her hip and cocked her head to the side, her ponytail swinging in the process. "No. Weren't you the one who blabbed to Reggie that Gladys liked him, and didn't you tell Savannah about the present that Blake was getting her when they found out she was pregnant? And the time—"

He held his palms up. "All right, all right, I give up. But—" he shook a finger at her "—I didn't tell the crew about us." He came to stand in front of her, his brows knitted tightly. He looked down into her eyes. "I should have listened to you," he said softly. "I let fear and ego mess with my head instead of listening to my heart and trusting you and my feelings."

Danielle felt a sick sensation sweep through her stomach as she listened to him confess to his faults, which were built on her lies. It took all she had not to break down and confess the whole twisted story. But she knew she couldn't, especially now that she had been truly validated as a member, one who was willing to risk everything to be one.

Danielle put a finger to his lips and slowly shook her head. "There was no way for you to know. It was just a colossal case of miscommunication."

He angled his head to the side and slid his arms around her waist, pulling her close. "What can I do to make it up to you?" he asked, bending down to plant a trail of featherlight kisses along her neck.

Danielle sighed breathlessly. Her eyes fluttered closed for a moment as she relished in his touch. "Why don't we take up this conversation in the privacy of our home," she whispered.

"There you go reading my mind..."

The instant the door shut behind them, Danielle and Nick were pulling off clothes, kicking off shoes, grabbing, kissing, stumbling and laughing all the way to the bedroom, where they collapsed onto the bed in a tangle of legs, arms and exploring tongues and hands.

Their hearty laughter slowly ebbed into low moans and deep sighs as the fever that heated their bodies rose by degrees and the playfulness shifted to heighten their sensual pleasures.

Danielle toyed with Nick, teasing him with tiny nibbles and long laps of her tongue along his warm flesh. Her fingers traced the hard outline of his chest, drifting down to his hard stomach to nestle for a moment in the downy soft hair that surrounded his pulsing erection.

"I have some making up to do myself," she whispered, looking up at him for an instant before she drew his length into her mouth.

A groan from deep in his throat rose up and punctuated the air. He gripped the sheets in his fist and forced himself not to fully bury his need in her throat.

Danielle worked him with long licks of her tongue, sucking him in and out, feeling his erection pulse in her mouth until he was a stroke away from exploding. The sensations grew so intense that he begged her to stop, holding her head in the palms of his hands to keep her from making him lose the last bit of control he had.

"I want you, Dani," he groaned. "I need to be inside you."

Slowly she crept up the length of his body, planting tiny kisses along his heated flesh until she was astride him. She taunted the tip of him with slow rotations of her hips allowing him to only barely touch her wet folds.

Then suddenly, Nick turned her onto her back, pinning her beneath him with his weight. He pushed her thighs wide apart with his knees and found his way home.

They made love off and on through the night, sometimes slow and easy and at others with a hunger that couldn't seem to be filled except with more of the same.

The light from the full moon slid in between the curtains, casting a soft glow in the room. A faint breeze gently lifted the curtains from the window.

Dani lay curled against Nick, her arm draped loosely across his chest. Tenderly he stroked her curves and realized how badly he could have screwed up simply because he couldn't let go of a past that denied him happiness. He wouldn't listen when she tried to explain. There was a part of him that believed that because of what happened with his father, he didn't deserve to be happy and if he was happy, it would be taken from him.

To avoid that, he wanted to strike first, and it had nearly cost him the woman he loved.

He held her a bit tighter, listening to the soft cadence of her breathing. Losing Danielle was something he would never risk again. In order to ensure that, he would have to be honest with her and let go of the ghost that haunted him.

"Babe," he said softly. "I want to talk to you about something."

Danielle snuggled deeper into the pillow and muttered something unintelligible.

Nick smiled ruefully, kissed the top of her head

and closed his eyes. Tomorrow was another day, he thought as he drifted into a deep, satisfied sleep.

When Danielle awoke the next morning, the space next to her was empty. Slowly she sat up, rubbed her eyes and sniffed the air. Hmm, bacon. Nick was busy in the kitchen doing his thing.

While he was busy, she decided to quickly check her PDA. Now that she and Bernard were on the same side, she could scratch him off her most-wanted list and direct her attention elsewhere.

She retrieved the PDA from her purse and immediately noticed the blinking light, indicating a message was waiting. It was from Bernard. He needed to talk to her right way.

With her eye on the door, she quickly dialed Bernard's number on her cell phone.

"I have some information, a lead," he said without preamble. "There's a couple—Jenna and Anthony Taylor—that have been on our radar for a while, but we can't prove anything. They're a little too low on my totem pole, but I have a gut feeling that they may be at the heart of your assignment. They live in a co-op on East 72nd Street. You need to get close to them."

"How?"

"You'll figure it out."

He disconnected the call.

Danielle sat on the side of the bed with the phone still in her hand. *Jenna and Anthony Taylor.*

The names sounded so familiar, but she couldn't place them.

She didn't have a shoot today, which was a good thing, but the flip side of that was neither did Nick. Generally on their days off they spent time together just hanging out, going to the movies, going shopping, visiting a new restaurant or, their favorite pastime, checking out new photography equipment. She knew that as soon as they finished breakfast, he was going to ask her what she wanted to do today.

As her thoughts went through a variety of scenarios she could tell him, the phone rang.

"Hello?"

"Just how long do you plan to make me wait before you tell me what the hell is going on with Bernard?" Savannah snapped into the phone.

Danielle tossed her head back and scrunched up her face. She'd gotten so caught up in the events of the day and night before that she'd totally forgotten to let Savannah know her mother wasn't in love with Jack the Ripper after all.

"Anna, I am so sorry, girl. Yesterday was crazy, to say the least. But I know I should have called you. First and foremost, everything is fine and that includes Bernard." She went on to explain all that had happened, up to and including her most recent conversation with Bernard.

"I still can hardly believe it," Savannah said. "Bernard is with Homeland Security, and it was my mother's idea all along. I'll be damned."

"Yeah, who you telling? I felt the same way. I guess that's why your mom is so good at what she does for the Cartel."

"I guess so," Savannah said in awe. "Now what are you going to do about the couple?"

"That's what I was trying to work out when you called. But I swear their names sound so familiar."

"Who did you say they were again?"

"Jenna and Anthony Taylor."

"Hmm, I wonder if they are the same couple that were clients of Nia's about a year or so ago. Remember some hotshot couple that had this fabulous party on a yacht?"

"Yeah, right," she said slowly as the recollection began to take shape. "I wonder if they are the same people."

"One way to find out."

They got Nia on the line with three-way calling.

"Sure sounds like them," Nia said. "Let me check my database to confirm the address. Hang on a sec."

Several moments later Nia returned to the phone. "It's them. I can't believe I was dealing with con artists," Nia said, more annoyed than alarmed. Her reputation was built on dealing with the crème of the crop. If word of this got out, her business would suffer.

"What are you going to do?" Nia inquired.

"I'm going over there, for starters. But first I've got to keep Nick occupied."

"How?"

"I'll let his new best buddy, Bernard, handle it."

Chapter 19

Danielle cruised to a stop on the opposite side of the street from 425 East 72nd Street. It was a twenty-story high-rise with rent hovering in the million-dollar category. She took out her camera from her knapsack and adjusted the telephoto lens, hoping she would remember the couple when and if she saw them. But just in case, she planned to take a picture of everyone who came in and out and then run the photos past Nia.

The doorman opened the door for an older couple to exit. Although Danielle was pretty sure they weren't who she was looking for, she snapped them anyway.

This process went on for about a half hour, when a

police cruiser slowed and stopped next to her car. At first she thought they'd stopped for a red light—until both officers got out of the cruiser. One approached her window; the other went to the passenger side.

Oh, Lawd. "Yes, Officer?" she said sweetly. Meanwhile cop number two was peering inside her vehicle.

"License and registration."

She swallowed hard. In her entire life she'd never been stopped by the police. She'd heard and read the stories of the "mishaps" of innocent drivers being pulled over by police for what they claimed were routine traffic stops. Oh, Lawd. She reached for her purse, took out her wallet and found her license and registration. She handed both to him with a soft smile.

"Step out of the van, please, miss."

Were they going to arrest her? Would she wind up a cause celebre for the good Reverend Al Sharpton? Or a statistic?

She slowly opened the car door and stepped out.

"We got a report that someone was sitting out here taking pictures," the officer said.

"Is this your equipment, ma'am?" the second officer asked.

She looked over her shoulder as he extracted her camera bag and camera from the passenger seat. "Yes."

The first cop was still looking at her paperwork

as if he were committing it to memory. Finally he handed it back.

"What are you doing here?"

"I'm a fashion photographer. I was simply scouting out locations for possible photo shoots…Officer."

"You have any proof of that?"

Her mind scrambled, trying to visualize the contents of her wallet. Then she remembered she still had the Michael Preston contract in her purse, which she was supposed to have filed away but for some reason never did. She leaned inside the car, dug around in her oversize purse and pulled out the folded manila envelope. She took out the contract and handed it to him.

"Michael Preston. The designer from that runway show?" he asked, mildly impressed.

"Yes." She beamed him a smile.

"My wife watches that show all the time." He looked at her with a new kind of respect. "What's he like?"

She was about to answer when she saw movement coming from across the street. She wanted to push the cop out of the way to be sure she was seeing correctly. It was that woman from the elevator—the one with the modeling agency.

"Ma'am?"

"Oh, I wish I knew. Every time I've gone to his office, I've dealt with his assistant." The woman got into a waiting cab, and it sped away.

"Yeah, I guess he can afford one, right?" He

chuckled as if he'd just shared a joke with his best friend. He handed her back the contract. "All right. You can go but I suggest you find another spot. Apparently the neighbors in this area don't take kindly to being photographed."

"Thanks, Officer," she said and wondered if he heard her heavy sigh of relief.

"Have a nice day. And good luck."

"Thanks."

The officers returned to their car and pulled off. Her entire body was trembling so badly she barely made it back inside her vehicle. She lowered her head to the steering wheel and drew in several deep breaths. She'd have to find another way, she thought, as she put the car in gear. What was that woman doing there? Was she a tenant? Was she visiting someone? And how much of a coincidence was it that she handled look-alikes and the people Danielle was investigating dealt in stealing identities?

She had the woman's card, somewhere. Maybe it was time to give her a call and use her Alicia Keys looks to her advantage. She put the car in gear and pulled off.

When she returned home, she was surprised to find Nick sitting in front of the television.

"Hey, I thought you and Bernard were hanging out for the afternoon." She put her bag on the table in the hallway and walked toward him. But the closer she came, the expression on his face grew clearer and she saw what he held in his hand. Her heart thumped with dread.

He flipped the small compact around his hand.

She came to stand in front of him, and that was when she also noticed her TLC kit sitting at his feet.

"I got back early," he said. "I wanted to surprise you with a romantic dinner." He turned the compact around in his hand again. "I found this on the floor in the bedroom. Thought I was helping when I went to look for this—" he nodded toward her case at his feet "—to put it back." He looked up at her stricken face. "You want to tell me what all this is, Dani, 'cause it sure as hell ain't makeup!"

The few seconds that ticked by felt like an eternity as Danielle tried to figure out how she could possibly explain what he'd found. Her brain grinded to a halt.

"Don't you have anything to say?"

Her shoulders slumped. She could spend the next hour weaving one lie after another that she could never take back and have to continue building their relationship on lies.

Slowly she sat down next to him. She was about to break every rule she'd sworn to uphold. It may ruin her future with the Cartel, but she wasn't going to ruin her relationship with Nick.

Danielle turned to him. "I know what I'm about to tell you is going to sound crazy. And I'm breaking a major trust to say anything." She drew in a breath as she put her thoughts in order. "If I'm going to trust you with what I'm about to say, then you need to trust me as well and not ask me any questions. Just listen."

"What?" he asked in disbelief. "I'm a technician, Danielle. I know electronic equipment when I see it. You can no more tell me this is a compact than you can say there's no racism in America! And you're going to sit there and tell me that I simply have to *trust* you and not ask any questions!" He jumped up from the couch and spun toward her. "What...the next thing you're gonna tell me is that you're some kind of spy or something?"

"Something like that," she said, noticing his stunned expression, which quickly turned to outraged laughter. "Danielle, please don't insult my intelligence." He began to pace. "Listening devices, burglary tools! Who are you?"

"Nick, please listen to me. That's all I ask. And when I'm done, if you still don't believe me...then I'll accept whatever decision you make. But at least give me a chance." She paused. "Please."

His jaw flexed over and over, making the veins in his temples pump. Finally he sat down and braced his arms on his thighs. "I'm listening."

More than an hour later, Danielle sat drained but surprisingly relieved as she waited for Nick's verdict.

He slowly shook his head. It was almost too crazy to comprehend. But the brilliance of it didn't escape him. Who would ever suspect the everyday woman to be a quasi-undercover agent? It's like the suburban housewives who run lucrative escort services during the week and take their kids to soccer practice on the weekend.

Nick turned to look at her, searching for any deception in her eyes but finding none.

She'd told him all she could reasonably tell him, leaving out the location of the Cartel, as well as the fact that not only was Savannah a card-carrying member, but also she was recruited by her mother, Claudia, who was one of the highest-ranking members in the organization.

Nick mopped his face with his hands. "How long have you been involved?" he asked.

"This is my first assignment, and I'll probably get kicked out because of this." She took his hands. "You have to swear to me that you will never, ever say anything to anyone. Please. It's one thing for me to mess up, but I can't ruin it for everyone else."

He nodded, then looked directly into her eyes. "You can trust me," he said with quiet sincerity. He opened the case at his feet. "I pretty much figured out what most of the gadgets were," he said, "but—" he lifted a bottle of what looked like shower gel and held it up "—what is this?"

She half grinned. "It's a sedative."

"Wow." He lifted the top tray, beneath which was an outline in the shape of a gun. "Please tell me that you're not carrying a gun around."

"No. I didn't get that far in my training. This was kind of a rush assignment."

"Is that where you've been this morning, on assignment?"

She nodded.

"Dani, I... This is all so crazy. I mean..." He turned to her, trying to find the words. "If you wind up with some kind of assignment that has you carrying a gun, I'd be insane with worry." He raked his fingers through his short ink-black hair. "And every time you walk out of the door and I don't know where you are..." His voice drifted off, but the implication hung in the air between them.

She studied the lines of anxiety that knitted his forehead. And then an idea slowly began to form. "We're a team, right?"

"Yeah, absolutely."

"And we trust each other, right?"

"Yes, but that isn't going to stop me from worrying about you."

"But what if...you helped me?"

His head jerked back in surprise. "Help you? But you said—"

"I know what I said," she interjected, cutting him off. "But I've already screwed up. This will probably be my first and last assignment anyway, so I might as well go out with a bang." A slow smile crept across her mouth.

"Let me explain to you what I have to do, and when I'm done, if you want to help me...then we go for it."

He tugged on his bottom lip with his teeth, a

habit he had whenever he was contemplating his next move. "Shoot," he said, quickly adding, "and I meant that figuratively."

Chapter 20

The following day Danielle made an appointment to meet with Reba McDonald, the woman she'd met on the elevator, then saw coming from the building that she'd been staking out. Reba was more than happy to make time in her schedule to "squeeze" Danielle in.

All she needed was a few minutes of alone time in Reba's office to plant a transmitter on her phone and, if she had time, a tracking device on her computer. After pulling into the parking garage, she walked the short block to the office building.

She checked the minicamera that was attached to the clasp on her purse and called Nick on her cell phone.

"Is the picture coming through?" she asked.

"Clear as crystal," he said from his spot in front of the laptop in their home office. "Babe…"

"Yes?"

"Don't do anything silly, okay?"

"I won't. And you either. If things get strange, don't play hero and call the police. They can't be involved. Understood?"

"Yeah, yeah. Hey, good luck, 007."

"Very funny," she said with a light laugh. "See you on the other side."

Danielle pushed open the glass doors and rode the elevator up to the twentieth floor. She checked the directional sign for room 2018. She made a left turn down the corridor, and it was the last suite on the right.

She knocked on the door and through an intercom was asked whom she was there to see. She gave them Reba's name and was buzzed in.

"Hi," she said, forcing more cheer than necessary into her voice and then realizing how nervous she really was. "I'm Danielle Holloway."

The young woman looked Danielle over and then smiled. "Yep, Reba said you looked like Alicia's twin. Have a seat," she said, lifting her dimpled chin in the direction of a white leather love seat embraced on either side by two glass tables, which were decorated with the latest celebrity magazines.

Danielle settled herself and took a cursory look around. The walls were adorned with photographs of celebrities, covering everyone from rap artists to Oscar winners and everyone in between.

"They look like the real thing, don't they?"

Danielle turned in the direction of the voice. Reba approached. She stood no more than five foot five in heels. Her gunmetal gray hair was cut to frame her rather angular face with the purpose of softening her square chin. She wore a fitted navy-blue suit that showed off her remarkable legs and narrow waist.

Danielle got up. "Are you saying that all of those photos are look-alikes?"

Reba nodded. "That's what I do. Sometimes a celeb needs a stand-in to get the press off them, and they come to me. Other times, it's for other reasons." She flashed a tight smile. "Come into my office and let's talk about what I can do for you."

Said the spider to the fly, Danielle thought as she followed Reba to her office.

"Make yourself comfortable." She indicated a chair placed beneath a circular table in the small but well-put-together office. Reba's desk was the focal point; it measured at least six feet long with a glass overlay beneath which looked like a massive collage of photographs. Danielle was most interested in the computer, which sat on the end of the desk.

Behind the desk, the twelve-foot windows displayed the might of towering Manhattan. There were several photos on the wall of Reba posing with some recognizable politicians, and the young actress from *Dreamgirls*.

"Are those real?" Danielle asked.

Reba chuckled. "What do you think?"

"I'm not really sure."

"Good, then I've done my job. Now, let me tell you what I think we can do. I cover everything from decoys to surprise guests for birthday parties. I think you would be great for parties."

"Really?" She hesitated, intentionally trying to give the impression that she may be broaching a sensitive topic. She leaned forward slightly. "Uh, you mentioned when we first met that these jobs pay very well."

"Absolutely."

"Well, I'm in a really bad financial bind at the moment. If I don't get a major influx of cash, I could lose my condo and my business. At this point I'd be willing to do just about anything." She sputtered a nervous laugh.

Reba studied her for a moment. She folded her hands on top of the desk. "I see." She continued to stare at Danielle so long and hard that she would have sworn that Reba was going to tell her she knew exactly why she was there.

A line of perspiration trickled down her back.

"I'm sorry," Danielle finally said. "I probably shouldn't have come here. You run a business and there's no reason to get you involved in my personal drama." She stood.

"No, wait. I think we can do business. How much money are you looking to make?"

"As much as possible and as quickly as possible. I'll do whatever."

"Are you sure about that?"

"I'm desperate."

"I'll have to do some checking, but I think I have the perfect opportunity. Give me a day or two to get back to you."

"Thank you so much," Danielle said profusely. Her time had just about run out, and she knew this may be her last chance inside this office. Tapping the phone didn't appear to be an option. The only other alternative was to plant a listening device somewhere in the office. She stuck her hand in her pocket and felt the tiny disk. She palmed it and stood, then quickly walked to the other side of the room to look up at the picture of Reba with the newest presidential hopeful.

"I still can't believe that's not really him."

Reba came up behind her. "That's why my business works."

Danielle spun toward her. "I better get going." She stuck out her hand, which Reba shook. "Thanks for talking to me. I'm eager to get started."

"So am I."

Danielle crossed the room to get her purse, and the instant Reba's back was turned, she stuck the recording disk beneath her desk and hoped that the signal would be strong enough to pick up something worthwhile. She straightened and walked to the door where Reba was waiting.

"Thanks again."

"You'll be hearing from me shortly."

"Great." She sucked in a breath and walked out.

The instant she was outside, she called Nick. "Well?" she said instead of hello.

"Got it all. Every angle."

"Did you get good shots of Reba?"

"Definitely."

"It was really kinda creepy seeing folks that are so recognizable but are simply look-alikes."

"Guess there are plenty of twins out there."

"And according to Reba she can help you make a mint for that very reason. I'll see you soon."

By the time she got home, Nick had already printed out the images that were taken with the miniature camera. "I still have no idea what Jenna and Anthony look like, but Nia does. They may be in one of these pictures, and if so, the connection is made." She turned to Nick and winked. "I need to get these pictures over to Nia so she can take a look at them."

"Mind if I ride with you?" His dark eyes raked over her.

Their gazes connected in a way that they hadn't before, seeing each other through different eyes in a new and different light.

She wrapped her arms around his neck and wiggled onto his lap. "I'd love nothing better," she whispered against his mouth before trailing the tip of her tongue tantalizingly across his lips.

He took her mouth in a long, slow kiss, pulled her closer, pressing her breasts against his chest. Danielle moaned ever so softly, running her fingers through his hair and pulling him deeper into the kiss.

With great reluctance he pulled back. "Keep this up and we won't be getting anywhere near Nia's house anytime soon."

She reached down and massaged the bulge in his pants. "That's the point." She gave him a devilish grin. "Nia can wait," she said, her voice thick with growing need. "But I can't."

More than two hours later, sexually satisfied and showered, they were on their way to Nia's house.

"Woman, if I knew you'd give it to me like that, I would have signed up for this spy stuff a long time ago. My legs are still shaking."

"I've been wanting to do it standing up against the wall for a while." She turned to glance at him. "But I suddenly felt the urge to be a little naughty. I got so turned on with this whole new vibe going on between us. I can't explain it."

"I can. It's about being open and trusting someone completely. Opens a whole new world. But you're right, working together like this on something a little illicit, a little dangerous, is a serious rush." His eyes narrowed. "I've always loved to watch you work, but this is different."

"I know. Just imagine if I had a gun."

They both laughed.

Shortly after, they pulled up in front of Nia's building.

"Don't forget—you don't know anything. You just took the ride to keep me company."

"Not to worry."

They hopped out of the car and went inside.

"Do you two always look so happy?" Nia asked as she ushered them inside.

"As often as we can," Nick said, hugging Danielle around the waist.

"Steve is in the living room watching something sports related," Nia said.

"Say no more." Nick headed toward the sound of screaming fans.

"So what do you have?" Nia asked, taking Danielle into the kitchen.

Danielle sat down and took out the envelope with the pictures. She spread them on the table.

"Do you recognize anyone? I mean, anyone you actually know—like Jenna and Anthony."

Nia peered and squinted at the pictures.

"Nia! For heaven's sake, would you please put on your glasses?"

Nia huffed, went over to the sink and took her eyeglass case from the shelf. She flounced back over to the table and began looking at the pictures, tossing them aside one by one. Then she stopped and looked closer at a group picture. She pointed at a couple standing behind a short woman with steel-gray hair.

"That's Jenna and Anthony."

"Are you sure?"

"Positive."

Danielle blew out a breath of relief. "That's the connection. Somehow the three of them are working this thing together."

"How are you going to prove it?"

"You're going to get me inside their house."

Chapter 21

"That's the plan, Nick," Danielle said as they lay in bed that night. "You said you wanted to help. I can't risk being the one to go over there and run into Reba."

"Does Nia know what's going on? I mean, really going on? Is she a member, too?"

"No." At least that part wasn't a lie. "She's not a member, and she only knows as much as she needs to."

He nuzzled her hair. "Hmm. Well, you know where to reach me. I'll be at the JCPenney studio tomorrow going over the designs for photographing."

"Right. I need to monitor Reba's office conversations until Nia can do her thing. Then I can get in there and grab what I need to take them all down."

Suddenly, he turned her onto her back and stared down into her eyes. A wicked smile bloomed across his mouth. "Humph, I love it when you talk dirty."

They both laughed until they were locked together in the oldest dance known to humankind.

Nia opened up her database and located Jenna and Anthony's number and dialed.

"Good morning, this is Nia Turner. Is Mrs…"

"Nia, hi—it's Jenna."

"Jenna! Hi, I'm so glad I got you on the phone. I know it's been ages since we've spoken. How have you been?"

"Fabulous. We just got back from Mexico earlier in the week. What about you? Planning any more fabulous events?"

Nia vaguely remembered that *fabulous* was Jenna's catchphrase for anything even remotely interesting.

"I've been great. Actually that's part of the reason for my call."

"I'm all ears."

"I was hoping that you'd be willing to do me a major favor."

"For you, no problem. Our circle of friends are still talking about that fabulous yacht party you put together."

Nia smiled with pride. That was certainly a signature event. Then her smile waned. At the time she didn't know she was dealing with a criminal. And even now, talking to Jenna, it was hard to believe that she could possibly be involved in something so despicable. What if she did what Danielle asked and Jenna was actually innocent? It could get back to her other clients and her business would be ruined. She'd be finished in New York, the city she'd built her business and reputation on.

"So what can I do for you?"

Nia hesitated. She could always tell Dani that she couldn't reach Jenna. Dani was obviously resourceful; she'd figure out something.

"Nia, are you still there?"

"Oh, yes, I'm sorry. I thought I was multitasking, but obviously I wasn't." She laughed nervously.

"You said you had a favor to ask. What is it?"

She drew in a long breath. "I was wondering if you would mind being part of…."

"Oh, thank you, girl," Danielle said when Nia called later that morning.

"It's all set for tomorrow at three."

"Thanks. Couldn't have pulled it off without you. You're the best."

Nia heard the relief in Danielle's voice, and whatever whispering doubts she'd had vanished. She wouldn't trade her friendship for all the business in Manhattan.

"That's what friends are for. Keep me posted. I have a meeting in twenty minutes. Gotta go."

"I'll call you tonight."

While Nick was off at the JCPenney studio, she spent the morning listening to Reba's office chatter. There was no doubt that she had a boatload of clients. But what she needed to hear was anything that would incriminate her in any way. She set the device to record when her cell phone rang.

"Hi, Dani, I didn't want to risk calling the house phone and get Nick." It was Bernard.

"Yes, he might get a little curious if you asked to speak to me instead of him," she said, her voice light and teasing.

"What did you wind up doing with that lead I gave you?" he asked.

"We're working it as we speak."

"We?"

She squeezed her eyes shut at her flub but realized that if they were going to pull this off, she was going to need his help and Claudia's. She told him the plan they'd worked out.

"Sounds like it can work. You know this is really going to piss off Jean."

"I know. I'm sure I'll be an afterthought when this is all over, but I had a choice to make—risk my assignment or my relationship. I found a workable compromise. He only knows what he needs to know."

"Then things must be pretty good between you and Nick now?"

"Better than good, actually."

"So you two talked?"

"What do you mean?"

"Never mind. I shouldn't have butted in. I'm sure Nick will talk to you when the time is right."

"Is there something I need to know?"

"Forget that I said anything."

"Too late now, Bernard. Can you at least tell me what it's about?"

"All I will say is that it's about his past. Something that happened to him and he's never been able to let it go."

Danielle was quiet while going over a host of scenarios about what it could possibly be.

"Don't say that I mentioned anything. Let him tell you on his own."

"I won't."

"Good. Give me a call when you have something."

"I will." She disconnected the call. Nick was the one who was so intense about being honest. Was that all just a crock of crap to put the guilt trip on her? If he was so in love with her, as he claimed, why could he tell Bernard his cold, dark secret and not her?

For the same reason she'd kept her own hurts and insecurities tucked away from probing eyes, the little voice in her head whispered.

She sighed. When this was all over, she and Nick were going to have to talk, really talk. She switched her attention to the conversation that Reba was having.

Danielle sat up straight. Reba was talking to Jenna and making plans to meet to discuss the next job. The call ended but Danielle knew no more than she had before the conversation started, other than confirming that Jenna and Reba actually knew each other. And now, for whatever reason, there was some kind of job coming up. That could mean anything.

She typed up her report, as sketchy as it was, and sent an encrypted e-mail to Jean.

"Honey, I'm home," Nick called out with laughter in his voice.

When she heard him, all the gloom and doom she'd felt about their relationship vanished. They both had their issues, their baggage, and it was going to take time to unpack everything. If he could go along with the craziness that was now her life and actually want to be a part of it, then they could certainly work out anything.

She got up from the bed and walked to the front of the house.

"You're back early." She came up to him and kissed him lightly.

"I decided to bring home the breakdown and work on it here."

"Is that really the reason, or did you think you might get left out of the action?" she teased him.

"Wellll." He drew the word out and grinned. "Anything exciting happen while I was gone?"

"Not really." She told him about the one-sided conversation she'd heard at Reba's office. "But we really need to go over what we're going to do tomorrow. We definitely can't make any mistakes. And I need you to get in and get out."

"I know, I know. Don't worry. Everything will be fine. You'll see."

Chapter 22

"All you have to do is get these hidden in the bedroom and living room. They'll pick up everything that's said. I don't want you to risk tapping the phone. But if you can, use this one," Danielle instructed, holding up a third device that looked like a black dime.

"I got it, I got it," Nick said and kissed her forehead. "Don't worry. And I'll even take some pictures while I'm at it."

"I just don't want you to get caught. We don't know what they're capable of."

"Everything is going to be fine. I better get going." He pulled her close for a soft kiss. "See you soon."

Nick arrived at the condominium on East 72nd Street. The doorman Danielle had mentioned was standing in front of the building. Nick called Danielle.

"I'm here," he said. "As soon as I'm done, I'll call you."

"Okay, good luck. And, Nick…"

"Yes?"

"I… Good luck."

"Thanks."

He grabbed his bag from the passenger seat, hopped out and locked the car.

"Morning," he said, greeting the doorman.

"Good morning. Who are you here to see?"

"Mr. and Mrs. Taylor."

"Are they expecting you?"

"Yes."

Nick followed the doorman to the front desk, where he called upstairs to the Taylors.

"You can go right up," he said, hanging up the house phone. "Apartment 2710."

"Thanks." Nick sauntered off. The first hurdle was over, he thought as he stepped aside to let a young man and his miniature terrier off the elevator. The big test was ahead.

He got off on the twenty-seventh floor and walked down the hushed hallway until he reached 2710. He pressed the buzzer.

Several moments later the door was answered by a stunning redhead who introduced herself as Mrs. Taylor.

"Nick Mateo."

"Please come in. And do call me Jenna," she said. "This is so exciting. Nia is such a wonderful woman. I was surprised that she thought of me," she continued, talking as she led him inside. "And remind me again why the young lady that Nia and Reba mentioned couldn't be here."

They entered an expansive sitting room that overlooked the Manhattan skyline. The furnishings were all in white, with low glass and gold-trimmed tables topped by glorious exotic flowers in crystal vases.

"Danielle was very disappointed that she couldn't make it, but she had a last-minute assignment come up. Hope you don't mind me," he added, turning on the charm.

Jenna blushed, her pale cheeks brightening. "Of course not. What red-blooded woman would mind having a handsome young man in her home?"

Nick grinned. "You're going to make an excellent subject," he said, looking deep into her green eyes.

Jenna stood straighter. "You certainly know what to say, don't you?"

"Only the truth." He walked around the space. "I'd love to get a few shots of this room before I get started with you and your husband, if you don't mind."

"Of course not. Can I offer you something to drink?"

"No, thanks. I'm fine." He began unpacking his bag.

"While you get set up, I'll go and check what's taking my husband so long."

"Sure."

The instant she left the room, Nick placed the first listening device beneath the table near the couch. That was when he spotted the phone. He hesitated. Should he take a chance?

He listened for voices coming his way. Quickly he took off the back of the phone and placed the disk inside the phone housing next to the battery, as Danielle had showed him.

He heard Jenna's voice drawing closer. He slid the covering back on and replaced the phone only moments before she returned, with her husband in tow. He grabbed his camera and began adjusting the lens just as the couple came through the archway.

"Nick, this is my husband, Anthony. Sweetheart, this is the photographer that is going to photograph us."

Anthony Taylor stepped forward. He was about sixty, Nick estimated, and was solidly built, had a full head of salt-and-pepper hair and sharp brown eyes. He stuck out his hand.

"Pleasure to meet you. My wife told me that we are to be subjects for an article on Manhattanites."

"Yes. Ms. Holloway was commissioned to do the project. And her mutual friend, Nia Turner, suggested you."

Anthony studied Nick for so long, that Nick began to feel as if the man could see right through his lie.

"I was telling your wife that I wanted to get some shots of the room first, and probably the rest of the house, before I take your photos. Some will be posed. Others I'd like more spontaneous."

Anthony checked his wristwatch. "How long do you think this will take? I have an appointment at five."

"I promise to do this as quickly as possible."

Anthony nodded. He turned to his wife. "Call me when you're ready. I have some calls to make. Nice to meet you," he said to Nick.

"This should take about twenty minutes, and then we can get started," Nick was saying, but Anthony was already walking away.

"Don't mind my husband," Jenna said, walking up to Nick, a little too close for his taste. "He can be a bit abrupt at times."

"I'm sure he's simply a busy man."

She stepped a bit closer and he could smell her soft but expensive-smelling perfume. Her green eyes sparkled.

Nick forced a smile and took a step back. "I should get started."

"Certainly. Mind if I watch?"

"Not at all." He adjusted his camera and began taking shots of the room from several angles, finishing up several moments later. "Can I see the rest of the house?"

"Of course." She led him through the eight-room suite, and Nick took photos of each of the exquisite spaces.

"This is an incredible place," he said, shooting the

final shots of the small home theater, all the while looking for other opportunities to set up the other device that he had in his pocket. He wanted it in a room that was frequented by both of them and where conversations took place, ideally the master bedroom.

"Thank you. And last but not least is the master bedroom."

The room was incredible to behold. One wall consisted of nothing but glass looking out onto the East River beyond. A lush melon-colored rug covered the center of the floor. An enormous king-size canopied bed dominated the room.

Nick walked over to the bed and casually set down his camera on the nightstand, then made a show of looking around. "I definitely want to get this room from the right angle." He returned to the nightstand, keeping his back to Jenna, and casually placed the disk under the lip of the nightstand. Turning back, he said, "A few shots and then I can get started with you and your husband."

A little more than an hour later, Jenna was escorting Nick to the door.

"Thanks so much for your time. As soon as we get the contact sheet done, I'm sure Danielle will be in touch to go over the photos with you."

"You won't be back?" she asked in a plaintive voice.

"Depends on my schedule."

"Well," she said, lowering her voice and touching his hand, "if you ever have some free time…you have my number."

"I'll keep that in mind. Nice to meet you…and your husband," he added with meaning.

She didn't miss a beat. "Oh, Anthony is *very* understanding."

"Have a good day and thanks again," Nick said, feeling that she would undress him right at the door if he gave him half a chance. He hoisted his bag on his shoulder and returned to the elevator.

As soon as he got behind the wheel of the car, he called Danielle. "Done," he said. "I'm on my way home."

Chapter 23

By the time Nick returned, Danielle was already tapped into the Taylors' home. She waved Nick into the bedroom.

She was seated in front of the computer with a headset on. Nick joined her on the side of the bed. She turned to him.

"We got 'em," she said. "I've been recording since you called me. The husband was on the phone with Reba. They were making plans for another gathering. Apparently, Reba uses her look-alikes to gain access to people's homes and parties, and that's when their IDs are lifted, everything from passports to driver's licenses. He told her he had her money for her and would meet her later in the week."

"Wow. Have you heard anything from Reba?"

"Not yet, but I told her how desperate I was to get some extra money. I hope that will be enticing enough."

Nick turned to her. "Thanks for trusting me to do this, Dani."

She stroked his strong jaw. "That's what it's all about, right? Trust?" She searched his eyes.

He leaned forward and kissed her. "It's everything." He paused and gazed downward, then at her. "I've been wanting to talk to you about some things for a while. The time never seemed right."

"What things?"

"About me...."

By the time he finished telling her about his father and the effect it had on him, tears were streaming down Danielle's cheeks. The idea that he'd been carrying this around with him all these years and feeling that he wasn't worthy of being happy tore at her heart. Nick was the most giving, most loving man she'd ever met. He deserved happiness and he deserved to be loved as no other man she'd ever known.

"Nick..." she choked out. "I didn't know."

"It's not something that I'm proud of. But sometimes the weight of it is so heavy I can barely breathe," he said, his voice growing thick.

"There was no way you could have changed what happened. And I can't imagine that your father would have wanted you to live your life filled with guilt about what happened to him. He couldn't have. He loved you."

Nick's eyes filled. "I know. I tell myself that, but that hole never seemed to fill." His throat moved up and down but no more words came.

She wanted to say the words she knew would make it okay. But she couldn't. They just hung in her throat. Instead she said, "It will be okay. We'll get through it together." She gazed into his eyes and saw the flicker of hope there. Leaning forward, she tenderly touched her lips to his. "I promise," she whispered.

He pulled her toward him just as the phone rang. They both sighed. Danielle reached for the phone.

"Hello? Reba!" Her gaze shot to Nick. "What do I need to do?" She listened in a mixture of shock and relief. "Fine. Tomorrow. I'll be there." Slowly she hung up the phone.

"Well, what did she say?"

"She said that the people I was assigned to photograph would meet me tomorrow and my money woes would be over. I need to contact Bernard. He'll know what to do from here."

She called Bernard and brought him up to date. He told her what to do and that if she followed his instructions this would all be over by tomorrow.

"Can you hear me?" Danielle asked as she parked across the street from Jenna and Anthony's condo.

"Loud and clear. Now remember, let them do the

talking. All you want to do is ask questions," Bernard instructed.

"Right." Her hands shook ever so slightly as she turned off the car. She reached for her purse and got out. "Here we go," she said into the mic taped to her chest and went into the building.

"Danielle, please come in." Jenna gave her a widening smile when she answered the buzzer.

"Thank you." She stepped inside and was both surprised and secretly delighted to see that Reba was there as well, seated next to Anthony.

Reba stood up and greeted her with a big smile. "Danielle." She turned to Anthony. "Didn't I tell you she looked liked Alicia Keys. I know we can make that work for us."

"Please have a seat," Jenna entreated.

"As I told you on the phone, Jenna and Anthony... help people. Sometimes with a new life or simply by providing them with the financial means to do so."

"I don't understand."

"It's quite simple, really," Anthony said. "We acquire property, cash, credit, homes by accessing other people's information."

Danielle feigned confusion. "Other people's information?"

"Yes, almost like a witness protection program," Reba joked. Everyone but Danielle laughed at her little quip. "All for a fee, of course, and a few favors from time to time."

"We've accessed the information from someone

who would be perfect for you," Anthony said. He opened a folder that was on the table. In it was a passport and what looked to be a credit card. "You can start your new life when you walk out of this door."

Danielle looked from one calm face to other. "I just start a new life as—" she looked at the name on the license "—Michelle Ingram."

"Yes, let's say that Ms. Ingram is out of the picture."

Danielle's heart thumped. "What do I need to do, I mean, you said, 'for a fee,'" she said, turning to Reba.

Reba smiled broadly. "We get a portion of the proceeds, which is how we continue to finance others who need our services and live the lifestyles to which we've grown accustomed." They all laughed.

There was a sudden loud bang, and the front door burst open. Bernard rushed in, followed by Claudia and a man Danielle didn't recognize, all with guns in hand.

Anthony leaped up.

"Don't even move," Claudia said.

"We've been watching you for a while," Bernard said as he went behind Anthony to put on plastic cuffs.

"I lot of people are going to be very happy to get their *real* lives back," Claudia said.

"There must be some mistake!" Jenna insisted.

"Take your hands off me," Reba shouted to the man who put her hands behind her back.

"Oh, there's no mistake," Bernard said, pulling

492   *Seduction and Lies*

out a tape recorder from the breast pocket of his jacket. He pressed Play and the damning conversation of moments ago filled the room for all to hear.

Jenna shot Danielle a murderous look. "I was a fool to trust you."

"I think it best that you keep your comments to yourself," Danielle said, suddenly feeling brave. "You're in enough trouble."

"Yes, and you will have plenty of years to think about it," Claudia added, shoving Anthony toward the door.

The cuffed trio was led out by Bernard and the third man.

Claudia turned to Danielle. "Are you okay?"

Danielle nodded, still shaken by the events of the past few minutes.

"You did a great job, Dani. You should be proud of yourself."

"I guess I will be when my heart slows down." She sputtered a nervous laugh.

Claudia grinned. "You'll get used to it. Come on, help me round up their computer and files."

"Who was that other guy with you and Bernard?"

Claudia grinned. "Oh, just a good friend of the family."

Chapter 24

Later that night, Nick and Danielle were in the tub with bubbles up to their necks, drinking wine and listening to a jazz CD.

Nick stroked Danielle beneath the water, and she squirmed in delight. "We're supposed to be relaxing, getting rid of stress," she teased.

"I am getting rid of stress. Can't you tell?" He caressed her breasts. "Are you ever going to tell me everything, about this organization?" he asked.

"If I could, I would. I've already messed up big-time by getting you involved. What I can tell you is that there may be times in my life and parts of it that I can't share with you. And it's not because I don't trust you or that I don't...love you."

"You what?"

She felt his heart pound against her back. She turned in the tub, coming up on her knees so that she faced him. "Love you," she repeated. "I love you."

"Do you really mean that?"

"From the bottom of my heart." And for the first time in her life, that enormous weight was lifted from her spirit. She had a man who loved her through thick and thin, not based on what she looked like or felt about herself but because of who she was, the woman she'd become.

"If we love each other, Dani, we can get through anything...even this spy stuff."

She leaned forward, linked her fingers behind his head. "I knew I loved you for a reason," she murmured before slowly lowering herself onto his erection. "There are some people I want you to meet," she said, moving slowly against him.

"Who?"

"My parents. I think you'll really like them, and I know they'll love you as much as I do."

The following morning Danielle received a call from Jean requesting that she come to the brownstone as soon as possible.

"If tomorrow afternoon works, I'll be there," Danielle said. "I have some business to take care of and it can't wait."

"I know," Jean said. "I'll be waiting." She disconnected the call and Danielle shook her head in wonder. What didn't that woman know?

The last time Danielle had been to this house was nearly ten years earlier. She'd walked away and never looked back, building her life of make-believe and blaming her parents for everything that was wrong in her life and with her.

She was a big girl now, a full-grown woman who had to finally face her own demons and own up to the hurt that she'd caused over the years.

Sure, she'd kept in touch at all the appropriate times over the years, with cards or phone calls, but this was different.

Nick clasped her hands and forced her to look at him. "It's going to be all right. I promise. Parents don't stop loving their children. And I have a gut feeling they're going to be so happy to see you that all the years apart are going to melt away." He gave her a lopsided grin and her heart thumped.

She swallowed over the dry knot in her throat and nodded her head.

"Come on, let's do this," Nick said, opening the car door, then coming around to open hers. He helped her out of the car and pulled her close. "Tell me again," he whispered against her mouth.

"I love you, Nick Mateo, with all my heart."

"Damn, I love the sound of that." He pecked her softly on the lips, and they walked toward the blue-and-white framed house.

Before they reached the front door, it opened and her parents stood in the archway.

For an instant no one moved. And then all at once her parents swept her up in their joined embrace, kissing and hugging their prodigal daughter.

Nick stepped aside and let them have their private moment. Finally Danielle turned, her expression luminous. Her eyes sparkled with tears.

"Mom, Dad, this is Nick Mateo."

Nick stepped forward with a big grin on his face.

Danielle's father stuck out his hand. "Pleasure to meet you."

"You as well, Mr. Holloway."

"Call me Joe."

"Well, are we going to continue this reunion on the steps, or are you young people going to come inside?" her mother, Carmen, asked, beaming at them both.

Several happy hours later, Danielle and Nick were on their way back to Manhattan.

"So this is where you grew up?" Nick asked as they rode through stately St. Albans, Queens.

"Yep, after we moved from Brooklyn. I used to play right in that park on Saturday afternoons," Danielle said, pointing to Addisleigh Park. "There was always something going on, concerts, tournaments." She smiled at the memories.

"Your folks are great." He glanced at her face for a moment. "You have your dad's eyes," he said softly, "and his strong-willed personality," he added.

Danielle laughed. "That much is true." And for the first time that she could remember in years she loved the sound of that.

"You don't know how lucky you are to still have a dad that loves you as much as yours does," he said wistfully.

"You did, too." She squeezed his hand. "And just because he's not here physically doesn't mean that the love he had for you wasn't real. You'll always carry that in your heart. And," she added, "now you have mine to love you, too."

He turned to her and smiled. "I like the sound of that."

"Yeah, me, too."

As they continued the drive home in a comforting silence, Danielle thought about her father's parting words as he hugged her.

"I told you a long time ago, sweetheart, that one day you would find someone who would love you for who you were, not who you appeared to be. You found him," he'd said, smiling softly. "Be sure to take care of him. Real love often only comes once in a lifetime."

"I love you, Daddy," she whispered, hugging him tight.

He kissed the top of her silky hair. "I know, sweetheart. I've always known."

Danielle sighed deeply, leaned back against the headrest and closed her eyes. Her father had been right all along. And if it took the rest of her life, she would ensure that her mom and dad never doubted her love for them ever again.

Chapter 25

Danielle sat straight as an arrow in the chair facing Jean. The look on Jean's face was so hard that Danielle would have bet money it would have cracked had she opened her mouth.

Jean turned her hard gaze on Danielle. "You did an incredible job on your first assignment. You used your instincts. I like that."

Danielle was so stunned she couldn't speak.

"Because of you, a major operation has been dismantled. My clients are happy and Bernard now has the information he needs to take out the next level. You should be proud."

"Thank you."

"But you broke every rule of the Cartel. You allowed your personal life to get involved. People could have gotten hurt. Fortunately, it worked out. It seems that you and Savannah have a way of breaking the rules and making this work for you." She handed Danielle a folder. "See if you can handle this one. And, Danielle…"

"Yes, ma'am."

"Try to keep the Cartel out of your bedroom next time."

"Yes, ma'am."

Danielle emerged from the brownstone walking on air. She'd accomplished much more than this assignment. Not only had she exposed those who worked to steal the lives and livelihoods of others, but also she'd found herself in the process. All these years she'd been searching for her own identity, hiding behind the lens of a camera, and she now finally knew without a doubt who she was—Joe and Carmen Holloway's daughter. That was what really made her proudest.

Nia and Savannah were waiting for her on the sidewalk in front of the brownstone. She greeted them with a broad grin.

"Well?" they asked in unison.

Danielle wrapped her arms around her two dearest friends in the world.

"I have so much to tell you both."

"Good stuff, I hope," Savannah said as they walked hand in hand toward Danielle's vehicle.

They all climbed in.

"I took Nick to meet my parents," she began as she started the engine.

Nia gave her a knowing look, which Savannah caught.

"What am I missing?" Savannah asked.

Danielle drew in a breath and eased out into traffic. "A long time ago, there was this guy named Michael...."

By the time they'd reached The Shop, Danielle had concluded her sad and sordid tale of her relationship gone terribly wrong.

"Dani, my God, you've been carrying that around all these years," Savannah said as they were shown their seats at their favorite booth. "I knew you and your folks weren't close, but I had no idea."

"Yeah, and I let it make a mess of my life, cut off my parents and harden my heart. I've been so scared of falling in love again, of being ashamed of who I was, that I nearly lost everything in the process."

"But you didn't," Nia said.

"And now you have Nick," Savannah said.

Danielle grinned. "Yes, I do. He still doesn't know everything about the Cartel, but he said that as long as we love each other, we can work anything out. And none of that changed after he met my folks."

"So it's finally official?" Nia asked with a gleam in her eye. "You're in love and not afraid to admit it!"

Danielle smiled. "And it feels damned good. If I

learned one thing through all this, it's that you have to be who you are. Accept yourself for who you are. And sticking labels and tags on people only separates you from them because underneath it all we're just people. And living a lie, a life of pretense, can only hurt you and everyone who cares about you."

"I'll drink to that," Savannah said, raising her glass of water.

The trio toasted to love and friendship.

"Ladies, lunch is on me!" Danielle announced.

"And I'll drink to that," Nia said.

When Danielle returned to her apartment later that evening, she couldn't remember the last time she'd felt so good about herself and the possibilities of the future.

She had a dream job, parents who loved her and the photo assignment of a lifetime, and when things got dull, she always had the Cartel. But most important, she had Nick.

She dropped her purse on the hall table and headed toward the bedroom, where she heard the sound of the television. Her heart skipped a beat just thinking about seeing Nick.

She opened the bedroom door; Nick was propped up on pillows watching the news.

"Hey, babe," Nick greeted her. He pointed to the screen. "They were just talking about a major identity theft ring that had been broken up. Thousands of people's personal information was recovered, but it's still going to take months to unravel everything."

Danielle came and sat next to him.

"Just think, you helped to pull that off." He hugged her tightly.

She snuggled next to him. "With your help."

He grinned. "Yeah, how 'bout that. So how was lunch with the girls?"

"Great. We were talking about planning Claudia and Bernard's wedding. She wants a fall wedding, which doesn't give us much time, but I think we can put together something really spectacular."

"Now that we've got our own hurdles out of the way," he began slowly, "there's no reason why we shouldn't."

Danielle frowned. "Shouldn't what?"

Nick disentangled himself and got up from the bed. He paced in front of her for a moment.

"Nick…what is it?"

He knelt down in front of her and took her hands in his. "I've been doing a lot of thinking… especially since we went to meet your parents."

Her heart thumped. *Here it comes,* she thought and didn't want to hear the rest, not after she'd finally opened her heart and soul. Not now. She couldn't breathe.

"Will you marry me, Danielle?"

For a hot minute she didn't process what he'd said. "What?"

"Will you marry me? Will you be my wife and

have our beautiful babies, be my best friend through thick and thin, make a life with me? Say yes, Dani."

Her spirit was so filled with awe and joy that the words wouldn't come. She cupped his face in her hands and looked deeply into his eyes.

"There's nothing in this world that I want more," she finally said, her voice thick and shaky with emotion.

Nick dug into his jeans pocket and pulled out a black velvet box. He opened the top and a sparkling diamond winked back at her. It was a simple setting, nothing fancy, but nothing was more beautiful.

He took her hand and slipped the ring on her finger.

Tears of joy spilled from her eyes.

"I hope those are happy tears," he said.

"Yes, yes, yes!" She pulled him to her, and they tumbled onto the bed, giddy with joyous laughter.

"I guess you girls will be planning two weddings," Nick said as he slowly undressed her.

"Absolutely." And she sealed her promise with a kiss.

* * * * *

**A brand-new miniseries
featuring fan-favorite authors!**

THE HAMILTONS *Laws of Love*

Family. Justice. Passion.

Ann Christopher	Pamela Yaye	Jacquelin Thomas

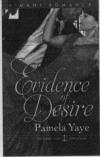

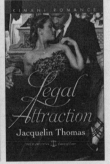

Available September 2012	*Available October 2012*	*Available November 2012*

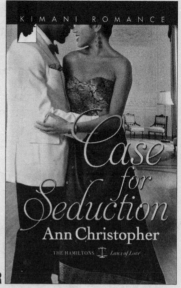

REQUEST YOUR FREE BOOKS!

2 FREE NOVELS
PLUS 2 FREE GIFTS!

KIMANI™
ROMANCE

Love's ultimate destination!

KROM11B

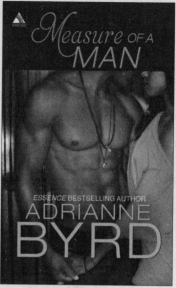